SEALFINGER

HEIDE GOODY

IAIN GRANT

1

"There's a bearded lady in the loft, dad."

"A bearded lady?"

"A bearded lady."

"In the loft?"

"I don't know which part of that sentence you're having trouble with."

"All of it, frankly."

Sam stared down at her dad.

Marvin Applewhite, Mr Marvellous himself, stood at the bottom of the loft ladder with a cup of tea and a faintly uncomprehending look. "I don't own a bearded lady," he said. "I'd remember something like that."

"You'd think," said Sam, doubtfully. She picked her way through the low attic space through the mountains of props, posters and memorabilia, a hoard of magical tat that never seemed to shrink no matter how much she cleared.

She brushed aside cobwebs real and imaginary, her

wobbling torch aimed at the bearded woman. When she neared, she realised her mistake. "Ah."

Minutes later, she had manhandled it down through the loft hatch and carried it along to the kitchen. "There," she said, standing it by the breakfast bar.

Marvin made a show of looking at it, squinting and widening his eyes. Even in his mid-seventies, he didn't wear glasses except for reading the finest of fine print. And by the looks of some of the red bills Sam had squirrelled away in her own private filing, Marvin Applewhite was not one for bothering with fine print.

"That's not a bearded lady," he observed.

"I can see that now," said Sam.

It was actually a mannequin, and might once have lived in a shop window, or been constructed by one of Marvin's prop-makers back in the day. She had killer cheekbones, sharp grey eyes and heavy eyeliner. And a beard.

Sam touched the papery mass. It flaked under her touch.

"What is that?" said Marvin.

"Wasps, I think." The paper nest covered her chin and neck, and had eaten away most of her lower face. There appeared to be a couple of desiccated insect corpses in there.

Marvin tutted. "Poor Consuela."

"Consuela?"

"Well, she had to have a name, didn't she?"

"But not any clothes?"

"She wore a spangly leotard, usually identical to whatever Linda was wearing. It must have perished." He tilted his head, a sure sign he was going off into some reverie. Sam indulged such things, but would have to snap him out of it before too long. It was gone eight o'clock and she needed to be at the DefCon4 office by nine.

"It was part of my version of the shell game trick," he said. "Three boxes on castors. Consuela went into one. Linda in another. A member of the audience or a celebrity guest in the third." He chuckled and sipped his tea. "I had Cilla Black in a box one night."

Name-dropping was always a sign of an oncoming anecdote. As Marvin took a breath for the next sentence, Sam leapt in. "There were some other wasp nests up there."

"With wasps in?"

She shook her head. "But I think there might be some rot. We'll have to look at it once we've cleared the loft."

He gave her a worried look and cast about at the boxes already cluttering one surface of the huge kitchen. This clutter was of her making, a work in progress. Items from his lifetime of hoarding, silently sorted by her into three groups: eBay, junk shop, and bin.

"You don't have to clear out this stuff." He placed a hand on a felt covered *thing* poking out the top of a box. "There are a lot of memories attached to these items."

"Dust, dad," she said. "The word is dust. This place needs to be tidy. People might come round."

"We've got guests?" he said.

Surveyors. Valuers. Estate agents. Hardly guests.

Duncastin' was an eight-bedroomed bungalow mansion at the end of Albert Road. It sat in several acres of land, bounded by high hedges on the road side, and a fence and dunes on the seaward side. So surrounded, it was hard to know it was there despite its size. It was an odd building: a curving snake of a house built around a winding hallway. Not even a proper bungalow, with its lumpy upper floor stuck onto the far end, as though the snake was sticking its head up to say hello. The white walls, the amount of exterior wood used in its construction (so vulnerable to rot and the sea air) and the veranda running along its entire length gave it the feel of a chain of holiday chalets which had huddled together for company.

"Danny La Rue was sick on that counter," said Marvin.

Unthinking, Sam lifted her elbow away. She doubted celebrity vomit anecdotes would add much value to the poorly maintained property. If her dad's debts were anything as bad as she suspected (and she had yet to get to the bottom of that), they would need every penny they could raise.

Maybe, just maybe, there would be something of value among the stage paraphernalia. Not enough to undo a lifetime of poor financial management, but enough to stave off the debt-collectors for a while.

"I've got the use of a bigger van later," said Sam. "Doing meals on wheels. I'll be able to take our bearded friend to the tip."

"Not Consuela," said Marvin, clasping the dummy with both hands. He saw where he had placed one of those hands and adjusted it appropriately.

"No one wants a bearded lady around the house," said Sam.

"But it was a stunning trick."

"I'm sure it was." Her phone buzzed: a work e-mail, a scheduled delivery, a parcel. "Parcel..."

"Three boxes," said Marvin. "Let me show you." He

started looking through the plastic recycling box on the drainer.

"No time, dad," she said. "Duty calls. Someone's got to earn the pennies." She kissed him on the cheek. "Back later for her."

"I'll put something in the microwave for tea."

"Not tonight. I'm out."

He made a silly face, waggling his eyebrows. "Out courting?"

"No one calls it courting anymore," said Sam.

"What do you call it?" said Marvin.

"What I'm doing tonight? Sheer tedium. StoreWatch meeting with bloody Sergeant Hackett at Carnage Hall."

"You might meet a feller," he suggested optimistically.

"Why do I need a man to be a drain on my time and resources? I've got you."

"Ha ha."

She kissed him again and left the house.

2

DefCon4 provided Sam with a company vehicle. When initially deciding to provide their regional offices with Piaggio Ape 50 vans, the wise heads at DefCon4 had perhaps asked for a vehicle which was cheap, economical, capable of transporting both people and cargo, and able to deal with both narrow streets and the crowded urban landscape. What DefCon4 purchased was a fleet of tiny three-wheeled Italian vans which drew amused looks. If it wasn't for the DefCon4 logo emblazoned on the sides, it could easily be mistaken for a miniature ice-cream van. In many ways, it reflected Sam's job: slow-going; while an outside observer would be hard-pressed to say what its main purpose was, or what it was generally *for*.

Sam drove from Albert Road, down Drummond Road, and cut through Barbara Road to the South Parade. The sun was rising over the sea, the line of wind turbines five miles out was a picket fence of silver spikes in the still-lifting haze.

As she drove up to the clock tower roundabout, the town was visible in all its early morning glory. Skegness. Skegvegas. Bright lights, small town. In the off-season, it was home to twenty thousand locals and retirees. In holiday season, home to over four million visitors, stuffed into crumbling Victorian B&Bs or caravan parks so big they had their own postcodes. Skegness: a mecca to the roll-up-your-trousers-and-paddle brigade of Nottingham, Sheffield and Leicester; to the fat, tattooed and (if they were lucky) sunburned, with a screaming toddler in one hand and a two-for-one cocktail voucher in the other.

To be thirty, single and living in Skegness was not something Sam had expected. To be thirty, single and living in Skegness without kids, a drug problem or incipient type 2 diabetes was perhaps something of an achievement.

She turned into Lumley Road, the main shopping street, and from there round the island by the train station to DefCon4's office. DefCon4's entrance was the narrowest of doors between the *Who Do You Ink You Are?* tattoo parlour and Cat's Café. She parked the Piaggio on the pavement directly outside. One of the few advantages of a vehicle which wasn't much bigger than a mobility scooter was no one was sure if it was allowed on the pavement or not.

She was required to check in at the office because the DefCon4 calendar app on her phone demanded it. Web-based calendar systems and GPS meant her employers could direct her with the minutest detail, even if actual human employers were never to be seen.

She unlocked the door and went upstairs to the first floor office. It was pretty large, containing four desks. All empty apart from hers. Well, one of the desks had a little name plaque on it for a Doug Fredericks, and because having a name plaque without a person to apply it to felt too much like having a ghost in the room, Sam had put a dusty cactus on the desk and silently declared both plaque and name belonged to it.

The loose carpet tile by Doug's desk had come unstuck again. Sam was sure she'd trip on it one day and brain herself on the edge of his desk, and that would be the end of her. She pressed it down with the ball of her foot. The residual tackiness of carpet glue held it in place, for now.

Her phone buzzed. The calendar item TEAM BRIEFING – SKEGNESS REGIONAL OFFICE went from red to green.

"Morning, Doug," she said to the cactus. When Doug Fredericks understandably failed to reply, she gave him a little fist salute. "Good briefing, Doug."

The rest of the day ran as follows:

11:00 – 14:00 – MEALS ON WHEELS – CONTRACTUAL OBLIGATION

16:00 – 17:00 – RECEIVE PARCEL CONSIGNMENT – BETA TESTING

18:30 – 21:00 – STOREWATCH BRIEFING – PROMOTION AND UPSELLING OPPORTUNITY

MEALS ON WHEELS was an easy and infrequent part of her job. The parcel was a mystery. StoreWatch was a chore, during which she was supposed to pretend that she cared about local business security, then try and sell DefCon4 alarms,

CCTV and other 'security solutions' to business owners in attendance. There were tougher and weirder days.

Sam drove the mile to the vehicle depot. DefCon4 contracted its vehicles out of a no-frills van and lorry hire place next to the town tip. She parked the Piaggio next to two vans outside the portacabin. She instinctively parked it next to the smaller one, to put them in size order. She wasn't a control freak or a neatness nut, but to do otherwise seemed deliberately perverse. In minutes, she'd be out again in the Transit van and no one would be any the wiser.

She went into the portacabin. The clerk was deep in heated discussion with a customer in a Seal Land staff shirt, seemingly about missing paperwork.

"And this is your *new* pre-hire damage check," said the clerk, sliding a sheet over to the man.

"Which shows no damage on the vehicle," said Seal Land. "What about pre-existing damage? There's a couple of dents in the side."

"So, you *have* damaged it?"

"No. They were already there. If you still had the original pre-hire damage check then—" He tapped the new sheet angrily. "This is a *mid*-hire damage check at best, mate. I've come all the way up from Cornwall. I've only got to drive five miles up the coast and I'm done. Me coming in, this is me doing you a favour."

Sorry," said Sam, cutting in. "Meal delivery. Usual van?"

"Take the Bipper," said the clerk, without even looking at her. "Keys are in the ignition."

Sam's heart sank. The Peugeot Bipper outside was a much smaller van. Consuela the mannequin would not easily fit inside, and definitely not alongside the meals on wheels trays she had to take. Yes, her dad had a car at home, but the E-type Jaguar in his garage probably hadn't passed an MOT this century and was far from ideal for transporting inflexible model assistants.

"Can't I take the Transit?" Sam said to the clerk.

"It's out."

"It's there," she said, pointing towards the car park through the wall.

"I can't let you take a vehicle without a pre-hire damage check," the clerk said to Seal Land.

"You didn't. And if you take a look at your pre-hire damage check—"

"This *is* a pre-hire damage check."

"—Without the damage marked that was already on it when I picked it up."

"And I'm supposed to take your word that the damage was already there?"

"No! That's what a pre-hire damage check is for!"

The clerk tapped the sheet again. "And *this* is yours."

"Look, sorry," said Sam, cutting in again. "If the Transit is back..."

"It's still out," said the clerk.

"But now it's back."

"Just take the van."

"Thanks. That's great."

Seal Land picked up a biro and started drawing vicious circles on the picture on the damage check sheet. "Dent. Dent. Dent."

Sam decided to leave them to it.

"Keys are in the ignition," the clerk called after her.

She gave him a wave, went round to the Transit and, prompted by the argument that the two men had been having in the portacabin, gave it a quick check-over.

Four wheels.

Only superficial marks on the body.

Nothing in the back but a weirdly fusty odour and a tarp over a large box, probably a tool locker, next to the partition between front and back.

Petrol gauge at least halfway full.

She was good to go, and still mostly on time.

The meals on wheels food came from a caravan park out to the south of the town, down a narrow road between cabbage fields which, shortly after the caravan park, gave up pretending to be a road and just petered out into nothing at all.

The caravan park's kitchens were used to cook the food for meals on wheels, although 'cook' was perhaps too generous a word. Much of it was long-life pots of a dubious substance which came from a distant factory. On several occasions Sam had asked why they didn't just make more of the meals they served in the holiday park's restaurants and bars. The answer was obvious of course: nearly all of the meals they served in the holiday camp were fried things with chips, and in the provision of meals on wheels guidelines, chips were forbidden. Sadly, glutinous mess from a foil packet was not.

Sam collected three high-stacked trays of hot meals and desserts, wedged them up against the tarp and whatever was under it at the back of the van, and left.

3

M eals on wheels was, Sam felt, a deceptive phrase.

Like the RNLI and the RSPCA, meals on wheels was such an established name that everyone sort of assumed it was an established and official body: some sort of government office existing to distribute food to the elderly and housebound. It was no such thing. Like the lifeboats and the animal inspectors, it had started out as an entirely charitable endeavour by well-meaning sorts, but unlike the RNLI and RSPCA, private sector forces had crept in and almost entirely taken over. Presumably there was little profit in sinking ships and abandoned kittens to draw capitalists in. Meals on wheels was a cash for nosh business, a Deliveroo for those who preferred their meals square and on proper plates.

The meals on wheels clients Sam catered for had signed up to a hot meal five times a week, with cheery banter and a friendly face as a very optional extra. Sam felt stopping and chatting with the elderly and isolated was a valuable part of the service, but her schedule, as administered through her DefCon4 app, had less sociable ideas.

The phone app beeped as she drove: her first visit of the day was Wendy Skipworth. She lived in a solitary cottage, up a small side road off a small side road, in Welton le Marsh: a village seven miles outside Skegness on the edge of the Wolds, at the point where the unremittingly flat and dull landscape began to show some promise of turning interesting. Like a Victorian lady lifting her skirts to show a bit of ankle. Mrs Skipworth's cottage had actual honeysuckle growing around the front door, as though she didn't realise it was a cliché.

Sam drew up on the gravel front yard and went to knock the door. The older woman waved at her from the bay window.

"Morning, Wendy," said Sam, brushing her feet on the mat as she entered. "Meals on wheels. Your menu choices today are salmon salad, bacon hotpot, lasagne, or cottage pie."

"I didn't like what you brought me yesterday," said Mrs Skipworth. "It gave me wind it did."

"Sorry to hear that," said Sam. "What did you have?"

"It was the special. What was it?"

"I wouldn't know," said Sam. "I only do every third Thursday. It's Karen who does the other days."

Mrs Skipworth raised her bowed head to look at Sam properly. She wore the doddery old dear act well, but Sam could see a sharp intelligence in her eyes. A Daily Telegraph, folded to the crossword page, sat on one arm of her chair. A spiral bound notepad sat on the other, covered with squares and writing.

"You're not Karen," she said with a ponderous certainty.

"I am not. I'm Sam."

"What happened to Karen?"

"Nothing," said Sam. "Karen has to take a break every few weeks."

"Why's that?"

Sam could tell her, but it was a long and stupid explanation. It involved timesheets and an anti-monopoly clause in the meals on wheels tendering contracts, meaning various costly things for the contractors if they provided a continuous service for more than twenty-one days, dodged by a legally suspect loophole involving the whole thing being subcontracted to DefCon4 one day every three weeks.

Sam simply said, "She deserves a break every now and then, don't you think?"

"Chow mein," said Mrs Skipworth.

"Did it have noodles?"

Mrs Skipworth nodded.

Sam knew some of the staff would push the easiest option as a 'special'. Glorified pot noodles seemed to turn up a lot, because all they needed was a little bit of hot water. They could make the client a cup of tea and prepare their meal in one easy hit. 'Broth' was another popular special. As far as Sam could tell it was a stock cube.

"There'll be none of that today," said Sam. "So, what do you fancy?"

"Bacon hotpot sounds all right," said Mrs Skipworth.

"Do I need to check your notes to see if you're on a low sodium diet?" asked Sam, her eyebrow raised. "You might be better with the salmon salad if you need to look after your salt."

Mrs Skipworth wrinkled her nose. "Cottage pie then."

It was a better choice. The bacon hotpot was a gloopy potato-based mess similar to the stuff campers might squeeze out of a packet into a billy can. There was no way it was more nutritious than chips. At least the cottage pie was chilled, which presumably meant it had been made locally. There were even some actual vegetables in it. She went out to the van and lifted the top lid to take out a cottage pie container. There was a strong fishy smell which competed with the fusty smell from earlier and was not at all pleasant. Sam wondered if the salmon salad was less than fresh.

She went back inside to put it into Mrs Skipworth's oven to warm it up. "Cup of tea?"

"Only if you're having one," said Mrs Skipworth, which Sam took as code for, "Yes, sorry to be a bother." There was a sudden rush of noise as Mrs Skipworth turned the television on.

The kitchen had a shelf on which stood six mugs decorated with stern-looking cats. Sam made cups of tea in two of them. She peered at the spiral notepad on the chair arm as she put the cup of tea down. Boxes with names in them – Edith Vamplew, Benjamin Greening, Thomas Osmond – arranged in rows and squares.

"Birthday party seating plan?" said Sam.

Mrs Skipworth laughed coldly. "It's my eightieth next year. Can't imagine any of these attending."

"You never know."

Mrs Skipworth leaned round her to watch the quiz show on the TV. "That Bradley Walsh has been getting right on my nerves with his laughing. He was better when he used to ride bikes if you ask me. Always playing the giddy goat now."

"I think you might mean Bradley Wiggins. He's the one that rides the bikes."

"Just testing," said Mrs Skipworth.

"You want me to draw the curtain? The sun's on the telly."

"Leave it," said Mrs Skipworth with the casual bluntness of the elderly.

"You sure?"

"I want to be able to see the ghosts in the churchyard."

"Ghosts?" Sam looked out the bay window. The cottage's slightly elevated position gave a good view across the road and a small village church.

"Now they're playing silly buggers most nights."

"Is that so?"

"Don't you look at me in that tone of voice, miss," said Mrs Skipworth. "I know what I see."

"Of course." Sam pulled out the menu card for the desserts and placed it next to the cup of tea in front of Mrs Skipworth. "Now, why don't you choose something for after?"

Mrs Skipworth studied the card. "When it says 'fruit-flavoured jelly pot', what fruit is it?" she asked.

Sam had no answer to that. She was certain no actual fruit came anywhere near the stuff. "Not sure," she said. "I heard that the carrot cake is good."

Sam checked on the cottage pie and went out to the van to find some carrot cake. As she approached the door she heard a scraping sound from inside. That was strange. She opened the door a couple of inches and peered in.

"*Blaaaark!*"

She jumped back at the noise, which was accompanied by a large, whiskered face peering out the door. The noise was halfway between a donkey braying and a world-class belch. The face was flabby and mottled grey, with big drooping whiskers. A seal! It had to be one of the biggest and ugliest she had ever seen. If a seal was ever cast as Pablo Escobar, the Columbian drug lord, this one would be in with a good chance, with its humourless expression and dark moustache. She stepped forward to look properly, but it lunged towards the door, making that appalling noise again.

"*Blaaaark!*"

As it rolled its enormous body, it spilled crushed boxes and food trays out of the door. The food from inside them had gone, along with chunks of cardboard and plastic, large bite marks in evidence.

"Oh hell!" Sam opened the door a little wider and saw the carnage within the truck. The tarp at the back had been thrown aside, revealing the remains of a wooden transport crate. The seal had eaten its way through nearly everything on the meals on wheels trays. When it wasn't attacking her, it seemed intent on cleaning up the rest.

She closed the door and stepped away. There were several problems here, but she needed to keep a clear head and not add to them by panicking.

She went back inside Mrs Skipworth's house and took the cottage pie out of the oven.

There was a seal in her van.

Sam slid the dinner onto a clean plate.

There was a grey seal in her van.

She brought the dinner to Mrs Skipworth on a tray decorated with stern-looking cats, like the mugs. "Here you go."

There was two metres and at least five hundred pounds of Atlantic grey seal in the back of her van.

"I like a bit of brown sauce with cottage pie," said the old lady.

I'm sorry, Wendy, you'll have to forgive me, but a large grey seal has somehow snuck into my van and I can't reach the condiments sachets.

Instead of saying that she searched the kitchen cupboards and found a bottle which looked as though it dated from this century. "Right, you eat up and I'll be back with your pudding in ... in a short while."

Sam stepped outside. She had to re-open the van to double-check.

"Blaaaark!"

"Oh, yes, it's still there." She closed the door and paced for a good few seconds. "A seal in the van. A seal in the van." She was sure that in several hours she would admire this as an excellent trick, worthy of Mr Marvellous himself, but right now—

Insanely, she was put in mind how, in high summer, ladybirds would appear in their thousands, everywhere; even where they could not conceivably be. "How did it even...? Through the air blowers?" Except it wasn't a ladybird. It was a bloody seal.

She pulled out her phone to call for help, though from

whom she had no idea, and saw that she had several missed calls from the van depot already. "Hi, it's Sam from DefCon4. Listen, that van I—"

"You took the wrong one!" exclaimed the clerk loudly.

"Did I? I mean, yes. Obviously, I can see that now. Although I'd be lying if I said I wasn't a little bit curious about how we came to have a massive angry seal in one of the vans."

"Guy from Seal Land is going absolutely spare."

"Does he want his seal back?"

"It's not that simple."

"I can drop him off."

"They've been moaning like anything because of timings and the vet's availability and yadda yadda. They want to re-schedule for the morning."

"I'm not keeping a seal until tomorrow morning."

"I told you to take the other vehicle."

"You told me to take the 'van'. You told me the van was out, but it was back, and you told me to take the van."

"You didn't even give me chance to do a pre-hire damage check."

"Oh, there might be damage now," she said.

"What have you done?"

"Did I mention the seal? It's huge! It's eaten all the meals. What am I going to do about them?"

"Hey, I do vehicles. Food is your department."

Sam thought he sounded a bit too pleased with himself at dodging *that* bullet, for having pushed her in front of it. She sighed. "Please pass me the contact details for the Seal Land guy. Maybe I can arrange to drop the thing off sooner."

"*Larry,*" said the clerk.

"And what's Larry's number?"

"*Larry's the seal.*"

"Larry the seal?"

"*Yes. I'll get the guy's number. And watch out. He can be vicious.*"

"The guy?"

"*The seal. The reason he's back here is because he got kicked out of some sanctuary in Cornwall for bad behaviour.*"

The was a thump and a creak and an unpleasant noise from inside the van.

"Did he eat all their food? Raid the cafeteria? Carry out carjacking's in the car park?"

"*If there's any damage to that van...*"

"It's all pre-existing stuff on the damage waiver," said Sam and killed the call.

She rang the kitchens at the caravan park. The phone rang and rang. She sighed, because she knew there was only one person there who was assigned to admin, and if they weren't there the others simply wouldn't answer the phone.

Sam inhaled deeply and prepared to open the door of the Transit again. She needed to see if there was anything she could salvage from the food that she'd brought.

"*Blaaaark!*"

If anything, the volume of Larry's cries had increased. He definitely had cake crumbs around his stinky fishy mouth. Could seals get a sugar rush? Sam immediately worried she had poisoned a wild animal by allowing it access to unhealthy food, then checked herself. This food was deemed ideal for the senior citizens of the area, so surely someone had decided it was all right? She edged towards one of the boxes which looked more intact, but Larry saw her intent and slammed his big blubbery body down in an angry protest at her invasion of his snacking space. The impact burst open another box, and Larry immediately started to consume the cold hotpot now dripping off every surface.

Sam sighed heavily and closed the door on Larry's decadent dining style. One thing was certain: no food was going to make it out through those doors unless it was inside Larry's belly.

She climbed into the cab. She could still use the vehicle with Larry in the back, and she needed to get some meals for her clients, including Mrs Skipworth – who probably thought she was washing up at the moment. She turned the van around and headed back up the lane. As she reached the top she had a thought and pulled over by the churchyard.

Options. She could give up and go home. There would be several hungry and potentially worried old people if she did. She could phone DefCon4's main office for guidance, but experience told her that would result in up to an hour battling the automated phone system before finally speaking to someone who would be unable or unwilling to help her. Since starting with Defcon4, every attempt to navigate their internal systems had met with failure, mainly because she was the only person in the area, and all too often the systems relied upon a chain of command which simply didn't exist in this rural outpost. She could go out and buy more dinners, yes. Which she would unsuccessfully try to claim back as an office expense and end up taking as a hit on her own personal finances.

How much money did she have? She looked in her purse. Eighteen pounds seventy five. She needed to find a way to replace the missing food for somewhere between zero and eighteen pounds. She gazed at the church, the drooping trees and the sunlit grass of the churchyard. To be a ghost in a churchyard like that... Yeah, sometimes Sam could envy the dead.

"Blaaaark!"

"Okay, Larry," she said. "Let's do this."

4

Sam went home.

"Dad!" she called as she headed to the kitchen. "It's only me, I'm not stopping, I just need to get something

He stood by the counter, reading the post. It was mostly junk and flyers, but he was reading it anyway.

"Back for lunch?" he said.

"Sort of. Dad, if you had to feed eleven people for less than twenty pounds, what would you do?" Sam fished three plums, a brown banana and a sad looking tangerine out of the fruit bowl. Then she noticed Consuela, the bearded mannequin. She was wearing a gold sequinned leotard. "She wasn't wearing clothes before."

"I put one of Linda's old leotards on her."

"What?"

Marvin Applewhite smiled sheepishly. "You're going to think me daft, but I thought she looked cold."

"Mad, not daft."

"It was going threadbare anyway and I don't think Linda plans to wear it again."

Linda, Mr Marvellous' stage assistant, was now a sixty-something retiree somewhere on the Florida coast, and who – after a career of wearing glamorous outfits and squeezing herself into magician's cabinets – had merrily decided to let herself go a bit.

"Oh, I can show you now," said Marvin.

"Show me what?"

He slid three white yoghurt pots he'd fished out of the plastic recycling across the counter and put one over the tangerine and the two others over plums.

"I need those," said Sam.

Marvin revealed each fruit again momentarily. "One, two, three. Consuela, Linda and my special guest star tonight, Miss Cilla Black!"

"I do not have time for this."

"Keep your eye on the tangerine – that's Consuela. Round and round they go..."

"I am in a hurry, dad!"

"A great food tip for you," he said.

"Really?"

Marvin slowly moved the pots around. Sam knew the slowness was a deception. He still had magician's hands. "Back in my youth, I liked to think I was part of the scene, one of the cool kids, but I rarely had the money everyone else did."

Sam hoped he wasn't going to launch into a lengthy bout

of his habitual showbiz reminiscing, as she just didn't have the time. She still had an eye on the tangerine though.

"I hosted a party," he continued, "booze was never a problem as people often brought their own, and a neighbour used to brew wine from things like dandelions and hedge clippings. But I couldn't afford to feed everyone, so do you know what I did?"

"What did you do?" she said

"I lowered the lights and smeared some week-old pate around a few bowls. I scattered them around the place and everyone assumed they'd simply missed the food while they were dancing or something." He tapped the side of his nose. "I even overheard Anita Harris telling everyone how delicious it had been."

"Enough with the name dropping," she said.

He stopped his pot shuffling and gave her a hurt look that only lasted an instant. "Where is Consuela?"

Sam tapped a pot.

"You sure?" he said. "So these other two are Cilla and Linda?"

She nodded.

Marvin picked up a heavy wooden chopping board and slammed it down on the Cilla pot, loudly crushing it.

"Dad!"

"Course on the stage, it was a sword straight through the cabinet."

"I was going to use that plum!"

"What plum?" he said archly. "You mean one of these?" He lifted one pot to reveal a plum and the second undamaged pot to reveal— "Where's it gone?" he said in a slightly baffled voice.

It took Sam a moment to realise this was not part of the act. "Not got time for this," she hissed.

"Must have rolled down the side of the counter. Yes, it's wedged down here behind the fridge."

While he searched for his lost plum, Sam searched the kitchen cupboards for anything that looked promising.

She dug out a pack of lentils, some tinned tomato soup and some stock cubes. It wasn't a brilliant start. She remembered something she had read in the paper about cooking without a kitchen. She boiled the kettle and popped lentils into her dad's thermos flask along with boiling water. It might come in handy. The fridge didn't hold much promise. A packet of cheese slices went into the carrier bag. If she found some crackers then at least it would make a snack.

Her father appeared in the kitchen. She hadn't even noticed he'd gone. "All right dear. I've put her in the back for you."

She turned slowly to face him. "Sorry, what?"

"Consuela. Cup of tea?"

She stared at her father. "The van?"

"Yes."

"And did you notice anything unusual at all?"

"Maybe you could take it to that junk shop up from the pier. They might give you something for it."

Sam rushed outside. If there was one thing possibly worse than having a misbehaving (yet protected) seal in the back of her van, it was the prospect of unleashing a misbehaving (yet protected) seal upon suburban Skegness. She opened up the van a crack to see if Larry had escaped.

"*Blaaaark!*"

She felt acute relief. How quickly she had come to accept that Larry was her passenger and she was responsible for his welfare right now.

She had a grey seal and a bearded lady in a gold sequin leotard in the back of her van.

Marvin stood on the veranda of the house.

"Everything all right, love?" he called.

"You are going to the opticians!" she shouted.

He held out his hands and felt about blindly. "Who said that?"

Sam gritted her teeth. "God preserve us from variety entertainers," she muttered. "Did you not see the seal in the back?" she shouted.

"Cilla Black," he nodded in agreement. "Scarborough Playhouse, 1972."

"And we're getting your hearing tested!"

Her app buzzed to tell her what she already knew: she was behind schedule. She drove away, aware that local pensioners were probably getting hungry by now. She drove to the express supermarket near the DefCon4 office and hopped out to look through the reduced section to find the bargains which were due to go out of date. There were several baguettes priced at ten pence each, so she scooped them all into a basket. A reduced pack of carrots and onions joined them. A pineapple for seventy pence.

"Yes!"

A mother with a pushchair stared at her.

"Cheap pineapple," said Sam.

She added some full price potatoes and went to the checkout. She'd spent less than four pounds, but still had to convert all of this into something edible. She knew about cooking, but when she cooked meals for herself and her dad, they mostly had something like a lamb chop and some vegetables. She needed help.

Cat's Café was just a couple of doors down. While Cat herself was something of a pain in the backside who simply would not shut up about her amateur dramatics group and dreams of becoming a playwright, she did know more than a little about cooking and wore her virtues on her sleeve. Sam nipped in.

"Morning, Cat."

Cat, working behind her glass fronted counter, had a willowy and somewhat wan appearance. Sam wasn't sure if it was the carefully cultivated pose of a would-be actor or the product of working long days in a greasy spoon café. Cat would argue vehemently that it wasn't a greasy spoon, pointing out the jolly yellow and blue farmhouse décor, the healthy options on the menu, and the frankly baffling array of coffees they offered. But if ninety percent of the clientele were coming in for sausage, egg, chips and a cup of builder's tea, then it was a greasy spoon all right.

"What can I get you?" asked Cat.

"Let me answer that with another question," said Sam. "If I needed to feed eleven people, and these are older folks, and all I had was around fourteen pounds and a bag of mixed ingredients to offer, what would you suggest?"

Initially Cat looked at Sam with suspicion, then with interest. "What ingredients?" she asked.

Sam felt foolish as she reeled off the list of things she'd bought in the supermarket. "Oh, and some lentils that are in hot water in this flask as well," she added, just to seal her reputation as a lunatic.

"Fourteen pounds will buy you the means to transform that into something splendid," said Cat. "Though I don't think this place's food licence covers helping strange women cook dinners."

"Am I strange?"

"Based upon available evidence. I shouldn't help you but..."

"But?" said Sam.

"I can't resist a challenge. Step round and we'll get you peeling some taters."

Sam slipped around the counter. She knew how to peel potatoes, so that was fine. What she didn't know was that the smell of carrots and onions gently sweating in a pan after being chopped up into tiny bits would be so delicious. What's more, when the tomato soup and lentils were added to them, they actually started to look pretty good.

"Now, there are two options," said Cat. "You can blend some of this into a pretty tasty soup, and serve it with a chunk of baguette. Add some sausage to the rest and serve with your spuds to make a main meal. It will be fine without the sausage if you have some vegetarians on your client list."

"Amazing," said Sam. "What shall I do with the pineapple?"

"Cut it up and give them all some delicious fresh fruit.

You've even got those cheese slices and bread for those who want something different. Here, these plastic tubs will hold your stewy soup."

They loaded the food onto some bread trays Cat had out back and Sam placed them carefully on the Transit's passenger seat. She'd told Cat the rear door was jammed shut, rather than try to explain about Larry. It sounded too outlandish, even to her ears.

Sam emptied her purse into the woman's hand and climbed up into the driver's seat.

"Get it to your clients while it's hot!" said Cat.

There was a loud thud from the back of the van. Cat looked sharply at Sam. "What's that?"

"Nothing."

"I 'eard it too," said a man walking by. "Have you got someone in the back?"

Sam had seen this scene on kidnap films. She knew better than to engage in explanations. "Double de-clutching," she said with an airy wave of her hand. "It's a bit tricky, this van."

"But you haven't even started the—" Cat began. Sam wound up the window and turned the ignition. She waved and drove off.

5

Sam resumed her rounds and delivered the meals to clients who were mostly scattered in the villages around Skegness. Mrs Donaldson in Sloothby who lived in a house that was too big for her and contained bedrooms kept in pristine condition for children and grandchildren who never visited. Mrs Clavell, a bitterly intelligent divorcee in Hogsthorpe who had kicked out her no-good husband after forty years of marriage. Mr Stewart in Huttoft, who had only come to the area to care for his elderly and isolated mother and, upon her death, discovered that being elderly and isolated was catching. Through villages and hamlets, Sam travelled with her deliveries, ignoring the bing and buzz of an app demanding she should be somewhere else, bringing some semblance of human contact to her clients.

There were some minor protests that there wasn't the usual choice of food and that it had arrived later than expected, but when they saw what she'd brought them most stopped complaining and ate up. Fresh pineapple was a particular draw. Sam resolved to look out for fruity bargains for her next trip out. Even Mrs Skipworth, who had been impatiently waiting for her carrot cake, was won over with a juicy slice of pineapple.

"Sorry it took me a while," said Sam.

"Did you have to go to South America to get it?" said Mrs Skipworth.

"It's been one of those days."

Sam was driving away from the last drop-off when her phone rang. She pulled up by the churchyard again to take the call.

"Delivery service," said a man's voice.

"Ah!" she said. "Do I have your seal?"

"What? No. Delivery service. I have parcel for DefCon4."

The parcel delivery on her to-do list.

"That's not due until four." She looked at the clock on the dashboard. "It is four. Sorry, I'm not there."

"I'm at your office."

"Yeah, I'm not. Sorry."

A police siren whooped on the road behind her. Sam made sure her handbrake was on. She didn't want to get a fine for being on her phone while driving.

"When will you be here?" asked the man.

In the wing mirror, Sam saw a policeman step out of his car. She recognised the round face and uncontrolled waistline. Sergeant Hackett. Cesar.

She stepped down from the van, phone to her ear. "I'm not going to be there for twenty five minutes."

"I have a schedule."

"Or you could bring it to me, then everyone's happy."

Cesar spoke into the chest radio hooked onto his stab vest. "Attending incident at the Frost construction site in Welton le Marsh. Stand by."

"I can wait for fifteen minutes, no more," said the delivery man.

"Twenty," said Sam. "Meet me halfway."

"Twenty," he agreed.

Cesar had his hand on his stubby yellow taser pistol.

"You wouldn't believe the day I'm having, Cesar," Sam said, conversationally.

He held his hand up to ward her off. "It's okay, Sam, we'll get this sorted out, I'm sure."

"I wasn't driving while talking," said Sam, holding out her phone.

"Just tell us where the ransom meeting point is," said Cesar.

"The what?"

"Twenty thousand, was it? That's a lot of money."

"I really don't know what you're talking about."

"Times are tough," he nodded, his voice filled with all the sympathetic understanding in the world. Was that the beginnings of a tear in his eye? "The price of things these days. I get it. You were desperate. You thought you had no other option."

"Desperate?"

"Please, Sam. Don't make this harder than it has to be. Now, have you hurt them in any way?"

"Why don't you ask me a question I can understand? Or

better still, leave it for a couple of hours because I'm seeing you at the StoreWatch thing. I've got to get this package—"

"Kidnapping," said Cesar, blurting it out like it had come from a dark and difficult place. "Have you abducted and imprisoned someone in the back of this van?"

The penny dropped. Someone had called the police – maybe the passer-by outside Cat's Cafe – a reasonable course of action given the situation. Throw in the least competent cop in the Lincolnshire Police and certain results were inevitable.

As understanding dawned, Cesar drew his taser.

"You are not going to taser me," Sam said.

"I really don't want to," he said fervently. "It hurts like billy bugger. I'm sure we can sort all of this out down at the station. Maybe over a cup of tea and a packet of hobnobs, eh?"

Sam wasn't sure how many kidnappers had been talked round with the offer of a cuppa and some biscuits. Although, this was standard Cesar operating procedure. Northern Ireland, Kashmir, the Middle East... Cesar probably believed all could be solved with a catering-sized box of PG Tips and an inexhaustible supply of digestives.

"Open the back door, Sam," he said.

"Well, hang on," said Sam. "You really need to understand what's going on here. Let me try to explain—"

"I'm sure there's a reasonable explanation for all of it," he said softly.

"Yeah, not sure about that..." she muttered.

Cesar took aim at Sam. "I'm sorry..."

"Okay, okay," she said, walking round to the rear of the

Transit and opening the door a crack. "Now, just peek inside to see what's—"

Cesar stepped forward and pulled the door open wide.

"Blaaaark!"

Larry reared up in anger at the intrusion, or possibly he'd run out of food and thought they might have some more. Consuela, tucked under one of his flippers, wobbled alarmingly.

Cesar squealed and raised his weapon instinctively. Sam pushed his hands and aim aside.

"You can't taser Larry!"

"Oh, my gosh!" yelled Cesar.

Larry roared and turned agitatedly on the spot, tipping Consuela out of the van and giving Sam a tail-flick of mushed food across the chest.

Sam tried to shut the door. It jammed on Consuela's legs. Sam pulled her free. Cesar grabbed the door. Larry lunged and momentarily sank his sharp canines into his hand.

"That is not normal!" wailed Cesar, wild-eyed with surprise and pain.

Sam forced the door shut. "It's Larry, the seal," she explained, although it wasn't much of an explanation.

"Flamin' Nora!" Cesar exclaimed, shaking his injured arm.

"Hold still. There's a first aid kit in the front."

Sam fetched it from the glove compartment. She cleaned Cesar's arm with antiseptic wipes. There were two rows of ragged little puncture marks where Larry had grabbed his flabby arm. Cesar sniffed, looking like he was trying to hold back tears.

"Larry's been expelled from his zoo or something for bad behaviour," she explained as she worked. "He's eaten all the food for the meals on wheels. He was on his way to be released into the wild when there was a van mix-up."

"A van mix up?"

"There was this van, and a little van, and I went to pick one up in my even littler van and..." Round and round they go, she thought.

The wounds were still bleeding. "You're going to have to go to a hospital," Sam said.

"Oh, I'm sure it will be fine," he said, his voice strangled by the pain.

"You're going to need a tetanus shot at least," she said, wondering if seals carried rabies like dogs. Or maybe TB like badgers.

"I don't understand," he said.

Sam shrugged. "Did I mention I've had a bad day?" She started to wrap a bandage dressing around his arm.

"At least it's not a kidnapping. Unless..." A stricken looked crossed his face. "Did you kidnap a seal, Sam?"

"Who would kidnap a seal?"

"Yes, quite right. But I'm going to have to insist that you drop the seal off—"

"I would love to."

"—then you and I will need to have a chat. Maybe over a biscuit."

"You need to go to hospital."

"He barely grazed me. I'll get my wife to have a look at it."

"You're injured."

"Erin's a doctor. A cup of tea and I'll be as right as rain."

"Go. To. Hospital. Are you able to drive?"

"Of course," he said.

"Good. I've got to collect a parcel. I will—" She was cut off by her phone ringing. "I'll be there in fifteen minutes, tops."

"Have you got our van?" said a voice.

"Wait." She glanced at her phone. "You're the seal guy."

"Is he all right?"

"Is *he* all right?" she repeated. Cesar had a seal bite in his arm, and her torso was liberally covered with a layer of mushed up food and – Sam sniffed and recoiled – something that had definitely come out of a seal's end.

"Can you bring him to the Seal Land sanctuary up at Anderby Creek?" said the guy.

"I know where that is. I've got a little job to do first."

"More important than animal welfare?"

She could hardly claim taking receipt of a parcel had priority, but she could do both jobs. Sam made to get in the van, then thought of her top. She wasn't going to drive around with that thick layer of crap sat on her chest. She stripped off her top, holding the neck hole wide so none of the vile stuff got on her face or hair.

Cesar stared at her standing in a country lane in her bra. "What are you doing?" he whispered. "Oh, Sam. There's no need for that. I can see your... Oh!" He covered his eyes in distress.

"Hospital!" snarled Sam. She propped Consuela up against the church wall and relieved the mannequin of her gold leotard, which had miraculously managed to survive an encounter with Larry unscathed.

"Sorry, doll," she said and left her by the wall with the ruined top at her feet.

Sam drove as fast as she could back to the DefCon4 office. Larry bellowed at her each time she took a corner. She still wasn't fast enough. She mounted the kerb outside the office, clipping the A-board for Cat's Café and knocking it flat. Still in bra and trousers, she nipped up to the narrow office door and opened it to find a 'Sorry we missed you' note on the mat. She looked at the time on it and swore.

The delivery man hadn't hung around at all.

Catching her breath, trying to find whatever shreds of calm she could, Sam stripped off her trousers and climbed into the leotard. She had to concede she didn't quite have Consuela's model physique, but it fitted, after a fashion. With her trousers back on, the leotard could pass for a shimmering top.

"And now the seal," she told herself.

Anderby Creek village was north, along the coast, past the big holiday camps and seaside amusements, up where the resort coast gave way to a stretch of wild and untouched shoreline. Along Roman Bank, the narrow coast road which edged the dunes, Sam saw advertising signs for a new housing development, Shore View, with a happy cartoon seal greeting potential homeowners. If Larry was typical of the local seals, they were far from ideal mascots.

Seal Land was a low, blue-painted building on the sandy lane nearest the beach. Even though she knew DefCon4 provided the alarms and security for the place, Sam hadn't been here in years, not since childhood. But she could still recall the smell of the place: saltwater on concrete, seaweed and urine. Two alpaca and a donkey were grazing on an enclosure out front. It might be called Seal Land, and operated ostensibly as a sanctuary and rehoming centre, but they had a variety of other animals on site to keep the tourists interested.

"Didn't you used to have penguins?" she said to the Seal Land guy waiting by the main entrance.

"Still do. Jackass penguins."

Sam tilted her head. "Are all your animals badly behaved?"

"Jackass is the species name," said the guy. "We've got penguins, alpaca, koi, tortoises, alligators."

"Seriously?"

"Rescued from a failed zoo in Yorkshire."

"And I thought a seal bite would be bad enough."

He pointed at the van. "Did he bite you?"

"No, not me, but..."

"You've got to be careful. You could get seal finger."

"There are seal fingers?"

"Bacterial infection. All the crap in seal's teeth. Causes inflammation and swelling of the bone marrow."

"Sounds nasty."

"Only way to treat it used to be amputation. Course, hardly anyone gets it. Average member of the public aren't likely to take one of our seals on a joyride round Skeg."

Sam felt the energy drain from her. "A stupid mix-up. I'm sorry."

The guy directed her to bring the Transit round to a double gate. "Back it in, up to the edge of the pool."

She did as directed. Inside the sanctuary itself was a crew

of Seal Land staff and a vet. Sam vaguely recognised him. She recalled he ran a veterinary clinic, horse stables and animal crematorium in Hogsthorpe, or some other village. The vet wore cords, wellies and a shirt and tie, like he believed all vets should dress like James Herriot. Seals basked in the evening warmth on other pools but this pool was empty.

"Larry doesn't mix well with others," said the Seal Land guy.

"The main concern is dehydration," the vet was saying. Despite the English rustic look, he had a crisp Eastern (or possibly Southern) European accent. "When did he last eat?"

The Seal Land guy was about to answer, but Sam jumped in. "He's definitely eaten today."

The vet raised an eyebrow.

"Salmon, hotpot, lasagne, cottage pie," she said. "Probably some carrot cake too."

"You fed him carrot cake?"

She shook her head. The vet looked perplexed.

"I thought he'd been in the back of a Securicor van today. I'd been told..."

"DefCon4 at your service." She did a little half-bow that almost certainly didn't help, particularly given the shiny gold top didn't lend much of an air of professionalism.

"Let's get the ramp up here," said Seal Land guy.

The vet and the seal volunteers flanked the doors and pulled them wide, standing to the sides of the board ramp to ensure Larry went straight down. The seal flopped down the ramp and over the low wall, plopping fatly into the pool. Streamers of lasagne sauce and gravy drifted off him.

"Blaaaark!"

It was a recognisable sound of joy, and Sam found herself warming slightly to the beast. Perhaps she'd just seen the wrong side of him while he was captive in the van? As if in response to her thoughts he surfaced right beside her, snapping and bellowing in a loud display of aggression. She took a hurried step back.

"You complete dick!"

"That he is," said the Seal Land guy. "That he is."

S am didn't have time to go home and get changed.

She had an hour in hand before the StoreWatch meeting at Carnage Hall. One hour was time enough to drive the van to the depot; to have an argument with the clerk about who was responsible for the smeary food mess, smashed trays and the remains of a seal transport crate that had been under the tarpaulin in the back; to leave the argument unfinished, collect the Ape 50 and drive it at full speed (twenty-nine miles an hour) down to the seafront and Carnage Hall.

Carnage Hall stood on Grand Parade promenade with the Pleasure Beach fairground behind it. At night it was wreathed in the firework-light display of street side illuminations, gaudy amusement display signs opposite, and the twinkling lights of the big wheel and Rockin' Rollercoaster behind. In all the Vegas lighting, you could almost forget it was in Skegness. Carnage Hall was a theatre, but also hosted three bars, a ground floor restaurant, and numerous function rooms. It billed itself as Skegness's premier entertainment centre, but still amounted to little more than a place where you could get a pie, a pint, and front row seats to whatever touring tribute act was currently in town.

She parked up at one of the few spots on the parade where it was legal to do so and went inside. According to the large poster in the foyer 'Antoine de Winter's Psychic Extravaganza' was on in the main auditorium, and there was quite a crowd of people waiting to get in. An information board said the StoreWatch meeting was upstairs in the Frank Carson memorial banqueting suite, so she pushed through.

The Frank Carson was a small room, only suitable for the most modest of banquets. It was set out presentation style with rows of chairs for at least forty people. Less than half of them were taken.

Sam scrawled her name on a badge and sat at the back. She was required to be here, and DefCon4 could track her GPS signal, but she didn't have to be a willing participant. Cesar set up at the front and handed out agendas. Sam was prepared to believe he had ignored her advice and not bothered with the hospital. More fool him.

She fidgeted uncomfortably as the meeting began. The leotard wasn't a comfortable fit. It was digging in at her shoulders and her groin. It felt like her blood supply was about to be cut off somewhere.

She was sufficiently distracted that she didn't notice the man sliding into a seat further along the row at first. She judged him to be an attractive looking guy: he had four limbs, two eyes, looked like he knew how to use soap, and didn't have the eyes of a serial killer. Sam's standards of personal desirability weren't as high as they once were.

"Am I late?" he said. "Struggled to get through that crowd downstairs. Who knew a psychic could be so popular?"

"The psychic, one hopes." Sam passed him an agenda from the seat next to her. She did it mainly to avert his attention while she tried to adjust the leotard one last time.

He scanned the paper briefly.

"I treat it like bingo," she said. "When we've ticked them all off, we get a prize."

"We get to leave?" he said.

"Precisely."

His name badge said: *Frost & Sons, Jimmy MacIntyre.*

The definition of madness, thought Jimmy MacIntyre that morning, is someone who keeps doing the same thing but expects different results.

He spooled out the measuring tape from the edge of Greg Mandyke's land, across the dusty track to the boundary fence of St Matthew's church. Five metres. Five metres exactly. Fifty centimetres short of council planning regulations.

He hissed bitterly through his teeth. He didn't swear. He'd already done enough swearing.

He released the tape-measure and it sprang back into the housing. The metal tape whiplashed noisily.

He walked down to the track towards the van. Seeing him coming, Wayne stubbed his cigarette out on the door and dropped it. "Is it good, mate?"

"Five metres," said Jimmy.

"But that's not enough," said Wayne.

"No," agreed Jimmy.

Wayne was a master of stating the obvious. His fat bald head apparently wasn't big enough to handle much else. No subtleties from Wayne. No lies. No original thoughts. Just a big cheery face, the loyalty of a Labrador and arms that could lug hundred kilo bags of builders cement all day long.

"What now?" said Wayne.

"We go meet Mandyke."

Greg Mandyke had agreed to meet them in, of all places, a greasy spoon in the town centre. His Tesla was pulled up on the curb, effectively blocking it for anyone who wasn't pencil thin. He got out to meet them. Greg – silver-haired, tanned and svelte – had once been a true grafter, but as his business grew he was to be found less and less on a building site and more and more on the golf course. Wealthy enough that he barely needed to work at all. Greg Mandyke was where Jimmy saw himself being in twenty years' time. Where Jimmy *had* seen himself being in twenty years' time, until Bob Frost's death.

"You're looking well, Greg," said Jimmy.

Greg slapped his midriff. "I live in the gym these days."

"I thought you were lucky to avoid prison after that nasty business a few months back," said Jimmy. According to rumours in the trade, and newspaper reports of the court trial, Greg had threatened to beat up a houseowner over unpaid building costs.

"I was," he said. "But I had a good solicitor. Got it down to a few hours of community service. And I'll be wriggling my way out of that, too."

"How's that, Mr Mandyke?" said Wayne.

"Doctor's note," grinned Greg. "Apparently I've got so many allergies there won't be any community service work they can force me to do. Burger?" He led the way inside without checking they were following. "Morning, Cat. Whatever these gents want. My treat."

"Aw, thanks, mate," said Wayne and clapped his hands together.

"From this place?" said Jimmy, nose wrinkled.

"Best in town," said Greg. "Part of my daily routine. Gym. Burger. Good and evil. Ying and yang."

"Ant and Dec," said Wayne.

"Exactly," said Greg. "Three cheeseburgers, Cat. Everything on them."

Watching the woman flip burgers on the hotplate made Jimmy impatient. He didn't want to eat greasy burgers while breathing cooking fumes. Jimmy didn't have time for this. He had a problem to fix, a deal to close.

"Greg, I wanted to talk to you about—"

"I know what you want to talk about," said Mandyke, commandeering a table. "Welton le Marsh."

"Yes."

"I've watched the houses going up. What is that? A dozen new homes?"

"Fourteen."

"Hardly in-keeping with the local rustic aesthetic, are they?"

"Rustic aesthetic?" This was coastal Lincolnshire. Round here local aesthetic was a static caravan, perhaps with a bingo hall or amusement arcade off to one side.

"You've done a good job of keeping Bob's business ticking over," said Greg.

"Not just ticking over."

"No," conceded Greg. "I've seen the proposed site for Shore View too."

"Nothing proposed about it. Bought, planning approved, the first of the pre-fabs already brought in."

"But you want to talk to me about buying a strip of my land."

Jimmy had the plans for the Welton le Marsh development tucked under his arm. He began to unfold them when the burger flipper brought three plated burgers to their table and Jimmy struggled to find room. He laid the plans out, holding them in place with his steel tape measure and a ketchup bottle.

"Welton le Marsh."

There was the road running through the village down past the churchyard of St Matthew's, and the little five metre access track Frost and Sons had been using for their construction vehicles. It continued past the big swathe of Mandyke's land and curved left up along Beck Lane and the edges of woodland and crop fields. A nice wide eight metre section of land had been highlighted, connecting the housing development with Beck Lane.

"I just want to nail down the details for the road we're going to build here," said Jimmy.

Greg said nothing, just bit into his burger. A droplet of grease dribbled on his chin.

"These are smashin'," mumbled Wayne as he ate.

"Are you not going to eat yours, Jimmy?" Greg said.

"We've got some leeway on the price, if that's an issue," said Jimmy.

Greg took another bite and chewed it thoroughly before swallowing. "I'm not selling," he said.

Jimmy guessed he was going to say that, but he was still stunned. "As I said, the price—"

"It's not the price. I don't want to break up that land. I've got my own plans."

"You agreed."

"Maybe. Even if I did, it was with Bob."

"And now it's me."

Greg shook his head. "Is it your company now?"

"No."

"Is Jacinda here?"

"She's at Shore View."

"Sending you out like her flying monkey?"

"I run things."

Greg ate the last of the burger and licked his fingers. For a lean guy, he could put food away. "I had the greatest respect for Bob Frost," he said. "The greatest. We used to golf together. Shooting out by Anderby Creek..." He looked away to the sky and the seagulls. "Nasty business that. In the end."

"For his sake then," Jimmy tried.

Greg refocused. There was a stern set to his face. "Thing is, Jimmy, you should know better than the rest of us. A verbal contract ain't worth the paper it's written on."

Wayne chuckled, a mouth full of food. "Good one, mate. Paper."

"I'm not leaving you in the lurch," said Greg. He traced a finger over the map. "You've got a route in here. Sure, you might have to reconsider that last house, but it will work."

Jimmy wanted to tell him that the track was too narrow, that the county council planners would not approve plans for a public highway of that width. He could tell him – but it would be a last desperate plea to get Greg to sell. Plan B would be scuppered, and Plan B was a shitty plan as it was.

"Come on, mate, play fair," he said. "What are you going to do with that land anyway? You've had it fifteen years or more. It was a bad investment on your part. Just bloody wasteland."

"Bad investment, huh?" Greg picked up a napkin and wiped the grease off his chin. "You think you belong at the top table, Jimmy? Think you can tell me my own business?"

"At least I don't threaten to hurt old people when my projects go over-budget," snapped Jimmy.

Greg licked at his teeth. "Get your things off the table. Eat your burger like a good boy." He dropped his napkin on this plate and left.

If he'd thought about it, Jimmy would have followed him out and keyed the Tesla's paintjob as Greg drove off, but he was too dumbfounded. He watched the car as it went.

"Fuck!" he spat and threw his burger onto the plate.

"No swearing in here," said the woman at the counter.

"Didn't you want your burger?" said Wayne.

Jimmy took out his phone to message Jacinda and saw she had already messaged him.

THIS CONTAINER IS FULL OF CAPITALIST WHORES. SHORE VIEW
ASAP.

"FUCK," he said.

8

It was a twenty minute drive north to the Frost and Sons development at Anderby Creek. Anderby was a nowhere place, a splash of houses, a dribble of caravans, a pub and a small store too eclectic to properly count as a village shop. It was an odd place and it attracted oddities. The Seal Land zoo was just off from the sea front. Up by the dunes they had a purpose built 'cloud observatory', which to Jimmy's eyes was nothing more than a raised platform with adjustable mirrors on the top. And, now, it had Shore View.

Anderby Creek's high street was just a poorly paved sandy track. Running off it at an angle was an even more poorly paved track that wound up into the dunes to the south.

"You ever been to Seal Land?" said Wayne. "I like seals."

"What's to like?" said Jimmy. "Dogs with flippers. Greedy bastards. And they stink of fish."

Wayne honked and clapped his hands like a sea lion and nearly lost control of the van in the process.

"Just drive," said Jimmy.

The track came out on the top of the dunes and the cleared space that was going to become Shore View. At first glance, there wasn't much to see, but a lot of groundwork had been done. Concrete foundations had been laid for forty accommodation units. Power lines had already been installed, with cables and junctions springing up next to each plot like twisted weeds of black plastic and copper.

At the furthest end was an unloaded shipping container. To one side was a flatbed truck; on the other was Jacinda's red coupe. Jacinda leaned against the bonnet and stared out to sea, a foul look on her face. Like the sea had some sodding nerve being so damned sea-like.

Wayne pulled up.

"Wait here," said Jimmy and jumped out.

Jacinda Frost, an only child and unmentioned daughter in Frost and Sons company, was a couple of years younger than Jimmy. While still an apprentice on Bob's building team, Jimmy had driven with Bob to collect the horse given to Jacinda for her sixteenth birthday. Jacinda had been a twig-thin teenager, and the horse had towered over her Jimmy recalled. A dozen years later, the horse was now dog food and Jacinda was still a twig: long, slender, brittle and thorny.

"My dad used to come shooting out here," she said, without looking at him.

"Yes. I remember."

"Set up clay traps and shoot out to sea. Not sure it was legal. I remember cold mornings. The mist."

Jimmy nodded.

"Is it sorted?" she said.

"Hmmm?" Jimmy had no intention of answering her if she was going to ask half-formed and ambiguous questions.

She faced him. "The access road. Greg Mandyke. Have you confirmed the purchase?"

"He's not selling."

Her huge eyes twitched. "Did you up the price?"

"He's not selling."

"Did you even try? You do know we need that land?"

"I do know that." Jimmy didn't add he'd known it long before she had ever shown an interest in her father's business.

"The business partners for Shore View will be coming to the Skegness and District Local Business Guild Awards next Friday."

"I know that."

"And they'll expect to see progress."

"I know. Hey, the first one's in place." He banged the side of the container. Flakes of paint came away on his hand.

"You got my text?" she said.

"Yeah. I assumed there was some autocorrect error. It said—"

"Open it."

Jimmy went to the double doors of the container. It was far from new, probably battered and corroded by decades of sea spray and ocean crossings. The bolts were stiff. Jimmy wiggled the second bolt loose. The door swung open.

"These were meant to be empty," he said.

"You don't have to tell me," said Jacinda. "I've got men coming in to fit windows and doors later today."

The container was filled with cardboard boxes, damp and mildewed. Each was printed with a jaunty cloud-like logo and the name *Capitalist Whore*. He opened the nearest box. The wet cardboard came away like tissue paper. Cardboard-backed blister packs slid over each other and fell in a heap at his feet.

He picked one up. Pink packaging, the same jolly logo, and behind the plastic a poseable plastic doll in hot pants and a crop top. "Knock-off Barbie dolls."

"Capitalist Whore," said Jacinda.

He read the packaging. "Made in China. I guess something got lost in translation. '*I have the dimensions you desire!*'" he read.

"We need Shore View up and running for when the business partners come."

"This is fixable," he said, tossing the Capitalist Whore back into the container.

She was unconvinced. "And we can't put the finance in place for Shore View unless we can finish up the Welton le Marsh development."

"Jacinda, I—"

She glared at him for using her name, like it was somehow an affront, an attempt at over-familiarity, even though he had called her by no other name in all the years he had known her.

She said nothing. In the silence, he thought of all the things he could have said to her. At the top of the list was the unhelpful comment that they shouldn't have stuck a spade in the ground at Welton le Marsh until the purchase of the access road land was confirmed. That this was a result of her hastiness. Okay, yes, she had been going through a tough time with the funeral and all, and yes, the deadline for the planning permission had been rapidly approaching and if they'd wanted to avoid months of delay and possible bankruptcy there had been no other choice but to start work, but...

"What did Greg say?" she asked. "What did Greg actually say?"

Jimmy chewed his tongue a second. "He said you should have been there yourself to talk to him."

"Doesn't he know I'm busy?"

Busy doing what? Jimmy screamed silently. The order books were empty. Apart from Shore View, Frost and Sons had no jobs lined up. There were men sitting idle, unpaid. They could be doing little jobs: driveways, block paving, loft conversions. There was nothing but the stalled Welton le Marsh development and this Shore View vanity project.

"Let's fix this." He went round to the flatbed truck's open driver's door. The driver, unshaven, a red bandana tied round his head like he was Axl Rose, was constructing a roll-up.

"It's, um, Ivan, isn't it?" said Jimmy.

"Yngve," said the driver.

"Right, Yngve. That container needs emptying."

Yngve Odinson licked the edge of his roll-up. "And I told tha woman that's not me job."

"But your dad – it is your dad, isn't it—?"

"Ragnar, aye."

"He's got a truck or something. He could shift this lot."

"Shift?"

"Gather it. Dump it. We don't need it."

Yngve regarded the roll-up and stuck it behind his ear, under the edge of his bandana. "I could call 'im. Make it disappear, aye?"

"Excellent. Just..." Jimmy dug around his wallet. "Fifty quid?" he said, knowing it was too low an offer.

Yngve snatched it from his hands, his eyes alight. "Fifty. It's gone. Fucking vanished."

"Good." As the Odinson man took out a phone to call his dubious family, Jimmy went back to Jacinda. "Sorted," he said.

"Of course, it's sorted," she said without a flicker of gratitude. "But what if the next container turns up with something in? Or the next?"

"Did you specify empty containers when you bought them?"

"I think it's kind of implied, don't you, Jimmy?" she snarled, then huffed. "It's just endless. By the way, you will need to be the face of the company tonight."

He was the face of the company every night. Every day and every night. Jacinda Frost's name was above the door, on the vans and, mostly gallingly, on the company papers but he, Jimmy, was the face of the company. "What's tonight?"

"StoreWatch."

"What?"

"The neighbourhood watch thing for local businesses," she said. "Meeting's at Carnage Hall at six."

He looked at his watch. "Why aren't you going?"

"Pointless talking shop," she said, with a derisory snort. "A waste of time."

"Then why am *I* going?"

"It's run by the local business guild. We have to show willing. I intend to claim the Business of the Year Award. Can't do that if we're not supporting the business guild's sterling work in the local area. Carnage Hall has a bar."

"Pardon?"

She tilted her head. "Have a drink. On expenses. I'm sure that will get you through the evening." She said it with huge generosity, as though she had offered him everything his heart desired. That she had no idea how little the pathetic gesture meant twisted in his gut.

"And Welton le Marsh?"

"It needs sorting," she said. "By all and any means."

"Yes?" he said, because her answer was no answer at all.

She breathed in sharply, impatiently, her little sparrow chest swelling. "The works access track. We make that our road."

"It's five metres wide."

"Have you moved the fencing on the church side?"

"As far as we can before we hit … more permanent barriers. Five metres."

"It has to be—"

"Five and a half metres. I know."

She stared at him. He met her gaze. Ten years ago he'd fantasised about sleeping with the woman, marrying her even. Now he was more likely to fantasise about throttling her and burying her under a patio.

"Do I have to come up with all the ideas?" she said. "And it's one beer."

"What?"

"One beer. Tonight. And get a receipt."

Jimmy bit down on any sharp response. "Of course."

Like verbal contracts and whispered promises, if it wasn't written down, it hadn't happened.

9

Jimmy vented his frustrations on Wayne all the way to Carnage Hall. It was like screaming into a cushion: momentarily relieving but ultimately unproductive. Wayne had heard it all before anyway. Jacinda's lack of business skills, her utter failure to manage people or situations, Jimmy's frustration that he, the disinherited surrogate son, was now nothing more than her gopher.

"Do they train them?" said Wayne, circling the clock tower roundabout and coming onto Grand Parade.

"What?"

"Gophers. Do they train them to do things? Is that why they call people gophers?"

"What are you talking about?"

Doubt clouded Wayne's expression. "Gophers. Aren't they...? The little things that pop their heads up and go 'meep'. Prairie dogs."

"Jesus." Jimmy could have wept. "Prairie dogs are prairie dogs. Gophers are gophers."

"They're different?"

"Yes," said Jimmy, then realised he had no idea if they were, or how. "We don't call people gophers because they're like gophers. They're gophers, go-fors. 'Go for this, go for that'. Gopher."

"Ah," Wayne nodded. "It's more 'Go do this, go do that'. Should call them go-dos." He pulled up outside an amusement arcade opposite Carnage Hall.

Jimmy looked at his watch. "This thing won't last more than a couple of hours," he said. "Pick me up here at eight."

"What we doing at eight?" said Wayne, lighting a fag.

Jimmy jumped down from the cab. "Just pick me up at eight." He slammed the door, muttering, "Fucking go-do."

He went inside the foyer, pushing through the early ticket holders for 'Antoine de Winter's Psychic Extravaganza' and took the stairs to the Frank Carson memorial banqueting suite.

Jimmy put his name on one of the prepared attendees name badges. The copper at the front waved with a bandaged hand for him to take a seat. Jimmy considered the assortment of minor businesspeople and shopkeepers – butchers, bakers, candlestick-makers – and sat near the back, one seat away from a lone woman who looked as happy as him to be there.

She looked up as he sat, giving him the briefest of smiles. She was dressed in a strappy gold top, like she was going out clubbing later.

"Am I late?" he asked. "Struggled to get through that

crowd downstairs. Who knew a psychic could be so popular?"

"The psychic, one hopes." She slid a sheet of paper over to him. "Agenda."

"Uh-huh." He scanned the list of items. Mobility scooters, fly-tipping, the seagull menace, travellers...

"I treat it like bingo," she said. "When we've ticked them all off, we get a prize."

"We get to leave?" he said.

"Precisely."

The copper launched into his presentation. Sergeant Cesar Hackett had a red sheen to his face and sweat on his brow, but it didn't appear to be nerves. He launched into his material with gusto.

Jimmy had suspected the copper was going to give them a doom-and-gloom rundown of the town's problems, paint Skegness as a town under siege from lawlessness and thuggery, with Cesar as its sheriff and the meeting attendees as his willing deputes. In that, Jimmy was wrong.

Cesar started off with a PowerPoint of photos of Skegness – and did he have photos. A whole narrative of photos. Skegness seafront, calm and peaceful at the beginning of the day. A child with some candyfloss. Pavements bustling with holidaymakers in the sunshine. Convoys of mobility scooters rolling down the promenade. A dog playing on the beach. Happy teenagers munching on donuts. Lager drinkers on park benches in animated conversation. A family gathered around a human-sized fibre-glass ice-cream. Smiles, cheeriness, sunshine. Nothing about crime. Nothing about lawlessness.

Stopping on a final picture of Skegness's mascot, the skipping Jolly Fisherman, Cesar turned to the audience. "Isn't it a lovely town, eh?"

There were a couple of nods, slightly more shrugs and an even greater level of complete indifference. When it became apparent Cesar wasn't going to immediately offer anything more than that, a woman on the front row put up her hand.

"What are you going to do about the mobility scooters?" she demanded.

"Do?" said Cesar.

"There's too many of them."

"Skegness is very popular with older people," Cesar agreed, smiling.

"They block the pavement. They go too slow."

"Do they go too slow or is everyone else in too much of hurry? People should take the time to enjoy things, look around."

"You don't think there's a problem?" said someone else.

Jimmy, who had experienced Skeg at the height of summer, thought there was a problem. One that could be solved if the young stopped breeding, the disabled stayed at home and everyone found somewhere to go other than Skegness seafront.

Cesar fielded inane questions about pavement usage, including why mobility scooters were allowed on the pavements if bicycles weren't, whether mobility scooters needed insurance like other motor vehicles, and whether the owner of the fibreglass ice-cream could sue someone if a careless scooter user knocked it over (which apparently someone had).

Bored, Jimmy scanned the room and silently played shag, marry, kill with all the women in the room. The woman in the spangly top next to him came out of the game quite well, not least because she didn't seem at all inclined to join in the general wasting of their evening by participating in the debate.

"If we're not going to do something about the problem with mobility scooters on the pavements, why's it on the agenda?" demanded an angry shopkeeper.

Cesar blinked the sweat away from his eyes. The man seemed positively unwell. "We are doing something, aren't we? We're discussing it. We're recognising our preconceptions and adjusting our perspectives. It's all fine really, isn't it?"

An irritated man on the front row stared at his agenda. "Fly-tipping then!"

"Ah." Cesar progressed his PowerPoint. His swollen bandaged hand seemed to be having trouble with the remote. He flicked through images of dumped rubbish bags, discarded mattresses in lay-bys – even an entire fitted kitchen.

"It's a bloody eyesore," said someone.

"And it's getting worse."

"No one wants to see rubbish dumped in our lay-bys," Cesar agreed. "And we don't know who's responsible—"

"Ragnar Odinson!" declared a man loudly.

"We don't *know* who's responsible," Cesar repeated.

"And his sons!" said another man. "The whole bloody family's at it."

"When are you going to lock them up?" said a woman.

"That Torsten Odinson is back out again," said another.

Cesar blinked furiously and gulped at a glass of water standing by the projector.

"Should've gone to the hospital," muttered spangly top.

"Is he all right?" said Jimmy.

"Bitten by a seal," she replied.

"A seal?"

"Probably got seal finger."

"You made that up." He used the momentary conversation to look at her stick-on name badge, trying to make it look like he wasn't peering at her tits. Sam Applewhite – DefCon4.

"Point is ... the point *is*," insisted Cesar with some difficulty. "Although the dumped rubbish causes a problem, when I went and looked inside this dumped kitchen unit, look who I found living inside..."

Jimmy's hopes that he would show them images of a cute squirrel family, or a pair of snuggling hedgehogs, were swiftly dashed. The next picture was of a cupboard full of filthy crud and half a dozen rats peering over the top of it. The phone camera's flash had given them a powerful case of red-eye, and it looked like the cupboard was home to Satan's own rat squadron.

"Jesus wept," gasped a woman.

"Life always finds a way," said Cesar. "It's beautiful, really."

"Dumping rubbish on our roads is not beautiful!"

"Oh, hell," muttered Sam. "Just remembered. I left a bearded lady on the side of the road."

Jimmy was about to ask her what the hell that meant

when Cesar, trying to take another sip of water, coughed, choked and had enough presence of mind to grab a waste-paper bin before throwing up. He retched for a good thirty seconds.

Sam Applewhite stood up. "You need to go to hospital!"

"No," said Cesar. "Erin told me not to make a fuss. Really, I'm—" He got no further before vomiting again.

There was the general unhurried chatter of people who'd realised their civic duty to a poorly soul was being called upon, and that the meeting was about to be cut drastically short.

"I think an alcoholic beverage is called for," said Jimmy.

"Not antibiotics and tetanus shots?" said Sam.

"I meant for me." He looked her up and down. "You need one too?"

10

J immy MacIntyre had no problem with women, and no problem getting women.

All a man had to do was show up at a nightclub or bar – the Tiki Club or Wellies – at a late hour and there'd be any number of drunk girls, come down from the Butlins holiday camp or the caravan parks, happy to get off with a suave-looking local lad. Hen parties and mums on the lash were the easiest of all: the first had come out with something to prove, the others with something to escape from.

Tackling sober women – sober and intelligent women – was trickier; particularly in a calmer, less alcohol-fuelled place like the Jim Bowen bar at Carnage Hall. Women had no idea how tough it was for a modern man, the fine line he had to walk between equality and chivalry. Even offering to buy a drink could be misinterpreted as chauvinism.

"What are you having?" he asked.

Sam drummed her fingers on the edge of the bar. "You sure?"

Well, he'd asked now, so he pressed on. "Absolutely." Adding, "It's on expenses anyway," to reassure her.

Sam twitched her nose. It was a cute expression. "Long Island Iced Tea?"

Jimmy glanced at the cocktail menu. Long Island Iced Tea: a five-shot cocktail.

"Well, I don't know if the expenses can stretch that far—"

"If it's a problem."

Damn it. Why did he have to bring money into it and make himself appear tight?

"No, it's fine," he said firmly. A little too firmly. "You asked. The lady would like a Long Island Iced Tea," he told the barman. "And a receipt."

The barman – in a waistcoat and a vintage white shirt, like he should be tending a bar in a western saloon or a paddle steamer – silently set about mixing the cocktail.

THEY TOOK a window table overlooking the gardens and fairground. Somewhere out there, in the black, was the beach and the sea. Far out there were suggestions of white and red flickering lights. Maybe the offshore wind farms, maybe a sand dredger, maybe even a container ship travelling across the North Sea to Belgium or Holland.

Jimmy raised his pint glass in cheers. Sam Applewhite of DefCon4 chinked her glass to his.

"So, tell me about yourself," he said.

Sam stirred her drink and wriggled in the seat. She had a restless energy, like she couldn't be still, couldn't be contained. "What's to say? My name's Sam Applewhite. I live in Skegness with my dad. I came back because... Well, that's complicated."

"Yes?"

"I came back to be with my dad. He's getting on a bit."

"Dementia?" he said, in his most concerned voice.

"What? No. Least I don't think so. He just needs a few things sorting out."

"And you've always worked for DefCon4?"

"Christ, no. It's only been a few months. Feels a hell of a lot longer. I sort of fell into it."

"And it's all this stuff?" Jimmy waved a hand to suggest the world of business and security. "Security guards and CCTV and stuff."

She shook her head. Her hair bounced softly. "Hardly any of it's that stuff. It's a big company. They've diversified a hell of a lot. Health and safety checks, prisoner transport, courier services, food deliveries..."

"Really? And you do all of that."

"Yup. It's only me and Doug in the office." She clutched her drink. Well, at nearly a tenner for a cocktail, Jimmy would want to hold onto it tightly too.

"Is Doug here?" he said.

"Doug doesn't get out of the office much."

"But you enjoy it?"

"The job?" said Sam. Another cute nose twitch, another sexy bum wriggle. "It pays. That's definitely the main motivator."

"Amen to that," he said, forcing himself to smile because most days he didn't feel like his job paid at all.

"And you do get to meet some interesting characters. There's a lot of local ... colour." She looked out of the window. "Some people who seem to not fit in anywhere else."

"And there's nowhere else to go," he said. "Skegness. End of the line."

She slurped through her straw, made a sucking noise in the ice and immediately stopped. "Wow. That went down quick."

"Another?" he said.

She dithered.

"Go on," he said.

"It has been a tough day," she said. As he reached for his wallet she added, "It's my round."

Jimmy downed his pint quickly.

SAM RETURNED WITH DRINKS.

"To the end of a tough day," he toasted.

"One of many," she said.

"There are other jobs out there," he suggested.

"But this job definitely has variety."

"I'll bet."

"Always got to think on your feet."

"Right."

"It's like..." She looked him straight in the eye. "What do you do when a seal has got into the back of your van and trashed all your deliveries while you've been chatting to some old dear about the ghosts she's been seeing in the churchyard?"

That threw him. Here they were having a nice little conversation and a nice little drink, he was thinking maybe if he got a third Long Island Iced Tea into her he could call up Wayne and tell him to not bother collecting him and Jimmy could spend the night exploring what was under that sequinned top, and then she goes and asks a nonsense question like that.

"Is that a real situation? Is that something that happened?"

"Come on," said Sam. "What would you do in that situation?"

"Er..."

He was saved from answering by her phone buzzing. She glanced at it, gave him an apologetic look and answered it. While she 'uh-huh'ed and 'yeah'ed, he checked the time. Seven thirty. He had thirty minutes in which to close the deal with this Sam and cancel Wayne.

She ended the call. "Sorry. My dad. One of his plums got stuck behind the fridge and he still can't get it out."

Jimmy winced but didn't ask.

"He could hear I was in a bar," she said. "Wanted to know if I was 'courting'?"

Jimmy grinned. "And are you?"

She looked a little concerned. "Right now?"

"Generally."

She drank while she thought. "There's an ex. Rich. Rich by name..."

"Recent?"

She tutted. "No. Months now. Years in fact."

"Oh, a while then..." He treated her to a half-smile, a charming little half smile that was meant to be partly sympathetic and partly an open invitation.

"I don't have much time for a social life," she said.

"But you're off out later," he said.

"Aren't I out now?" said Sam.

"I meant..." He nodded at her top. "You look dressed for a night on the town."

She fingered the edge of the top, lifted it away a centimetre. The woman was a tease. "This? I came straight from work."

"Oh," he said, surprised. "It's a very ... striking top."

"Not company uniform or anything."

He pulled a face, a magnanimous 'I'm easy' kind of expression. "Where'd you get it?"

"Well ... I'm not sure I'll be wearing it again. It's actually out of my dad's old things."

"Your dad wears a lot of sequins, does he?"

"Ha ha. His props cupboards. He used to be a stage magician."

Jimmy thought the name Applewhite had rung a bell. Applewhite, Applewhite... "Marvin Applewhite? Your dad is Mr Marvellous?"

"Was. He's retired now."

Jimmy grinned. "So that makes you ... Little Miss Marvellous? Do you know any tricks?"

"I can show you the Amazing Disappearing Sam if you don't change the subject."

He held up his hands in submission, pint in one hand. "I like you, Sam," he said.

"That's good. I like me too," she replied and looked at her drink like she wasn't used to saying such things sober.

"I'm meant to have a work thing later," he said.

"At this hour? You're a builder, right?"

"Management," he corrected her. "My lad's supposed to be collecting me at eight."

"Not got long," she said.

"Unless I get a better offer." It was a clumsy choice of words.

"Offer?" said Sam.

"You eaten tonight?"

"The day I've had has put me off food a bit."

"We can skip dinner."

She frowned at him and drew back in her seat. "I barely know you, Jimmy."

"What do you want to know?"

She was still and silent.

"I'm sorry," he said. "I was too upfront. I'm too honest for my own good."

"No," she said, suddenly alive again. "Honesty is good. Upfront is good."

"Right," he agreed, smiling. "You've got to know where you stand these days."

"Right."

"You can get into a lot of hot water over a misunderstanding. What's said on the spur of the moment can be open to a lot of misinterpretation."

"Indeed."

"It's all about honesty."

"Sure."

"Clarity."

"Yes."

"Consent."

She coughed and took a sip of drink. "Consent. Yes."

"As I say, Wayne's picking me up in—" he looked at his watch, clicking his tongue "—fifteen minutes. But I would much rather spend the evening with you."

"That's really nice, Jimmy," she said, then scowled. "Not 'nice'. That's a nothing word. Lovely? Just as bad. Look, I'd love to have some more drinks and..." She pursed her lips. Her hands hovered in her lap, like she was itching to shove them down her trousers. "Jimmy, I just want to get out of these clothes and into bed—"

"Okay, okay," he said, clapping his hands together. "Let's see where the evening takes us, but cards on the table—"

"That's not what I was going to suggest..." she said.

"It's fine," he reassured her. "Don't be embarrassed. I like a woman who knows her mind."

She regarded her glass, drained the last of the cocktail and stood. "This has been..." She searched around for a word. "Nope. Got nothing."

"You're leaving?" he said.

"Oh, I certainly am. You and Wayne have got work to do. Thanks for the drink."

She walked off in a determined manner, a gesture spoiled somewhat when her shin collided with a low table. She corrected course and carried on, looking back to see if he'd seen her. Jimmy had seen her all right.

11

"Bloody cockteases the lot of them," said Jimmy, getting into the van.

"Who?" said Wayne.

"Women?"

Wayne clearly gave this some thought as he drove down the parade. Jimmy could almost see the cogs turning, smell the gears burning. "All of them?" said Wayne eventually.

"All of them."

"Wow."

Jimmy huffed deeply. "Welton le Marsh."

Wayne looked at him.

"We've got stones to move," said Jimmy.

Jimmy let the van rock him on the night drive out of town. Two pints wasn't enough to make him drunk, not even close, but it gave him a freedom of thought, a fluidity and lucidity that rarely came to him sober. He thought about that bloody Sam Applewhite. He thought about the other frustrations of the day. Greg Mandyke refusing to sell, Jacinda Frost's arrogance and naivety, an access road that was half a metre too narrow to pass council planning regulations...

Welton le Marsh was in darkness when they arrived. It was too small a village to have its own street lighting. There were lights on in the pub and a couple of the cottages, but from the churchyard onwards it was dark. Wayne pulled into the building site access track. The part-finished houses on the development were just about visible, black silhouettes like castle ruins against a grey-black sky.

Jimmy jumped out, felt a moment of beer-induced wobble, took a piss off the side of the track onto Mandyke's property, and joined Wayne at the back of the van. Wayne was fixing a headtorch on his own huge bonce and passed another to Jimmy. He glanced to the land on the other side of the track. The fence was made of wooden posts bound to each other with barbed wire.

"We've moved the fence posts as far as they'll go," said Wayne.

"Fifty centimetres," said Jimmy. "That's all we need. Fifty centimetres. Then we get the surveyors out, get the maps redrawn, pass planning and... Get that barrow. Pass it over to me when I..."

He carefully stepped over the fencing, holding down the wire with both hands and making sure he didn't snag his trousers on the barbs. Wayne passed him the wheelbarrow and the shovels, and climbed over too. Wayne got his boot caught somewhere and fell over onto the thick grass.

"I'm not happy about this," he muttered.

"You should watch where you're going," said Jimmy.

"Not that." He got to his feet and brushed at his hands under torchlight. "The stones. It's not right."

"No one cares," said Jimmy. "No one will notice. We've already done one." He cast his headtorch along the boundary. "Four, five... We only need to move six of these."

The stones along the boundary fence were old and weatherworn, none of them less than a hundred and fifty years old. No one cared. No one would care, as long as they didn't break them or leave tell-tale marks in the earth.

"This one first," said Jimmy, jabbing a spade into the earth to cut out a rectangle of turf to fill the hole the stone would leave behind.

"What if someone sees us?" said Wayne.

"What if we don't get this done?" replied Jimmy. "You want to tell Jacinda?"

"Not me, mate. She scares me."

Jimmy grunted in agreement as he dug. "You know that shotgun she shoots off in her office? The twelve-bore Purdey?"

"I've heard someone say it was the one Bob used to—" Wayne didn't finish the sentence.

"Exactly," said Jimmy. "Her own dad. She's a nutter. Now, create some wiggle room round the stone. Come on. I don't have to tell you to do everything. Show some initiative."

Wayne didn't move.

"Get a shift on," said Jimmy. "Sooner we're done..."

"There's someone watching us," said Wayne.

"No there isn't." Jimmy looked round.

In the not-quite-black of night, the outline of a person

was clearly visible against the wall by the road. The figure was perfectly still. There was no telling if they were facing towards or away from them.

Jimmy reversed the shovel in his hands, holding it like a club or an axe. "Some nosey bastard," he said to Wayne.

"I don't like this," said Wayne.

"You mentioned."

Jimmy approached cautiously. "Oi, mate!" he called out as he neared.

The figure didn't move. Jimmy stepped closer. Wayne followed.

"Oi, mate! What's your game, eh?"

Still nothing. There was quiver in Jimmy's guts. He told himself such quivering had far more to do with beer than thoughts of ghosts and zombies and any of the other impossible creatures of the night.

As he got nearer still, within shovel-striking range, he saw there was something odd; something very wrong. The figure – clearly a person: his headtorch picked out the glistening hair, the pink cheeks, the scruff of an unruly beard – was not moving at all. In this dark, rural spot, his mind uncontrollably leapt to images of corpses, cadavers unburied.

"Mate?"

He prodded the body with the tip of his shovel. It slipped sideways and fell to the ground with a hard thump.

"Jesus Christ!" said Wayne. "What did you do to her?"

"Her?"

Making sure Wayne was very much beside him, he approached the low wall and clambered over it into the lane.

His toe clipped something hard, plastic. He looked down. He shuddered at the sight of the wide eyes, then realised they were painted on.

"It's a dummy!" he said, almost yelled. "It's a bloody shop dummy!" The beard around its chin appeared to be the remains of some insect hive. He remembered something Little Miss Marvellous, Sam Applewhite, had said. "Bearded lady. Shit!" Annoyed, he whacked at it with the shovel, gouging a deep gash in its solid neck. "Bloody thing!"

"Someone's watching us," said Wayne.

"It's a dummy," said Jimmy, slowly and firmly.

"Nah, mate. There."

Wayne was pointing back across the churchyard, to a cottage on a side road. There was a bay window. A figure stood in the window, backlit by houselights. Their arms were raised, making a shield over their eyes as they looked out into the night.

Jimmy considered what they had just seen, what they might think they had just seen. A figure by the wall, struck down from behind by a man with a shovel. If they called the police, there would be questions. Even if Jimmy managed to explain away the business with the dummy there'd be questions about holes in the ground and fence posts and...

"Gotta get over there," said Jimmy.

"What are you doing?" hissed Wayne.

"Smoothing things out."

Jimmy had no idea how he was going to do that, but he was going to do something. He marched round the churchyard towards the cottage. He gave a cheery wave as he approached. He could see it was a woman, and from the frailty of her movements he guessed it was an old lady. She closed the curtains to shut him out as he came to the driveway.

He rapped at the door.

He waited long enough for an elderly woman to shuffle to the door and answer it, but there was no reply.

He rapped again.

"Hello?" He bent to the letterbox and lifted the brass flap. "I just wanted to check you were all right."

Still nothing. He tried the door handle. It was locked. Worth a shot.

He stood and turned to Wayne. "Go round the back. See if we can get in that way."

"Why?" said Wayne.

"Just need to sort this out. Don't want the cops involved or anything."

Wayne scurried away.

"We're all right in here, thank you," came a woman's voice through the door.

Jimmy forced a laugh. "I was just worried about what you might have thought you'd seen."

"No, no. Thank you. Goodnight," she said.

"It was just a dummy. I think my friend, Sam, left it there by accident."

"Sam?"

"Yes. She works for DefCon4. I think she was—"

"The meals on wheels lady?"

That's her!" he said with relief. "Sam Applewhite."

"Oh! Oh." There was the click of a latch and the door

swung open. The old woman blinked and recoiled as his headtorch shone in her eyes.

Jimmy whipped it off. "Sorry, miss."

The woman, dressed in a quilted house coat, considered the mud-smeared man on her doorstep. "Mrs."

"Sorry?"

"Mrs Skipworth," she said. "It's very late."

"We didn't mean to alarm you," he said.

The house was cluttered, overstuffed in that way that could only be achieved through a lifetime of accumulation. Plump armchairs and piles of magazines. Shelves crowded with photographs and knick-knacks and books.

From the far side of the house there was the rattle of a back door being tried. Concerned, the old woman turned and shuffled through her living room toward the kitchen.

"That's just my friend," said Jimmy, following, spade still in hand. "We were worried." His eyes happened to fall on a spiral notepad on a chair arm, an arrangement of boxes on the top page, each with a name in. It took him a moment or two to realise why he recognised some of them. "Shit!"

Mrs Skipworth saw him looking, registered the alarm in his eyes and reflected it back at him. She stepped up a gear in her hurried totter to the kitchen.

"Wayne!" he shouted.

There was the smashing of glass. The woman started to make a fearful cooing noise as she fled. Jimmy went after her. A hand slipped through the broken glass of the back door as Wayne let himself in. Mrs Skipworth switched directions around the kitchen table, like this was some weird geriatric chase and she could possibly lose them by running round furniture.

"Stop her," said Jimmy.

Wayne stepped forward. He had his shovel held high. Jimmy could see what he was going to do. He had time to shout out, but his brain had frozen. Wayne struck out. Mrs Skipworth crumpled. A flailing hand reached out and knocked two cat mugs off a draining board by the sink. The cups made more noise hitting the floor than she did.

Mrs Skipworth was laid out between kitchen table and sink. Her housecoat had ridden up to expose wrinkled knees and sparrow legs dotted with liver spots. Jimmy didn't need to check her to know she was dead. He had seen the life fly out of her when Wayne smashed her face in.

Jimmy was suddenly out of breath. "Wayne," he gasped. "What have you done?"

12

Wayne stared at the body, his mouth working. "I ... I ... I..."

"Yes," said Jimmy.

The alcohol in Jimmy's system had turned instantly to acid. His whole body wanted to throw up, to rip off its skin, to empty the sickness inside him all over the floor.

"I ... I..."

Jimmy staggered with faltering movements. A part of him, little Jimmy MacIntyre – the one who'd sat up straight in school assemblies, who wanted to join the cub scouts – that little Jimmy MacIntyre wanted to kneel beside dead Mrs Skipworth, check her pulse, give her chest compressions to bring her back to life. Another part, older and wiser and more cynical, was telling him to run. Run far and fast and never look back.

"Why did you kill her?" he said.

"I didn't," said Wayne.

"You fucking did!" hissed Jimmy. Immediately he thought his voice was too loud; that their every word and movement was being heard.

"You told me to show some initiative," said Wayne.

"Do not pin this on me," Jimmy whispered.

The older, cynical, wiser part of Jimmy's mind was gaining traction. It was a black and inky thing: cold, lurking in a cave at the back of his mind. Now it seeped out, reaching over him with enfolding tentacles. Options presented themselves, coldly and rationally.

They could call an ambulance and the police, tell them a version of the truth which fitted the facts. They were working late, saw a woman at a window for whom they were suddenly concerned. Jimmy had knocked on the door, spoken to her and... He couldn't make a broken kitchen door and a shovel to the face sound like anything other than murder, or manslaughter. You hit an old lady with a shovel and you definitely went to prison.

"We can sort this out," he said.

Option two was a slight variant. Wayne had hit her, Wayne had to pay the price. Who could say why Wayne had chosen to go round the back of the old biddy's house and club her in the face? Jimmy had no idea what he was going to do. Maybe Jimmy had even tried to stop him.

Wayne stood with his shovel still raised. There was a square of blood on the underside of his shovel. There were even two empty patches for her eye sockets, a jagged line for her upper jaw, like the shovel was a horrific version of that fucking Jesus shroud thing in Italy. Blood dripped on the floor between his dirty, mud-caked feet.

Wayne was the killer. That much was obvious.

Except, thought Jimmy, when the police questioned him, Wayne wouldn't be slow in mentioning the graveyard, their secret night-time job, and the access track to the building plot. The Welton le Marsh building site, the Shore View development, Frost and Sons – what little remained of Jimmy's career and financial well-being would all tumble down like dominoes.

Shop Wayne to the coppers for murder and Jimmy would be out of a job, ostracised by the industry, penniless, and probably still liable for some criminal offences.

Unless, of course, Wayne didn't get to speak to the police.

Wayne had just killed an old woman. Jimmy had seen him. Perhaps Jimmy had tried to stop him. Perhaps, shovel in hand, he had reacted instinctively to protect the old dear and keep the mad killer at bay. Jimmy raised his own shovel...

"What we gonna do?" said Wayne.

Wayne might have been an idiot, a fat idiot at that, but there was muscle under that flab. Jimmy could easily imagine that it would take more than a couple of taps with a shovel to crack Wayne's egg-like noggin. Jimmy did not want to find out if he was up to the task.

"We sort this out," he said, lowering his shovel.

"But the old lady..."

"Yeah, she was old," he said, or the cold, dark and calculating something inside Jimmy said. "She was nearly dead anyway. It was a mercy killing. And she shouldn't have been spying on us, anyway, should she?"

"No..."

Jimmy mentally assessed the room, looking beyond the

crumpled saggy mess on the floor, at the marks they'd left behind, the things they might have touched.

"Put your work gloves on," he said, taking his own from his back pocket. "Touch nothing. We're cleaning up."

"Cleaning up," nodded Wayne.

There was a dishcloth on the draining board. Jimmy grabbed it and went out through the living room to the front door. Do things in order. Be methodical. He went outside. The cold, the sudden exposure to the night and the thought of potentially hundreds of eyes watching him, made him shiver.

He had knocked on the door. He wiped it where his knuckles and fingertips might have touched the surface. He had entered the door. His hand might have brushed the door frame and door here, or maybe *here*. He wiped vigorously.

He went inside. He had touched nothing in the living room. But there was the notepad and the names. The names...! Bloody interfering bitch! He ripped off the top sheet and then, because he'd seen those old police shows, ripped off a half dozen more sheets in case the impression of the pen carried through. He stuffed them all in his pocket and went back to the kitchen. Wayne was looking at his phone.

"What are you doing?" asked Jimmy.

"Looking up how to conceal a death," said Wayne.

"You are fucking kidding me."

"Look." Wayne held up the phone. "There's a WikiHow. With pictures."

Panic exploded in Jimmy's brain. Mobile phones. The police could track them, couldn't they? Something to do with the nearest transmitter masts or something. Would the police be able to tell they were here? Or would that only apply if he made a phone call?

Jimmy whipped out his phone, ripped off the protective case and tried to remove the battery. The damned thing was a sealed unit! No access. The SIM card then.

The card was encased in a little side compartment. He scrabbled at it with his fingers and then saw the little hole. "Pin!"

"What?" said Wayne.

"I need a pin." He pulled open a kitchen drawer, then another, a third. A paperclip! He unfolded it with clumsy gloved hands and waggled it in the side of his phone until the SIM card came free. He shoved both it and the phone in his pocket.

"It says here that most people are killed by someone they know," said Wayne. "That's good news."

"What?" said Jimmy.

Wayne pointed at the dead woman. "Do you know her?"

"No."

"See?" said Wayne and smiled. "Step two—"

"Sorry? Step one in concealing a murder is make sure you don't know the dead person?"

"Yeah. Step two, don't leave DNA at the scene."

Jimmy paused. "DNA. We'll have left some."

"I didn't notice," said Wayne.

"Hair."

Wayne brushed his bald scalp.

"Spittle," said Jimmy. "Even a little. Blood. You cut yourself at all?"

"No."

"No," agreed Jimmy.

"It also says semen," said Wayne.

Jimmy swore under his breath. "I don't think either of us spunked on her, Wayne. Or did you get really excited?"

"But it says..."

"Sure. It says."

"Step three, leave the body where it is. Don't get any of its DNA on you."

"We can't do that," Jimmy said.

"It says we shouldn't move it."

Jimmy mentally retreated from the moment, into the dark cave at the back of his mind. It was a calm place, where emotions and fears could not enter. Jimmy suspected he might just be going into shock, but he retreated to the cave nonetheless, letting the dark rational thoughts, its squidly tentacles, wrap around him and take over.

"We can't leave her here," he said. "When she's found, they'll see she's been murdered."

"I didn't murder her," said Wayne. "I just killed her."

"Same difference," said Jimmy, thinking yeah, whatever happened, Wayne was shafted. He killed her. He was the one who'd used his bloody phone in her house, Googling how to dispose of corpses. If anyone was going to pay for this screw-up, it was Wayne. One way or another.

"Maybe we can make it look like an accident," Wayne was saying.

"You bashed her head in with a shovel, Wayne. I'm no criminal pathologist, but I'm pretty sure even the most gormless copper won't miss the massive dent in her skull. There's bone fragments in her hair, for God's sake."

"Then we make it look like a random attack."

"Random attack? By who?"

Wayne shrugged. "Bandits?"

"Bandits! What the Jesus fuck, man?"

"I dunno," said Wayne. "They used to have Vikings round here."

"A thousand years ago! The police find this body they're going to be able to work an approximate time of death. They're gonna know it was after ten-fucking-sixty-six!"

"I'm just coming up with ideas," said Wayne. "WikiHow says—"

"Screw that. Go to the van. Bring a tarp and some of that decorators carpet protection roll."

"The see-through one or the blue one?"

"We're going to wrap up a body for transportation. What do you think?"

Wayne took a guess. "The blue one?"

"Yes, the bloody blue one!"

Wayne hurried out. Jimmy found himself alone with a dead body. Except he wasn't alone. In the cave, the dark squid-thing was with him, holding him in its loose but certain embrace.

13

Sam had filled eight boxes with items she had found in the attic and various cubbyholes and nooks dotted around *Duncastin*'s sprawling rooms. Whether they were valued mementos, possible antiques, nearly worthless junk, or entirely worthless tat was a matter of judgement. At breakfast time, Sam perched on a stool at the kitchen counter, simultaneously sorting junk, eating toast, and keeping an eye on the screen of her laptop.

Her dad hovered, ostensibly tidying the kitchen, but occasionally moving items from the boxes at the tat end of the spectrum and into the 'to be kept' box. He looked at the map on her screen. "What is that?"

"It's my lorry," she said.

"Oh, we own a lorry now, do we?"

"It's delivering a parcel for work. I've had it redirected here after I failed to be in for it yesterday. I don't want to miss it."

Marvin Applewhite looked at the screen again. "It's just round the corner, down Drummond Road."

"I know."

"You could just pop round and knock on his window."

Sam gave a tight, bitter smile. "I did. It's not there."

"It is," said Marvin and pointed at the screen.

"On there it is," she said. "It's been there for two hours. I went down to meet it but it's not there."

"Where is it then?"

Sam raised her hands, sharing her mystification at the ways of the universe. She posted the last piece of marmaladed toast into her mouth, then spotted something in one of the boxes.

"Er, dad...?"

He looked. A pair of small handcuffs dangled from her fingertip.

"These would fit a child," she said.

"I suppose they would."

Except they were proper handcuffs, with a ratchet locking mechanism. "I think these need explaining, dad."

"Winter of nineteen seventy-five. I was doing panto, Aladdin, at the Wolverhampton Civic. Roger De Courcey and I were the Chinese policemen. We got the kids up on stage to sing a song in the second act."

"Chinese policemen? You?"

"It wasn't considered racist in those days. I don't know if you can even call Chinese policemen Chinese these days."

"Depends if they're Chinese," said Sam.

"Well, it was me and Roger De Courcey, so no."

"And you handcuffed children when they came on stage?" said Sam, worried.

"No, although that would have been good." He caught her glance. "It was a different world back then. But, no, the handcuffs were for Nookie Bear, Roger's puppet. We'd arrest him, lock him up, do a little escapology turn. We had a lot of fun. He was an absolute gentleman."

"Nookie Bear?" said Sam.

"Both of them," said Marvin after some thought.

14

Wayne turned into the Elysian Fields Caravan Park. Built to the south of the town, in a stretch of land caught between crop farms and unattractive sand dunes with only one narrow road in and out, Elysian Fields Caravan Park was the end of the line as far as holiday accommodation went. The quality of the caravans didn't help. A few were mobile trailer caravans, now wheelless and raised on bricks. The rest of the static caravans were grimy and tarnished things, seemingly only held together by the mould and mildew. Elysian Fields was the place where caravans came to die.

Jimmy didn't reckon anyone came to the place for a holiday. It was too far to walk to the delights of Skeggy and had very little to offer on site. There was an open air swimming pool that was only three feet deep, yet you still couldn't see the bottom. You'd only book a holiday let in Elysian Fields if you hated holidays and yourself. The people who lived here, slack-faced troglodytes the lot of them, were probably permanent residents, serving penance for murky undisclosed sins.

Apart from the Odinsons. The Odinsons were different, holding themselves apart from the rest of the caravan park. They had what amounted to a compound at the furthest corner of the site. There was a tightly parked row of trailer caravans which, upon closer inspection, were clearly unoccupied and merely there to form a wall. A chain barrier was strung across the only gap in that wall, beyond which was the kingdom of the Odinsons: a small warren of caravans, sheds, workshops, and enough space to park a motley assortment of trucks, lorries and heavy machines.

Wayne stopped the van a distance from the chain barrier.

"What's the matter?" said Jimmy, which was a bloody stupid question on reflection. Right now, everything was the matter.

They had spent the small hours of the night wrapping the old biddy in layers of plastic, then wiping and rewiping the floors and counters and anywhere that blood had splashed or might have splashed; anywhere they had touched or might have touched. They swept up the broken glass and smashed cups from the kitchen floor and stuck a piece of cardboard in the kitchen door to replace the glass, with what they judged to be the right skill level for an elderly woman. They checked the coast was clear before dawn – rechecked it and triple checked it – before bringing the van round to the cottage and loading Mrs Skipworth into the back, wrapping her up further with wiring and plastic sheet so she looked less like a corpse. A nightmare of a night, covering up a pointless death.

"You sure about this?" said Wayne.

"Sure how?"

"Using the Odinsons."

Jimmy gave an exasperated huff, not least because he wasn't sure at all. "The Odinsons do a lot of work for us, and they do it no questions asked. They dumped all those Barbie doll things for us yesterday. Vanished. Gone."

"It's just ... they're a bit dodgy," said Wayne.

"Exactly. They are dodgy. They are underhand. And they work for cash."

An Odinson, dressed in nothing but tracksuit trousers and an open leather jacket, slouched up to the chain barrier and waved the van forward.

"They frighten me," said Wayne.

Jimmy looked at him. "They frighten *you*?"

He was surprised. The Odinsons were coarse and rough and, for the most part, mad as a bag of ferrets, but he'd always regarded Wayne as being socially closer to the Odinsons than himself. They were all working class, but Jimmy considered himself to belong to the noble, aspiring working class. A common man done well for himself by the sweat of his own brow. One day he'd own a house outright and, if he ever had kids, they'd be the type to go to uni and become doctors or barristers or something, be able to hold their heads up high among the great and good of society. Wayne was definitely part of the non-aspiring working class: a skilled grafter for sure, but perfectly happy as long as he had a pint in one hand, a pie in the other and Sky

Sports on the telly. The Odinsons ... well, they were some distance even below that. What they did for a living – it was hard to call it work, and they weren't exactly grafters. They belonged to that perplexing underclass which would put in extraordinary amounts of effort to avoid doing regular work. Extremely busy doing nothing, or at least nothing good.

The Odinson waved more vigorously. Jimmy could see the man mouth the words, "For fuck's sake."

"Can we trust them?" said Wayne.

"If we pay them," said Jimmy. "Drive, man. I'm knackered and I want this to be over."

Reluctantly, Wayne rolled the van forward, through the fortified wall of caravans and into the Odinson compound. There was a central open space surrounded by the clan's caravans and huts. Free-roaming chickens flapped away, squawking, as Wayne circled and parked. The leather-jacketed Odinson closed the chain barrier behind them.

There were numerous Odinsons already out and about in the compound. All turned to look at Jimmy and Wayne. Jimmy had met many of them before, although he would be hard-pressed to say which. Ragnar Odinson's children and grandchildren kind of blended into one another. There was definitely an Odinson 'look'.

In a corner of the country where deep-fried chips with every meal came as standard, and the average person tended towards obesity, the Odinsons were conspicuously slender creatures. It was possibly down to genetics. It was more likely because the Odinson adults seemed to exist on a diet of little more than tobacco and alcohol. The Odinson men were either unshaven or badly shaven. The few Odinson women had long lank hair and did not smile.

The exception to this was Astrid Odinson, Ragnar's wife, who was rotund, jolly, and probably the only one of the entire tribe who knew how to use a napkin.

The other distinguishing feature of the Odinsons was their hands. Their hands were always busy. One Odinson watched the van while cleaning car parts by the open bonnet of a probably stolen vehicle. A grubby Odinson child picked and gnawed at a bread crust while sitting in a caravan doorway. Another Odinson slouched against a vehicle shed, his hand flicking a butterfly knife open and closed like he'd seen it in a movie.

"Okay, here goes," said Jimmy and stepped out. "Morning!" he said to everyone and no one. You never knew which Odinson to address until one presented themself.

An Odinson stared at him blankly and picked food from between his teeth.

"I've got some rubbish that needs dumping," said Jimmy.

A man in a bandana appeared at the steps of the largest shed. More of a hall, really. Jimmy was ninety percent certain it was the driver he'd spoken to yesterday.

"I've got something else," said Jimmy. "Yngvar, isn't it?"

"Yngve," said the man.

"Right. Stuff that needs dumping."

Yngve Odinson came down the wooden steps unhurriedly. He kicked a chicken out the way as he strolled over to the van.

"Doors, Wayne," said Jimmy.

Wayne jumped out and opened the rear doors to show

Yngve the plastic-wrapped corpse. Yngve sucked on a roll-up and regarded the long bundle. Jimmy had already decided if the Odinsons recognised it as a body, he was just going to drop dead on the spot, have done with it.

"What is it?" said Yngve.

"Asbestos," said Jimmy.

"Is that so?"

Jimmy thought it was an excellent cover story. Finding poisonous asbestos in old walls was a common hazard in the building trade. It was expensive to dispose of legally, and only an idiot would open a container of asbestos to check that was what it really was.

Yngve nodded thoughtfully. "Tha wants it dumpin'?"

"Like it never existed," said Jimmy. "You got rid of those dolls?"

"Capitalist Whores," grunted Yngve. "Me dad says tha underpaid me for that job."

"Fifty quid we said."

"Underpaid." Yngve nodded at Mrs Skipworth. "Two 'undred quid for thee."

"Two hundred?"

"If tha wants the job doing right. And I won't say tha underpaid me."

Jimmy could have argued, but he'd have happily paid double to make this situation vanish. He opened his wallet.

Yngve whistled. Two Odinsons scurried over and hauled Mrs Skipworth out. She didn't bend at the knees or waist, or give any obvious signs she was anything other than a long bundle of building waste. None of the Odinsons gave a flicker of suspicion.

"And you'll do it today?" said Jimmy.

"Like the dollies," said Yngve, taking Jimmy's cash.

Jimmy and Wayne couldn't get out of there fast enough. Mud spun beneath their tyres. Odinson children cheered and ran after the van for the first hundred yards.

"It's done now," said Jimmy.

Wayne was breathing heavily. He nodded, the folds in his fat neck wobbling. "Can we go for breakfast?"

"We're going to power-wash the back of the van first. With bleach. Get every crumb of DNA evidence out. Then we're going to bin and burn our clothes. We'll switch into some of the decorating coveralls."

"Not my Yeezys."

"Your what?" said Jimmy.

"Yeezys." Wayne attempt to raise his foot to show Jimmy his trainers, but he had neither the room nor the flexibility. "They were proper expensive."

Jimmy felt a knot of tension inside him. He wanted to argue but he didn't need to. They had swept and mopped that kitchen floor. There were no footprints in the house.

"Then we make sure they're clean too," he said. "Microscopically clean."

"Then can we go for breakfast?"

Jimmy just wanted to go to bed, but maybe breakfast was a good idea. The whole episode needed putting to bed, and a greasy Full English would be a way to reassert normality.

"Wherever you like," said Jimmy. "My treat."

"You're the best, Jimmy."

Jimmy didn't feel it.

15

S am stood behind the front door and watched the delivery man approach through the frosted glass. She was poised, ready, as he reached for the doorbell. As the bell dinged, Sam snatched the door open before it got to the dong.

"Yes, I am here," she said. "Good morning."

The man nodded. He had a little *Sorry, you were out when we called* card ready in his hand. Sam thought he looked decidedly disappointed he wasn't going to be able to deploy it.

"Parcel?" he said.

"Yes," she replied.

He went back down the stone steps to his van and returned with a box not much smaller than a washing machine, although clearly considerably lighter. Sam took receipt of it awkwardly and angled it through the doorway. Once she had battled it through to the hallway, she returned to provide the delivery guy with a signature and waved him off.

She half-carried, half-shoved the large cardboard box through to the kitchen.

Marvin regarded it with interest. "A bit of a double standard, isn't it?"

"How so?" she said.

He inclined a head towards the boxes on the side, filled with his belongings. "You're clearing out my things because you say we need the room."

"That's not it exactly, dad."

"And then you just replace it with your things."

"This is a work thing," she said and heaved it up onto the counter.

"What is it?" he said.

"No idea. Work sent it. Apparently I'm to beta-test it."

"What does beta-test mean?"

Sam frowned. "I think it's the testing you do after alpha-testing."

"So, test it again?"

"I guess so."

He rolled his smiling eyes. "I do wish people would just say what they mean rather than make up new words."

Sam found the knife she'd used to spread jam on toast, licked it clean and used it to cut the tape seals on the flaps. Marvin leaned forward as she opened it. A small avalanche of polystyrene packing chips spilled out. Inside were sealed bags of black plastic components. Sam picked up a single sheet of paper marked with the word *Instructions*. The one and only instruction was to go to a website.

"Does it need assembling?" said Marvin.

She was about to answer when she recognised the tone in his voice. This was the tone of a man who'd spent a large portion of his adult career creating or constructing stage props; the tone of man who still had, in his study, an Airfix model of the Supermarine Spitfire he'd glued together as a boy in nineteen-fifty-something.

"It does," she said, neutrally. She fetched her dad's tablet from the living room, propped it up on the counter and told him to type in the address. "I'm going to put some of your things in the back of the van."

"Did you sell Consuela?"

She had to stop and think for a moment where she had left the mannequin. When she remembered, she said, "I will be collecting her later."

"You haven't just abandoned her at a bus-stop, have you?"

"Er, no."

"I told you, you should try the junk shop up from the pier."

"Right you are."

She carried a box of stage magic tat out to the Piaggio on the driveway. When she returned, Marvin had got the video working and he was being lectured by a bearded Californian in an on-line video.

"—glad to know you've bought a MySky smart-drone. Have you got the pre-packed tool kit ready?"

"I surely have, Hank," Marvin said in a bad American accent. He held up a tiny pack of screwdrivers and Allen keys that had come with the box.

"Then let's begin constructing your MySky smart-drone," said the Californian. *"And we're going to have fun doing it. Because making things is fun, isn't it?"*

"Rootin' tootin'," said Marvin.

"Now, take out the body panel 'J'. This is going to be the undercarriage of your MySky smart-drone..."

Sam silently waved her dad goodbye. There was a grin fixed on his face as he sorted through the components in the box. Some men never grew up. Actually, in her experience, no man ever truly grew up.

16

Jimmy and Wayne played whack-a-croc before breakfast.

There was a greasy spoon café near the far end of Skegness Pier. As piers went it was not an impressive specimen. There was the building housing the arcade video games, the narrower section housing the gambling machines, the tuppenny cascades and the greasy spoon, and then the boardwalk which just about got its stanchions wet when the tide was in.

There was a whack-a-croc machine down the noisier end of the arcade, between the camel racing game and a basketball game which spewed out prize tickets if you scored enough baskets. Wayne wanted to play whack-a-croc. It was an old ritual, to be performed before they ate at the pier café. Jimmy had no appetite for games or breakfast, but if it helped draw a line under the horrors of the last twelve hours, he was all for it.

He gave Wayne the fifty pence for the machine and then, while a jolly Cajun tune played, watched one of the planet's slowest-reacting men get outwitted by an automated game for two minutes. Wayne whacked his foam-padded mallet frequently and hard, but the snapping green faces were still too quick for him.

The machine spat out four yellow tickets on a strip. Wayne carefully pocketed them.

They looked at the prize counter on the way to the greasy spoon. Even the lollipops and novelty pencil-tops required hundreds of tickets. Wayne lingered over the Xbox games console behind the glass. Fifty thousand tickets to buy that. That was a lot of games of whack-a-croc.

Jimmy ordered Full English breakfasts for the pair of them. The café operated in a narrow galley kitchen, squashed to the side of the pier building's final section by coin pusher cascade games and test-your-strength machines. Jimmy only ordered a breakfast for himself to keep Wayne company, surprising himself when he polished it off with ease.

They took a brief walk along the pier. Wayne lit a cigarette and took deep breaths, like he was a man just released from prison.

"You done good," said Jimmy.

Wayne just looked at him.

"All behind us now," said Jimmy.

The wind farm filled the sea view end to end. There was a faint haze in the miles between the pier and the massive turbines. Jimmy could just make out a gas platform on the horizon beyond the wind farm.

Wayne spat over the edge and into the sea. "We moving the rest of them stones tonight?"

"When you're ready," said Jimmy.

He became aware of little pink dots in the sea, some distance out. They speckled the waves, glinting in the morning sun. Sometimes, rarely, you could spot a seal head popping up. They weren't pink, though. These were too far out, and too many to be human swimmers.

Jimmy squinted. He rummaged in his pocket for twenty-pence and put it in the coin-operated telescope next to him. He swung it round and tried to find the dots again. A dozen fixed grins smiled at him as they bobbed on the tide.

"Oh, shit," he whispered. "Capitalist Whores."

"What?" said Wayne.

Jimmy's mind raced. A cargo container full of knock-off Barbie dolls; the Odinsons told to get rid of them permanently. Jimmy had assumed they'd go to landfill somewhere, but maybe the Odinson version of permanent disposal involved driving down the coast some distance and dumping the rubbish in the sea at high tide.

There were hundreds of Capitalist Whores floating on the sea, coming in with the tide. Thousands of them.

And then a thought that should have occurred to him much sooner walloped him, and walloped him hard. "The body!"

"What?" said Wayne.

"They're just gonna dump it in the sea—!"

He could see the unwanted dolls were going to wash up along the shore, all around. He did not want that to happen with the remains of Mrs Skipworth.

"We've got to stop them!" he said and began to run back up the pier towards the promenade and the parked van.

17

S am parked her Piaggio outside the *Back to Life* junk shop on the corner of Scarborough Avenue opposite the entrance to the pier. As she got out, there was commotion on the other side of the road. Two men in workers overalls running out of the pier building. The taller one shouted savagely at his shorter, tubbier mate to keep up. They ran to a Frost & Sons van parked at the roadside. She recognised the taller one as Jimmy MacIntyre. Were they running to an emergency building job? Or were they running away from a botched job? Sam watched them accelerate away.

She had a bunch of her dad's junk in the back of the Piaggio, but she needed to check out the shop first, see if it was the kind of place that could and should take her dad's old knick-knacks. Browse casual; that was the first order of business.

She pushed open the door and stepped inside. It took a

moment for her eyes to adjust from the brightness of the sunny morning. It was a larger shop than she had imagined, arranged in very broad categories. If John Lewis decided to sell second-hand junk, they would probably lay out their shop something like this. She strolled through the kitchenware, recognising crockery patterns from decades ago. There was a peculiar pull to these almost-forgotten fragments of the past – the irrational urge to get the sugar bowl matching her granny's favourite teapot, even though her granny had been dead for some time.

The back wall was a gallery of terrible art. Prints that were popular in her childhood made her grimace. Further along was a collection of mounted needlework, representing many hours of dedicated but terribly misguided work. Portraits and landscapes shared the odd, pixelated look that resulted from being rendered in stitches, but several had the added horror of bizarre coloration. Presumably because whoever made them had a limited pool of threads. Sam marvelled over a picture of the queen mother. If she squinted at it long enough, the blue colours of the hat and dress she was wearing dominated the composition, and the horror of the rest of it took a back seat. Unfortunately, when she looked at it properly, the face, neck and pearls had a bizarre, unblended look. As if someone had applied raspberry ripple ice cream to a canvas and then put a pair of startling blue eyes in the middle.

"Admiring my crapestry?" said a voice beside her.

"Sorry?" Sam turned to see a woman in a baggy jumper.

"Crapestry," said the woman. "Crap tapestry."

She had a friendly, open face and a sharp glint in her eye,

although Sam thought she looked tired. The woman's hair was tied up in the manner of one who tied up their hair because it was easier than either washing or brushing it. Strands of loose blonde hair hung around her face. She looked like she wanted to crawl inside a giant cup of coffee and not emerge until the caffeine had done its work.

The woman smiled. "Delia." She held out a hand.

Sam shook it. "Sam."

"It's becoming quite collectible."

"Sorry?" Sam realised she was talking about the horrifically ugly needlework. "No. Really?"

"It really is. For one thing, nobody's making it anymore. I guess before we had the internet or dozens of telly channels you'd do this sort of thing to pass the time. You don't see the elaborate pictures much after the seventies."

Sam nodded. The things did seem to be of a certain vintage.

"So people are latching onto it as a thing. Buying the weirdest ones and putting them up in the loo or whatever. This beauty will get snapped up soon, and that lumpy cat over there. People love a slightly deformed cat."

"Do they?"

"Much sought after by the crapestry aficionados." Delia began sorting through a box of tat under a display counter.

"I can sort of see the appeal," said Sam. "Like collecting deliberately naff ornaments."

"Ah, we have a special on naff ornaments!" Delia indicated a nearby shelf with an elaborate if languid *ta-da* motion. "A free paper bag to hide your purchases from the taste police."

Sam laughed. "I wanted to ask. Do you buy things?"

Delia nodded. "As opposed to scavenging them out of bins, where they rightfully belong, you mean?"

"Oh, I didn't mean—"

"Joking!"

"Right. Of course."

"Sometimes I will buy things from people. I'll warn you though, I'm cheap. Nobody ever got rich from selling me their stuff. I tend to take the things that people are glad to get rid of."

Sam looked up at the wall and nodded. "Fair enough."

"The other thing that I do here is rent cabinets. You see over on the other side?"

Sam looked: there were some tall glass cabinets. One had displays of jewellery and the other had camera equipment.

"I rent those out for forty pounds a month. When something sells from out of your cabinet, you get the money."

They looked well-suited for things that were small and valuable. None of her dad's stuff really fell into that category.

"I think we're probably looking at the scenario where I don't get rich," she admitted. "I've got a bunch of my dad's things in the van. I've got a ton more at home."

Delia took a moment to conjure a solemn face. "I'm sorry for your loss."

"He's not dead—"

"Oh!"

"—I'm just getting rid of his junk."

"His nineteen fifties porn collection?"

"Ew! No."

"Shame. That stuff is worth something." The shopkeeper shook her head. "Yes."

"Yes?"

"If you're in the town I can come out and have a look, give a valuation. Some stuff I can sell for you. What I can't, I can upcycle."

Sam frowned. Delia beckoned her over to another room. Sam hadn't spotted the entrance as it was behind a beaded curtain and assumed it was off-limits.

"My upcycling room." It looked a bit like a workshop and a lot like a dumping ground for items that didn't make it into the display cabinets at the front of the shop.

"I do projects of my own," said Delia. "Make things to sell in the shop and on-line. I also run workshops, but the magic all happens right here."

Sam was aware of upcycling. From what she'd seen before, it mostly seemed to involve taking perfectly good wooden furniture and painting it in ugly shades of chalky paint. This was different though. She peered at the piece of furniture closest to hand. It looked like a coffee table made from a vintage suitcase. It turned out to be exactly that. The lid still opened when she tried it.

"Handy for storing bits in," she observed.

Fairy lights featured in a good many things. There was a hanging light fixture that was surely the glass door from a washing machine hanging from chains, with coiled-up fairy lights twinkling magically inside it. There were interesting, tactile rugs draped across the larger pieces of furniture and hanging from the wall. Sam realised, on closer inspection, they were woven from strips of fabric that had once been clothing.

"I like it," said Sam.

"Like it?" said Delia. "That's ... polite."

"No. Really. I mean, it's crazy, but I love it. What are you working on at the moment?"

"Well, I'm mulling over some new treasure," said the woman. "It seems these things have been washing up all along the shore. I've had them brought to me by several people and I've got loads of them now." She opened a massive plastic storage box which was filled with dolls. They all had the same face, although the hair and outfits differed.

"Can I interest you in a Capitalist Whore, madam," said the woman.

"Um, what?" said Sam.

18

It took Jimmy a full minute to realise why his mobile phone wasn't working and he couldn't call the Odinsons. He'd taken the SIM out at Mrs Skipworth's. He'd stuffed it in his pocket. He'd stripped off his clothes when they cleaned out the van.

"I've burned my SIM!" he hissed.

"What you do that for?" said Wayne.

"Not on purpose! Give me your phone."

Wayne slowed as he fished around for his phone.

"Keep going," said Jimmy. "Head to Elysian Fields!"

19

"Capitalist Whore," Sam read the logo stamped into the back of the doll's neck. "Not the greatest marketing line ever."

"It might account for why they all ended up in the North Sea, though," said Delia the junkshop owner.

"But they're so realistic," said Sam, sarcastically. "Works of art." The faces were a sort of Disney-Manga-Kardashian concoction of giant bambi eyes and bouncy-castle lips. "Sorry - North Sea?"

Delia shrugged. "I collected at least a hundred while on the beach with Milly and Alfie this morning." The way she said it, Sam wasn't sure if Milly and Alfie were dogs or children. "Maybe fell off a container ship somewhere."

Sam couldn't deny she was curious. "What are you going to do with them?"

"I have a few ideas. Obviously, there will be a light fitting.

A bicycle wheel. Hang the heads from the spokes and interlace with fairy lights."

"Obviously."

"I also have a picture in my mind of a translucent resin toilet seat with these dolls swimming around in a circle. I'll need to press them a little bit flatter, but I think it will work if I use heat."

"You're going to press a doll to make it flatter?" Sam asked, trying not to sound too judgy.

"I am."

"Can I watch?"

"Sure! Pop through there and put the kettle on, will you? Let's mess up some Capitalist Whores!"

It turned out the kettle boiling was for doll-squashing.

"Go and find a shallow dish that looks like a couple of dolls could lie down in it," said Delia. "Bonus points if you find a plate to fit inside."

Sam went to mooch through the crockery. She quickly found a Pyrex casserole dish and a transparent Pyrex plate that would fit inside it.

"Ooh," said Delia, "I love that you found a plate we can see through, and monitor progress. Now we pour the boiling water onto the dolls and squish them good."

"Got it. The technical term for what we're doing is 'squishing them good'. I'll be sure to remember that." Sam leaned on the plate, but it soon became quite hot.

"Let's pop a weight on there," said Delia. "Look! I can see they're already softening into something new and interesting."

"New and interesting indeed." Sam stared at the dolls'

flattened faces, looking very much as if they were screaming in anguish at the torture being inflicted upon them. "It's a shame really. First forced to be sex-workers and now this. Some women just can't get a break, can they?"

"Necklace?" Delia asked. Off came the heads of several dolls. Delia used an awl to make holes in them so that they could be threaded onto a strip of cord. They each put one around their necks.

"Cool! Do you have any ideas for the bodies?" asked Delia.

"Can we link their arms together?" Sam picked a couple up and tried it out. "Maybe a toast rack from their legs? We get them all to lie down in a line and kick up like synchronised swimmers."

"Hah! Love it."

They fiddled around for a few minutes. What they eventually ended up with looked like a very impractical toast rack.

"Yeah, maybe I wouldn't trust Capitalist Whores with my toast anyway," said Sam.

"So quick to judge your fellow woman," Delia tutted.

"You could give them colourful body tattoos and sell them as wine glass markers."

"Wine glass markers?"

"At a party everyone has one, so when they put their glass down they know which is theirs. Mostly they're little circles of wire with beads, but a Capitalist Whore could work – like a pole dancer on the stem of the glass. My dad's got a load of wine glass markers, still in the packet would you believe?"

"Ah, would that be some of the stuff you want to sell?"

"It would," said Sam, carefully. "But that might be considered normal. Most of it is quite ... unusual."

"Oh, I'm intrigued already," said Delia.

20

"Foot down, we need to catch him!" Jimmy hissed.

"It's a forty limit here," said Wayne, "and the sign says there might be horses and carriages as well."

"Wayne, I need to stress to you that carriages will be nothing compared to what will happen if Yngve Odinson dumps that body like he dumped those dolls. It'll be washed up on the beach before you know it and the police will have a party with the forensic evidence we've wrapped up in that bag for them."

"But he said he was going to make it disappear."

Jimmy could have slapped him. He could have slapped himself. "I guess the Odinsons aren't as clever as they think they are when it comes to disposing of unwanted rubbish!"

They had raced to Elysian Fields and managed to get through on the phone just as they drew up at the chain gate in front of the Odinson compound. They quickly learned that Yngve Odinson had driven off with the plastic-wrapped Mrs Skipworth. It taken an extra ten minutes and a fistful of bank notes to ascertain that Yngve had driven south, to the village of Friskney, and the long track leading down to the coast. They set off in hot pursuit.

"Van." Jimmy pointed at a Vauxhall van ahead.

"Is that them?" said Wayne.

"Could be."

Jimmy leaned over to flash the lights and sound the horn. The Vauxhall kept moving.

"Fuck's sake," muttered Jimmy, and leaned on the horn, flashing the lights repeatedly. Eventually the Vauxhall stopped and they pulled alongside it.

Wayne lowered his window. The face looking out at him was extremely alarmed, glancing nervously between Jimmy and Wayne. It wasn't Yngve and it certainly didn't have the Odinson 'look' about it.

"What's your game?" said the driver.

"Jimmy, I think this might be the wrong van," said Wayne.

"Window up, drive on," said Jimmy through gritted teeth. He should be tearing Wayne a new arsehole right now for using his name in what might turn out to be an incriminating exchange, but he knew the idiot would take ages to cotton on. What's more Wayne was absolutely guaranteed to simply forget and do it again, the next time.

Wayne accelerated round the Vauxhall. They passed through Friskney village and down the sea lane. They scanned the horizon for the Odinson's vehicle.

"Is he going to Jacinda's house?" said Wayne.

"Or nearby," said Jimmy.

Jacinda Frost's house was out this way, on the edge of the Wash in a landscape entirely reclaimed from the sea, where the world was flat and featureless. The kind of landscape that made farmers (and builders, it turned out) start to question their life choices and look at their shotguns in a meaningful way.

There was a dirty white speck near the horizon.

"There!" said Jimmy. "Floor it!"

Flooring it on the narrow sea lane was potentially dangerous. They could end upside down in a dyke wide enough to swallow the van whole. Although if they drowned that would be the end of their problems. Jimmy held onto the door handle as the van bounced along at fifty, sixty, sixty-five....

Ahead, the Odinson van had reached the end of the tarmacked road and was heading across a grooved track towards the sea. As Wayne followed, Jimmy saw Ministry of Defence signs staked into the ground but was jolting around too much to read them.

Wayne flashed his headlights. Jimmy honked the horn. The van ahead stopped.

The man who jumped down was wearing a red bandana. Jimmy nearly vomited with relief.

Yngve Odinson had a joint hanging from his fingertips. "Is there a problem?"

Jimmy walked up to him. Wet sandy soil clung to his shoes. "For one, I don't want you smoking that shit while you're working for me," he said.

Odinson shrugged.

"Need that package back," said Jimmy.

"But tha' said…"

"We'll talk later about why that is. Open the back."

He turned back to Wayne and gestured for him to get the van open.

Yngve opened his own van. Jimmy was looking once more at a wrapped body he thought he'd seen the last of.

"Wayne, move it over." Wayne lumbered round. "Make sure there's nobody coming, for Christ's sake."

Wayne picked the body up effortlessly and put it back in their van. There was a Tesco bag for life in the way, but Wayne shoved the body in regardless. It ended up wearing the bag like a pair of boots, or maybe a hat. Jimmy wasn't sure which end was the head. That small act of carelessness grated on Jimmy's nerves, but Wayne didn't even notice.

Sea birds wheeled overhead, cawing. Jimmy looked round in case anyone was watching. There wasn't another soul in sight, probably not another human being for miles. If Jimmy knew which direction to look, he'd probably spot Jacinda's house on the horizon. He could see why it made an ideal fly-tipping spot.

"No one ever comes down here," he said to Yngve.

"No. All used to be an RAF bombing range. Public can't come down here. Unexploded ordnance." Yngve wandered over to a brown lump in the mud and kicked it. Jimmy flinched.

Yngve grunted, as though when the whatever it was didn't explode it was a major disappointment.

"Jesus," said Jimmy.

Yngve took out a cheap lighter and lit his joint.

"I told you not to smoke that shit," said Jimmy.

"Not working for thee now, am I?" Yngve shut up the back of his van and got in.

21

"This house is amazing," said Delia. "It's like someone had a bunch of cute bungalows and squashed them all together into one mad building."

"Mad is about right," said Sam.

She had driven Delia back to her dad's house, shown her the boxes of oddments set aside for the junk shop. While her dad made tea for them all, she had taken Delia deeper into the house to point out some bits of furniture she was fairly certain her dad didn't really need. Sam would have to work on him a bit before he'd give them up, but it didn't hurt to start the conversation.

"So why the big clear out?" asked Delia, while they were away from the kitchen.

"Oh, you know," said Sam. "I want to make dad's life a bit easier for him. It'll be much easier to clean if it's de-cluttered."

She liked Delia a lot, but she'd only just met her, and wasn't ready to share her suspicions that her dad was having some financial trouble. He was evasive when she asked him directly, but the running costs for this place had to be a major drain on his pension. She had no idea how bad the financial situation actually was, but if he needed to downsize his house, he'd never sell this one while it looked like the cluttered home of an eccentric who'd been collecting magical paraphernalia for decades.

"Your dad's really into his stage magic," said Delia.

"It was his job."

Delia paused, frowned. "I thought I recognised... Marvin Applewhite?"

"That's him."

Delia mugged in delighted surprise. "Mr Marvellous himself."

"I tend to call him 'dad'," said Sam.

"He looked different on the telly."

"Well, he was younger then, wasn't he?"

Delia chuckled. "So, tell me about this," she said, pointing at a low table which had symbols carved around the sides.

Marvin entered the room carrying a tray set with tea things. "Ah, a woman with an eye for an interesting piece! Let me tell you about the time I won this in a bet with a man from Haiti."

"Ooh, please do!" said Delia.

"Kerry Packer had a private poker game at his hotel in London," said Marvin. "Everyone else had folded, and there was just me and this quiet Haitian man in a Panama hat. I couldn't get a read on him at all. It was very tense. The stakes just kept going up and up. I had an E-type Jaguar at the time and the keys to that went on the table against the promise of this piece of furniture." He patted the table. "Luck was on my side that evening and I went home with both Jag and the table. It's ebony of course, and much older than the town of Port-au-Prince where he came from. He told me it belonged to a friend who was a *houngan*, a priest in their Vodou religion. He used it for various rituals and—"

"It's a nice table, dad," said Sam. She couldn't be sure, but wasn't this one of the pieces that he'd had made back in the day for his stage act?

"So much history," said Delia, running her fingers across the carvings. "Are you very attached to it?"

"I'm very attached to all of my things," said Marvin with a smile. "But of course I can't keep them forever. When I die it will be a nightmare for Sam if she has to deal with all of—"

"Dad," said Sam reproachfully. "That is not the reason for sorting things out. We need to make life simpler for you where we can."

"Well, I can definitely help you with the boxes of things in the kitchen," said Delia. "Take your time with the other things."

"Those boxes have real magic in them, you know," said Marvin. "Be careful they don't fall into the wrong hands, won't you?"

Sam rolled her eyes and nudged her father. "You're not on stage now! I think Delia can handle them."

"I will take great care," said Delia solemnly. "I might concentrate on selling some of the costumes first then build up to the magic things." A thoughtful look came across her face. "You know what, though? There's so much stuff here, it might be worth setting up a temporary online store, selling to the nostalgia crowd."

"Is that a thing?" asked Sam.

"It certainly is. You must have seen how popular those tribute band nights are at Carnage Hall. A little trip down memory lane is worth money to people. The only magic tricks you can buy in the shops these days are hopeless plastic novelties."

"Ah, it's an underappreciated skill set, that is very true," said Marvin.

"We could even make some little videos of Marvin demonstrating how a thing works," said Delia, taken with her own idea. "Give people a direct link to someone they recognise from back in the day. You'd definitely get a lot more money for these bits and bobs online if we did something like that."

Sam looked at her dad. "Have you got the time and the energy for that, dad?" she asked.

The answer was written across his face. He'd already trotted through to the kitchen and rummaged in the box for something to work with. "Is the camera rolling?" he asked.

Delia wasted no time. She pulled out her phone and pressed a couple of buttons. "Ready when you are, Marvin."

"I want to show you one of the most basic magic tricks. Of course, I can't reveal how it's done, but with the right equipment and a little research, you'll be able to work it out. Watch carefully. I take these four rings. You can clearly see that they are solid, separate and very strong, yes?" He chinked the rings together and clattered them between his hands. "Now, if you have studied the magical arts, you can do some very special things with these rings. How is this possible?" A ring dropped, linked to one of the others. Another dropped and another. He held them up, all four of them linked together. "Is this magic? What else can explain the change? Can we transform them back into solid and separate rings?" He gathered them up in his hands and presented them one by one. "Yes! Yes we can."

Delia stopped the video and applauded. "Bravo, Marvin!"

"Very good, dad," said Sam. It had been ages since she'd seen him perform a magic trick, and it seemed to have put some colour in his cheeks. "What are your thoughts then, Delia?"

"I have an online shop already – extends my physical shop's reach, or footprint, whatever. I think I could create a sister site for this, make it more specialised. If we made some more of these videos and split the profits fifty-fifty, how would that be?"

"Sounds great," said Sam.

"Sixty-forty," her dad said at exactly the same time.

"Deal," said Delia.

Sam laughed. She was amazed at the idea they'd get any money at all, but her dad had an eye for an opportunity – always had done.

"Oh, I've got an idea!" said Delia. "Have you got some plastic tumblers or pots?"

"Yeah, I think so," said Sam, bending to look in a cupboard. "How many?"

"Three," said Delia.

As Sam stood up with three plastic beakers in her hand, she saw Delia had taken off her necklace and was unthreading a doll's head from it. She put the head down on the kitchen counter. "What about it, Marvin? Can we do 'find the lady' with an actual lady?"

Marvin took the beakers from Sam with a wink. "Can I do that? What do you think? Nothing easier than making a woman vanish, is there?"

22

Jimmy stared blankly at the maddeningly flat landscape.

"We could bury her here," said Wayne. "We've got shovels in the back."

Jimmy felt his chest tighten. "Did you not hear the bit about the unexploded bombs in the ground?"

The look on Wayne's face suggested he wasn't afraid of those odds. "Then somewhere else—?" He clicked his fingers.

"Don't," said Jimmy.

"What?"

"You're going to say the graveyard in Welton le Marsh."

"What's wrong with that?"

"You want us to bury the dead woman in the graveyard next to her house."

"It's full of dead bodies. It'd be like camouflage."

"Old bodies. Ancient graves. You turn over six feet of fresh soil, someone is going to notice."

Wayne fell silent.

"And don't suggest the building site either," added Jimmy. "Not Welton le Marsh, not Shore View. That's just pointing the finger at ourselves. We get rid of Mrs Skipworth, we do it right and we do it permanent. I don't want someone in Welton digging up their garden for a patio in twenty, thirty years' time and finding our handiwork. We need a permanent solution."

"We could get a boat and dump it out at sea," said Wayne.

"And have it wash up again? No." Jimmy tried to compose himself. "What do they do in films? Come on. We must have seen a hundred different ways to dispose of bodies."

"Well," said Wayne, "how about *Dexter*? He takes the bodies out to sea and throws—"

"*Different* ideas from films," snapped Jimmy.

Wayne was quiet for a minute. "What about dissolving it in acid like in *Breaking Bad*?"

Jimmy nodded. "It needs quite a bit of time, space and specialised equipment that we don't have. Can't pop down to Homebase and buy a hundred gallons of acid. Anything else?"

The working of Wayne's mind was a ponderous affair, one Jimmy often thought he could almost hear, like the grinding sound an old car made climbing a steep hill.

"Pigs."

"What?"

Wayne turned to him. "Pigs, like in that gangster film

where they all talk in daft accents like they're off EastEnders. Grind the body up and feed it to pigs."

"We don't know any pig farmers," said Jimmy with a sigh. "Not any who will let us feed a body to their animals."

There was a shimmer on the horizon. The tide was coming in out there, fast and low.

"Come on, let's turn this around and go home," said Jimmy.

"Seals," said Wayne.

Jimmy looked over his shoulder, in the irrational belief Wayne had spotted something. "What?"

"Seals are a bit like pigs. We've got them round here."

"And do we know any friendly seal ... farmers who will let us feed them a body?"

"Yes."

"What?"

"Seal Land."

"You've got contacts?"

Wayne shook his head. "I did a job for them a while back. On the side, while we were laying hardcore for Shore View. Concreted in their gateposts on the big front gates. Heavy things. Bolts, padlocks, the lot."

"And you've got keys?"

Wayne shook his head again, but he was smiling. "There's a big gap round the back of the gateposts. It's all show really. Can't drive a vehicle in without the keys, but you and I and the old lady can get in."

Jimmy considered this. "Those fuckers'll eat anything," he said. "Heard one tried to eat a cop yesterday."

"See?" said Wayne.

Jimmy nodded. "Drive."

As the vehicle bumped up the rough track, Jimmy sat back and let the motion rock him. He tumbled into the dark cave of his mind, let something else do the thinking for a while.

23

Sam watched the video now uploaded to YouTube.

"Watch carefully as I put the lady beneath one of these cups," said Marvin. *"You can clearly see which one it is, yes?"* Hands on the table tilted the middle cup to reveal the head of the Capitalist Whore, staring petulantly. He moved the cups around, slowly, so it was easy to follow which cup had previously been in the middle.

"At this point, if I were running a street hustle, I would ask you to put some money on the table and point to the cup containing the head." The camera angled up to his face and he gave a conspiratorial wink. *"But since we're on friendly terms, I'll just ask you to tell me which one you think it is."*

Delia's hand came into shot to point confidently at the cup on the left.

"This one?" Marvin lifted the cup to show that it was empty. *"So sorry. It appears that you're wrong."*

The video ended.

Delia re-entered the living room, phone in hand. "That's it. The husband is in charge of bedtime duties tonight."

Bedtime duties? It had barely gone five o'clock. Sam guessed Alfie and Millie were children; young ones at that.

"So, you'll stay for another?" said Sam, jiggling the pitcher of homemade cocktail.

"You can twist my arm," said Delia, flopping into a chair. She gestured at Sam's phone. "What do you reckon? Nice little trick demonstration."

"It's not quite Sunday Night at the Palladium, but yeah, it works."

"Then I think we have a new product for the store. Find the Lady kits! It could be popular. I just need to get hold of a few more of those dolls."

Sam poured Delia's drink. "And that's your job, is it? Turning tat into things you can sell?"

"Upcycling," Delia enunciated slowly. "It's a good thing. And what exactly is it you do? You a magician's assistant? His agent?"

"Dad and agents...?" Sam scoffed. "I work for DefCon4."

Delia's brow creased. "The armoured van people?"

"That's some of what they do. You've seen my van. I don't get to transport gold bullion around the place, or anything."

"So, what do you do?"

"Whatever this thing tells me." Sam waggled her phone. She scrolled through the days ahead. "Health and safety inspections. Supervising community service workers."

"You run a chain gang?"

"Not quite. It's a broken job for a broken company, with just me and Doug Fredericks to mind the office."

Delia sipped her drink. "Doug. Doug. That's not a young guy's name, is it?"

"I've no idea how old Doug is," said Sam honestly. She wasn't sure what the lifespan of the average cactus was. Nonetheless, she caught the drift of Delia's question. "I am currently a single lady."

"Happily single?"

Sam swirled her drink and said nothing for a while. "My ex," she said eventually. "My last ex – God, that makes it sound like there's been a lot – Rich, his name was. It ended when it should have done."

"Right after you took all his money?" Delia joked.

Sam gave her an exaggerated look. "Thereby hangs a tale. It's not an exciting tale, but it's one where the ex becomes extraordinarily wealthy not long after we split up."

"Ouch."

Sam shrugged. Money would have made very little difference to that story. "And you?"

"No, I'm not extraordinarily wealthy," said Delia.

Sam rolled her eyes. "You're not single. There's a husband somewhere."

"Currently reading *Funny Bunny's Magic Show* to our litter and granting me a little time off." She stretched to emphasise the point, put her feet up on a coffee table, remembered herself, and put them down again. "I'm sorry, they don't let me out much."

There was a sudden wordless shout from the kitchen.

Sam shot up, realised that a glass and a half of lazily assembled cocktail had gone straight to her legs, and made her way to the kitchen. "Dad! Everything okay?"

Marvin stood at a distance from the drone on the counter, his arms spread as though waiting to catch a beach ball. He didn't appear to be hurt.

She looked at the drone. "You finished it?"

Marvin found his voice. "Hank and I together. Team effort I should say."

Delia crowded in behind Sam. "That is a big helicopter," she noted.

"That is a MySky smart-drone," said Marvin proudly. "Three kilograms of high speed, self-directing drone technology. With a top speed of forty-five miles per hour, wind resistance of twenty-six miles per hour and a maximum operating ceiling of five thousand metres above sea level. Four lithium batteries provide over ninety minutes of flying time, guided by an on-board intelligent navigation system controlled by your secure app." He pointed at the tablet on which a control program was open.

"And it's a very shiny helicopter," added Delia. "And DefCon4 want you to have it because...?"

Sam checked the instructions on her phone. "Just to beta-test. Build it, fly it and maybe they'll roll it out for surveillance jobs or something."

"Fly it as in...?"

Sam looked out the window. There was still plenty of light. It had been a clear calm day weather-wise.

"We should fly it," she said. "To the garden, dad?"

Very much like a boy with a brand new kite, Marvin picked up the drone and followed Sam and Delia out of the house. It might have been lightweight, but it was a wide thing, and Sam had to steer her dad around the corner of the house to avoid a minor collision.

"Wow," said Delia upon seeing the rear gardens.

It was a common reaction, Sam had discovered. *Duncastin'* had more land attached to it than the average school playing field. Sam was never sure if people's surprise was at the size of the garden or its state of wild abandonment. It was certainly varied. Conifer trees down one side, the struggling remnants of several palm trees and tropical fronds down another. In between, grasses, wildflowers and encroaching dunes fought over the ruins of what deliberate landscaping there had been.

"Careful," said Sam. "There's a fishpond somewhere. Rumours of a tennis court somewhere over there. Possibly lost tribes of indigenous people as well."

"She exaggerates," said Marvin.

"There was a party here in the late nineties," said Sam. "A conga line went in there and never came out again."

They followed the natural path through the least overgrown sections to a grassy hillock just before the dunes. Marvin set the drone down reverently. Sam swapped the glass and pitcher of cocktail in her hands for the tablet under Marvin's arm.

"If you don't mind, dad," she said.

He looked at the cocktail. "No, not at all." Then he saw the tablet. "Oh, no, not at all. I'm merely construction crew. You're the boss."

Sam explored the app briefly.

"How do you control it?" asked Delia.

"Um – you don't. You program in a flight route and off it goes. Automated. Like CCTV but in the sky."

"Just what we need."

Sam inputted a route. "Something simple to start. Straight up, circle for a hundred metres, and ... go."

The drone's four rotors buzzed into life. Delia gave a little start and then giggled at herself. The three of them stepped aside as it rose, wobbly at first and then with confidence. It tilted and flew off towards the dunes and the sea.

"A hundred metres?" said Delia.

"Hmmm."

The drone was flying on in a straight line. It had reached the shoreline and was carrying on.

"Did I build it wrong?" said Marvin.

Sam stared at the tablet, which was of no help.

Evening seagulls scattered as the drone flew out over the shallow waves.

"Where's it going?" said Delia.

Marvin looked about and tested the wind with his finger. "Norfolk. Possibly." The drone was little more than a black dot now. "If the batteries last that long," he added. "It's supposed to head back to base when its batteries are low, but it might be too late by then."

Sam sighed and began mentally composing the explanatory e-mail to her faceless superiors.

Marvin poured a glass of cocktail and sipped it. He pulled a face. "What is this?"

Sam tried to recall. "Cointreau, crème de cassis, gin, more gin, lemonade. It doesn't have a name."

Marvin took a further reflective sip. "All Glory Is Fleeting," he suggested.

"That'll do."

24

Jimmy and Wayne pulled up outside Seal Land in the dusky light of evening. They had spent the intervening hours doing a great deal of nothing, apart from a brief stop at Morrisons to buy some snacks, and Dutch courage in the form of half a bottle of cheap whisky. Now, at eight o'clock, the whisky had been drunk, the Seal Land staff were long gone, and the few shops in Anderby Creek had shut up for the night. Jimmy wanted to have some daylight to help them gain entry. He didn't want to spend another night stumbling around in the dark.

Wayne hopped out and went round the side of big double gates that looked like they should be the entrance to Jurassic Park, not a poxy local zoo. He came back a moment later and waved to Jimmy.

Jimmy opened the back of the van. Wayne, nineteen stone of flab and muscle, hoisted Mrs Skipworth over one shoulder. She wasn't heavy anyway. The body was disturbingly light, like something had physically vanished from her at the moment of death.

Wayne led the way round the gatepost. He was absolutely right: there was a two feet wide gap, half hidden by a gorse bush and a ragged end of chicken wire. They walked past the admin centre towards the main attraction.

"I think I came here as a child," Jimmy said.

"Did you like it?" said Wayne.

"I don't remember," he said. "Do children like anything for more than ten seconds?"

"I like it," said Wayne as though that settled the matter.

Ahead, in the gloom, were the seal pools. The smell of the seals and their fishy meals was unmistakeable. Jimmy realised at least some of it was coming from Wayne.

"What have you got there?" he asked, pointing. Wayne had the old woman's body over his shoulder, but a Morrisons carrier bag swung from his other hand.

"Brought some fish," said Wayne proudly. "It was reduced, so I thought it would help us get them seals' attention."

"Jesus Christ, Wayne. We've brought them a fucking body to eat. If you fill them up with cut-price cod so they don't want to eat the old lady, you know I'm going to make your life not worth living, don't you?"

"I like seals," said Wayne quietly.

They walked down a concrete ramp and entered the pool area. There were three seals in what looked like a sizeable pool. They all reclined on fibre glass rocks on the far side. Wayne opened a little gate to give them access to the poolside. For hopefully man-eating creatures, the security measures were fairly flimsy.

"There's only three of them. Where are all the others?" Jimmy asked.

Wayne read from a chalk board. "'Elton, Kylie and Beyonce remain in the sanctuary pool, while most of this year's rescues have now been released at the nearby shore. Visit our website for a chance to—'"

"Fuck," said Jimmy. "Can three seals eat a whole body?"

Wayne dropped the body to the floor and started to remove the wrapping. "Let's try it," he said.

Mrs Skipworth rolled out onto the fake rocks by the pool, her face mottled and her eyes wide. Jimmy took an involuntary step back and sat on the short poolside wall. He stared at her face, felt himself melt away in her presence until only detached clinical Cold Jimmy remained.

Wayne picked Mrs Skipworth up by her shoulders and flipped her into the pool. It was a deep splash, far bigger than her bird-like frame warranted.

"Come and get it, seals!" called Wayne. "Nom nom!"

The seals remained on their rocks, with only the briefest of glances to indicate they had even noticed the disturbance.

Jimmy shook his head silently. He could see it was a terrible idea, born from desperation and tiredness, and fuelled by fear and bad whisky. Mrs Skipworth lay at the bottom of the pool, a shadow, rocked slowly by the currents.

That's me, thought Jimmy. That's me. He wished himself into a cold, dark, silent space and unconsciously held his breath. To disappear, to sink beneath the surface and be gone from things, felt like the best possible thing in the world at that moment.

Of course, he had to breathe again, and when he did, he spoke. "We need to get that body out from the bottom of the pool. The seals won't even be able to smell it down there."

Wayne jumped into the pool and ducked down. He re-appeared a moment later with the old woman's body in his arms, like the most careless romantic hero who'd almost let the love of his life suffer a violent and bloody death before rescuing her from the water. He plopped her down on the side and considered the problem.

"I've got an idea," he said.

"Another one?"

Wayne took a folding handsaw from his pocket. Without warning he sawed off one of the woman's fingers.

"You're out of your fucking mind!" said Jimmy.

"Nah, this will work."

Jimmy bit down on further words, unwilling to dwell on the sight any longer, in the very real belief that he ran the risk of puking. He looked away. When he looked back, Wayne had pulled one of the fish from his Morrisons bag and was ramming the woman's finger into its mouth. This was worse, this was definitely worse.

"Come on then! I know one of you will eat this!" shouted Wayne. He threw the fish over towards the reclining seals and it plopped into the water. Jimmy watched as the seal closest to them finally slid bonelessly off its rock and disappeared under the water. Two seconds later it surfaced, gulping down the fish.

"It worked! Did you see that?" crowed Wayne.

"Just wait up for a second!" said Jimmy. "I don't know how many fish you've got in that bag, but I'm willing to bet it's not enough for us to hide a whole body inside. We'll be here all night just chopping it up."

"Nah, it'll be fine."

"Fine?"

"We just need to give them a taste for old lady, then they'll come and finish the rest. You watch."

From anyone else, that might have sounded like callousness or outright sadism. From Wayne it was just a bear of very little brain working on a solution to the current problem.

Wayne repeated the fish trick with another two fingers, then he sawed off three toes to push into the last fish in his bag. The seals ate the fish hungrily, before retiring to their rocks to sleep off the excitement.

Jimmy looked at his phone. He'd been looking at it intermittently all day, automatically checking for texts or calls from Jacinda, but without a SIM the phone remained predictably silent.

"Wayne, it's nearly ten o'clock. All you've got rid of are a couple of fingers and toes. I know fellas down the Ship Hotel who'd have guzzled that down without a thought if you doused it with chilli sauce and handed it to them on a kebab."

"Oh, good idea! Closing time is—"

"—That's not an actual suggestion! We're *not* doing that!"

Wayne's face fell.

Jimmy looked across at Elton, Kylie and Beyonce. He wondered which was which, and who had eaten the most of

Mrs Skipworth. He decided the seal on the rock must be Beyonce. There was a lot of attitude in its expression, and it definitely had a curvy booty. Beyonce and her backing singers looked at Jimmy. He could feel them judging him. Fucking celebrities.

"I need you to wrap this back up and put it in the van," Jimmy told Wayne, pointing at the body.

"But the plastic's all ripped now."

"We'll look around. There's sure to be a store room with some bin bags or whatever."

Jimmy stepped back over the wall and walked across the public spaces to the nearest building. Night had fallen, but even out here, miles from proper civilisation, orange light pollution gave a shape to the darkness. Wayne got ahead of him and found a light switch as he went inside. There were leaf patterns on the wall and a musty, humid quality to the air. An ambiguous sign invited them to come look at FROGS, ETC.

"Reptile house," said Jimmy.

Seconds later, Wayne shouted. "Hey, Jimmy, you'll never guess what they've got in here!"

Jimmy ignored him, but Wayne's voice continued in excitement.

"Apparently it's a myth that piranhas strip the flesh from a skeleton in seconds. They are mostly scavengers."

"Oh, for fuck's sake." Jimmy ran. "Wayne! Don't mess with those things! I don't care if it says they're tame as fuck and they use them for a kiddies' petting zoo! Stay right away from them, do you hear?"

Jimmy burst through plastic hangings designed to keep

the heat in, and into an exhibit area that was a lazy designer's idea of a rainforest. Uneven fake stone flooring, a bamboo bridge, several deep pools crowded with waxy-leafed plants. Wayne was over the far side on the rocks between two pools.

"Get out of the piranha pool, Wayne," said Jimmy calmly.

Wayne waved his hand. He was holding a roll of black bin bags. "Cleaning cupboard back here," he grinned.

"Good, now come on."

Wayne walked back between the two pools. "It's okay, I'm staying well away from them," he said.

"Good."

Three things happened. Jimmy noticed that the non-piranha pool had a stubby dark log floating in it. The stubby dark log moved independently towards Wayne. Wayne walked too far from one pool and too close to the other, and his foot slipped on the fake rock slope. Jimmy could not rightly say which of those events happened in what order. But the log opened a hinged jaw and lunged at Wayne with a sickening speed.

Wayne screamed.

Jimmy saw its eyes, yellow ovals, and the glimpse of a triangular tooth or two as it clamped down on Wayne's shin.

"Jimmy!" screamed Wayne.

Jimmy was just about processing that the thing was an alligator, or a crocodile, or something.

"Help me!"

Jimmy's first instinct was to run. His second was to stand and watch. After the day he'd had, his concern for his fellow man had almost trickled away entirely.

Wayne flopped down, half-in and half-out of the pool,

the alligator worrying at his leg with the tenacity of a terrier at a bone. Another alligator stirred at the bottom of the pool. Five feet long, maybe more.

"Jimmy, shoot it!"

"I haven't got a gun."

"Shoot it!"

"I haven't got a gun!"

The situation was bad. It was worse than bad. Yet Jimmy, whilst stunned, was oddly unmoved. Wayne had killed a woman. They had concealed her death. They had fed a number of her digits to the local seals. Now, Wayne was having his foot eaten by an alligator. It seemed to be part of the natural order of things.

By the far safer path, Jimmy ran round the pool to the cleaning cupboard Wayne had found. It was a storeroom; there was nothing useful like a taser or a tranquiliser gun. Jimmy picked up a net but put it down again. It was more suitable for scooping up tiddlers and would definitely not hold an alligator. He grunted with frustration at the quality of equipment and picked up a broom instead.

"Wayne, you're going to be all right," he said, approaching the pool.

"It's trying to drag me over to the deep bit," said Wayne, tearfully. "I'm not sure I can stand up for much longer, I feel funny. And it *really* hurts!"

The alligator – and now, looking at the thing, it was no more than four feet long, probably only a baby – thrashed and back-pedalled and tried to haul the big fat man in.

"Right, first things first then," said Jimmy. He held the broom out to Wayne. "Haul yourself up."

"Yes, Jimmy," snivelled Wayne.

He managed to claw himself onto the pool edge, drawing the alligator along with him.

"Now, sit down while I have a think."

"You kidding me?" said Wayne. "I'm supposed to sit here and watch while this thing eats my leg?"

"Wayne. Sitting down will stop you falling into the water. If you fall in the water then it will chomp on your neck, or drown you, or whatever."

"Oh, Christ, Jimmy. I'm sorry. I'm sorry for what I did to the old lady's fingers."

"Shush. Now let me think. Is it alligators where you can prise open their jaws?"

"That's sharks, isn't it?"

"No, you hit sharks on the nose." Jimmy was momentarily and unhelpfully put in mind of the whack-a-croc game on the pier. "Why don't you prise open its jaws?".

Wayne reached down, his hands shaking. "Oh, its eyes! I can't look!"

"It's best if you look. You can do this."

Wayne grasped the alligator's jaws. "It's wet!"

"Of course it's wet. It lives in the water."

"Are you sure about this?"

Jimmy considered lying. "No. But try it anyway."

The alligator reacted to the attack by writhing swiftly and violently. It turned out Wayne's bulk wasn't enough to hold him in place. Wayne slid into the water and Jimmy wasn't sure what was happening for a long moment. Then Wayne powered towards the edge, propelled by his giant arms, the alligator giving chase.

"Get away!" yelled Jimmy, using the broom to bash the thing on the head.

Wayne made it to the edge, hauling himself onto the pathway, panting fiercely.

Jimmy looked at him. There was a ragged stump where the lower portion of his leg had been. The alligator sank into the shallows, presumably to feast upon Wayne's foot. Jimmy finally gave into the urge that had been bubbling under for a while, and vomited copiously on the tiles.

"Jimmy," said Wayne, woozily, as blood leaked from his severed leg. "My Yeezys..."

"Your what?"

Wayne waved a weak hand indistinctly towards the pool and his missing foot.

"Yes, sure," said Jimmy. He didn't want to break it to Wayne that he was unlikely to be using that trainer again. Jimmy certainly had no plans to fight an alligator for it. "I need to stop your bleeding, get that body back in the boot, and get you some medical attention."

He stopped short of mentioning the clean-up tasks that needed to be completed before morning. He also didn't dwell too much on the fact that the medical attention wasn't going to be from an orthodox practitioner. No way was he taking a one-footed man to A&E while they still had a body to dispose of.

Jimmy's mind retreated further into the merely functional. His life became a list of tasks.

It reminded him – reminded that small section of conscious, feeling human – of the time a mate had entered them both for a half marathon. Thirteen miles was an impossible distance for the casual jogger to comprehend, impossible when he got stitch after the first two miles, and his shins started to burn after three. The only way to survive it was to break it down, mile by mile. Get to the next mile marker, get to the next drinks station. When all the body wanted to do was cry out in anguish, and the brain could no longer remember how things had come to this – why it had seemed like a good idea at the time – it was all about dividing the torture into manageable chunks.

- Put a tourniquet around Wayne's calf to stop him bleeding everywhere.
- Tell Wayne to shut the fuck up.
- Wrap up the old woman's body in plastic again.
- Drag the body to the van and load it in the rear.
- Get Wayne to the van.
- Discover that Wayne can't hobble round the gate post in his condition.
- Break the lock on the gates and open them up.
- Put Wayne in the van.
- Tell Wayne to shut the fuck up.
- Check the crocodile or alligator or whatever it was is still in its damned pool.
- Use a mop and pool water to wash away the worst of the blood in the reptile house.
- Check that the cleaning cupboard is shut and the break-in covered up.
- Double-check on that alligator. That's right – alligator. There was an information sign.

- Use the hose reel by the side of the seal pools to hose down any blood Wayne had trailed across the Seal Land compound.
- Wind in hose. Wipe down any possible prints.
- Go out, closing the gates.
- Get in the van with Wayne.
- Tell him to shut the fuck up or, *Jesus Christ*, he was going to be left to bleed out on the roadside.
- Reverse round and drive towards Roman Bank and the main road.
- Head towards the riding school in Hogsthorpe and Sacha's clinic.
- Search for Sacha's number.
- Call Sacha and tell him it's an emergency.
- When Wayne asks if the Sacha on the line is the same Sacha who is Jacinda's horse vet, tell him again to shut the fuck up.

25

S am was awakened by the slamming of the front door. She was drunk and tired, but the sound of exterior doors in the night cut right through to the cavewoman centres of her brain. She was up before her body had time to protest, padding through the long house. She would have picked up a heavy ornament to use as a weapon on a potential intruder, but probability dictated the person she'd be most likely to brain with it would be her dad. Besides, all the decent heavy objects had been moved to the junk boxes for reselling.

She entered the front lounge and found the sofa where Delia had drunkenly crashed was empty. There was a note scrawled on the back of the drone assembly instructions.

THANKS FOR A GREAT NIGHT. *Got to go. Bloody husband!*
  Delia

. . .

SAM RE-READ IT, decided there was nothing further to be gleaned from it, and went to bed. On the way, she stopped at the kitchen for a much-needed glass of water, stopped at the toilet for an even-more-needed pee, and checked her phone.

There was an alert from the DefCon4 app.

An alarm had gone off at a property where DefCon4 managed the security: Seal Land at Anderby Creek. A perimeter alarm had been triggered. In her limited experience, most alarms were false alarms – technical faults or human error. The package Seal Land were signed up to meant the same alert would be sent to the property owners and the police. There was nothing for her to do. They'd call her if she was needed.

Sam went back to bed and dreamed of a drone, flying over dark waves for eternity.

26

Jimmy helped Wayne hobble over to the vet's office. By all rights, Wayne should be in a wheelchair, but Jimmy didn't have one in the van, and vets had no use for them. Wayne had lost a lot of blood, in spite of Jimmy's best efforts at a tourniquet, and much of it was pooling in the van's footwell. Jimmy had tried to staunch it further by wrapping duct tape around the stump, but the loops of tape just became a baggy sock to carry the blood in.

Sacha's veterinary practice was next to the stables he part-owned with a farmer, out Market Rasen way. It was a decent distance from Hogsthorpe village, far from any prying eyes. It was the middle of the night and the world was comfortingly dark. The light of the vet's surgery was a beacon.

"Hey, Sacha," said Wayne with a pale, giddy grin. He tried to wave and nearly fell out of Jimmy's arms.

"Wayne, you aren't looking so hot, my man," said Sacha,

standing in the light of the doorway. He had a crisp, cultured accent. Jimmy didn't know what country the vet was originally from, although Sacha had told him it was one that no longer existed, but never revealed more than that.

The two men hobbled in. In the clinical light of Sacha's workspace, Jimmy realised his own legs were as soaked in blood as Wayne's. More clothes to go in the fire.

Sacha looked at the extent of the damage in alarm. "You should be in the hospital."

"I told you on the phone," said Jimmy through gritted teeth. "We don't want any attention. We can't do the hospital."

"Yes but this..." Sacha waved a hand over Wayne's ragged stump. "This is bad. If we get complications, I don't want to be—"

"It's fine," said Jimmy. "None of this will come back to you, and we'll make sure you're compensated."

"Jacinda knows?"

"We'll see you right." He was deliberately vague on who 'we' referred to. "If anything goes wrong nobody needs to know you helped him."

"Yes, but I have a reputation to uphold."

"Exactly. You've treated horses with bad leg wounds, right? This is just like that. Tidy up the wound. Fill him full of antibiotics and pain killers and we're all good."

"I shall decide on the appropriate course of treatment," said Sacha with a sniff. "He is not a horse and this injury... Let's get him up on the table."

With some difficulty Jimmy and Sacha lifted him to the table. Wayne whimpered.

"We will soon have this sorted out for you," said Sacha. Jimmy thought it must be strange for Sacha having to explain what he was doing to his patient, as they weren't normally human. He'd heard someone say that Sacha liked to sing opera to the horses when he treated them, especially when inseminating the breeding mares. He wasn't sure if that was true. Maybe that's what they did in his country which no longer existed.

Wayne struggled to sit up. Sacha pushed him gently back down.

"I need to walk," said Wayne, feebly.

Sacha pulled a nakedly honest face. Vets didn't have to put on a brave face for their patients. "Yes, but you have no foot. At least not one I can see..."

Wayne was having none of it. Even in his weakened state he fought to sit up.

"Can't you knock him out?" said Jimmy.

"With this kind of trauma, the risk of shock..." Sacha injected Wayne swiftly and unfussily. "Methadone to take the edge off. Hold him." Sacha ripped away what remained of Wayne's lower trousers, then went at the wound with a number of scissor-like clamps.

Sacha loosened Jimmy's tourniquet, showing no panic when blood spread across the table and onto the floor. He fixed a superior rubber tourniquet and put further clamps on the wound. "Janet or Esther?" he asked.

"What?" said Jimmy.

"Which alligator was it? I've treated both."

"We didn't stop to ask questions!"

Wayne groaned loudly. Sacha gave him two further

injections. "Fentanyl for the pain and antibiotics. There will be a high chance of sepsis."

Jimmy couldn't tell if Sacha was informing him or narrating his own actions.

Sasha produced several clear bags of what Jimmy assumed was some sort of intravenous fluid. One by one he broke them open to wash out the wound.

Wayne gasped. "What will I have?" he whispered.

"Pardon?" said Sacha.

"Will it be like a bionic leg?"

Sacha hesitated. "Sure, but you need to heal first, my man. Afterwards there will be options—"

"No!" yelled Wayne, throwing Sacha's arms aside and lurching upright. "I can't wait around like a cripple. I gotta have something I can walk on. What can you do?"

"Let's talk about this when—"

"No!" Wayne pitched himself off the table and crashed to the floor, tipping over a set of drawers as he went. Metal instruments and kidney bowls of blood-stained cleaning materials cascaded everywhere. He unbalanced a metal and plastic half-gun, half-funnel device, and Sacha dived to save it.

"Careful! This is expensive."

"You need to do something I can use right away," Wayne whined. "You gotta!"

Wayne proceeded to drag himself across the floor, levering himself along with his stump, attached clamps clanking on the floor with every movement. Jimmy looked on in something closer to amazement than horror, wondering how he could stand the pain.

"I don't get this with the horses," Sacha muttered.

"Fuck's sake. Just tell him he can have a bionic leg," hissed Jimmy.

"Yes, but of course," said Sacha. "Back on the table first."

They wrestled him back up onto the table. It was doubly hard the second time around as the floor was slick with Wayne's blood; littered with dressings and equipment. Sacha swept them aside and hit Wayne with more painkiller injections. After cleaning the soiled wound once more, Sacha set to the edges of the wound with a scalpel, slicing away chunks of flesh. Here, here, here... A pile of meat built up in a dish to the side. Jimmy suspected he wouldn't be able to face diced ham again any time soon.

"Debriding non-viable tissue," Sacha said. "Avoiding possible necrosis."

Sacha fell into a simple, quiet rhythm. Wayne was still conscious but calmer, muttering something unintelligible except for the occasional utterance of 'foot'. From scalpel to needle and thread, to soft dressings and bandages, Sacha sealed up and contained Wayne's wound.

After what felt like no time at all, but measured by the debris on the floor and surfaces around them, was clearly more than an hour later, Sacha stepped back. "He is stable," he said.

"My foot," said Wayne.

"Is no more, my man."

Wayne rumbled deeply. "My bionic foot."

"Rest is what you need."

Despite the pain and the drugs, Wayne pushed himself up once more.

"There might be something," said Sacha hurriedly. He stepped into a back room and returned with something that looked like a cross between a surgical support and an umbrella stand. He held it up and smiled wanly at them both. "Here we have the answer, my friends."

"What is it?" said Wayne.

"I have used this in procedures where it was necessary to provide emergency support to the patient," said Sacha. He sounded a little evasive to Jimmy's ears, but Wayne was loving it, a grin spread across his pale face.

"So, I can use it straightaway?" he asked.

"Yes, but only because you insisted," said Sacha.

"Where on earth did that metal contraption spring from?" said Jimmy. "I've seen it before."

Sacha patted the thing proudly. "Do you remember Miss Frost's favourite stud, Horn of Plenty?"

"Yes," said Jimmy. "Oh. Oh right."

Horn of Plenty had been an outstanding stallion, Jacinda's long-standing favourite. He had broken a leg in a steeplechase and Jacinda had gone berserk with grief. Jimmy didn't have much to do with the horses on a day-to-day basis, but he had heard whispered accounts down the pub about the multiple attempts to save Horn's leg. None of them had been successful, so the horse had been fitted with some kind of leg brace. From what Jimmy could recall, the horse had trouble lifting it, and could barely walk. But he could still service the mares, which became his full-time occupation. Jimmy had often wondered what sort of a life that was for the horse.

"It is my own invention," said Sacha proudly.

"But if this is Horn's leg brace, what's he wearing now?"

"This was mark one," said Sacha. "The spring clasps kept unspringing, so I made mark two. Not that we need Horn of Plenty anymore." He picked up the funnel-gun apparatus he'd saved from Wayne's delirious rampage. It had a little TV screen mounted on the trigger end.

"And that is...?" said Jimmy.

"Insemination gun," said Sacha. "With endoscopic camera for precise delivery of sperm."

Jimmy blinked at the thing. The barrel was eighteen inches of pointed steel. Jimmy imagined Sacha would have to sing some fucking charming opera before most mares would let him come anywhere near them.

Sacha put the gun aside and showed the leg brace to Jimmy. "This one will be fine for your man though. He won't need it for long."

"Cos I'll get better, right?" said Wayne.

Sacha gave Jimmy an easily readable look.

"Er, yeah," said Jimmy.

"That's right," said Sacha, equally convincingly.

It was a good job Wayne was pumped full of drugs. And stupid. It was a really good job Wayne was stupid.

27

Sam parked her Piaggio van outside Seal Land and sipped the drive-thru coffee she'd picked up on the way over. It was definitely coffee, but didn't taste of anything recognisable. It was basically the liquid version of a picture of a coffee. But it was scalding hot, and the touch of it against her lips and tongue was enough to wake her a little more. She and Marvin and Delia had been toasting the sadly departed drone long after midnight. Sam thought she recalled they'd even attempted to mix another pitcher of All Glory Is Fleeting, but they'd definitely got the measures wrong.

She did not want to get up that morning but, electronically prodded and poked by the DefCon4 app, Sam had dragged herself up to contend with the day. The calendared items on her app consisted of a team briefing and a number of residential property inspections. There had also been an unkillable alert regarding the security systems at

Seal Land; even a message from the client that they needed someone to attend. Thus, hungover and with scalded lips, Sam got out of her tiny vehicle and walked to the Seal Land entrance.

A police car stood outside the open double gates. Sam wandered past it on her way inside. A searing orange sun was rising over the far wall of the zoo compound. Sam's unhappy brain winced enough to make her shield her eyes.

"We're not open yet."

She blinked and saw it was the Seal Land guy from the other day. She fumbled for her ID, quickly giving up looking for it. "DefCon4," she said.

"Oh, God, it's you. You've not come to kidnap one of our other seals?"

"Ha ha," she said, deadpan. Hangovers and humour didn't mix. "The alarms. They keep tripping."

"I think it's just a system fault, but the police are here anyway and doing a general check."

There was a sudden and urgent shout from across the site. Swiftly followed by another loud voice. A woman emerged from a building marked *Frogs, Etc.*

"Guy, you need to see this," she called. Sam realised that the Seal Land guy was also the Seal Land Guy.

"So maybe not a system fault," Sam said to Guy. She could hear the disappointment in her voice. A system fault would have allowed her to just prod a few buttons on the alarm controls, maybe put in a call to a maintenance contractor, then head to the office and let Doug Fredericks assume command for an hour or two. If there had been a break-in, there might be actual work to do.

As they walked towards the reptile house, Sam scanned the site, recalling what she knew. The place had no CCTV. Seal Land had only forked out for trip alarms on the exterior doors, gates and the largest outward facing windows. In the event of an investigation, she'd be able to provide no information other than where and at what time the break-in had taken place.

She followed Guy through to a humid windowless space, a cheap attempt to recreate a twilit rainforest. Sergeant Cesar Hackett was leaning over the side of a pool and fishing around with the handle end of a mop.

"What's going on?" said Guy. "Those are sensitive creatures."

"Hoop-la!" declared Cesar as he hoisted something out of the pool. Below him, a five-foot alligator swished its tail in irritation at the disturbance.

Cesar carefully swung his dripping catch round to the crazy paving pathway. It was a trainer, ripped and ragged around the heel, but definitely a trainer. It had a Morse code dot-dash tread and the manufacturer's logo stamped into the sole. "Someone's been a bit careless with their shoes," he grinned.

"Did someone fall in?" said Sam.

Cesar looked round and realised he had a small audience. He gave Sam a comforting look. "I'm sure nothing so dramatic."

Guy approached the pool and studied it thoughtfully. "We would know if a visitor left with only one shoe, wouldn't we?"

"Maybe it fell out of a shopping bag," Cesar suggested.

Pool water trickled down the mop and onto the dressing around Cesar's seal-mauled hand. He picked at the damp bandage.

"And no one's been eaten, have they?" asked Sam.

"An alligator can't eat a human that quickly," said Guy, but turned to his colleague. "We might need the vet out again."

"Not to cut them open?" said Cesar, horrified.

"What?"

"Like that bit in *Jaws*. Maybe we'll find a licence plate in one of these guys."

"What? No! If they've eaten a shoe or clothes... It could make Janet or Esther seriously ill."

Sam crouched beside the trainer. "Perhaps someone dropped it in. Deliberately."

Cesar scoffed. "An Adidas Yeezy Boost 350? What kind of person would throw away a shoe like that?"

"As opposed to the kind who would feed themselves to an alligator?"

"I'll call Sacha," said Guy. "He'll need to check them over. Are we okay to open today, sergeant?"

"Hmmm?" said Cesar.

"Is this a crime scene?"

Cesar laughed. "No. Of course not."

Guy and his colleague stepped out to prepare for opening. Sam took out a pen and prodded the shoe.

"You can touch it if you like," said Cesar. "It won't bite."

"Fingerprints," Sam replied and tipped the trainer upright. "It's heavy. I think there's something in there."

"Waterlogged probably," said Cesar and picked up the trainer. "It is heavy," he agreed. "A good shoe, the Yeezy."

"And how do you know so much about trainers?" asked Sam. "You don't look the ... athletic type."

Cesar drew himself up. She wasn't sure if he was trying to puff out his chest with pride or pull in his considerable gut. "Can't a man be a servant of the law and a follower of fashion?" he said. "There is something in here, you're right."

He jammed in his fingers and wiggled them about. "Seems stuck." He up-ended the shoe and rapped it sharply against the floor. Something, pink-white and lumpy flew out of the heel, bounced limply on the ground, and rolled down the short slope into the pool. A sinuous alligator – Janet or Esther, Sam didn't know – shifted in the water and snapped it up.

Cesar looked at Sam with the expression of a man who hoped she hadn't seen what had very obviously happened. "That was nothing," he said.

"That was a piece of foot and at least three toes," said Sam.

"It'll be fine, I'm sure."

28

The alarm at Seal Land had been set off by the double gates being opened in the night. The only additional sign of a break-in was the central latch on the gates had popped from its socket, an act that would have been easily done by only a moderate amount of force if the L-shaped ground bolts weren't secured.

"Could have been the wind," said Cesar. "A strong off-shore gust."

Sam thought of the drone test flight. "There was no wind last night."

It didn't matter to her. She disconnected the gate zone from the site's alarm system and said she'd have it reinstated once the gate was fixed. Cesar had bagged the ripped shoe (telling no one there had probably been the rest of a foot inside) and declared he would be making an appropriate investigation. Sam assumed that would involve making himself a cup of tea and forgetting all about it. In all honesty,

Sam didn't care. The power of the purely nominal cup of coffee had already worn off. She needed a recharge.

She drove back into Skegness with every intention of getting a fresh cup of caffeine from Cat's Café before tackling the rest of the day. This plan was slightly derailed by the sight of an Odinson waiting outside the DefCon4 office door.

Even before taking the DefCon4 job, Sam had heard of the Odinsons. Their name was a byword for low-level criminality in the town, a universal local scapegoat for every petty anti-social act. They were invoked so often, used as an answer for the otherwise unanswerable, that they had become a slice of folk belief. They were, in the minds of most, as real as the tooth fairy; as nebulously defined as the bogeyman.

Since then, Sam had met several of them in the flesh. Their slapdash attitude to parentage, their fluid attitude to family structure and general uniformity of appearance meant even with official records to hand, it was not easy to tell them apart. On the noticeboard upstairs, behind an OS map of the local area, Sam had built up a visual family tree of the Odinson clan with photographs, string and drawing pins. It had a lot of gaps in it, and the string was forced to travel in genealogically unlikely loops and swirls in some places, but she wasn't aware of anyone else making such an effort.

For once, she half-suspected she knew this Odinson. The leather jacket and stained T-shirt were standard Odinson uniform. The crimson harem trousers and plaited beard were not. He looked like a Hell's Angel extra from Aladdin.

"Morning," she said. "Ogendus, right?"

He jutted his chin in greeting. Silver ornaments woven into his beard jiggled. "Ah need to talk ta thee."

Ogendus was one of Ragnar's sons. Definitely – almost definitely – one of the patriarch's oldest offspring.

"I need a coffee," said Sam. "But I need to step in the office a second."

Ogendus nodded. Sam unlocked the door, ran up the stairs to the office and waited for her DefCon4 app to buzz and automatically tick off the morning team meeting. She saw the loose carpet tile had sprung up again.

"Back in a bit!" she said to Doug Fredericks, then went down and locked up again.

She led Ogendus into Cat's Café. "Americano, please," she said to Cat.

"Coming right up," said Cat. "How are you today?"

"Coping," said Sam. She didn't reciprocate the question. Asking Cat anything would turn into an excuse for Cat to talk about the play she'd been working on ever since Sam had known her. "A drink?" Sam asked Ogendus.

"Aye, a tea would be grand," he said to Cat.

Cat looked at him with worried disdain, clearly glad there was a serving counter between her and him.

"And some toast would be champion?" said Ogendus, turning it into a question for Sam.

"I think I can stretch to toast," she nodded.

"An' toast then." Ogendus looked at the menu board. "An egg to go on it. And some bacon on t'side. Tha got black pudding?"

Cat shook her head.

"Tha's no way to run a café, is it?" he said. "I'll just have a couple of sausages an' all, then."

Cat looked to Sam. Sam didn't have the energy to argue. She waved her assent, ordered a sausage roll to go for herself, and sat in a window table. Ogendus sat opposite her, putting his hands together on the table in front of him, as though he thought that's how people should behave in proper meetings. The tattoos on his knuckles, now interlaced, spelled out *LHOAVTEE*. Sam didn't bother to start the conversation. She could wait him out or wait for her coffee. Whichever came first.

"Ah just had to tell thee," said Ogendus. "My lads didn't do it."

Sam nodded. The coffee and the tea arrived. Cat retreated rapidly to her kitchen to cook a breakfast. Sam sipped the coffee and it was good, proper, cleanse-the-soul coffee. "Do what? You might need to narrow it down a bit."

"I'm just sayin'."

"Yes," she agreed. "What are you saying? What haven't your lads done?"

"The burglary at t'seal place."

Sam was surprised. "How did you know...? Burglary?"

"Whatever," said Ogendus. He clutched at a stylised hammer pendant hanging at his chest from a leather strop. "I swear on almighty Thor that me lads are innocent."

"Yes, yes," said Sam. "I'm sure you do."

"Do not deny my fervour, lass!"

"You'll keep your voice down in this place or I'll be forced to have words!" she retorted hotly.

Sam wouldn't usually get confrontational with a man

twice her age and a very loose attitude to conventional morality, but she was hungover, she had to present herself as an authority figure in front of the Odinson tribe, and this man, despite his manner, had come to her in the manner of a supplicant.

"You think your boys are going to be blamed?" she asked.

"They allus get t'blame," he said simply. "You Saxons allus blames us. An' Torsten is tryin' his best."

"Ah."

It made sense now. Partial sense at least. Torsten Odinson – young, blond, beefy, with a softer heart and brain than he'd care to let on. Torsten Odinson was currently subject to a community payback order. Something about an argument outside a pub and an assault. DefCon4 had a regional contract for overseeing community service, and Sam had the power to refer people back to court if she thought they weren't meeting the terms of their court order.

"Has Torsten been picking fights in pubs again?" asked Sam.

"He 'as not," said Ogendus firmly.

"Then he has nothing to worry about," said Sam.

"As long as tha knows that. Me an' the lads are tryin' to do right. We're applying for a new 'ouse from the Saxon social. Not one of them B an' Bs, but our own 'ouse. Do right by me lads."

"Away from the Odinson compound?" said Sam.

Ogendus said nothing to that. It didn't matter. The idea that he and his sons could get a housing association place, or any other kind of social housing, was a pipe dream. If children and single parents, particularly single mothers, were at the front of the housing queue, then adults, especially men, living as a family or not, were at the back. There weren't enough spaces to accommodate existing needs, here in Skegness or anywhere else. Ogendus Odinson and his offspring could keep their noses clean for the rest of their lives; the chances of getting any assistance with housing was virtually nil.

Ogendus began heaping teaspoons of sugar into his tea.

"And how did you know about the break-in at Seal Land?"

Ogendus narrowed his eyes. "Are police scanners illegal?"

"Let's pretend they're not," said Sam.

"I 'eard that daft apath Hackett's gonna get some evidence tested. Though 'is inspector ain't impressed."

"Right."

Cat clattered in the kitchen as she served up.

"I don't think anyone's going to blame your sons," said Sam. "Although, if one of them is missing a trainer and a few toes, you let me know."

Her phone buzzed. The caller ID came up as KAREN MoW and it took Sam's struggling brain time to recall who that was.

Cat came round the counter with a large fry up for Ogendus and a paper bag for Sam.

"I've got to take this," said Sam, standing. She took the sausage roll off Cat and then, because hangovers made her cruel, said, "Cat's writing a play, Ogendus."

"Oh, tha's one of them there authors?" said Ogendus automatically.

"You read?" said Cat, surprised.

"I ... can."

"It's a work of youth theatre set after a cataclysmic disaster," said Cat. "Less of the hero's journey, more the heroine's journey. My beta-readers at Skegness Operatic and Dramatic Society say it's a sort of Hunger Games, but I don't want to pigeonhole it as science fiction. I think it's got more of a non-linear experimental quality. I couldn't even begin to properly describe it..."

As Cat began to earnestly describe her indescribable play, and Ogendus's breakfast cooled before him, Sam slipped out and answered the call.

"Hey, Karen. What's up?"

"Hi," said the regular meals on wheels woman. *"How's things? I've got a question about last week's meals. Mrs Skipworth."*

Mrs Skipworth. The woman in Welton le Marsh with the grumpy cat cups and the ghost sightings in the graveyard.

"Yes. Ah..." Sam wondered if she'd have to explain a series of events that involved an anti-social seal, a bearded mannequin and a lot of ruined dinners.

"Did you see her when you did your rounds?" said Karen.

"Yeah. She made a complaint or something?"

"Not at all. She didn't answer her door yesterday. I made a note of it. She's got a niece or something in Grantham, but I wasn't aware she'd gone away."

"I saw her," said Sam. "She was in fine spirits."

"Right." There was an uncomfortable hesitation on the line.

"Listen, I've got to go out there at some point," said Sam.

"I need to pick up Consuela. Um, a friend. I could drop in and check on her."

"*Would you?*" said Karen with undisguised relief.

"Sure." Sam took her phone away from her ear for a moment to look at her calendar. "I've got a house check to do first, but straight after, yeah. I'll head out to Welton."

29

J immy woke up late. It had been a long and extremely unpleasant night.

He couldn't take Wayne home. He didn't want Wayne's mum or sister asking questions about what the hell had happened to the man's foot. The truth would have been out in seconds and, though they might not have called the police, they would have taken him to the hospital, which would have amounted to the same thing. No way was Jimmy taking Wayne to his place either. This horrid business had invaded Jimmy's personal space, his mental space, far more than he liked. No, Wayne wasn't coming home with him.

He had considered booking them into the Premier Inn by the pier, but even with the automated check-in console and a low likelihood of facing awkward questions from staff, it still seemed a step too far. And so they had come to Shore View.

The fitters had come in and put windows and doors on the first cargo container, turning a crappy, rusting box into a crappy, rusting building. With plastic-wrapped fibreglass insulation rolls Jimmy had constructed two narrow beds and then, exhausted, he'd slept.

Wayne snored loudly in the other bed. Any other time Wayne's appalling snoring would have driven Jimmy mad, but right now he was grateful the man was still alive. Sacha had seemed a little uncertain about some of the doses he was administering. The vet's usual reference point was a horse, and it had been hard for Sacha to determine what size pony Wayne was equivalent to.

Letting Wayne snore on, Jimmy got up from his sweaty, plastic-wrapped bed and stepped outside.

The beach stretched for forever in either direction, Skegness town was lost in a haze to the south. The sun was high. The sea sparkled and almost looked blue for once, rather than its usual palette of slate grey and estuary brown. A stiff but not unpleasant breeze wafted in from across the waves. The world looked bearable. The vile deeds of the past days had not gone from his mind, the body was still in the back of the van, and the cold and calculating part of Jimmy which had carried him through the worst of it was still there, asleep in its cave at the back of his mind. But, for a moment, he could rise above those things, put his life on pause, and appreciate the sun and the sea.

He went to the tiny site office, filled the kettle from a water drum, and put it on for a cuppa. He took two brews back to the half-finished container house. Wayne was stirring.

"Hey, mate, how you feeling?" Jimmy asked.

"Thirsty," said Wayne, starting to sit up.

"Take it easy. I've brought you a cuppa. You need to rest."

Jimmy made him a pillow of another fibreglass pack and passed him his tea. Wayne sipped. His face lacked colour and there was a sweaty, lemon-yellow sheen to his skin.

"Whoa, cool," whispered Wayne.

Jimmy followed the big lad's gaze down to the end of the bed.

One foot still had the trainer on from yesterday, while the other ended with the bizarre brace Sacha had fastened on. It wasn't just held on with a strap. Clickable bands, like the fastenings on ski boots, clamped it to Wayne's leg. His stump was a mass of dressings, nestled tightly within the framework of Sacha's ironmongery, giving him a peg-leg but no foot.

"I'm Robocop," grinned Wayne. "This is even better than a bionic leg."

"Is it? Yeah."

"Sacha's brilliant."

"Yeah, about Sacha. We probably don't want to mention his name too much when we talk about this stuff."

"Look at me!" declared Wayne, ignoring Jimmy completely. He pushed off the bed and lurched forward onto his braced leg. He hit the floor and somehow did a very ungainly version of the splits. "Ooh, ooh. Help me, Jimmy!"

"Fuck's sake, Wayne," hissed Jimmy. The cold squid uncoiled in his brain-cave and prepared to take over. Jimmy forced it back. "Look. Rest up a little bit, for crying out loud."

"I'm fine," said Wayne. "Cup of tea'll sort me right out. We got a body to get rid of, haven't we?"

"You're not wrong," said Jimmy, "but that'll keep for a while. Drink your tea."

30

Sam's phone beeped a reminder as she bit into the sausage roll. The accommodation inspection. No time for the sausage roll now. She put it back into the paper bag and stuffed it into a pocket. The address was about half a mile away. She could get there on foot if she hurried.

She glanced around the houses after some serious power walking. She was looking for Lavender Court bed and breakfast. Inspecting accommodation facilities which were used for benefits claimants was another thing DefCon4 had scooped up in its efforts to step in where local government faltered. If the likes of Ogendus Odinson and his sons were at the back of the queue for social housing, the people at the front weren't necessarily going to be placed in flats or houses of their own. Skegness had an abundant supply of bed and breakfasts and cut-price hotels. Placing claimants in those had originally been a convenient stop-gap, but was now a deliberate part of housing policy.

Sam scanned the names as she walked. *Sunnyside, Elrond House* and yes, *Lavender Court*. She went to the front door and tried the handle. It was locked, so she rang the bell.

It was answered by a teenager wearing earphones. "Yeah?" he asked.

"I've come to do the inspection," said Sam. "Maybe I need to speak with the owners?"

The teen issued a grunting sound that Sam interpreted as "Do come in, I'll find them for you," but more closely resembled the noise her office chair made when she sat down too quickly.

He led Sam inside and into what was probably the breakfast room. He closed the door and disappeared. Sam waited for a moment or two, but he didn't return straightaway. She decided she might as well get on with the inspection while she waited. She consulted the notes on her phone.

COMMUNAL FACILITIES: CHECK FOR CLEANLINESS AND SIGNS OF OVER-OCCUPANCY.

THIS FACILITY COULD ACCOMMODATE thirty guests, so she looked around for signs that it was home to more than that. There was a door at the back of the breakfast room which led into the kitchen.

Much of the inspection focussed on a basic hygiene assessment. She started with the cooker. It looked very basic to cope with thirty guests: one of those odd little ranges which turned up in some of the older houses. Not as functionally rich as an actual AGA, but some people swore by them. She opened the oven door to check for grease. Something in the dark cooed: a fluting 'plibble plibble' noise.

She recoiled and pushed the door shut.

She'd had quite enough of opening doors and finding unexpected creatures on the other side in the past week. The likelihood of there being a seal in the oven was very low (of course, she would have said the same of finding a seal in the back of her van), but seals did not go 'plibble plibble'. In truth, she couldn't think what creature did.

Curiosity – damned stupid, uncontrollable curiosity – made her open the door again. Cautiously this time. But it wasn't just her curiosity that had been roused. The moment the oven door was open, two small long-legged birds flapped out and jumped to the floor.

Sam fell back in renewed surprise.

The birds, grey and scruffy, with long legs and long necks, but no more than a handspan in height, padded across the floor like velociraptors.

"What the hell are you?" she said softly.

They ran together under the table and behind a large dresser.

"And what were you doing in the oven?" she demanded.

The dresser was one of those decorative ones with rows of mismatched plates on display. Animals in the food preparation area was a big no-no, an instant fail for the inspection, but she couldn't leave things like this. She wondered where the teenager had gone, but she was worried about opening the kitchen door to go look for him, in case the birds escaped. What on earth were they anyway? She was not an expert on birds, so all she could say with certainty was that they were bigger than a magpie and smaller than an oven-ready chicken.

"Here, chookie chookie!" she tried in a low voice.

The warbling sounds from behind the dresser continued unchanged. She would need to flush them out, or move the dresser to get access to them. She looked around for a broom or something she could poke at them with. There was no broom, but in a corner was an old-fashioned feather duster. She'd never seen one made from actual feathers before. Mostly the ones in pound shops were rainbow-coloured plasticky stuff. Her dad loved to wield one on a monthly purge, ridding the house of any cobwebby traces. This one was made from huge, luscious feathers mounted on a cane. When new it had probably looked like a burlesque accessory. Now it was just dingy and sad. Still, it would do for getting tiny birds out from their hiding place. She held onto the feathery end and poked the handle into the gap hiding the birds. She slid it along gently, not wanting to hurt them. She heard an increase in volume indicating she had reached them, so she changed her grip on the feathers, intending to sweep the thing round and brush the birds out to the front of the dresser where she could see them.

Something touched her hand.

She looked down. The biggest spider she had ever seen edged from between the feathers onto her hand. She screamed involuntarily and threw down the feather duster. She wasn't afraid of spiders as such, but she was as vulnerable to a jump scare as the next person. She cursed her lack of self-control as she heard the birds scrabbling in alarm and making even more noise. It sounded as though they were making their way up the wall in the gap behind the dresser.

"Oh, no you don't."

She was worried they would hurt themselves, either by getting crushed in an impossible space, or by falling down and smashing themselves on the floor. More than that, she was gripped by the challenge of a task needing completion. She grabbed hold of the dresser and tried to drag it away from the wall. She'd make enough of a gap to retrieve the birds, then push it back into place. It moved much more easily than she had expected for such a weighty piece of furniture. That turned out to be because the top and bottom were separate pieces. She'd put all of her weight behind pulling the top part, and now it skated across the cupboard it sat upon. She watched in horror as it toppled over, sending plates smashing to the floor.

She stood for a long moment, expecting the door to open and someone to come and investigate the noise; find the catastrophic mess she'd made. The house remained silent.

"Get birds back, sort out mess," she muttered. "Don't stop to worry about it. Just get on with it."

She returned her gaze to the dresser. Without the weight of the top half, the bottom part slid out easily. She found the birds cowering in the gap. She addressed them on hands and knees.

"Come on now. Come out to Aunty Sam."

The birds – ostrich chicks? Really ugly chickens? –

looked at her, tilted their little heads and made 'plibble plibble' noises, but didn't move.

"Come on!" she snapped. That didn't work either.

She rolled back on her haunches, considered the situation, then took the sausage roll from her pocket. She tossed a flaky crumb under the dresser. One of the birds approached, bent-kneed comedy footstep after comedy footstep and pecked at it.

"That's it," she said. She threw down more. Crumbly pastry and morsels of sausage meat.

The dinosaur manner of the creatures was unmistakeable and fascinating. She absurdly hoped the presence of pork sausage wouldn't turn them into ravenous carnivores. The little birds were easily drawn by both pastry and sausage, until they were close enough for Sam to scoop them up, popping one in a nearby bucket while she grabbed the second one. The bird fought against her with its scratchy over-sized feet. Its friend gamely tried to jump out of the bucket. It was like juggling with balls that fought back. Eventually she managed to put them back inside the oven – it didn't seem right but it was at least a place of containment.

Sam located a bin bag and started piling smashed crockery into it. A thought occurred to her and she fished in her pocket and drew out the business card for Delia's junk and upcycling shop. She dialled the number and munched on the sausage roll as it rang.

"*Back to Life,*" croaked a voice.

"Delia, it's Sam."

Delia groaned. "*Don't talk to me. I'm not your friend.*"

"What?"

"*Friends don't get friends drunk on fancy cocktails and drain cleaner.*"

"I did not give you drain cleaner."

"*Then why does my mouth taste of zesty lemon and bleach?*" Delia grunted at her own silly joke. "*I love your dad.*"

"Me too. But try living with him."

"*I've got my own circus and my own monkeys, thank you. Hey, and sorry about dashing out. My hubby got called out for work in the wee small hours.*"

"Not a problem. Look, I need some help."

"*Does it involve me moving?*"

"Maybe."

Delia groaned again. "*What?*"

Sue looked at a large piece of crockery on the floor. "Do you have any Meakin plates?"

"*Yes, I do. What kind?*"

Sam took at picture of a large fragment and sent it over.

"*Ah,*" said Delia. "*I sense a story behind this.*"

Sam sighed. "I have such a story to tell," she said, "but is there any chance you could bring a big pile of Meakin plates, and maybe some other ones too, and meet me at Lavender Court bed and breakfast?"

"*Crockery-based emergency. I can do that,*" said Delia. "*I can be there in five. Maybe ten. I'm slow this morning. Fifteen. May need to stop for a pee and a tactical chunder. I'll want the full story later, mind.*"

"Over a glass of wine?"

Delia groaned once more and hung up.

31

There was no work being done on the Shore View site, nothing to be done until the next containers came in, so there were no workmen about. Jimmy walked the mile down the track to buy food. He picked up chocolate bars, crisps, pasties and Tic Tacs from the corner shop. He ate two mint Tic Tacs on the walk back to get rid of the unclean taste in his mouth.

Wayne was sitting up when he returned. "Food, yay! I'm starving!" He shovelled in the food as fast as he could manage.

Jimmy thought Wayne was acting awfully chipper for a bloke who'd lost a foot and been patched up by a horse doctor. He still had that sickly sheen to his face, but his vitality was surprising.

"You used one of those painkillers patches?" Jimmy asked, looking round for the fentanyl drugs patches Sacha had given them.

"Yeah, they work pretty good," said Wayne, shoving half a Mars bar in his mouth.

"You used just one, right?"

"Just one. Don't want to get an overdose."

He pulled up his trouser leg, cut off at the knee, to reveal a two-by-three grid of patches stuck onto his leg as a single slab.

Jimmy nodded. "Right. That'd be bad."

Shit. Jimmy hammered out a rapid message to Sacha: WHAT SHOULD I DO IF WAYNE HAS PUT ON TOO MANY PATCHES?

Sacha replied a minute later: THE FENTANYL?

YES.

FUCK. HOW MANY?

SIX.

FUCK.

Jimmy waited for a further reply before responding: ELABORATE.

Sacha's next message was longer: YOU HAD ONE FUCKING JOB. WAIT IT OUT MY MAN AND DON'T LET HIM SLEEP FOR AT LEAST FOUR HOURS. GET HIM TO DO SOME GENTLE EXERCISE.

Jimmy replied: I CAN'T TAKE HIM FOR A JOG.

JUST GET HIM TO MOVE ABOUT. NOTHING TOO STRENUOUS.

OKAY

WORST CASE: IF HE PASSES OUT YOU NEED TO RELEASE THE SUPPORT AND DROP HIM OFF AT A&E.

Jimmy shuddered at that. Release the support? He had no idea how to do that, and the one thing he knew he wouldn't be doing was diving under those dressings and looking for whatever butchery Sacha had carried out on that leg.

"Hey, Wayne," he said cheerily. "How would you like to get out in the fresh air?"

"Bit sleepy after that food," said Wayne. "Might have a nap first."

"No," insisted Jimmy. "A trip out will do you the power of good. You need to make sure your bionic leg is up to scratch in the real world. Am I right?"

"What, like in a running race?" asked Wayne, swaying gently.

"What? No!" Was he stoned? Yes, he probably was. "No running races for a while. Just a bit of light exercise. We'll do something fun."

"We've got work to do," said Wayne. "I know that, Jimmy." He was slurring his words, his head lolling.

"Work, yeah. We've got a body to dispose of you know. It's pretty urgent. Come on, walk with me."

Jimmy inserted himself under Wayne's meaty armpit, which was pretty rancid with stale sweat. He pushed up and Wayne tottered lumpily along for a few steps and out the door.

Wayne giggled at the sound of his metal peg-leg crunching on the building site hardcore.

"To the van," said Jimmy, struggling slightly under Wayne's weight. "Let's just get some practice. One, two, three."

He marched Wayne to the van, desperate to keep him moving.

"Lean here." Jimmy propped him against the side of the van. "I need to clean this out."

The passenger footwell was still mired with Wayne's

blood. Some of it had dried. Much of it was still a thick, uneven soup. Jimmy washed it out with water from the site office. It cascaded over the door sill, pink with congealed lumps of dark red.

"S'like the fountain in the ghost train," slurred Wayne.

"What?" said Jimmy.

"Ghost train. At the fairground. I could..." He blinked and staggered but kept upright. "Should I be in the ghost train?"

Wayne's mind was off somewhere else, but as long as he was awake Jimmy didn't care. The floor of the van was sort of clean. The white hard core stones were now stained a rosy pink.

"The rides, Jimmy, when can we go on them?" murmured Wayne.

"In a minute buddy, in a minute."

Wayne levered himself away from the van and stumbled several steps, ungainly but upright. Jimmy couldn't believe he could actually walk with that thing on, but Wayne was built like an ox, and hardly seemed to notice the impediment.

"Hey Jimmy, I had the best idea," said Wayne.

"Yeah?"

"Yeah."

"What was your idea, Wayne?" When he was firing on all cylinders, Wayne's ideas were not the greatest. Whatever drivel he was about to suggest, while high on horse tranqs, was going to have to be filed under 'not on your life'.

"You know we have to get rid of a body, yeah?"

"Yes, we do. You remembered well, Wayne."

"And you know how we're gonna ride the ghost train because it's my favourite, yeah?"

"Ri-ight," said Jimmy, really not sure where this was going.

"Well how about we unwrap the old lady, take her with us on the ghost train and *leave her in there*! So when people go round on the train they just see a creepy-ass lady looking like she's a dead person. Because she *is* a dead person."

"Wayne, that's—" Jimmy thought for a moment. It was ridiculous. It was definitely not a long-term solution, but it could get her out of the way. What was the saying? Hidden in plain sight. Cold Jimmy, the creature in the dark of his brain, stirred.

"That's not a terrible idea," Jimmy heard himself say. "Let me think about how we'd get her over there."

Wayne grinned goofily; whether it was at the idea of going on the ghost train, or that his idea had been deemed a good one, wasn't clear.

32

S am had tidied the smashed crockery. Her phone rang.

"*Where are you?*" asked Delia. "*I'm at Lavender Court.*"

"Yes. I'm coming to the door."

"*I'm already in. I even made them let me see the kitchen.*"

"No, no, I'm..." A new fear gripped Sam. A dawning realisation crept towards her, but she pushed it away. "Can you just go to the front door?"

She slipped through the house. There was still no sign of the teenager. She peered out of the front door and saw Delia, two doors down. She came round to join her, a weighty cardboard box in her hands. "This is Lavender Court House," she said pointing at the sign. "That one there is Lavender Court!"

Two doors down people waved.

Sam nodded back wordlessly. "That's just stupid."

"I can see how a person might get confused," said Delia. "A hungover person."

"Can't blame everything on alcohol." Sam looked at the box. "Plates?"

Delia handed her the box and Sam retreated to the kitchen. Delia followed her and Sam indicated the bag of smashed crockery and the empty dresser.

"You did a proper number on these, didn't you?" she said, removing plates from the box and slotting them onto the dresser with practised ease.

"In my defence, anyone could have made the same mistake," said Sam.

"They could have broken into the wrong house, decided to drag the furniture around and smash up all their plates?"

"When you say it like that—"

The kitchen door opened and a man with a bushy moustache walked in. "Hello. You've come about the turkeys?"

He held out his hand and Sam shook it without comment, trying to process what was going on. Delia shook his hand as well.

"Turkeys, of course," said Sam. "Baby turkeys."

"Just a couple of poults, aye. My son let me know you were here. Wish he'd use the damn phone rather than a text. I didn't see it for a good three parts of an hour. Did he show you the birds at all?"

"No," said Sam. "It's not a problem, really."

The man made mildly exasperated noises about the uselessness of his son while he bent to the oven door.

"Been keeping them in here. How my gran used to do it.

Incubated them in the oven. Though these ones are ready for the garden."

He plonked a bird into Sam's arms and another into Delia's. The bag of smashed crockery hanging on Delia's arm made a rattling noise with the movement.

"Sorry," said Delia. "My shopping,"

They spent a few minutes looking over the birds. Sam tried hard to think of a sensible-sounding question to ask, but she had nothing. Eventually she knew she had to bring this to a close.

"It's very kind of you to show these to us, but I think I've decided turkeys are not for me."

The man nodded. He took the birds and addressed them solemnly. "Not today my lovelies."

"I'm sure you'll soon find their forever home," said Delia with an indulgent smile.

"Forever home?" The man's eyebrows rose. "Ready for slaughter in another ten weeks I'd say. Though they'll be fine till closer to Christmas."

"Wait a minute," said Delia. "Let's not be too hasty, Mr....?"

"Vamplew. You think you might like to take them?"

"How well do they get along with cats?"

33

There were three places providing mobility equipment hire in the local area. Two were legitimate businesses which catered for tourists, and the third was run by the Odinsons. It was situated on the coast road running down from Anderby Creek, through the Chapel St Leonard sprawl of caravan parks. It looked like the dodgiest biker-run chop shop in the whole of Lincolnshire, but instead of cars or bikes they dealt with second-hand mobility aids.

With Wayne in the front and Mrs Skipworth still in the back, Jimmy pulled up out front. One of the Odinsons sat on the step of the low building. He had no idea which one it was. A son? A grandson? A nephew?

"I need a wheelchair or a scooter," said Jimmy, popping a Tic-Tac. "It's for someone pretty, er, heavy. What have you got?"

The Odinson took the cigarette from his mouth and

ground it out under his heel. He beckoned Jimmy into the building.

It was a workshop-cum-showroom, looking every bit as dreadful as the outside. Whether they dragged them out of skips or found them unattended outside shops, the equipment arrayed came here to moulder and die. Or be bought by desperate mugs like him.

Jimmy moved towards the least disgusting items. There was an old-fashioned wheelchair which looked as if it had been stolen from a hospital. There was a lighter-weight wheelchair that was definitely designed to fold, but looked as though it had been retired from a rich career of off-road wheelchair rallying and nobody had bothered to rinse off the mud, or repair the many buckled struts since its last outing. It was unlikely to take the weight of the slenderest person without collapsing. He turned his attention to an electric scooter. It was one of the folding ones with what looked like a motorbike seat. It was possible to imagine how you might fit two people on there.

"That one," he said to the Odinson. "How much?"

"Five 'undred."

"Not a chance."

The Odinson sniffed.

"I'll give you seventy five if you can prove the battery's not dead," said Jimmy. "That'll be the most money you'll make out of all this worthless junk in a month."

Odinson walked back outside and lit up again. Jimmy waited, biding his time.

"'Undred," called Odinson from outside.

Jimmy paused. "Done. If the battery's good."

Jimmy wheeled it outside and lifted it into the back of the van alongside Mrs Skipworth's corpse.

A hundred quid for a scooter. That on top of the money he'd paid to have her body dumped, and the extra he'd spent getting her undumped. His wallet was starting to look thin. If this was how much Britain's ageing population was costing it was no wonder the country was in trouble.

34

The Piaggio was the ideal size for one person. One. It might have had two seats but in terms of elbows and knees, one was the preferred level of occupancy. Four was definitely pushing it. Two of those might have been turkey poults in a box on Delia's knee, but two humans and two birds – scratching, warbling little birds – definitely felt like over-occupancy.

Sam had to gently push the box away so she could indicate right for the Welton le Marsh turning and a second time to turn the indicator off.

"And this woman?" said Delia.

"Wendy Skipworth," said Sam.

"The plan is just to knock on her door and when she answers say, 'Oh, you are here, that's all right then'?"

"Pretty much."

Sam steered into the side road running alongside the

church and the new housing development. Frost and Sons. She grunted in recognition and the memory of her brief meeting with Jimmy MacIntyre.

"That's Consuela." She pointed at the naked mannequin laying down next to the wall.

"Poor girl looks cold," said Delia.

"You're worse than my dad."

Sam pulled round the corner and onto the short gravel driveway of Mrs Skipworth's cottage. Delia slid out from under her rattling, babbling box of turkeys to join her.

Sam went to the door and knocked, then went to the bay window. "Curtains are drawn."

"People draw their curtains sometimes," said Delia.

Sam hummed doubtfully. "She liked to have good view of the churchyard and the ghosts."

"Ghosts. Right."

"What she said."

Sam looked across the garden at the line of sight from the lounge window to the church and the edge of the building beyond. "Probably just workmen." She knocked at the door again, louder now. "Could be in bed."

"Could be dead."

"That's the spirit," said Sam sarcastically.

She tried the front door. It was locked. It had been unlocked when she'd previously visited, although that in itself signified very little.

While Delia stepped back and shielded her eyes from the sun to scan the upper windows for signs of life, Sam circled the house. All the downstairs curtains were drawn, the roller blind pulled down in the kitchen. She tried the back door: also locked. The back door had a grid of Georgian-style window panes. The one nearest to the door handle was broken, the pane replaced by a piece of cardboard taped into place. Sam didn't remember it from the previous visit, but it was a minor detail and not the kind of thing she would necessarily have noticed.

She weighed up the pros and cons of housebreaking for a moment, then tried to push in the cardboard cover. It was stuck down well, but with increased pressure at one corner it slowly levered away to allow her hand access.

"What ya doin'?" asked Delia cheerily.

Sam gave a little start. "Breaking in."

"Uh-huh."

Sam felt her way inside, angled her hand down, found the door handle and the key and twisted it.

"And just to be clear, this is entirely your idea and I'm only here because you were giving me and my turkeys a lift."

"Yes, if it bothers you that much…" Sam saw Delia had her phone held out. "What are you doing?"

"Videoing it. So when it goes to trial, they know none of it was my idea."

Sam sighed and looked directly at the phone. "Yes, dear jury, this was all my idea. We're going to check that Mrs Skipworth is still alive."

The door opened and they entered. It was the same kitchen Sam had been in previously, delivering and preparing meals on wheels – the same shelf of cat mugs, the same antiquated oven – and yet, somehow, it now felt different, as though the act of entering through a different entrance with a different purpose made it alien and strange.

"Mrs Skipworth!" Sam called. "It's Sam from Meals on Wheels!"

There was no reply and Sam moved through into the lounge. Things were much as they were when she had last been here. The cluttered neatness of a sole occupancy home.

"Post on the mat," said Delia.

She stood in the tiny hallway. There were a few letters and a couple of Daily Telegraphs in their shrink-wrapped packaging. Sam looked through them. The oldest was from Friday, the day after Sam's visit.

"Wendy!" she called up the stairs.

They progressed upstairs together. Two bedrooms and a bathroom, all empty. The beds were neatly made. At the bedside of one was an old alarm clock with a luminous dial and a fading colour photograph. The photograph was of a family on a beach, half a dozen people clustered around two deck chairs. It was possible one of the people in the photograph was Wendy Skipworth, maybe one of the dark-haired women in swimming costumes, but the quality of the image made it impossible to tell.

"That's nice, that is," said Delia.

"Her family, I guess," said Sam.

"I meant the clock. Ingraham folding travel clocks. Worth a bit."

Sam tutted. "She's not here, is she?"

"Unless she's hiding in the cupboard."

They made their way downstairs. Sam locked the back

door again through the broken pane and pulled the piece of cardboard back into place as fully as possible.

"There's a niece in Grantham," said Sam as they walked back round to the drive. "I could call her. Or I could just let Karen from Meals on Wheels know."

"What was your main concern?" said Delia. "That she'd had a fall and couldn't reach the phone."

"I suppose."

"Or had died in her sleep and was just lying there waiting to be discovered."

"I hadn't put that much thought into it."

"Point is," said Delia, "you've done your neighbourly duty. Oi, Twizzler!" This last was shouted at a turkey poult which had jumped up onto the Piaggio's tiny dashboard.

"It better not be pooping in my van," said Sam. "I've had enough animals crapping in vehicles for one lifetime."

"I don't know how he got out," said Delia.

Sam shook her head, exasperated, and looked round at the environs. As though some clue to Mrs Skipworth's whereabouts might present itself.

"I need to pick up the mannequin," she said as Delia tried to round up the escapee turkey in the cab. "Don't want to be accused of fly-tipping."

Delia seized the bird. It flapped frantically for several seconds before Delia managed to get it back in the box with its sibling.

A feather stuck to Sam's lip as she got in the driver's side. She spat it away and started the engine. "And you can't call a turkey Twizzler," she said. "It's insensitive."

She reversed off the drive, went back up the side road and

into the lay-by. Consuela was leaning against the wall in a decidedly louche fashion. Sam was surprised that the people of the local parish had let a naked and shameless woman lounge in their village for so long.

"I don't know if I've got room in the back," she said.

Delia hopped out. "Nice looking mannequin. Could be a Greneker. Shame about the damage."

"It's a wasps' nest."

"I meant that slice taken out of her neck."

Delia was right. There was a narrow wedge-like cleft in her neck, like someone had taken an axe to her. Sam crouched beside her and touched the wound, wondering what could have caused it. And then she saw the footprint next to it.

The lay-by next to the church wall was slightly lower than the road. Fallen leaves and other crud had gathered in it to form a light damp topsoil. Pressed into the soil near Consuela's head was a footprint. There was nothing specifically extraordinary about that, but for the fact she had seen that dot-dash trainer tread earlier in the day.

"Yeezys," she said.

"What?" said Delia.

Sam felt a puzzling sense of prescience come over her and she didn't know what to do with it. An empty home, a damaged mannequin, and a distinctive footprint. And, elsewhere, a training shoe found at the bottom of an alligator pool with a tread she was certain would match this. There was no meaningful link between any of them and yet, with a certainty built on no foundations at all, she was suddenly convinced something untoward had occurred.

"I think something bad has happened to Mrs Skipworth," she said.

"Like what?" said Delia.

Sam took a photograph of the footprint in the muck and shook her head. "I don't know, but I think it's something very bad indeed."

35

S carborough Esplanade ran between Skegness Pier and the Pleasure Beach fairground. Jimmy wasn't sure what an esplanade was, but he was prepared to bet it didn't mean a narrow and badly tarmacked cul-de-sac. With the pier-side lawns on one side and a succession of bars, tattoo parlours and arcades on the other, Scarborough Esplanade was as close to the fairground he could park without actually driving into it.

Jimmy pulled on the handbrake and turned to Wayne. "We're here. We're gonna put Mrs Skipworth in the ghost train, yeah?"

Wayne nodded, but his face was slack. He looked like he was thinking about taking a nap right there. The damned horse tranquilizers were still holding sway.

Jimmy tapped Wayne's face, and not gently either. "Listen, this was your plan, remember? I'm going to unwrap the old biddy so we can get her out and put her in a scooter, like she's a relative or something, yeah? All I need is for you not to lose your shit and it will all be fine. Understand?"

Wayne nodded again.

"Tell me you understand," said Jimmy.

"Sure. Understand."

"Now sit there, just for a minute."

Wayne's open mouth spilled drool onto his lap, but Jimmy was past caring about the minor stuff. With the back doors facing a solid wall covered by a mural of images straight out of a saucy seaside postcard, Jimmy could open the back doors and create a four-sided enclosure that kept him unseen.

He pulled the scooter out of the back and lifted the dead pensioner from the van and onto the scooter. The corpse was no longer stiff and she flopped inelegantly into the seat like a cheap drunk. Her face had a waxy sheen that was verging towards silver green, like old bacon. Eventually she was on the scooter. He wrapped a blanket round her and pulled a woolly hat over her head. He really didn't want to look at her face's weird colour out here in the bright sunshine, although it would look great inside the ghost train.

He left her momentarily and closed one rear door to go round to drag Wayne out to meet her. "Come on now, check out these wheels, Wayne. You get to drive."

"Cool!" said Wayne and clattered round to look. Step, clank, step, clank. "It's electric, yeah? Can I make it— Wait. Is that the dead body?"

"This was your idea, man, and it was a fine idea. It just depends on us keeping our cool. Now get on the scooter behind Aunty Pat and make sure she can't fall off."

"Aunty Pat?"

Jimmy gestured at the body on the mobility scooter. "Aunty Pat. Aunty Pat loves the funfair."

Wayne got on the scooter and nearly fell off. Jimmy held him up. There was a sudden parp of flatulence. Unashamedly bold and brassy, it rang clear like the trump of doom. Jimmy wasn't sure if it was Wayne's tortured and medicated innards or escaping gas from the corpse. Whichever it was, Jimmy, a man who had experienced the vilest portaloos and most vulgar brickies in the building trade, was assailed with a sickly sweet stink that caused him to retch.

"Fucksticks," he gagged.

"I'm ready," said Wayne, apparently oblivious.

"Yeah, let's try to pretend she's a real person, you know," said Jimmy. "Let's not squash her to death. I mean, not to death but— Hey!"

Wayne had tried out the scooter controls and run the vehicle into the remaining open door.

"Back up, back up," said Jimmy.

He closed the door and, fearing his drugged and deranged accomplice might veer off at any moment into a wall or the front pages of the next day's papers, accompanied the scooter through the gap between a tattooists and an abandoned candyfloss shop into the fairground proper.

High season had passed, but there was still life in the fairground. The Gold Mine runaway train rollercoaster rattled around its track next to the dodgems. The Dumbo flying elephant ride serenely carried toddlers and parents in the shadow of the spinning, flipping, g-force inducing

FreakOut ride. And, just beyond the pirate ship (closed for refurbishment), was the ticket kiosk and ghost train.

"Ghost train then, yeah?" said Jimmy. "Aunty Pat can't wait, can you, love?"

He wanted to hurry this along for any number of reasons, including his lack of faith in the scooter's battery life. He got Wayne to follow him to the kiosk, and while Wayne tried to perform donuts on the scooter, he bought three ride wristbands from a woman with *Libby* on her nametag.

"All full price?" asked Libby.

"Yep. All adults," said Jimmy, shifting a little so Libby couldn't get a good view.

"Here you go."

"Thanks, Libby." Jimmy turned around. "Pop one on your wrist Wayne. You too Aunty Pat." He held her cold dead hand and slipped on the wristband, trying to keep a smile on his face.

As they came up to the ghost train, a teenage attendant approached. Jimmy brushed off his efforts to help. "I'm their carer. We have some very unusual needs here, so give me some space, will you?"

"If you want, I can—"

"Some space, man."

"If your ... mum? ... isn't well enough to get on the ride then—"

"She's got that Bell's palsy thing. Affects her face and limbs. But she loves the ghost train. You just make sure it's extra slow. My patients have got those, um, cognitive difficulties."

"I don't know if—"

"Libby in the kiosk said it would be fine," said Jimmy firmly. "Don't want to get done for being anti-disablist, do you?"

"Libby said that?"

Jimmy gave him a fierce look. "Go ask."

The lad backed away, eyes fixed on Wayne's drooling face. "I'll ask," he murmured.

"You do that," said Jimmy. As soon as the boy had turned away he wrestled Wayne and Aunty Pat into a carriage, leaving the scooter at the side. Wayne's metal leg brace wouldn't fit properly inside the carriage, so he hung it off the side.

"Here we go," said Jimmy and pushed the big green button on the operator's console. Jimmy climbed in the second row of seat of the moving carriage and then they were through the noisy swing doors and lurching into the darkness.

"Hey it's a skellington!" shouted Wayne. "Look Aunty Pat!"

The piss poor day-glo spectre dangling in front of them looked like it had been picked up from a clearance sale at a costume shop.

"Yes, it's a skeleton," said Jimmy.

"What? Is there another one? Oh wow, Jimmy, this is so scary, I almost forgot we got a real dead body with us."

"Shut up. Now, look. You see that pink demon thing against the wall up ahead?"

"Where?"

"There! I—" Jimmy jumped up, stepped out of the practically crawling carriage and hit a red and yellow electrical knock-off switch he'd spotted on the wall. The car stopped dead. The pink light over the demon went out and they were in utter darkness.

"Ooh, it's really scary now," whimpered Wayne in a little boy's voice.

"Let me..." Jimmy fumbled out his phone and switched it to torch mode.

"And I think I've sat in something wet," said Wayne. "Did I wet myself?"

Maybe he had. Maybe he hadn't. Maybe vital fluids – formerly vital fluids – were leaking out of Mrs Skipworth and across the seat. Jimmy didn't want to think about it.

By torchlight, he pulled the woollen hat and the blanket off the corpse. Its escaped stink enveloped him. For a moment, the insanity of the situation took hold of him and he began to panic. Then, from his mind cave, a tentacle of brutal emotionless certainty soothed that panic away. They had done terrible things, crossed legal and moral lines, and now this was the world they inhabited. One where hiding a decomposing granny in a ghost train was both normal and necessary.

"Over there. Go Wayne!"

Wayne clanked out of the carriage and hauled the dead body with him. He carried her over to the wall where the rubbish pink demon leered, above a set of prison bars through which a bunch of mediocre zombies reached out for liberation, or brains, or whatever zombies craved. Wayne manhandled the corpse round the bars and arranged her so that she had an arm poking out through the bars with the other zombies.

He beamed proudly at Jimmy. "I could do this Jimmy! I could make ghost train rides for a job, look!"

"Come on," urged Jimmy. "Hurry up and get back in!"

Wayne clanked over towards the carriage and tried to climb back in, but Jimmy could see he was having trouble.

"What's the matter?" he asked.

"The metal thing is caugh— Aaaargh!" Wayne howled.

Jimmy jumped out of the carriage to take a look. To his horror he saw Wayne's metal leg brace was crushed between the metal carriage wheel and the rails.

"Crap! How did you manage that? Look, we'll pull when it moves again, yeah?"

"Moves?"

Jimmy twisted the key in the knock-off switch. The mood lighting came back as the carriage trundled into life. Jimmy shoved Wayne, hauling on his waist. He came free, although the bellowing sound coming from him was far from appreciative.

Something crunched. Wayne fell into the carriage and onto his seat. Jimmy climbed in behind. "Now act natural."

"I've put my hands in the wet stuff!" said Wayne.

As the carriage pulled through the hanging plastic and wooden doors of the exit and back into sunlight, Jimmy was already concocting his explanation to the ride attendant. How there were suddenly only two of them; how Aunty Pat had decided to go on the Waltzer instead. Walked off without her scooter? Yeah, she did have sudden bursts of energy...

Jimmy looked up at the teenage attendant. There were no questions, no claims they'd gone on without supervision. The lad just gave them a single chin-tutting nod of acknowledgement and let Jimmy do all the hard work getting Wayne out of the carriage again.

Wayne flopped onto the scooter seat. All the excitement and exercise seemed to have brought some life and focus back to his expression. "I feel funny, Jimmy," the useless lump said.

Jimmy looked at Wayne's foot brace. It was a funny shape now. Whereas before the metal was generally round, it was definitely squashed into an elliptical shape, and the flesh was kind of squeezing out of the metal bits.

"My leg hurts. You got any painkillers?"

"Sure thing, man," said Jimmy and passed him the box of Tic Tacs. "Knock yourself out."

Wayne downed two. "They're minty."

"Funny that."

36

Sam dropped off Delia and her new pet turkeys at her home, a small detached house next to the large Otterside Retirement Village. The front garden was overgrown and appeared to be producing a large crop of plastic garden toys. A ride-along Little Tike car lay in the long grass. A stubby plastic slide leaned out of an untended hedge.

"Least the turkeys will have some entertainment," said Sam, nodding.

"They'll be in the back garden. Do turkeys eat grass?"

"Thinking it'll save on buying turkey food?"

"Thinking it will save having to buy a new lawnmower." She put a hand on Sam's arm. "There'll be a rational explanation."

"You can probably look it up on the internet," said Sam.

"I meant about the woman. Mrs...?"

"Skipworth."

"Right. Don't let it get to you."

Delia got out and proceeded to the front door. Sam mulled over what Delia had said. She was absolutely right. That didn't stop her driving straight from Delia's house and round to the police station on Park Avenue.

She parked in a spot that only a Piaggio could fit in and went inside to the front desk. The police officer at the desk nodded in greeting.

"Is Sergeant Hackett in?" asked Sam.

The woman frowned. "Perhaps I can help."

Sam produced her company ID card. "DefCon4. I want to talk to Cesar about a break-in I was called to earlier."

The woman's eyebrows rose as though it was deeply implausible anyone would seek Cesar Hackett out for any reason, but she picked up a phone and dialled. "Yep. Someone at front desk to see you. A—" she gestured for Sam's ID again "—Sam Applewhite. Applewhite, like the magician. Uh-huh."

She hung up. A minute later, Cesar appeared through the security door, his seal-bitten hand still wrapped in a dressing. "Sam. Just in time. You can help me with something."

"Er, sure."

He led her through the building. The police station was a cube of pebble-dashed concrete, odd but boring. They continued the odd but boring theme going inside. There were grey carpet tiles which looked like they had been installed half a century ago. There were grey polystyrene ceiling tiles almost exactly the same shade. It gave Sam the uncomfortable impression that gravity could reverse at any moment and life would go on uninterrupted in the upside down building. It made her want to hold onto something for support.

The journey from the front desk to Cesar's was long and circuitous. They eventually wound up in an office space barely wider than a corridor, tucked between the boiler room and the station gym. The plate on the door said PERIPHERAL DUTIES. On a wonky desk looking like it had been reclaimed from a skip there was a computer, a kettle and a missing cat poster with a blank central area with the words *insert picture of missing cat here* written in biro.

"Someone's cat gone missing?" said Sam.

"Has it?" said Cesar.

"No. I'm asking."

He looked at the poster. "No, that's just the template. All missing cats. They come through this office."

"In search of rats?"

Cesar frowned and then said, "No, I mean the paperwork."

"I know. I was being facetious. I wouldn't have thought the police would show much interest in missing cats."

"You'd be surprised what work I get involved in."

Sam didn't know how long Cesar had been working in Skegness, or where the force had posted him earlier in his career, but there was something about the pokey office, the cat poster, the vague PERIPHERAL DUTIES nameplate on the door, and her limited understanding of Cesar's skillset that made her wonder what his precise function was within the Lincolnshire Police. If she was to hazard a guess, and it would be a cruel guess, she would imagine he had been put here, out of the way, where he could do minimal damage and be safely forgotten.

"We need to talk," she said.

"Indeed we do," he said and put the kettle on. It rattled noisily as it began to heat. "We need a cup of tea if you're going to help me." He pulled a sheet from his drawer. "Third round competition," he said.

Sam looked at the sheet. It was the cascading tree-diagram of a knock-out competition, but where there might normally be team names or individual competitors, there was something else entirely.

"Coffee creams versus malted milk?" said Sam.

"It's going to be a tough one," said Cesar and removed two unopened packets of biscuits from his desk drawer. "True, neither's going to be in the final. There's some heavyweights – your bourbons, your Fox crunch creams – that neither stands a chance against. But which of them is better?" He found two cups on a shelf and peered inside them to see if they were clean.

"This is what you wanted me to help you with?" she said indignantly. "I came on proper business!"

"Oh?" he said, surprised.

"That trainer at Seal Land. I've seen a print near a house where a woman's gone missing and—"

"The trainer?" said Cesar and sighed. "It's done. It's dusted. It's been bagged and filed away as evidence."

"I'm not sure how, but I think a crime's been committed."

Cesar was genially shaking his head before she even got to the end of the sentence. "No, no, no, no. It's all fine. It was just a trainer."

"There were toes!"

"Could have been a screwed up tissue."

"We were both there!"

Cesar shook his head again. "If you've been a police officer as long as I have, Sam, you realise that, in the long run, things just sort themselves out. Society is like a machine, the world is like a machine. It just keeps ticking along."

"Is this your excuse for doing nothing?"

Cesar looked affronted. "Doing nothing? We oil the machine. We guide things, a touch here, a nudge there."

Sam prodded the cat poster. "By finding missing cats?"

"Small acts make a big difference." The kettle clicked off. "Now, I judge biscuits on five criteria. Taste, texture, crumbliness—"

"The trainer," said Sam.

He sighed again. "It's like everyone's worried about that global warming. As I say to my wife, if it was really all that bad, then the government would do something about it. And she's a doctor and she agrees with me. If we all just stop worrying, relax a little and—"

"A woman's gone missing," Sam seethed.

"You know this?"

She wanted to say 'yes' but stopped herself because it wasn't true. She screwed up her face in annoyance.

"Now, how do you take your tea?" he asked.

She exhaled angrily through her nose. "I would just like to see the trainer."

Cesar paused and looked at directly. He had the round, well-meaning face of a complete idiot. A mooncalf, her grandma would have called him. He was a well-meaning soul but that just made his unhelpfulness all the more annoying.

Cesar nodded slowly and pulled a circular bin from under his desk. He removed a trainer-sized object wrapped in a Morrisons carrier bag.

"You said it was filed as evidence," she said.

"The circular file," he said and gave her an embarrassed grin. "But I did bag it, see?"

She snatched the trainer from him, unwrapped the supermarket bag and pulled the wet trainer out.

"There's no evidence a crime has been committed," said Cesar.

There was a receipt for coffee cream and malted milk biscuits stuck to the heel of the trainer. Sam ripped it away and looked at the sole. She compared the Morse code pattern on it to the picture on her phone.

37

T he body was hidden. Sort of. Sort of out of sight and sort of out of mind.

Jimmy knew it was time to attempt to re-engage with the real world, even if that unfortunately involved going to speak to Jacinda Frost. His phone had been kaput since the night they'd killed Mrs Skipworth. There were probably a thousand texts and a dozen angry voicemails waiting for him in the telecommunications ether.

The Frost family home was near the village of Friskney, a dozen miles south of Skeg. It sat in a featureless landscape that had been reclaimed from the sea over the years and had little use except as a nature reserve and RAF bombing range.

Bob Frost and his wife, Di, had owned various villas out in Spain and brought a smidgeon of that Spanish feel back to the house they built on the bleak fens. It was a Brit's interpretation of Spanish style. British brick painted white, sloping red roofs. A peculiar driveway that swept up over a humpbacked bridge, round to the first floor entrance, so the ground floor was accessed through an archway tunnel. Cartwheels had been pinned to the front walls. Hanging baskets of pink bougainvillea hung from the eaves. It was kitsch. It was ugly.

And while Bob and Di had been alive it was Jimmy's second home.

Now, Jacinda didn't let him through the door. Jimmy never even saw her in there. She was always in the big office shed out back. Jimmy pulled round to the chalky yard at the rear of the house. The yard was huge – there was no pressure on land use round here – and was fenced off twenty yards further on with warning signs about RAF land and unexploded ordnance.

"Wait here," Jimmy told Wayne as he got out.

Wayne popped another Tic-Tac 'painkiller' and nodded.

There was the report of a shotgun; one barrel, then the second. She was in a shooting mood.

Jimmy stilled himself and went into the shed. Bob had constructed the shed to be an office and a workshop. It was fifty feet long, and at one time had been kitted out with workstations, power tools and table saws. That had all been cleared out by his daughter. The desk and chairs, the computer and phone, had all been moved to the centre of the single room. The remainder was bare concrete floor and cinderblock lined walls.

Various sections of the wall were pitted and scored by shot. When they were almost blown through, Jacinda had them replaced. There was a small mountain of grey rubble out behind the building. She had also erected a number of cinderblock pedestals around the place. An eclectic array of objects had graced those pedestals: vases, garden gnomes, old TVs, potted plants. None of them lasted long.

One of the lads on site once told Jimmy about these places they now had in the cities: rage rooms. Hipsters and other stupid urban wankers would pay top price to spend ten minutes in a room with some breakables and a baseball bat. And Jimmy knew more than one bloke who had a dartboard in their office with an ex's face, or a hated footy team's picture pinned to it. Jacinda Frost has simply combined both these things and added a shotgun.

She stood by her desk, red ear-defenders on, the over-and-under shotgun broken over her arm as she reloaded.

"Jacinda!"

She had her back to him and appeared not to hear. He approached her carefully.

"Jacinda!"

When he was close enough to touch her, she whirled, snapping the shotgun closed in reflex. Surprise made her large eyes, accentuated by heavy mascara, larger still. "Where the hell have you been?" she said.

"Phone problems," he said.

"It's been two days, Jimmy."

"I've been busy."

"Those stones in Welton moved?"

"No, but—"

"That was job number one, Jimmy."

"And it needs doing ... covertly."

"You can work nights, can't you?"

Before he could answer, Jacinda turned away, took aim at

a wooden carving on a pedestal. Jimmy wasn't fast enough putting his hands to his ears. The boom echoed off concrete walls and came back in painful force. The wooden carving, a stylised praying woman, exploded into splinters so fine it was little more than smoke. Jimmy recalled it having pride of place over Bob and Di's mantelpiece.

Jacinda turned and took out a cheap brass golfing trophy with her second shot. A piece of shrapnel pinged off the far wall, nearly bouncing as far back as Jimmy. It was the little model golfer's head.

Jacinda broke the shotgun and lowered the ear defenders around her neck.

"Listen," he said. "When we do that job, we have to make sure no one finds out."

Her eyes narrowed, heavy black ovals. "Does someone know?"

Jimmy found he had the mental strength to meet that gaze. "No," he said, which was true. The word 'know' was present tense, and whatever Mrs Skipworth might have seen, there was nothing present tense about her anymore.

"Then you get on with the job," said Jacinda. "I've got a guild event Wednesday night."

"Oh, you don't want me to go to that one then?" he said, flippantly.

She laughed. "You? Ready to grease the wheels of business, are you? I've got to sway a few more people before the voting. The backers say they're definitely coming to the awards evening."

"They'll back the Shore View project regardless."

"Oh, I'm glad you're so confident," she sneered. "Without

Welton plots sold there isn't the funding for Shore View. Without something to show at Shore View, the backers won't uphold their end of the bargain. Without our out of town friends supporting it, there won't be any tenants in those damned container homes and our current cashflow situation will become terminal."

"Sure."

"It's a line of dominoes, Jimmy."

"Yeah..."

"Any tiny slip-up could ruin it."

She pulled spent shells out of the gun with long fingernails.

"Wayne killed a woman," he said.

He didn't mean to say it. Or, he did mean to say it, but his brain didn't give him any advanced warning.

Jacinda eyed him cautiously. "What?"

"Wayne killed a woman. An old fogey in Welton. She saw us. We went to talk to her. Wayne panicked. He whacked her with his shovel."

Jacinda picked up two fresh shells from the box on her desk. "And?"

"And?" he asked.

"And?"

"We've disposed of her. Hidden her for now. No one else saw us. We left no trace."

"Anything else I should know?"

Jimmy considered the question. "Wayne had his foot bitten off by an alligator. He's sat in the van now. Wayne, not the alligator. We had Sacha stitch him up so you might get some odd calls from him about that. And ... yeah, that's it."

Jacinda reloaded the gun slowly. The shells dropped into place with audible taps. "And if Wayne is arrested...?" she said.

"Then they'd find out about our, um, jiggery-pokery in Welton, at least."

"The dominoes."

"Exactly."

She nodded and took a deep, cleansing breath. "Everything you've just told me... I'm going to pretend you didn't tell me. If anyone asks, this conversation never happened. I hate you for even thinking it was acceptable to tell me."

"I understand."

"Nothing stops this deal," said Jacinda.

"You can't make omelettes without breaking some eggs," he said.

She snapped the gun closed forcefully. "Fuck omelettes. Fuck eggs. We're doing good here. Building houses, giving people a fresh start."

She raised her ear defenders, took aim at a piece of *Home Sweet Home* embroidery in a glass frame that had once hung in the family hallway and blasted a hole through its centre, utterly obliterating the middle word.

"Get a new phone," she said before taking a second shot which tore the frame apart completely. "And move those stones. Pronto."

Jimmy left, his ears ringing.

38

Human beings were like magic tricks, thought Sam as she sorted through the collected papers making up her dad's finances. Human beings drew the eye and invited interest. Other people were fascinating – their lives, their views, their personal quirks, their histories and back stories. It was human to be interesting. And be interested. And, like stage magicians and their tricks, human beings invited others to look, but only at certain aspects. Look at this, not that. Pay no attention to the mysterious curtain at the back of the stage. Humans presented what they wanted the world to see and tried to hide the rest.

But humans, like magic tricks, were too interesting and one could not help but want to delve deeper, to go behind the curtain and see...

Sam first recalled uncovering the secret to one of her dad's magic tricks when she was about six or seven years old.

It had been at rehearsals for a variety show in London. Sam remembered little of it, except that her dad had a five-minute set (between Joe Pasquale and Lulu) and on one of her visits on a rehearsal day, while her parents were arguing in loud whispers some distance away, she had stepped on stage, smiled at Linda (who was smoking a crafty cigarette) and looked at the apparatus for zig-zag girl illusion. The illusion involved Linda being locked in a cabinet and the middle section slid out to the side, thus apparently cutting Linda into thirds.

"Oh," six-or-seven-year-old Sam said in sudden realisation. "When that box is moved, the bit at the edge, the black bits – there's still enough room for you to stand in that and still be in all three boxes. If you stood really straight and held your tummy in."

Linda gave her a wry smile. "That's why you never see Aunty Linda eating chips, munchkin." She contemplated her cigarette. "No calories in these, though."

Young Sam had been struck with what she later recognised as guilt. She had peered too closely without asking; she had uncovered something hidden about her father the great magician and somehow it had ... diminished him.

Here and now, a quarter of a century later, in the dining room of *Duncastin'*, with a near complete picture of his financial situation, she felt that same guilt, the same sense of invasion. All laid out in painful tiny details.

There were bank statements with ever decreasing balances. There were long-term investments, stock portfolios and even a pension: all been cashed in. There were hire purchase agreements and reclaimed goods. There were letters from stage prop companies either making payment for returned items or demanding money. There was a letter from an American organisation, signed 'Magic' Kingdom, reminding him of his financial obligations. There was even a little note from the window cleaner dated only a couple of months ago, thanking Marvin for being his customer for years and reminding him the previous month's final payment was still due. Sam grunted at that; she thought the windows had been looking grubby of late.

There were some hard conversations ahead and tough decisions to be made, including the almost unavoidable sale of *Duncastin'*. But for now she could make a positive and practical contribution to the situation. Sam went through to the kitchen and filled the bucket from under the sink with hot water and a squirt of washing up liquid.

"What you doin' there, pardner?" said Marvin, unable to snap out of the faux-American chirpiness he'd been practising on her all morning. He sat at the kitchen table, in an identical position he'd been in last week, surrounded by the components of a drone, the American instruction video playing on the tablet before him.

"I'm going to wash the windows," said Sam. "Are you going to talk like a cowboy all week?"

"I surely am," he said. "Oh, and there was a phone call for you earlier."

"Yes?"

"A Holly Skipworth in Grantham. She said she hasn't spoken to her aunt – Wendy, was it...?"

"Wendy Skipworth," Sam nodded.

"She hasn't spoken to her in a few weeks. Reading between the lines I gathered they're not particularly close. Not spoken to her in a few weeks and this Holly wants to know if she should be worried."

"No," said Sam, immediately thinking that probably wasn't true. "No," she repeated softly. "I'll give her a call and tell her everything's all right."

"And is it?" said Marvin.

Sam smiled. Damn, the man could read her at times. "I don't know. But maybe it's none of my business. Too bloody nosy for my own good. Always wanting to peer behind the curtain."

"What curtain?"

"Ignore me," she said and went outside to clean windows.

Duncastin', sprawling and winding bungalow that it was, had far more windows than Sam cared to count, but some time and three buckets of water later she had nearly completed a full circuit of the house.

"Is this another thing DefCon4 has you doing?" It was Delia, coming up the path and looking very pleased with herself. "Washing windows for retired stage magicians."

"Trying to avoid paying for a window cleaner." Sam dropped her squeegee in the bucket.

"I brought you a gift." Delia waggled the shopping bag she carried. "Well, it's for you and your dad. Something for the house."

"This had better not be a turkey," said Sam.

"No, it's something I made."

"Dad's in the kitchen. I'm sure he'll want to see as well."

Delia followed Sam indoors. Marvin was unpacking more electronics from their plastic bags.

"Howdy, Delia!" he said

"Morning, Marvin. A new drone? Where did that one come from?"

"It arrived by courier," said Sam. "Several of my tasks have been re-scheduled to get back on track with this beast. It seems the company really wants to use these. I thought there would be more questions about what happened to the first one, to be honest."

"It means I get to spend more quality time with Hank," said Marvin, looking up from the scattered components. "You know, I'm not only talking like him now, I swear I'm starting to dream about him, too."

"Dad's loving it, obviously," said Sam. "Dad, Delia's brought a gift for us."

Marvin sat up straight. "Is that so?"

Delia put her shopping bag down and bent to lift something out. "I was inspired by your lovely garden, so I've made a prototype windchime, and I wanted you to have it."

She pulled away the tissue wrapping with a small *ta-da* flourish and revealed her creation. It hung from a metal loop; the top part formed from something that might well have been recycled wire coat hangers. It was the hanging parts which caught the eye though. Twelve dolls' heads bobbed from lines of transparent filament. They all hung at different levels, facing in different directions. Did their pouty precocious faces look mildly put out to have parted company with their bodies? Sam thought they did.

"I have you two to thank for the latest upcycling idea," said Delia.

Sam prodded one of the decapitated Capitalist Whore heads. It tinkled lightly. "It's amazing! There's something I don't quite understand, though. Aren't windchimes normally metal things that hit other metal things?"

"Yes," said Delia, "but obviously that wasn't going to work here. I bought some little bells and popped them up inside the neck holes."

"Huh," said Sam, peeking inside. "Clever."

"Well, I hope so, because I bought a thousand bells."

"What?"

"I need to make a profit from these. Economies of scale. You have to take risks to expand your empire. One of these days I might even end up taking the right risk at the right time." Delia gave a small helpless shrug. "I can't help it if the world's not ready for some of my top innovations. I brought musical plant potholders to the people of Skegness, but I think it's fair to say they did *not* embrace them. I brought them crisp packet holders, but they ignored those too. So now it's the turn of Capitalist Whore windchimes."

"You might want to re-think the name," said Marvin.

"Wait, go back to the crisp packet holders," said Sam. "What on earth were those?"

"Ah!" said Delia. "It's a well-documented problem in coastal towns that seagulls nick your food, right?"

"Right."

"So, my working hypothesis was if you took a shiny, crinkly packet of crisps, which the seagulls recognise as a tasty snack, and disguised it with a velvet pouch, it would throw them right off the scent."

"So, does it work?" asked Sam, fascinated.

"I used it lots of times, and a seagull *never* stole my crisps," said Delia proudly.

"What did other people think?" asked Marvin. He'd put down the drone parts to listen.

"Dunno, never sold one. Not a single one. Like I said, the world is not ready for that kind of innovation."

"It could be a very niche product," said Sam, trying to imagine a world where she would carry round a velvet pouch just in case she wanted to enjoy a bag of crisps. "I think the windchimes are a great idea, though."

"I need to sell quite a few to use all—"

"Eighty odd—" chipped in Marvin. "You'll need to sell just over eighty windchimes to use up all those bells if you bought a thousand."

Sam stared at him. How was it possible that her dad, who feigned deafness or senility in the face of his mounting household bills, was clearly capable of mental arithmetic faster than she could pull out her phone and use the calculator?

Delia had obviously already done the maths because she nodded glumly. "I haven't even got enough dolls' heads, if I'm honest."

A thought struck Sam. "Are you part of the Skegness and District Local Business Guild?"

"No. Why?"

"They might be able to offer you some services. They're supposed to help businesses like yours."

"They're like freemasons, aren't they? Always been a bit nervous of joining stuff like that to be honest. Same with the Women's Institute."

Sam looked at her. "How are those things even a little bit alike?"

Delia put down the windchimes and used her hands to form an imaginary bubble. "It's like you have these people over here. They are the ones who know what they're doing and join clubs and stuff to prove it. Then you have these people over here," she made another bubble with her hands, "and they are the ones like me. They are doing their own thing and basically just pretending they know what they're doing."

"I have a working hypothesis about that," said Sam with a small smile. "I think the reason the people over here seem to know what they're doing is that they join clubs so they can learn from each other."

Delia did not have an immediate response to that. She gave a small shrug. "Maybe."

"Listen," said Sam. "There's a meeting tomorrow night ahead of the business of the year awards on Friday. I'll be going. Come with me. Just have a look."

"Oh, I don't know."

"Buy you a drink?"

"Are you a guild recruiter?" said Delia. "You have to tell me if you are."

"Maybe," said Sam. "Or maybe I just want to take a friendly face along with me to the meeting."

"Implying the others are unfriendly...?"

"You won't regret it."

HEIDE GOODY & IAIN GRANT

"Let me work out where to hang this delightful thing," said Marvin, picking up the windchime and taking it out to the garden.

"And I'll make us a brew," said Sam.

"Trying to sucker me in with your offers of tea and your folksy charm," said Delia.

Sam filled the kettle. Delia looked about.

"And your gorgeous house where there aren't children's toys on the floor everywhere. And no one's screaming or yelling at each other."

"Is it that bad?" said Sam.

Delia grunted. "Swap. Find out."

Sam put the kettle on the stand. Every family, every house, had its attractions and its secrets. She wondered if Delia would be so keen to swap if she saw the state of her dad's finances and the hard choices that lay ahead. She took down three mugs and looked at them.

"Are you busy at the moment?" she said.

"Define busy."

"Take a ride with me. I need to go look at something."

Delia nodded wisely. "You see, this is how it goes. First you join the guild, then you're going for a car ride. Next thing you know, you've got blood on your hands and you're putting horses' heads in people's beds."

"The local business guild is not the mafia."

"And the mafia is just a family business association, sure."

39

They were halfway to Welton le Marsh before Delia twigged where they were going. "The old lady's house?"

Sam nodded. "Something's not right."

"Poking around old lady's houses isn't right. I thought you went to the police."

"I did. The trainer they found in the alligator pool at Seal Land is a match for that print by the churchyard wall."

"And?"

"That idiot, Cesar Hackett, has refused to investigate the matter."

Delia winced at her harsh comment. "If the police don't think this trainer thing is significant then—"

"Cesar doesn't think anything's significant. He thinks crimes are like chicken pox. If you don't scratch it, it'll just go away by itself."

"Whereas you can't resist scratching an itch?"

"Ha ha," Sam huffed, then gave a genuine laugh. "Okay, so I've got a curious streak. I can't leave a job half done."

"Job?"

"I can't leave a mystery unsolved." The fifth car in a row overtook her slow Piaggio van, beeping as it accelerated past. "On my eighth birthday, I had a cake with candles. And I remember blowing the candles out and my dad asking me what I'd wished for. I said 'To know who Jack the Ripper was.' They laughed and gave me funny looks." She looked at Delia. "I just wanted to know, I guess."

Delia's expression was doubtful but sympathetic. "Fine, we go visit the old lady's house again. As long as we're not breaking in to poke around."

"Then you stay outside as lookout while I break in and poke around."

Delia groaned.

At Mrs Skipworth's cottage, Sam knocked on the front door again, just in case the woman had returned, and the mystery of her disappearance was nothing more than a last minute coach trip to Scarborough. When there was no reply, Sam went round the back, pushed through the carboard taped over the back door window, and let herself in.

"You're just contaminating the crime scene, if that's what it is," said Delia at her shoulder.

"I thought you were staying round the front as lookout," said Sam.

"*You* said that. I just said it was a bad idea to break in and poke around."

Sam went to the shelf of stern-looking cat mugs. "It occurred to me while I was making tea."

"What did?" said Delia.

"There's four mugs here. There were six previously. There's two missing."

"That's some expert arithmetic you're doing," nodded Delia. "And?"

"There's two missing," Sam repeated.

Delia tried to look supportive. "A lost trainer. Two missing mugs. This isn't exactly coming together as solid evidence. Not unless you think a one-legged man broke in here to steal some rare and valuable cat mugs."

Sam took one down. "Are they valuable?"

Delia looked at the underside. "Modern factory-made stuff."

As Sam put it back, Delia flipped open the bin by the sink. "They're in here. Broken. The one-legged man came in, broke some mugs, and left."

Sam rushed to the bin. She half reached in to scoop up the shards. "Let's—"

"Glue them back together?" said Delia, reading her thoughts. "Why? What's going through your brain, Miss Marple?"

Sam sighed wearily. "Don't you just think something is a bit ... off?"

"This..." Delia waved her hands about, fingers splayed. "Creeping round old lady's kitchens. Yeah."

Irritated, by herself more than anything else, Sam walked through to the living room.

"I came here on Thursday," she said, narrating her actions rather than speaking to anyone in particularly. "She was sat by the window, looking out." Sam peered out the gable window, past the Piaggio and over to the church yard. "She wanted the cottage pie. She was doing the crossword. She was talking about Bradley Walsh and Bradley Wiggins and the seating plan for something or other."

Thursday's Telegraph paper, folded to the crossword page, was in the magazine rack next to Mrs Skipworth's armchair. The notepad was still on the arm of the chair. The top page was blank. Sam picked it up. The page above, the one with the names, had been ripped off.

"Huh."

The tear across the top didn't run through the holes for the spiral binding. It was a sloping tear a centimetre underneath. Sam recognised it would be easy to get paranoid and read secret meaning into any detail, but it struck her that Mrs Skipworth had been fussy enough and organised enough that she wouldn't have ripped it off like that.

"Where is it?" she muttered.

She looked in the wastepaper basket by the chair. It contained nothing but a screwed-up tissue. She went back to the kitchen and the bin.

"Oh, we *are* going to glue them back together," said Delia as Sam pawed through the bin, sifting contents onto the table.

"It's not there," said Sam.

A dash upstairs, a look in the tiny pink bin beside the bathroom sink, an inspection of the council wheelie bin outside and it was confirmed.

"You're being weird," said Delia. She corrected herself. "More weird. Weirder. What's going on?"

Sam stood beside the kitchen table, closed her eyes and

took a deep breath. "There was a notepad," she said calmly, eyes still closed. "She'd drawn boxes on it. A dozen, a couple of rows. Several names. Like a seating plan for dinner or ... I don't know, names in tents."

"What names?"

Sam could see them in her mind's eye. She could see the shape of them. But like written words in dreams, the more she tried to focus on them, the less certain they became. "I can't remember."

"And why is this list important?"

"It's gone. It's definitely gone."

"So? Why is that significant?"

"No reason," said Sam. "Except it has gone. A woman who hardly ever leaves the house has gone and that list of names has gone with her."

"Which means?"

Sam clutched at the air but she had nothing.

40

Murder – or death at least – had done something to Jimmy. It had touched him in a way few other experiences had. It was a door he had walked through and now there was no way back. There were few other things he could compare it to. Sex, maybe. That day after Mandy Yaxley's fifteenth birthday party, after those ridiculous fumblings on the floor of her parents' conservatory, he had been changed. Not in some stupid 'Now You Have Become A Man' way but he had shed the skin of childhood and entered a world of sin and furtiveness and dirty biological urges, and he hadn't seen anyone or anything in the same way again.

The death of Mrs Skipworth had done something to him, and he'd never see anyone or anything in the same way again. Wayne, popping pills and mints indiscriminately, had the air – the stink! – of death on him. The fat idiot not only had a sickly feverish sheen about him, but his sickness oozed through his pores, hung about him. Like the rot of death had already moved in.

And most disturbing about it all, Jimmy didn't care. In the immediate aftermath of Mrs Skipworth's death, he had retreated into the dark cave in the seabed of his mind. He had become Cold Jimmy, operating only as needed. Perhaps he'd been in shock, but the changed mental state hadn't dissipated. As the days went on, he found himself retreating further. He had shed another skin of innocence. There was still the outer shell of Jimmy, walking, talking, getting the job done, but the true Jimmy was now way down inside, wrapped in the tentacles of his own certainty, watching the discarded skin, the outer shell. Cold Jimmy, going about the business of putting things right.

They had spent the day at the Welton le Marsh construction site. Jimmy set Wayne up in one of the houses, with a kettle and a radio, and left him there while he got on with work. Genuine work that needed doing around the site. He had brickies and roofers and sparkies lined up to get on with finishing the houses, but for today it was just him. He had things to attend to before allowing the lads back on site.

When evening fell, he drove to the nearest corner shop and picked up some snack foods for a miserable dinner. He returned to find Wayne in a folding chair in the half-finished house, sat utterly still, gripping the arm rests. He stared at Jimmy, high on painkillers or delirious with pain.

"Will you put me in the ghost train, Jimmy?" he whispered.

"What?"

"When I'm ready, will you put me in the ghost train too?"

"What are you on about?"

"I think I'd be dead good at it."

Wayne inhaled deeply, then saw the bag of food. Jimmy gave him an unheated chicken tikka pastry slice and a bottle of Vimto. Wayne scoffed the slice like he hadn't eaten in days.

Now it was dark outside Jimmy headed to the edge of the building site, and the access track that was still fifty centimetres too narrow. With a headtorch and a shovel, he set about changing that. Cold Jimmy set about changing it. Old Jimmy hid, skulked in the cave of his mind and watched.

41

Over the next day, the mystery of what had happened at Mrs Skipworth's house gnawed at Sam like a toothache. It didn't help that her DefCon4 app had updated several times during the last day so that it could prioritise the drone tasks. She had the rest of the day to assemble and prepare it, and because her dad was doing that at home, it left Sam with plenty of time to just sit in the DefCon4 office, stare at the wall, and think about questions that had no answers.

To distract herself, she reorganised the office. She did some cleaning: dusted the two empty desks, then cleaned around Doug Fredericks, even giving his needles a little light dusting. Doug Fredericks was, as best as she could tell, a powder puff cactus, a tall rotund thing, seven inches in height and covered in sharp yellow spines. He didn't need much looking after, but she carefully dusted him nonetheless.

When she'd done all the dusting she could usefully do and stuck down the loose carpet tile yet again, she reorganised the filing in the filing cabinet. This did not take long as the filing (in a slightly sticky filing cabinet) consisted of three sections: Sam's expense receipts, a sealed plastic folder entitled OPERATION BUDGIE – DO NOT REMOVE OR DESTROY, and DefCon4 employment records for the office staff. These records included the real Doug Fredericks and other former office staff Sam had never met. Despite her natural curiosity she never browsed through them, not wishing to disturb the ghosts of the past.

Unable to let the matter of the shoe and the missing woman go, Sam phoned the Pilgrim Hospital in Boston, Grantham and District Hospital and Lincoln County Hospital, and asked if anyone had been treated in the past week with a missing foot. Unsurprisingly, each hospital told her they weren't permitted to give out such information. The operator at Lincoln County suggested she should take her enquiry to the police. That, Sam thought (but did not say), was not going to help.

Bored beyond reason by late afternoon, Sam even had an office fire drill. This involved shouting "Fire!", running to the top of the stairs, looking back forlornly at Doug and calling out "I'll send help!" before hurrying downstairs and assembling at the fire drill muster point. Which just happened to be Cat's Café. Sam sat in the window table and drank a hot chocolate while she ticked off fire drill and emergency procedure training checklists on her app. Cat tried to engage her in a conversation about her latest improvised theatre project, but Sam ignored her.

When Sam returned to work, she found Delia and a heavy rectangular parcel on her office doorstep. "Okay, I'll come," said Delia.

Sam blinked at her.

"The local business guild event thing," said Delia. "Tonight, yeah?"

"It is," said Sam. She picked up the parcel. "Want to come in and see the nerve centre of DefCon4's regional operation while you're here?"

Together, they went upstairs.

"Say hello to Doug," said Sam, gesturing at Doug's desk.

"Er, hi Doug," said Delia dutifully.

Sam opened the parcel. She had been sent a big pile of DefCon4 flyers to distribute to potential local clients. "Here," she said, giving one to Delia. "In case you foolishly decide you need DefCon4's services."

"No, this looks good," said Delia. "These people offer so many services. Scalable business solutions for a small monthly subscription, including risk consulting, event security, training services."

Sam rolled her eyes. "You know this is all me, don't you? At least for this area."

"You can do all of these things?" Delia asked.

"Apparently, I have access to the requisite training material if I find myself with a development need," said Sam, quoting from one of the cryptic and incredibly unhelpful emails she had received in the past.

"Well, that's pretty good," said Delia. "Getting new skills is—"

"—Except I've never been able to access it," said Sam.

"Something about not being on the trusted domain for the company's network, because the IT person who was supposed to do it can't get out here because of working time regulations. I don't even know what that means, but I can't get past it."

"And what's clown management?" asked Delia, pointing at the flyer. "Is the circus in the Guild of Small Business Owners?"

Sam looked and groaned. "No, it's supposed to say 'crowd management'. That's what comes of using spell check instead of getting an actual human to look over something."

She looked at the clock on the wall. Two hours to the local business guild meeting.

Sam searched around for a felt tip. "Let's see how many of these I can correct before the meeting."

"We," said Delia. "How many *we* can correct."

"Don't you have better things to do?" said Sam. "A family to spend time with?"

Delia blew a stray strand of hair away from her eyes and dropped into a chair. "Have you never thought I might be doing this to avoid spending time with my family?"

Later, with five hundred corrected flyers in her bag, the pair of them headed to Carnage Hall.

"I should have dressed up a bit," said Delia as they passed through the theatre foyer and towards the Jim Bowen bar.

The bar was closed to the public for the guild event. The member of staff on the door wasn't checking IDs or invites or anything. Sam simply gave the man an 'I'm here on business' look and went through.

"You don't need to dress up to come to these events," she said.

"Some of these people are in suits," said Delia.

Sam looked around at the half full bar. "That's people who've worn suits all day. You'll probably see people come here in overalls as well."

"I don't think so," said Delia. "It's got the word 'guild' in it, for heaven's sake. That does not speak of overalls to me. It speaks of pearls and twinsets and—"

"I'm getting the idea you might be nervous about this," said Sam.

"No! Not me, I'm fearless." Delia made a visible effort to calm herself, then she turned to Sam. "I bet all your guild friends have Audis and Mercs and Beemers. These people are actual businesspeople, with plans and investors and whatnot."

There was some light mingling going on in the room, and several people had drifted into knots of conversations. There was also an undeniable bit of class distinction going on. People Sam knew who were shopkeepers had drifted together in one clump, with hairdressers, beauty therapists and manicurists as a distinct (and well-presented) off-shoot. There were the financial services people, and the loosely associated estate agents, solicitors and pawnbrokers. Publicans, club owners and holiday park managers suffused the room, confident in their businesses' dominance of the local economy. And although there were no people actually in overalls, the tradespeople – the electricians, the plumbers, the builders and mechanics – were a clearly defined bunch, some of whom had succumbed to stereotype and already moved from the free (albeit cheap) wine onto pints of beer from the bar.

"Some people think the trappings of success is the same thing as success," Sam said, then thought about it. "Yeah, well maybe it is, some of the time. But look at you. You are clearly motivated by your passion for re-use and invention."

"I'd quite like a nice car as well," said Delia.

"Would wine and nibbles do in the meantime?" Sam asked.

"Oh absolutely!"

They snagged a glass of wine each.

"Cheese and pineapple on sticks!" said Delia, a massive grin on her face. "It's like the last thirty years of culinary history totally passed this place by."

"Lincolnshire folk know what they like," said Sam.

"How many can I take before I look greedy?"

"Nobody's judging you here," said Sam. "At least, not until it's time for the businessperson of the year awards. You can fill in a form while you're here. Tonight is the last chance to vote."

Sam picked up a form while Delia arranged speared cheese and pineapple chunks in between all of her fingers. She held out a fist bristling with cocktail stick claws as they walked away from the table. "Look at me! I am like that superhero fella, but with useful snacks!"

"Hey, Sam, I didn't expect to see you here!"

Sam knew that voice. Her stomach lurched. "No way," she murmured.

She turned slowly.

Oh, hell, she thought. It was him. Months since she'd last

seen him, years now since they'd broken up. A mop of carefree black curls and the lingering tan of a man who had spent a lot of time in the sun.

"Rich." She coughed in surprise and drank a mouthful of wine to wash it away. "Wow. I didn't expect to see you here either."

Why would she expect to see him? This was Skegness. Rich was St Tropez, Cannes, Miami, Capri. Rich was not Skegness. Even here, among the local movers and shakers, he stuck out like a sunbather at the D-Day landings.

She stared at him for a long, confused moment, at the easy cocksure grin on his face, the tailored suit, the shirt unbuttoned halfway down his chest, the scallop shell on a leather thong hung round his neck. "Why *are* you here?" she asked, after a moment.

Ex-boyfriend Rich smiled and made an expansive gesture. "Local business meeting, isn't it? Came to see who's around and what everyone's up to."

"No, no. Not just here. Why are you in Skegness. No scratch that. Why are you in Lincolnshire, or even England, come to that? I thought you were living in Nice, or Los Angeles, or somewhere?"

Rich nodded carefully. "Citizen of the world, aren't I?" he said and laughed. "I'm re-thinking things. Don't want to make hasty life choices, so I'm here for a while, looking at business options. Got this amazing plan for a seabed tourist attraction." He nodded at Delia. "Is this a friend of yours?"

Sam turned. "Sorry. Delia, this is Richard Raynor. He and I—" She nearly froze again. Delia knew. Rich knew. Why say it? "—A long time ago," she finished. "Delia here's a friend and a local businesswoman."

Rich held out a hand. Sam saw Delia's face drop as she tried to disguise the fact her hand was currently a cheesy hedgehog by holding it behind her back.

"I'm Rich," he said.

"I heard," said Delia, reaching out boldly with her left hand. "We're thinking of introducing a secret left-handed handshake. What do you think?"

Rich took Delia's left hand in his and shook it gently. "I think I would very much like to know where I can get some of those amazing cheese and pineapple sticks." He gave Delia a conspiratorial wink that made her blush.

"I like your necklace thing," she said.

He fingered the shell lightly. "Found it while scuba-diving in Costa Rica. The simple things in life give us the most pleasure, eh?"

Sam wasn't sure there was anything simple about scuba-diving, and she was pretty certain he had found it on a beach in Vietnam. Maybe, once you've walked on every beach and dived in every sea, they all blurred together.

"Must leave you for a mo," he said to them both. "I've got to go shake a few hands, pose for some photos. I think someone wants me to be the keynote speaker at Friday's awards event." He pulled a pretend bored faced before heading off.

He clasped hands and patted shoulders as he made his way through the crowd, as if he were familiar with everyone there. Perhaps he was.

"He's rather gorgeous," said Delia, giving Sam a nudge in the ribs. "I mean seriously, he looks like a swimwear model."

"He's got a pot belly under that suit."

"But he's certainly charming."

"Superficial charm is all very well," said Sam primly. "It's not everything."

"No, you're right," said Delia, sipping her wine. "I mean, if he was a millionaire as well, that would change things, right?"

Sam sighed and gazed into her drink, wondering how the hell she could change the subject.

"Really?" said Delia. "You're joking. You said he became wealthy but... Millionaire?"

"And some. You know that UK rich list that gets published every year? Well, he's been in the top fifty ever since he invented the Crap Trap."

"What, that stupid plastic thing for picking up doggy doo?"

"That's the one."

Delia was silent for a minute. "And he's doing the speech at the awards, as well?"

Sam slumped against the table. "Probably talking about some of his charity work. He's worked with slum kids in India, built a hospital in Africa. Last I heard, he was setting up a renewable energy plant somewhere in central America."

Delia nodded. "How long have you known him?"

"Years," said Sam. She tried to tot up how many on her fingers and gave up. "A long time. He didn't really change though, when he got rich. He's always been a bit – what would you call it? – full on."

"Like how? Party animal or drama queen?"

"I should lay off him, Delia. I've moved on."

"Yeah, that was a mistake."

Sam slapped Delia's arm. It was a playful slap, but it came packed with hurt feelings.

Delia shoved a pineapple cube in her mouth and chewed. "I'm saying it as I see it. A rich, fairly hot ex-boyfriend. There's got to be some regrets."

"He's just not in my life anymore, so I don't want to rake over all the stuff that happened between us."

"Fair enough," said Delia. "Although for someone who's not in your life anymore, he seems to know what you like to drink." She nodded towards Rich who was walking back towards them with two extravagant glasses, which were trailing smoke as he walked.

He smiled broadly as he handed over the drinks. "I couldn't go without offering you these. I have my own mixologist with me, to make things a bit more interesting."

"Mixologist," said Delia, taking hers gleefully.

"Cleopatra. She's a wizard. This here's a cocktail of my own humble invention. You'll see it features some dry ice to give it a level of drama. Would you two ladies do me the honour of testing it for me? If you don't like this one, or if you want some more, just go and find Cleopatra at the far end of the bar and tell her I sent you." He winked and walked off.

Sam glared at the steaming thing in her hand. "That," she said. "That's the thing he used to do which drove me mad."

"Huh? Getting you the nicest drink available on the east coast?" asked Delia and slurped with enthusiasm.

"Deciding things for me. Honestly, it seems cute at first,

but trust me, it gets old when you never get to choose anything for yourself. Just because someone has already decided what the best option is." Sam mimed the air quotes around 'best option'.

"I wish my other half would be more decisive, to be honest," said Delia. "A bit more forceful too, if you know what I mean."

Sam sighed. "I sound bitter and ungrateful, but I'm not." She sipped her drink. "You're right, this is very good." She hated it for being so good. "Here, let me introduce you to some people."

She escorted Delia across the room to Alistair Green, chairman of the guild, who was hanging around the edge of a group of chatting members. Mostly farmers or holiday park owners, Sam would have guessed. Although there was an angular young woman with large eyes who was aggressively trying to hold court among them. The woman's voice was strident, rude even, but Sam understood the difficulty of a woman trying to be heard among a group of men.

Sam peeled chairman Alistair away from the group with a jerk of her head.

"Saving me from Jacinda's political campaigning?" he said, with a smile for Sam and a genial eyebrow raise for Delia.

"Hmmm?" said Sam.

Alistair inclined his head at the chatting group. "Intends to be the businessperson of the year. Have you both filled out your voting forms?" He gave Delia a little frown.

"Delia here is a potential new member," said Sam.

"Fresh meat!" declared Alistair with easy-going relish.

"She wants to hear all about the perks of membership while I distribute some of these flyers."

Delia gave Sam a look of shocked abandonment. Sam responded with a tartly mocking look in reply, not sure if Delia understood it was revenge for the lightly hurtful comments and utterly true comments Delia had made about her ex-boyfriend.

Sam drifted around the bar, leaving flyers for DefCon4 in strategic locations, propped up on ledges and at the tables where people would sit afterwards.

She drifted along the bar to where Rich's pet mixologist had set up. Sam had perhaps expected to find a cabaret act that involved juggling cocktail shakers and pouring ingredients from a great height; what she found was a petite and very intense woman with an encyclopaedic knowledge of drink and a willingness to indulge her curiosity.

"Rich said you could fix me up with a drink," said Sam.

"He pointed you out to me," said Cleopatra.

Sam smiled politely, seething inside, as though Rich had baited a trap with alcohol and Sam had walked right into it.

"Now, I could rustle you up something of your choice," said Cleopatra. "Or I could take you through this cheesy app that matches cocktails with your personality."

Sam shrugged. "I'm always open to new things. I like mixing new cocktails myself."

"From recipes?"

"Just whatever I fancy."

Cleopatra nodded slowly. "And how does that work out for you?" she asked, neither condoning nor condemning.

"Hit and miss. Mostly miss."

Cleopatra chatted to her amiably, mixing spirits, liqueurs and flavourings before presenting her with a *Life's What You Make It*. Both were apparently Cleopatra's own inventions. Sam sat back on a bar stool and made deliberately pleased noises to show her approval.

A woman pushed in beside Sam at the bar with little appreciation for personal space. "Get me something classy," she said.

It was the young angular woman who had been dominating the conversation elsewhere. Jacinda someone. She wore dangerously high heels and seemed in an awful hurry. Not a good combination.

"I'm sorry, I'm just here as Mr Raynor's assistant," said Cleopatra. "You can get a drink from the main bar."

"She's got one," said the Jacinda woman, meaning Sam.

"And she's one of Mr Raynor's friends."

Sam, who was enjoying the alcoholic headrush of her cocktail, asked Cleopatra, "Is Rich footing the bill for these?" When Cleopatra nodded she said, "Please, make the lady a cocktail."

Sam could feel the laser-beam scrutiny of the woman's large eyes.

"Thank you," said Jacinda with the icy reserve of someone who wasn't sure why they had to thank anyone for anything.

Cleopatra dropped blackberries, egg white and a host of other components into a shaker and rattled it vigorously. She poured out the liquid, now a viscous and foamy black, into a coupe glass.

"What the heck is that?" said Jacinda.

"A *Body Bag*," said Cleopatra and slid it over to her.

Jacinda eyed the mixologist as she sipped the dark drink. "That actually tastes nice."

"Of course," said Cleopatra.

"And that taste..." She smacked her lips and licked her teeth.

"Activated charcoal."

"Impressive."

Something seemed to relax in the intensely tense young woman, and she looked at Sam and the pile of remaining flyers. "You a guild member?"

"I am," said Sam.

"Voted for the businessperson of the year yet?"

"Not yet."

There was a business card in Jacinda's hand. A moment later, it was in Sam's.

JACINDA FROST

FROST & SONS

PROPERTY DEVELOPMENT AND HOUSING SOLUTIONS

"AH," said Sam and then, "Thank you," for want of anything meaningful to say. "You've got that development up at Anderby Creek."

"Shore View," Jacinda nodded. "Homes for eighty families. Affordable homes at that."

"And this would be the point where I suggest you consider DefCon4 for your on-site security."

Jacinda Frost looked once again at Sam's flyers and picked one up. "I thought you just did security vans."

"Oh, we do everything. Site security, premises checks—"

"Clown control?" said Jacinda, reading.

"If you like. Live seal transportation, crockery replacement, murder investigations."

"Murder investigations?"

Sam laughed at herself. That *Life's What You Make It* had gone straight to her head. "Sorry. That's definitely a sideline."

"Murder?"

Sam shook her head. "A woman I know in Welton le Marsh. She's gone missing. I've got a trainer from a one-footed man and some names missing from a notepad."

"What names?" said Jacinda. Her tone was sharp and demanding. Clearly she was interested, but who wouldn't be interested in a real life murder?

"I can't remember," said Sam. "It's nothing. Forgive me, I think I might already be tipsy."

"Of course." Jacinda downed her Body Bag and hurried away – paused a second, turned, said, "Remember to vote for me," and hurried away.

Delia plonked down next to Sam. "Who's that?" she asked.

"Her name's Jacinda Frost," said Sam.

"Ah, her."

"Her?"

"Her dad was Bob Frost, the building guy. You wouldn't

know him necessarily. Except a year or so back – it might have been money worries, or depression or something—"

"Yeah?"

"I think he was into his shooting. You know, pheasants and grouse. Bang, bang."

"Okay, I see where this is going," said Sam.

Delia gave a little sigh. "She inherited the company."

"And wants to make a name for herself. She ask you to vote for her as businessperson of the year?"

"Nope, but I am now a signed-up member of the guild," said Delia. "Alistair gave me a form to fill out. I'm supposed to write business goals on them."

"Uh-huh."

"Well, that's a joke obviously. Come on, you've seen my place. It doesn't make any money."

"Well, I think it's great you've joined and are now one of us." Sam dropped her voice to a zombie monotone. "One of us. One of us."

"Thanks," said Delia. "And we must now celebrate." She nodded at Sam's empty glass. "You're liking the cocktails then?"

"The woman's a genius."

Sam gestured to Cleopatra and made general cocktail summoning gestures. Cleopatra began to work her magic.

42

Jimmy answered his ringing phone. He had a new SIM card in the phone and hundreds of waiting texts and voicemails when he'd finally reconnected to the network. He deleted nearly all of them without replying. Even now, up to date, he felt disinclined to respond to communications. Isolation was preferable. If he didn't talk to people, then he couldn't betray himself. Stay hidden, in the dark, he told himself.

However, this phone call was from Jacinda and there was no hiding from her.

"Yes?"

"*The woman in Welton,*" hissed Jacinda. "*Someone is investigating it.*"

"What?" said Jimmy.

"*A woman from DefCon4. She's investigating it.*"

"DefCon4?" Jimmy thought, then it clicked. Little Miss Marvellous. Sam. She of the spangly top.

"She says she has clues!"

Jimmy wondered how Sam Applewhite could possibly know anything other than the barest details. The body was safely hidden. They'd cleaned up the house good and proper.

"She's not a threat. I know her. She's just a gopher in a dead-end job."

"She's looking for a one-footed man!"

"How...?"

"You need to get to know her a lot better," said Jacinda, still hissing and rasping with rage and worry. *"Where are you?"*

By the minimal moonlight coming in through the newly installed windows, he could see Wayne sprawled on the makeshift bed. The cargo container home was filled with the man's stink. Jimmy had been sitting silently in the dark ever since nightfall. He hadn't eaten. He hadn't turned the lights on. He'd just been sitting in the comforting, silent dark.

"Shore View," he said.

"Yes, well you need to be back in town and sorting out this mess you created. I am not going to prison for you, Jimmy MacIntyre."

She hung up. Silence resumed.

43

Rich slid onto a stool next to Sam and Delia as the women worked on Delia's application form together, while trying to find inspiration in a fresh round of cocktails. Sam was supping another *Life's What You Make It* and Delia had been presented with a violently fruity *99 Red Balloons*. Rich tipped a finger at his pet mixologist and Cleopatra began to make him a drink.

"Application form," he read over Delia's shoulder. "Business goals."

"It's a bit of a struggle," said Delia.

"Let's have a look." He whisked the paper from under her hands and scanned it for a second. "So, your business goal is to 'spend enough time in the shop to avoid household duties and family in general'?"

Delia looked sheepish. "Maybe I wasn't taking it as seriously as I should have."

"No, I like that playful tone," said Rich. "And I think there's probably a perfectly legitimate goal hidden away in there if we go looking."

"You think?"

Sam said nothing. The two of them had been perfectly happy coming up with their own half-arsed ideas of what was right and Rich – same old Rich – just came along and inserted himself into proceedings.

"You could simply re-phrase it as 'optimise my work/life balance'," he suggested. "But I feel as though that's not quite right for you."

He stared at Delia, deep in thought. Delia seemed quite happy to stare right back.

"*Husband!*" Sam coughed.

Delia tutted. Rich smiled.

"Is there perhaps a little bit of 'establish my personal boundaries and ambitions, ensuring my family learns to respect and support them'?" he said.

Delia looked shocked. "That's ... that's really good."

"Write it down," said Rich. "Write it down and it's one step closer to being a reality." He turned to Sam. "And what are your business plans?"

She tapped her pile of flyers, several of which were now soggy with spilled alcohol. "Not my business. I don't need goals."

"Hence the attention to detail," He placed a finger on an obviously corrected typo.

Sam took it back. "It pays the bills."

"Not knocking it," said Rich. "There's been times in my life when I've been in desperate need of some clown management. At least I know who to call now." He folded a flyer and put it in a pocket. "What have you got on this week then, assuming the clowns are looking after themselves? Is it risk consulting, event security, or training services?"

Sam laughed, despite her attempts to despise him. "Tomorrow should be a fun day. I'm co-ordinating some community service work."

"Chain gangs breaking rocks on the side of the road?"

"A beach clean-up."

"Nice," said Delia. "You might find treasure."

Sam opened her mouth to comment if treasure took the form of broken flip-flops and bits of nylon rope, then it would be rich pickings. She closed her mouth again, realising those things probably *were* treasure to Delia, and shrugged. "Come and see if you're curious. We can divvy up the treasure."

Rich smiled at them both as he stepped away. "I'll be on the beach tomorrow too. Lifeguard duty. See you there."

"Sure," said Delia.

Sam rolled her eyes. She watched Rich move through the room, working the crowd, being best buddy to everyone in the world.

"Lifeguard?" said Delia.

"I have no idea," said Sam. "Not even going to ask."

"Right," said Delia, drumming fingertips on the bar. "Gonna hand my application in and then call it a night."

Sam checked the time and groaned. "Beach duty at nine a.m."

"And it won't do for the community service lady to turn up late or, indeed, hungover," said Delia.

Sam groaned again because it was true. "I hate you."

"Careful now, or I'll report you to the guild."

"You do and I might consider not voting for you as businessperson of the year," said Sam, waving a voting slip at her.

44

The voice of Hank's gently reassuring Californian tones filled the otherwise silent rooms of *Duncastin'*. Marvin was in the kitchen with the drone on the table in front of him, a morning coffee in his right hand and a plate of toast at his left.

Sam took a raincoat from the cloakroom and came back through the kitchen, checking her bag and pockets for all the things she needed for the day.

"You using this?" she asked, holding up a coarse building supplies bag she'd found.

"What is it?" said Marvin.

"Dunno. That's why I asked."

"It was blowing around the garden. Must have come from somewhere."

"Most things do. I was going to use it to take supplies to the beach."

He made an open 'be my guest' gesture.

"I thought you'd finished that," she said, pointing at the drone.

"I have," said Marvin.

"But..." She pointed at the tablet on which Hank's assembly video was playing.

"Oh, I just like to have him on for company."

Sam couldn't tell if he was joking or not. "He's just telling you how to build a drone."

"It's not what he's saying; it's how he's saying it," said Marvin. "You shouldn't underestimate the power of a soothing voice. I did a run at the Bristol Hippodrome with Max Bygraves. I could listen to him tell his stories all night. I did sometimes. Couldn't tell you a single thing he said, but what a voice!"

Sam shook her head.

"You off courting again?" said Marvin.

"In waterproofs and wellies on a weekday morning? No. It's work. Wolla Bank. Someone's got to earn the pennies, haven't they?"

Marvin gave his daughter a quizzical look. "If you're short of a bob or two..."

Unexpected, those words nearly broke Sam's heart. The papers making up her dad's finances; the bills with an inescapable amount of red ink. Was the man blind to the truth or wilfully ignorant?

"Dad?"

"Yes?"

She tried to hold his gaze as she plucked up the courage to speak and found she didn't quite have enough courage to look at him and speak at the same time. "Cards on the table—"

Marvin tapped the table edge, clicked his fingers, and there was a playing card in his hand.

"Jesus, dad!"

"I mean I used to get applause in the old days, but I'll settle for blasphemy."

"You're in financial trouble, dad."

He put the card down. "Everyone is these days. It's the credit crunch."

"That was years ago and I'm not talking about everyone. You. *You* are in financial trouble. There's a mortgage on this house that you haven't paid off yet."

"It's a big house."

"That you can't afford to pay off."

"I'm sure it's just one of the back bedrooms left to pay for. Maybe that and the patio."

"It's not funny, dad."

Her dad – Mr Marvellous, the clown, the magician – who always had a ready smile and ready words, dropped his smile and looked at her directly. "What is it then, Sam?"

There was worry in his eyes. Worry and anger. Sam couldn't help feeling like she was betraying him, treating her parent like a child.

"How should I feel about this situation?" he said.

"It's frightening," she replied. "You could lose your home. More. I'd be frightened."

"And what use is that?" he said coldly. "What use is fear?" His mouth twisted into an ugly expression. He stabbed at the computer tablet, pausing the video. "Shut up, Hank. No one asked you anyway."

"I don't mean to upset you," said Sam. "But there's some hard financial realities you just can't ignore."

"I'm not ignoring them."

"You're doing a very good impression of someone who is."

He flung away the card he'd magically produced. It vanished into nothing before it left his fingertips.

"That's what I do!" he said with a quiet bitterness. "You think this external persona is the real me? All of me? Misdirection, Sam. You think I don't know why you've been going through my bank statements? You think I'm just some stupid old man?"

"No...."

"I've got cards up my sleeves, Sam. I've got solutions."

"That's great. I'll—"

"We'll sell the Jag. Number one."

"Really?"

"That will bring in seventy thousand pounds, easily."

"But you love that car."

He waved her concerns away. "What's it doing except gathering dust in the garage?"

"The memories..."

He scoffed. "What memories? Apart from some unspeakably filthy behaviour with a *Top of the Pops* backing dancer, what memories?"

"No, but..." She was going to say something else, something pertinent and meaningful, but got side-tracked by an entirely unwanted mental image of her dad and one of

Pan's People (or maybe Legs & Co) in the tight confines of his E-type Jag.

"There. It's decided," he said. "I don't need to cling onto the past. When a thing is done with, I'm happy to get rid of it." He prodded the drone as though to push it away. Its little rubber feet squeaked on the tabletop. "It's finished. Why don't you take it to the beach and give it a test flight?"

The MySky drone was a wide thing, but it would probably just about fit in the back of the Piaggio. "You want to come watch?" she asked.

He shook his head slowly. "You go. I'll be fine."

45

There was something glorious about tarmac, thought Jimmy, immediately recognising he was clearly very tired. Of course there was nothing glorious about tarmac. Nonetheless, it was deeply satisfying to see a layer of hot black asphalt concrete being poured over the stubby branching roads that made up the Welton le Marsh housing development.

The hardcore sub-base had been laid the day before, and now the tarmac was being poured by a company out of Boston. Normally, Jimmy might have considered using the Odinsons for a job as simple as that (not much caring where they had 'sourced' their materials), but after the fiasco with the old woman's corpse, he was going to steer clear of them for a while.

The tarmac crew worked their way from the corners of the miniature estate and back to the existing road, filling in cul-de-sacs and drives before they tackled the access road.

Jimmy stood at the side of the access road, now crucially fifty centimetres wider than it had been two days ago.

When the tarmac was down, a neat black covering from kerb to kerb, he would consider this nasty business done. The Welton job – the grafting, the building, the murder, the disposal – would be almost behind him. They would sell the houses, all in various stages of completion, new families could move into the area. People would be happy. Everything would be done.

His phone buzzed with a text.

It was Jacinda, calling him to the Shore View site.

He turned to Wayne, sitting on the verge in a folding deckchair, drinking a box of Ribena with a straw. In its squashed peg-leg contraption, Wayne's stump was mostly invisible beneath soiled bandages. Where it poked through it was a deep purply-black, and shiny, like a tray of offal in a bad butcher's window.

"Jacinda wants me at Shore View," said Jimmy. "You'll be fine here."

"Got me juice. Catching some rays. What more could I want, eh?" said Wayne.

Two feet, thought Jimmy. "Then later, we'll take you home and get you properly cleaned up. Fresh clothes, eh?"

"Smashing," agreed Wayne.

"And we'll remember to tell your mum and your sister the right story about your foot. Crushed by an earthmover, yeah? And that you've spent the past week in the Pilgrim Hospital."

"I'll tell 'em it weren't bitten off by an alligator."

"No one's mentioning any alligators," said Jimmy. "At all."

"It's a much cooler story though," said Wayne, moodily.

"We can't say it was bitten off by an alligator," said Jimmy. "Because then people will ask questions."

Wayne nodded reluctantly. "What about a tiger? I hear they've got a tiger out at Candlebroke Hall. Coulda been bitten off by a tiger."

"Fuck's sake," said Jimmy and went to his van.

46

W olla Bank Beach was eight miles north of Skegness on the Anderby Road, just half a mile shy of Anderby Creek. Sam parked in the sandy car park on the leeward side of the high dunes. The council had been as good as their word and put two empty dumpsters in place to take the rubbish.

She had a clipboard full of names, gloves, hi-vis vests, litter picking grabbers and plenty of rubbish bags. She left them all in the van. She still had time before the community service offenders were due to arrive, time enough to perhaps set up and test the drone.

She got it out, carried it through the gap in the dunes onto the wide featureless beach, and put it down. She planned to set it up on a repeating grid search pattern, right across the beach. If the documentation's claims were correct, the live video feed would be sent directly to her phone, as well as backed up to cloud storage for later review and analysis. The battery – ninety minutes of flight-time – ought to allow it to cover most of the beach clearance effort.

Sam spent a few moments double-checking everything she had set up (or the pre-flight checks as she now thought of them) before she sent it off. The drone was programmed to come back to base when the battery was low. And by base Sam meant the phone with the controlling app. She assumed it wouldn't just try to land on her head. As long as it didn't take a suicidal one-way trip out to sea like its predecessor, she'd be happy.

It rose from the sand, looking majestic in the early morning sky. There was a brief moment of anxiety as a seagull swooped down to check it out, but the drone continued its ascent before moving out across the beach. It began to follow the set flight-path pattern, making slow turns across the sand. Sam checked the live feed and was staggered to see a clearly useable video stream.

"Huh. Actually works."

She could zoom in and out if she wanted. She zoomed in on what she thought might be a seal, but it was a bin bag. Well, at least today's activities would sort that out.

She was tempted to build on this nascent success by sending the drone back to buzz her dad, so he'd pick up on the good news, but she didn't want to disturb it now it was doing exactly what she needed. She closed the app and went back to the car park to collect the more mundane parts of the day's equipment.

A Tesla had pulled up near her van. A middle-aged man,

sunglasses pushed back over his receding curls, walked over. Sam looked at his jeans and polo shirt and was certain they hadn't come from anywhere local.

"Morning," he said, pointing at her collection of litter picking gear. "Here for the beach clean-up. Do my bit for a good cause."

"Community payback," she corrected him. She had no intention of rubbing his nose in it, but thought it better to be clear: this was compulsory. A punishment handed out by the courts, not a voluntary piece of charity work.

"That's the one," he said smoothly. "Greg Mandyke." He leaned forward and tapped a name on her clipboard.

"Great," said Sam. "Grab yourself a hi-vis and a pair of gloves out of the bag." She waved at the large white bag that she had dumped everything into.

He hesitated. "Is that a builder's delivery bag?" he asked.

The name of a local builder was written on the side, so there was really no denying the bag's provenance. "Yes, it is," she said.

"Only, I've got dermatitis," he said, in what she understood to be the tones of a man who really didn't have dermatitis but openly defied her to say otherwise. "My hands are really sensitive. If there's been cement in that bag, I guarantee my hands will be red raw by the end of the day."

Sam peered into the bag. "Let me find some for you." She pulled out a pair that were still in the cellophane wrapper. "Here. These are new and wrapped. They should be fine."

"Ah, well. New and wrapped brings a different kind of problem. Did you know that there are all sorts of chemical finishes on new items of clothing? It's a complete nightmare for people like me. Especially if they've been wrapped. They need to off-gas."

"They need to what?"

"Off-gas. It's where any solvents evaporate and disperse. It's one of the reasons that many of us have toxic homes and workplaces. I'm surprised you're not more familiar with the issue, given your role as a public servant."

Sam looked at him. "Why don't I consult the employee handbook to see how I should handle this for you?" He looked pleased at this. Sam wondered if he thought he was going to be able to avoid his day's community service. "Ah, here, we are," she said, leafing through. "When providing PPE to a client, make sure they are suitable for the purpose and the person. The health of the wearer must be taken into account. If there is any doubt as to the wearer's health, the DefCon4 occupational health officer must be consulted."

"Marvellous!" said Greg. "Do I need to make an appointment?"

"Oh no, not at all. The occupational health officer is right here," said Sam. "In fact, it's me."

"What? But you clearly don't understand my condition. Are you a doctor?"

"I think I understand it well enough to make a recommendation," said Sam firmly. "My recommendation is that you should go ahead without gloves. You'll be fine."

"Of course I won't be fine," he huffed. "There could be needles or anything out there. There's a risk to my health if I don't wear gloves."

"As the leader of this offender management team, I have done a risk assessment."

"Have you? Where's the paperwork?"

"A dynamic risk assessment."

"Which means what?"

"It means I thought about it in my head. And what I thought was if you use one of these grabbers, you will never touch any rubbish."

Sam held out a grabber and he took it, frowning.

"I could refuse," he said.

"And I could tell the court you refused," she said. "Entirely your choice, Mr Mandyke."

Other offenders were turning up now. There were three Odinsons walking towards her across the top of the dunes, two men and a woman. She consulted her clipboard to check which ones were expected. Oddly, only two were listed.

"Names please," she said. It wouldn't do to get them wrong.

"Odinson."

"Odinson."

"Odinson."

All three wore deadpan expressions, not even a smirk. Sam wasn't sure if they were messing with her or not. "Torsten?" she asked.

The tall blonde youth with tattooed arms gave a nod.

"And Hilde?" The red-headed young woman gave her a pinched look and the tiniest of nods.

Sam ticked her list. then looked up at the last one, who she finally recognised as Ogendus. "So why are you here?"

He grinned at her. "'Reckon I might help me lad." He nodded at Torsten. "And me niece if she needs it."

"Help with what?" asked Sam. "Obviously, I'll be here to support everyone."

"Aye, but 'e gets agitated with authority figures. I'll just keep an eye out."

Sam nodded reluctantly and moved across to meet with the other woman on her list. "Name?"

"Stacey Wheelan," said the woman, her hair flopping from a piled-up bun on the top of her head. "Is this gonna take all day?"

"You're committed to three hours minimum," said Sam.

"That's like forever."

"It's three hours."

She called for everyone to gather round and addressed them. "I'm Sam Applewhite. I'm part of the offender management team."

"Sounds like she's the entire offender management team," muttered Greg Mandyke.

Sam conceded this with a nod. "Budget cuts. Nonetheless, the courts have a job for us to do. We have an area of beach to clear between Wolla Bank and Anderby Creek. That's up by that tall house over there. You won't be signed off from this activity until it's done to my satisfaction. So, if it's all done in three hours' time, you can go. Otherwise we stay until the job's done."

Greg raised a hand. "How will we know if it's good enough?"

"Excellent question," said Sam. "I will be looking for a

beach that is free of rubbish, and for all of that rubbish to be bagged up and returned to this area here."

"So we've got to go there and back?" said Ogendus Odinson.

"Indeed. Well spotted. I will inspect the beach using various methods." She glanced up to the sky but couldn't see the drone. "Also, I will be on hand to supervise and address any issues."

"What about health and safety?" said Greg.

"Very important," said Sam. "I hope it goes without saying that you need to stay out of the water."

"I can't swim," said Torsten Odinson.

"It's like three feet deep for half a mile," said Greg. "If you're drowning, just stand up."

"Let's just stay out of the water, eh?" said Sam. "There are not very many hazards otherwise."

"Seals," said Hilde Odinson.

"Aye," nodded Ogendus.

"Are seals a hazard?" said Stacey.

"Heard one attacked a copper t'other day," said Ogendus. "Ate a man's foot an' all."

Stacey whirled as though a killer seal might be sneaking up behind her right now.

"Ate it up and shat it out," agreed Torsten.

"There are no killer seals on this beach," Sam assured them. "You need to be more mindful of sharps. If you see something that looks sharp or noxious, use the grabber to pick it up. You must all wear a hi-vis so I can easily identify you. Grab the equipment you need and make your way onto the beach."

They all walked onto the sand and Sam divided the area into sections so they could each get started.

"The tide is right out now, so if you start down by the sea you can tackle that part while it's exposed," she said to Torsten and Ogendus, who had adjacent sections, at southern most end.

"Why do that?" asked Torsten. "Tha's daft, I reckon. Tha's making the job bigger'n it needs to be. If we start up here, the beach'll get shorter as we go."

He ambled off, cackling lightly. Sam didn't argue. She walked over to where Hilde Odinson had already filled her bag. She dragged it heavily towards the car park.

"Wow, so full already?" Sam asked.

Hilde nodded. "Loads of dolls everywhere. Might need stronger bags. These're poking holes with their arms and legs."

Sam shaded her eyes and looked down the beach. There was a line marking where the sea had turned at high tide. She walked towards it. As she got closer, she could see that instead of the usual line of seaweed and shells, there were hundreds, possibly even thousands, of Capitalist Whore dolls. They were tangled with each other, with seaweed, and colourful bits of nylon rope. She pulled out her phone and called Delia.

"You know that treasure you were after?" she said.

"*Uh-huh.*"

"Turns out you might be in luck. I'm looking at something like a cross between an art installation and a doll orgy right now."

"*Ooh, where are you?*"

"Wolla Bank. Making our way north."

"I will pop down. Are we talking a carrier bag full, or a bin bag full?"

Sam stared at a line stretching as far as she could see. "We're talking more like a cargo container full."

47

There were now six containers on the Shore View construction site, and a seventh being off-loaded by Yngve Odinson and his flatbed truck. Jimmy crossed to Yngve.

"No weird dolls in this one?" said Jimmy.

"All sorted," said Yngve without looking round at him.

A black dot in the sky caught Jimmy's eye. He looked up at the rolling white clouds, but didn't see it again.

"There you are," said Jacinda, striding across the chalky hardcore ground from the site office.

"Yes." Jimmy didn't have the energy to deny the obvious or pay any attention to Jacinda's implied rebuke. He pointed over to the new containers where a group of builders were fitting windows and door frames. "You've called the lads in. I could have done that."

"You weren't available," she said.

"I was busy," he said, loading the last word with a wealth

of meaning that encompassed property crime, murder and body disposal. "And if you'd come to me first, I'd be able to point out where they're going wrong."

"Wrong?" said Jacinda defiantly.

"Just a couple of things. Firstly, some of these containers are already rusting through."

"We'll apply some filler and give them all a paint job."

"Secondly, and I know this is a minor thing, aren't there meant to be holes in the walls before the windows are fitted?"

He pointed at two blokes – Steve and Justin – who were fixing a frosted bathroom window over a wall of corrugated steel.

"You think we're idiots?" snapped Jacinda.

Jimmy said nothing. He let her own damning question hang in the air.

"The backers are coming down to the site on Saturday after the awards ceremony on Friday. They are going to want to see more than one completed housing unit. Windows will be installed, walls will be painted. That first unit, which you left in a terrible state inside – it's like two hobos slept in it – that unit will have internal walls put up, flooring laid, plumbing and electrics installed. All the fittings, decorated, and furnished with show room furniture."

"Within three days?" said Jimmy. "How do you expect to achieve that?"

Jacinda smiled and spread her arms to indicate Jimmy himself. Her smile was a cruel thing, a lopsided slit in her darkly beautiful face.

"I'm not the hands-on type," she said and backed away to the site office. "But I expect results." As she reached the office door, she turned. "And I need a decent coffee machine in here," she shouted.

Jimmy swore softly, feeling an anxious tension in his chest. Having Jacinda Frost as a boss was more stressful than covering up a murder. He walked to the edge of the dune and looked out over the beach, hoping to recapture some calm. The golden sandy beach sparkled in the morning sun. In truth, it was no more golden, no more special than the builder's sand they used on site, but distance made it beautiful.

He took deep breaths, stretched and thought about the massive task Jacinda had laid before him.

Oh, it was all feasible. They could get a few of the young lads on the filling and painting work. Stud walls would go up quick enough. There'd be no time for plastering, but a lick of thick emulsion would be good enough for a quick inspection. They'd find flooring, but it would have to be a simple batten and plywood surface for now.

Shore View: a week ago only a plateau of loose foundations on top of the Anderby dunes, now taking shape as the container village it was destined to be. In the clear light of late summer, it could be mistaken for idyllic. Dozens of economical, cottage-like homes in a quiet corner of the country, with views of the sea and the rising sun. It would look and feel different in the autumn and winter, though. Winds would sweep in from the east bringing storm surges and Siberian temperatures. The east coast avoided much of the country's rain – spent long before it crossed the Peaks and the Pennines – but a hard dry winter would soon make the residents of these steel boxes regret moving here. And that's when they'd realise the true disadvantage of being eight miles from the nearest town or supermarket in a county with next to no public transport.

He'd pity the people who were going to live here, if he could summon the heart to care.

A black dot in the sky again. He kept track of it this time.

It wasn't a seagull. It was too dark and moved wrong. For a moment or two, he wondered if it was a bird of prey, the way it hovered. But that wasn't right either.

His eye was drawn down along the beach. Half a dozen people in bright hi-vis were approaching from the south along the sand.

48

S am walked around to make sure everyone was getting on with the clean-up. She walked over to Greg who looked very unhappy and was waving at her.

"I can't do that part of the beach," he said, pointing towards the sea.

"Why not?" asked Sam.

"It's wet sand. I understood that we were operating only on dry sand, otherwise I wouldn't have worn my espadrilles. They'll be ruined if I go down there in them."

Sam gave him a long hard look, to see if he was joking. Apparently he wasn't. "Well, you're going to have to think of something," she said. "You can take them off, you can leave them on; or maybe you can get one of your staff to bring you some more suitable footwear."

"Staff?" he frowned. He pointed up to where the Odinsons were gathering Capitalist Whores up near the dunes. "You could swap me with those crusties over there. They've got boots on."

"They're doing the section they've been given," said Sam, "and you need to clean the whole of your section. Wearing the wrong shoes will not get you out of it, I'm afraid."

He scowled and turned back to his bag, which was half full of dolls. "This is playing havoc with my lower back, you know."

"Bend at the knees," said Sam, demonstrating for him. "You'll thank me later. It will help your back."

He did not look grateful, but slipped off his expensive shoes and reluctantly went down onto the damp sand. "I'll have to spend an hour in the jacuzzi to soak away these aches," he complained as he went.

Sam checked her phone, pleased to see the app was still showing good clear footage of the beach as the drone swept up and down. On the screen, she saw a pair of figures approaching from the south. She glanced back along the route they'd taken from Wolla Bank and saw Delia approaching and next to her—

"Ugh!" Sam muttered.

Rich Raynor was with her, wearing long orange swimming trunks and a bright red bomber jacket.

"Are you a lifeguard or going to a fancy dress party as David Hasselhoff?" said Sam.

Rich grinned. "Oh, the Baywatch look? Ha. Good one."

"I've already pointed it out to him," said Delia.

"Seriously, is that the uniform they gave you?" said Sam.

"I'm a freelance lifeguard," said Rich. "Bought it myself."

"A what?"

He tossed his dark curls and looked out to sea. "Wherever there are waves, I'll be there. Danger calls to me."

"You're mad. That's not a thing…"

He laughed. "Of course it isn't. But I did buy the uniform. Bought them for the whole RNLI lifeguard team. I'm not going to be saving lives in speedos and cheap polyester."

"And you've apparently come as a beach-combing Ghostbuster?"

Delia gave a proud twirl. "Like it?" She was wearing something that looked like a bell-shaped rucksack made out of loosely-woven rope. "I've had this lobster pot out the back for ages. I knew it would come in handy. A couple of belts looped through as shoulder straps and it's transport for any number of sea-soaked dolls."

"Any number?"

"Well, as many as I can carry," said Delia with a shrug.

"The young woman here told me there were dozens of shapely dolls on the beach that needed rescuing," said Rich. "I came ready to rescue damsels in distress." He grinned to show he was joking. "But I'm happy to help your new friend, Delia, here."

He gestured to a plastic sledge he had been pulling behind him, and the equipment laid across it. Delia bent to grab a ball of string and a bag of elastic bands from the sledge, shoving them into the deep pockets of her cargo trousers.

The community payback team had covered most of the distance between Wolla Bank and Anderby Creek. Off to the left, atop the nearest dunes was a levelled area on which half a dozen steel cargo containers had been placed. Sam would have assumed they'd just been dumped there, but there were workmen moving around the site and, it would appear, they were fitting uPVC windows and doors to the containers.

Sam took out her phone and played with the drone app to see, just out of curiosity, if she could get it to have a closer look.

"Shore View," said Rich, still lurking. "That's Jacinda Frost's new development."

Sam felt a small but unshakeable annoyance at Rich. Their relationship had been some time ago now and although she hadn't exactly returned to Skegness to get away from Rich, there was a part of her that felt it was unfair he had somehow followed her here.

"You are well up on local business affairs," she said.

"Thinking of reinvesting in the local area. Got my eye on some property opportunities."

"Going to buy a caravan park?" she said.

"Actually, got my eye on something much much bigger." He put his arms on her shoulders and turned her towards the sea, pointing. "Buying myself some real estate out there."

Sam squinted. "You're buying a wind farm?"

"Further out. Got big dreams."

Sam shrugged. There were no islands between here and the European mainland. Wind farms, oil rigs and gas platforms, but nothing else. Unless he meant he was planning on buying Belgium.

"Hope it makes you happy."

He touched his shell necklace. "Material things don't make you happy," he said.

"Try telling that to homeless people. I need to get on."

She went to check on the offenders she was supposed to be overseeing.

Stacey's part of the beach was looking very clear. Sam nodded with approval, but then paused. It wasn't just good and clear, it was utterly empty. The line of tidal detritus Sam had seen before had disappeared. She went to find Stacey.

"How's it going?" she asked.

"Fine," panted Stacey. "Filled six bags so far. Stacked them over there."

"Let's have a look." Sam opened the bag that Stacey had at her feet. There was a sodden pile of seaweed in the bottom. "You know you don't have to clear up the seaweed, don't you?"

"We're cleaning the beach, ain't we?" said Stacey. "Disgusting. Shouldn't be allowed where kiddies play."

While Stacey went full tilt at stripping the beach, the Odinsons cleared their sections with a slovenly fatalism. Greg Mandyke trudged on the shoreline, bag and picker in hand.

Delia and Rich walked along the high water line, dolls loaded in Delia's eccentric backpack. It was clear Delia had already taken on more dolls than she could easily manage. The lobster pot was full, with dolls sticking out everywhere, as if Delia had rammed them into every gap, twisting them so that they stayed in place. Rich had a miniature mountain of them on the sledge he pulled for her. Delia's current problem clearly stemmed from the fact she could no longer get her lobster pot rucksack onto her back. The Odinson girl, Hilde, had even dug a small pit in the sand so that Delia could stand a bit lower and hitch it onto her shoulders, but it wasn't working.

"Can I help?" Sam asked.

"The more the merrier," said Rich.

Sam grunted as she lifted Delia's pot the crucial extra few inches, so that Delia could fasten her shoulder straps.

"Yes!" shouted Delia, as she got it secured. She took one step and promptly fell over backwards. "Bugger."

She wriggled over onto her front and tried to stand up. Rich extended a hand and Delia got cautiously to her knees.

"I know what it needs," said Hilde Odinson.

"Yes?" said Delia.

"It needs balancing out. I've got some elastic bands. I've a plan."

The plan turned out to be using the rake as a balancing pole. It was strung with pairs of dolls at either end, fastened together with an elastic band, and suspended like an old-style butcher's display from the rake's shaft.

"That actually works," said Delia. "Very clever."

"I likes making things," said Hilde and went on with her duties.

"Nice girl," said Delia.

"Doing community payback," Sam reminded her.

"What for?"

Sam tried to recall. Specific offences didn't always come with the paperwork. "Stealing telegraph poles."

"Out of the ground?"

"Before they were put up. I believe her defence was she didn't know anybody wanted them."

The sledge was piled with dolls, so as Delia trudged

slowly across the beach, she had Capitalist Whores hanging from every part of her body as Rich pulled another large load of them behind her. Delia occasionally staggered from side to side in order to maintain balance, but she mostly kept moving forward.

"So, is this how multi-millionaires spend their time these days?" Sam asked Rich.

"Labels don't define me," said Rich serenely.

There was a panicked shout. "Help! Help!"

Stacey stood up at the highest part of the beach, not far from the ugly cluster of dunes, hands clutched in her hair like a Hammer Horror scream queen.

Sam hurried forward. Rich ran beside her, leaving his doll toboggan with Delia.

"She's not drowning," Sam gasped as she jogged.

"Damsel in distress though."

Sam didn't want to turn the race to get to Stacey into a competition, but she sped up, not wishing Rich to get there first. By the time they got to Stacey, Sam was on the verge of collapse. She heaved in great lungfuls of air, while pretending not to be out of breath.

"Stay back!" Stacey was wild-eyed. She stood in a wide-legged stance and held her hands high, not wanting anyone to mistake what she was saying. "I think it's a landmine!"

Sam and Rich looked down at the sand three feet in front of her. There was a small round object, with a dusting of sand across it, embedded in the beach. From what Sam could see it was a dull black colour, with a flat circular top, and tiny concentric ridges stepping slightly down into the ground.

"It's just a lid or something, isn't it?" said Sam.

"Don't be complacent," said Rich. "Think like that and then it's step, click, boom. We need to call this in."

Stacey's shouts had drawn in the other members of the beach clearing party. A couple of men had come running down from the Shore View site.

"Can everyone stay back please," said Sam. "I'm sure it's nothing."

"It's a landmine," said Rich.

"I'm sure it's nothing to worry about."

"Oh, suddenly she's the landmine police too," muttered Greg, loud enough to be heard from a safe distance.

"Right, I'm not the landmine police." She sighed and wondered if DefCon4 had bomb disposal as one of its listed services. It seemed possible.

Stacey was starting to video the scene. The Odinsons appeared to be taking bets.

One of the men from the site was drifting towards them. He approached Sam. "What's the situation?"

"It's —" She recognised him as the guy from the StoreWatch evening. "Jimmy."

49

"Hey up, Sam." Jimmy gave Little Miss Marvellous a smile and nodded at the half-buried thing in the sand.

"Almost certainly not a landmine—" said Sam.

Landmine. Jimmy heard the word and it had no impact on him. After the week he'd had, nothing had the power to shock him any more.

"—Although I really don't know what it is," Sam finished.

The curly-haired lifeguard chap spoke up, zipping his phone back into a pocket. "I have alerted the authorities and they are sending someone. They have asked us to clearly mark the position of the suspect object, then to retreat to a safe distance."

"What a good plan, Rich," said Sam. "Everyone, up to the dunes. I'll find something to mark the spot."

"I worked in Senegal with some of the charities who clear land mines," said Rich the lifeguard. "The advice given there is for whoever discovers the mine to mark its position with a pair of branches, or something that will stick up from the ground."

"Heads up, Saxon," said a red-headed Odinson girl and tossed something to Rich. It was a Capital Whore doll. The damned things filled the litter pickers' bags. They seemed to be bloody everywhere.

"That'll do nicely," said Rich and stabbed the Capitalist Whore into the ground. If the circular device was a landmine, he did it too close and forcefully for comfort. But nothing exploded.

"There," said Sam, "Landmine Clearing Barbie is on duty now. Up to the dunes."

The party trudged up to the level of the grassy dunes. Jimmy walked with them and stayed close to Sam.

"You know, I can't see why there'd be a landmine on this coastline," he said.

"Exploded ordnance all the way up and down this coast," said Rich.

"Sure," said Jimmy. "Old World War Two bombs, and the RAF bombing ranges." He thought of the area to the rear of the Frost house, of Yngve Odinson's favourite dumping spot.

"Exactly," said Rich.

"Not landmines," said Jimmy.

"You'd be surprised," said Rich.

"I would."

The group plonked themselves among the brittle dry grasses of the dune.

"This delay counts towards us hours, don't it?" said a young Odinson.

"It better," said a man.

Jimmy realised it was Greg Mandyke. Builder, businessman, access road denier. Jimmy grunted in amusement. So much for wriggling out of community service. "Morning, Greg," he said.

Greg Mandyke gave Jimmy a begrudging head nod of greeting.

So Greg Mandyke was reduced to picking up rubbish for the courts. He was barefoot as well, which somehow tickled Jimmy.

Greg followed his gaze. "Crap. I've left my espadrilles down there."

Sam was looking down the beach. "Delia...!"

On an otherwise deserted beach, a woman with a huge rucksack thing and heavy pole was trudging on the wet sand. She struggling with her burden and making her way up the beach.

"She doesn't know," said Sam. She started down the slope of the dunes to call to her, warn her. "Delia!" Sam shouted, waving her hands.

The woman, Delia, waved back like it was a greeting and made directly towards Sam.

"Delia!" Sam waved more vigorously and ran.

Running was a bad idea, thought Jimmy but said nothing. To confirm it, near the base of the dune slope, Sam stumbled.

The reflexes of the human body are a remarkable thing. The speed and mental agility needed to, say, catch a thrown object or run over uneven ground was something robots and computers struggled to emulate. The body's ability to respond to emergencies, at speeds faster than conscious though, was something quite special. The human body was also capable of acts of automatic stupidity. When stumbling towards danger, while the conscious mind could recognise that simply dropping to the ground was the fastest way to stop, the body's in-built reaction was to trying to correct and compensate.

Sam stumbled towards the landmine. Her knee gave way and she stumbled further, step after desperate step, flailing. Eventually, she pitched forward into the sand. She landed heavily, pretty much right in front of the Capitalist Whore doll they'd shoved in the sand.

"Oops," said Jimmy.

Sam froze in a prone position.

Rich began to run down to her. Jimmy found himself tagging along. "Don't move!" he shouted.

"I think I'm on the device!" Sam called back.

"I think you're on the mine!" shouted Rich.

Jimmy skidded to a halt at her side.

"Try not to move," said Rich.

"Gee, really?" mumbled Sam.

Jimmy walked round, taking stock of which parts of her were touching the ground. Her forearms were supporting her top half, but her chest was very slightly elevated. Her left leg was in full contact with the beach, but her right leg and hip were twisted slightly away.

"Where exactly is it, in relation to my body?" she asked.

Jimmy continued to circle as he peered down at her.

"What's going on?" said the woman, Delia, approaching.

"Get her away!" Sam hissed.

Rich was on his phone, urgently calling someone. Jimmy didn't much care what he did as long as he didn't do anything stupid.

"I would say that it's underneath your face," said Jimmy slowly.

"You what?" she grunted against the sand.

"Stay very still. You should resist the temptation to have a look."

"Why?"

"Because I might be wrong."

He crouched down beside her. He wasn't frightened. He could no longer recall the last time he was truly frightened.

Here was the woman who, according to Jacinda, was the only one showing an interest in the death of Mrs Skipworth. Here she was, prone and helpless. And if there was a landmine underneath her...? Well, that would certainly be a solution to the problem. In truth, Jimmy wouldn't really mind if the landmine went off right now, killing them both. A split second of heat, they probably wouldn't even hear the bang. It had a definite appeal.

"I want to move," said Sam. "I've got cramp. We need to do something."

"I'm on the line to someone now," said Rich.

"Jimmy," Sam breathed. She sounded tired. "I've got an idea. Slide your phone under my face and take a picture. We can see if anything's there."

It sounded like a monumentally bad idea. An invitation to set the device off.

"Okay," said Jimmy. He took out his phone. "Let me take a

picture right next to your face. We might be able to see what's underneath."

"Please."

Jimmy moved closer and crouched right down beside her head until he could smell her hair, the floral shampoo she'd washed it with. He brought his phone closer to her cheek.

"Flash or no flash?" he said.

"I don't care!"

"Close your eyes then."

She closed her eyes.

"Right, let's see," he said. "Huh—"

"'Huh' what?" said Sam.

"Lincolnshire police bomb disposal are on their way," said Rich.

"'Huh' *what*?" repeated Sam impatiently.

Jimmy looked at the image. "I can confirm your face is just above the thing. It's got writing on it that I can see from the side. Promatic? Hang on."

"Oh, I'm hanging," she said, anger masking her panic.

Jimmy googled on his phone. "I think it's safe."

"Safe how?" she said.

"Let's not be hasty," said Rich. "This thing could go off in our—" He snapped his mouth shut.

"Faces," said Sam. "You were going to say faces."

"Well, it isn't," Jimmy assured them.

"You sure?"

"It's a clay pigeon."

"A clay pigeon?"

"Yeah." He looked back to Shore View and thought of Jacinda and her dad. They probably weren't the only ones to have used this spot for some illicit shooting practice. He angled the phone to show her the picture he'd taken. It featured a large, unflattering profile of Sam's cheek and nose. The disc below had lettering around the centre: *Promatic*.

Sam took a deep breath. "Right, stand back, just in case."

"Are you absolutely sure?" said Rich. "Because it wouldn't be beyond credibility for a munitions manufacturer to make both mines and shooting equipment."

Sam straightened up, gasping with relief. She looked at the thing in the sand and blew gently on its surface. Jimmy could see the lettering clearly now. Sam pulled it out of the sand and scrambled to her feet, holding it high.

"It's all right everyone! Not a landmine!" She dropped the clay pigeon into one of the nearby black bags.

"You all right?" asked Jimmy.

"Never better," said Sam, stretching. Her face was white, though. It reminded Jimmy of Wayne's ghastly complexion.

"You know, you look like you could do with a drink," he said.

"Bit early for alcohol, isn't it?"

"I was thinking a cup of tea. But sure, whatever you fancy."

She gestured at the community payback group, who were slowly, reluctantly, getting to their feet. "I've got this lot to deal with."

"Their time's not up yet?" he said.

"Did you say our time was up?" Greg called down from the dunes.

"I did not!" Sam shouted back. She looked at Jimmy. "You seem to know that guy."

He shrugged. "Greg Mandyke. Builder. Semi-retired, I think."

"Really? He said he was allergic to cement dust."

"Is that so?" said Jimmy archly. "Almost as if he was trying to get out of doing his community service. And after the way he treated that customer."

She gave him a puzzled look.

"Over-charging for a simple extension and then – what's the phrase? – demanding money with menaces when they couldn't pay up."

Her mouth set in a hard line. "Is that so?"

"Oh, yes."

He watched her stomp back up the dunes. Jimmy returned to Shore View, cutting across the dunes at an angle. Jacinda stood at the edge of the levelled site, watching him with a fixed scowl.

"Got time to play on the beach?" she said sarcastically.

Jimmy returned her snide expression. "That," he said, pointing back, "is Sam Applewhite. She's the one you said was looking into that 'business' at Welton?"

Jacinda looked at the group on the sand. "And?"

"Maybe I'll go on the charm offensive and find out what she knows."

50

Greg was complaining loudly about something as Sam approached, but she didn't care anymore. She didn't care about him personally, and she'd had more than enough of the community payback session. She could legitimately end the day's activities when they got back to the car park. She would sign them all off and everyone could go home.

"He's got them!" Greg said, stabbing a finger in Ogendus Odinson's chest. "He's got my espadrilles!"

Ogendus contemplated the rope-soled shoes hanging casually from his fingertips. "Tha's sayin' they're yorn?"

"Obviously mine," snapped Greg and made to get them back.

Ogendus lifted them out of his reach with a casualness that masked his quick reflexes. "I don't see your name in them, Saxon."

"Because I'm not a six-year-old."

"Maybe you want to get them DNA tested. I say it's finders' keepers."

"You didn't find them."

"I found them on the beach."

"Where I'd put them!"

"Abandoned them, eh?"

Greg turned pleadingly to Sam. She didn't have the energy for this, and certainly had no sympathy for Greg Mandyke, but she did need to present herself as an authority figure. However, before she could speak, Rich cut in.

"If they had washed up on the shore, technically they could count as flotsam or jetsam."

"Aye," said Ogendus.

"I put them there with the intention of collecting them afterwards," said Greg.

"That's lagan, that is," said Sigurd.

The Odinsons behind him mumbled in agreement.

"Lagan?" said Greg.

"Lagan," said Ogendus.

"He's right," said Rich. "Although if you find any salvage you need to inform the Receiver of Wreck."

"That's a thing?" said Sam, who couldn't help but be caught up in the bizarre conversation.

"An' I was just about to do that very thing," said Ogendus. "Don't want a get fined for doing owt improper." He nodded deferentially at Sam.

"Would this cover Capitalist Whores?" asked Delia, waggling her haul.

"That it might," said Ogendus to much murmuring from his family.

"They're fucking Gucci's!" squealed Greg. "They cost five fucking hundred pounds!"

"An' the Receiver of Wreck can determine if they're yorn," said Ogendus.

"Can we go home now, please?" said Stacey.

Sam nodded. "Back to the car park."

Greg spasmed in confused rage. "Is no one going to help me get my espadrilles back?"

"Receiver of Wreck," said an Odinson simply.

"We'll sort it at the car park."

After the excitement of the morning, it was an uncomplicated pleasure to walk back along the beach to Wolla Bank.

"You gonna need a drink after today?" said Delia.

"I think I already had an offer from that builder back there," she said.

Delia glanced back. "The slightly hunky dark-haired one."

"If you say so."

Back at Wolla Bank car park, the bin bags of rubbish were put in the council dumpsters. It was an impressive haul of shoreline crap, be it flotsam, jetsam, or whatever dog-walkers and holidaymakers had thoughtlessly left behind. Delia emptied her haul into the boot of her own car. There was an animal cage on the folded down back seat.

"You taking those turkeys everywhere with you now?" said Sam.

"Twizzler's got a little limp. I was going to take him to the vet."

"He's probably just faking so you take pity on him and don't eat him for Christmas."

Sam signed off the hours for all the participants. Most of them she'd be seeing again to finish off the hours still owed. Greg Mandyke came to Sam demanding she resolve the espadrille problem, but even as he began speaking, she pointed out the Odinsons had vanished into the dunes, taking Greg's shoes with them.

"Police matter now," she said. "Try Sergeant Hackett at Skegness police station. Missing espadrilles will be right up his street. Assuming you can prove they're yours."

"How do you expect me to do that?"

"Like Cinderella," suggested Delia. "You know, but with espadrilles. If the shoe fits..."

Sam was struck by a curious thought. She still had the single trainer wrapped in a carrier bag in the back of her van. If local hospitals weren't going to help her in the search for a one-footed miscreant, maybe there was another way of finding out who the shoe belonged to.

"Which vet are you taking the turkeys to?" she called to Delia.

"Why?" said Delia, shutting her boot.

A white van pulled up onto the car park.

"Hunky builder alert."

Sam gave her a silly scowl and went over to the van as Jimmy wound down the window. "Forget something?" she said.

"That drink, perhaps?"

"Didn't our last drink together end awkwardly and really badly."

"Not *really* badly," he said. "And this is just a daytime 'settle your nerves after a traumatic experience' drink. We can still do a cup of tea. I know a place on the promenade that does the most disgusting hot chocolate and whipped cream combo."

"Astonishingly tempting."

"That's a yes."

"I've got an errand to run first," she said. "A crazy idea's just occurred to me."

"Not just fobbing me off?"

"No," she assured him. "After the morning I've had, a restorative hot chocolate sounds good. A nice quiet innocent drink. I've had enough drama and near death experiences for one day."

Her phone buzzed in her pocket. She took it out. It was the drone app.

"Battery depleted. Returning to base," she read. "Ah."

She looked round, wondering where the drone might be. And then it hit her.

51

W hile Delia drove her to the veterinary clinic in Hogsthorpe, Sam rubbed her temple again and detected the beginnings of a bump.

"Honestly, there's nothing there," said Delia. "Barely a scratch."

Sam made a doubtful noise. In the back of the car, the drone sat next to the cage, unsullied from where it had dive-bombed her. Twizzler the turkey made noises at the drone and strutted up and down in his cage. He was either trying to impress a would-be mate or ward off a rival. Either way he was going to be disappointed.

"Here," said Sam and pointed at the turning.

The vet's clinic was in a long low wooden building attached to stables, set between a rough paddock and a neatly laid out show-jumping arena.

"Man must have some money," said Delia.

"If people are willing to pay him to give their Christmas dinners a medical check-up..."

Sam helped Delia with the cage, walking it together through the front door of the clinic. The receptionist held the door for them to go through to the consulting room.

The vet, Sacha, looked up from his computer screen. He tucked a knitted tie into his shirt to put it out of the way.

"Ah, but this is Twizzler, yes?" he said and smiled at the two women. He had a dapper manner and perfectly combed hair to go with that crisp accent and the folksy country vet look he clearly cultivated. He flipped open the cage, scooped the bird out with ease and looked him over.

"He seemed to be limping," said Delia.

Sacha pulled an interested face and put Twizzler down on the examining table to watch him walk.

"Careful. He might run away," said Delia.

"Yes, but I have..." Sacha picked a pad of pink post-its from the side counter and put them on the table.

Twizzler tilted his head as he considered the post-its, then pecked at them. He ripped the top one off with his second peck and seemed most put out that there were more underneath.

"They are fascinated by bright colours," said Sacha, crouching to inspect the bird while it played. He poked Twizzler and forced the bird to take a few steps. As he did, he looked up at Sam. "I've met you before."

Sam had hoped he wouldn't recognise her. The situation hardly put her in a good light. Maybe he wouldn't remember the details.

"You fed carrot cake to a seal," said Sacha.

He did remember.

"Er, yes. That's me. I didn't do it on purpose."

"Yes, but fed it to him all the same." He stood, picked up and upended Twizzler to look at the base of his feet, and put him down again. "I could clip his claws if you like."

"Do they need clipping?" said Delia.

"No," smiled Sacha. "But it might make you feel better. There's nothing wrong with him and I'll be charging a consultation fee anyway."

"I didn't know if turkeys often had foot complaints."

"No. And not many turkey owners come to me with just one turkey." He played his fingertip around Twizzler's beak and the inquisitive bird tried to peck at him. "Handsome fellows like this usually only need to live long enough to put on some weight, ready for the oven. Is he a pet or is it a Christmas bird?"

"Um, I've not decided yet," said Delia.

Sam gave her an openly unimpressed look. "I knew it! You said you were buying him to eat..."

"He's so cute though," argued Delia.

"Yes, but what's important is that he's well cared for while he's alive," said Sacha.

"Er, speaking of feet," said Sam.

"Yes."

"Did you get called out to the alligators at Seal Land? I know the Seal Land guy, er Guy, said he was going to call you."

Sacha nodded slowly. "Don't tell me you had something to do with that too?"

"I was just curious. One of the alligators ate a foot, or at least part of a foot."

"So they say."

"I was just wondering how long it would take the foot to, er, pass through the alligator."

Sacha frowned at the unusual question.

"I wondered if the bones would turn up?" said Sam.

"In its faeces?"

"You want to root around in crocodile poo?" said Delia.

"Alligator," said Sacha and mimed an alligator jaw with both hands. "Different skulls and teeth. And no."

"No?" said Sam.

"An alligator's stomach acid is unbelievably powerful. Soft tissues are dissolved within hours. Bones are eventually reduced to nothing."

Delia gave Sam a disbelieving look. "Were you going to try to piece them together? Do a morbid Cinderella thing and go round looking for a man whose bones matched?"

"It was an idea. A theory."

"Stupid-ass theory," said Delia.

"I'm sorry," said Sacha. "If a man has his left foot bitten off by an alligator, it might take a week or more for it to be fully digested but, no, there will be nothing left after."

Sam shrugged and sighed.

Sacha picked up Twizzler and clipped the tips of his claws with a pair of nippers. The turkey made no complaints, only chirruped at the vet with curiosity.

"There," said the vet. "Good as new."

Sacha presented her with a couple of leaflets on poultry

care and held the door for them as Delia carried the cage back through to reception.

Sam paused halfway out the door. "You said left foot."

"Sorry?" said Sacha.

Sam gathered her thoughts. "You said … if a man has his left foot bitten off by an alligator…"

"Yes?"

"How did you know?"

"Jeez," said Delia, at the counter and looking through her purse for payment card. "Are you trying to do a Columbo on the vet?"

Sacha laughed. Sam didn't.

"You knew," she said.

"You must have said," smiled Sacha.

"No. I don't think so."

"Someone did."

"Only me and a police officer saw the shoe, and I don't think he was keen to share it with anyone."

"If you'll forgive me, I am quite busy."

Sam immediately felt silly. She was accusing the vet, and of what? Knowing it was a left trainer they had fished from the pool? Making a fifty-fifty guess or a blind assumption? And to what end? What did it matter if the vet knew? It clearly wasn't his foot.

She looked past him through the open door at the consultation room and the long steel table.

It was a fact that this place was close to Seal Land. That didn't mean anything in and of itself but if – *if* – one had suffered a traumatic foot injury in Seal Land and urgently needed to seek medical attention, one could do far worse than go to the nearest vet. Especially if one didn't wish to face the kinds of questions that would inevitably come from turning up at A&E with a foot missing. So, if someone had been involved in Mrs Skipworth's disappearance and then, for reasons entirely unclear, tangled with the nasty end of an alligator, one might indeed end up on that steel table.

"Was he a big man?" she said. "Was there a lot of blood?"

"You will have to forgive me, but I am very busy." Sacha closed the door between them.

He hadn't answered her question, but he didn't need to. In that moment before the door closed, she clearly saw it in his face. He wasn't confused, or angry. The vet was terrified.

"What the hell was that about?" said Delia.

"I don't know," said Sam.

52

Jimmy came over with two paper cups stacked high with squirty cream, chocolate flakes and sprinkles. He put them down on the circular metal table in front of the *Ice U Love* stall and took the other seat. The stall was at the junction of Tower Esplanade and the narrow promenade called North Bracing, nestling in the shadow of the tall lifeboat rescue building.

"That's your super-deluxe hot chocolate combo with two shots of mint chocolate Baileys liqueur and all the extras," said Jimmy.

"Hmmm?" said Sam, lost in thought.

"Super-deluxe hot chocolate combo with two shots of mint chocolate Baileys liqueur and all the extras."

"Sounds awful," she said absently, wondering how she could tackle the drink without having to eat all the cream off the top first.

"You okay?" he said. "That drone didn't give you concussion?"

She shook her head. The drone was in the back of the Piaggio, parked up next to Jimmy's van fifty yards away – big van, little van, like mother duck and duckling.

Sam took out a flake and used it as a spoon to eat the fluffy topping.

He gestured at her temple. "You've got a bump coming."

"I knew it!" she said. "But Delia insisted I didn't."

"That a work thing? The drone?"

She nodded. "Just testing it out and sending a report back to head office."

"Your company has its fingers in a lot of pies."

"Too many."

"But you've not got a big office."

"Nah, just me and Doug."

"So, how's your week been?" He tried to sip his own hot chocolate and got a big foamy cream moustache.

"Varied," she said. "It must be nice to have a simple job like building."

"Simple?" he said, eyebrows raised.

She backtracked. "I don't mean you're simple. And I don't mean it's easy either. I mean..." She sighed. "You build a house and there it is, a house. There's got to be some satisfaction in that."

"There used to be," he said. By his expression Sam guessed he'd said something he didn't mean to. His face shifted as he tried to compensate, and Sam realised with abrupt clarity there was a deep, deep fatigue in Jimmy's eyes that she hadn't seen the last time they'd met. It wasn't merely tiredness; it was the thousand yard stare of a man who had endured too much.

"Used to be?" she said softly.

"Bob Frost was an excellent boss," he said, the words spilling out. "He treated us as family. All of us. More of a dad to me than my own dad. He looked after us, made sure there was work for all of us."

"I hear he, uh—"

"Killed himself?" Jimmy nodded. "Too much robbing Peter to pay Paul. I think. He never said. Never confided in anyone. Maybe over-extended himself with the plans for Shore View."

"Oh, I thought you'd only just started building that. It's just a bunch of containers up there at the moment."

Jimmy wrapped his mouth around the dissolving cream and practically inhaled it. "Years of planning. The number of committees these things have to go through for a project of that size."

"Some containers on top of a dune?"

"Those containers will become homes," he said, his tone sharply defensive.

"Shipping container homes?"

"They've been doing it in London for a few years now. Stack 'em high, fill 'em with poor people who can't afford modern rents."

Sam had dug her way through the cream to the actual hot chocolate. She sipped. There was a sharply minty alcoholic kick to it. "I suppose the housing problem is as acute here as it is anywhere."

Jimmy grunted, amused. "They're not for locals. Not

these ones."

"Oh?"

"You set out to create a project like this – and there will be other sites if this a success – you need people all ready to move in. Councils – Doncaster, Scunthorpe, Leicester – they'll pay a chunk up front to get homeless benefit claimants out of their authority and into our container villages."

Sam was surprised, then wondered why she should be. Shipping the unwanted, the unemployed, out from the cities to the back end of nowhere was something the government had been doing since the Second World War. It was just Skegness's turn to be on the receiving end. "It's still homes for those who need them, I guess," she said.

"Anyway," said Jimmy, "you changed the subject. You were telling me about your week."

"Was I?"

He nodded. "What have you been up to?"

It felt like an oddly phrased question, clumsy. Sam couldn't work out why. "The usual."

"Wild seals in the back of your van..."

"Okay, not quite."

"No meals on wheels this week?"

"It's only one week in three."

"But you must get to know the old folks well."

"I'm probably one of the few friendly faces some of them get to see. Me and Karen."

"Who's Karen?"

"The regular meals on wheels lady."

"Karen who?"

Sam frowned. "Why do you want to know?"

"Wondered if I knew her."

Sam shook her head, unable to remember Karen's surname, and drank. The powerful minty liqueur got stronger the further down the cup she drank.

"No, no meals on wheels this week. No seals. Although I did end up chasing turkeys around a kitchen."

"A kitchen?"

"The wrong kitchen. It was meant to be Lavender Court, or Lavender Court House. Even now I can't remember which one. There were turkeys, plates got broken and then Mr Vamplew the owner..."

She tailed off. The name stuck in her brain. It was an odd surname for certain, but why it should suddenly chime with her wasn't clear. Vamplew.

"Edith Vamplew," she murmured.

"Sorry?" said Jimmy.

Sam could picture it now. Rows of boxes drawn on Mrs Skipworth's notepad with a name in each box. One of them had been Edith Vamplew, Sam remembered.

"Excuse me, I've got to google something," she said and pulled out her phone.

"No problem," said Jimmy, reflexively looking at his own phone. "Shit."

"What?"

He stared at the screen for a long time. "Problems. Loose ends."

53

Jacinda wouldn't discuss her problem on the phone, insisting Jimmy come out to the house. Another round trip to squeeze into Jimmy's shrinking day. The woman was unnecessarily needy. Between her and the increasingly impaired Wayne, Jimmy felt like the carer for a band of invalids. That left him no time to himself, and no time to find out what Sam knew.

A swing round to pick up Wayne—

"Yes, I'm taking you home later, and what are we not going to mention?"

"The alligator."

"Good."

"Or the tiger."

"Right. Or the tiger."

—and then straight down to the Frost house in Friskney.

Jacinda was, as always, in the office building out back. Jimmy couldn't hear shooting this time. That didn't necessarily mean the encounter would go any better. He left Wayne in the van and went indoors.

Jacinda sat at the desk. To one side was a map of the Lincolnshire coastline, with Shore View and the other proposed container village sites marked on it. On top of that, splayed across the desk, were a number of postcards filled with dense, neat writing. Jacinda murmured to herself, fingertips on the postcards. She didn't look up as Jimmy approached.

"You said it was urgent," he said.

She ignored him and continued her almost inaudible reading.

"Did you want me?" he said, pointedly.

"I'm going over my acceptance speech," she said. "Businessperson of the year awards tomorrow. I have delegations from Nottingham and Doncaster City Councils to show round Shore View the day after. I am under a lot of stress."

"Sure," he said.

Jacinda cleared her throat as though summoning energies from deep within. "Five days ago there was a conversation which never took place."

"Eh?"

"And during that conversation you said no one saw you kill the woman and that you left no trace."

"Right, is this about that woman? Sam? Because I was actually talking to her when you called. She's just being nosy. She's not police. She's not been given authority to investigate—"

"She was at Sacha's clinic in Hogsthorpe, asking if he'd

treated a man who'd had his foot bitten off."

"How the fuck...?"

"You said she knew nothing!"

"There's nothing for her to know!"

"That's not the worst of it!" Jacinda shouted, pushing herself to her feet. "Sacha is suddenly fearing for his livelihood and reputation. He's thinking of going to the police and confessing his part in things!"

"Did he say he was?"

"He intimated as much."

Jimmy shook his head. "What does that mean? Did he say it? Did he say, 'I'm going to go to the police and tell them what happened'?"

"You think we can risk that?" In fury, she pushed her speech cards away. Maybe she expected them to fly up in a dramatic cloud, but they simply tumbled along the desk like breeze-blown leaves. "This can't come back to me!"

"It won't," he said.

"Oh, really?" Her mouth twisted like she had a bad taste in it. "Why did I trust you? You're just a fucking brickie!"

"Trust me?" he said and stepped back as though wounded. "Why did I end up working for a brainless girl who only runs this building company because her dad was stupid enough to top himself without making sure the right person was put in charge!"

That hurt. He could see it in her eyes. That fucking cut her deep. And it felt good.

"How dare you!" she snarled.

"I fucking dare because even though we are going to get away with this, if there is a sliver of a chance the old woman's death is going to be pinned on me, I will make sure you go down with me!" Thinking on his feet, he pulled his phone from his pocket. "You think I haven't been recording every one of these little conversations that supposedly hasn't happened? Huh? Fucking stupid bitch."

She stared at the phone. She had eyes like a doll, huge and lifeless. A Capitalist fucking Whore.

"We are wedded together," he said. "In this and everything else. I'm your bloody partner now. For better or worse."

She was silent for a long moment. "We need to salvage this situation," she said eventually, quietly.

Seething with residual rage, Jimmy nodded.

"We need to silence any potential leaks," she said.

He nodded again.

Jacinda raised three fingers and ticked them off. "Sacha. We can't risk him going to the police."

"Agreed. I'll talk to him."

"'Talk to him'? Is that code for something."

"What? No. I can talk to him. Make him reconsider."

Jacinda ticked another finger. "Sam Applewhite."

"We don't know what she knows."

"But she clearly knows too much."

Jimmy looked at the third finger and blinked.

"Wayne," said Jacinda.

"Really?"

"You think we can ever let that one-legged pillock go back to his mum, that we can rely on him to keep his mouth shut."

Jimmy pressed his lips together. Cold Jimmy stirred at the back of his mind. Out of all three of the potential problems,

Wayne was the most unpredictable. Besides, Jimmy had no love for him. Any residual sympathy or friendship he'd had for the man had been washed away by prolonged exposure to his injury and his stupidity. Wayne was like a wounded dog; it'd be kinder to put him down. Jimmy looked at the shotgun with Cold Jimmy's eyes.

"But Sacha first," said Jacinda.

Jimmy nodded slowly. If the worst situation arose, Jimmy would have to kill all three of them. But he didn't have to kill them all himself. He could get Wayne to off the vet. Sacha could put Wayne out of his misery. Dominos.

"We'll do it tonight," he said.

54

It was dark by the time Jimmy pulled up outside Sacha's place in Hogsthorpe, but the lights were on and there was only one vehicle in the parking bay. He placed a phone in the big man's hand. Wayne's hands had that sickly infected look now.

"Now, you stay here. If I need your help to put the frighteners on Sacha, I will call you."

"And I'll come in."

"If I call you."

"Is he going to have a look at my leg?"

"Does he need to? Does it hurt?"

Wayne shook his fat head, the action sending waves of sweaty, diseased, unwashed stink rolling off the man. "It doesn't hurt. It's more like I can't feel it all that well."

"Yeah? What do you mean?"

"It's not just my leg, it's my other leg and all over. I think

Sacha gave me superpowers. I feel really light. I'm sure I could fly if I jumped off something high up."

"I don't think so, mate," said Jimmy. He leaned over and pinched the flesh at the top of Wayne's leg. Wayne didn't react at all, just carried on gazing out of the windscreen into the distance. He considered the notion that if Wayne died from a raging infection there would be no need to kill him. Jimmy wasn't sure if that was a relief or a disappointment.

"You come if I call you," he said.

He got out and crossed to the clinic. A lamp over the doorway created a cone of light in the dark. Jimmy pressed the doorbell. Soon, he saw movement through the frosted glass and Sacha opened the door.

"Jimmy?" he said, the surprise in his voice unmistakeable. Was his guard up? "What are you doing here?"

"We need to talk."

"Yes, but is this about—?" He stopped and looked past Jimmy. "Wayne, my man. You don't look well."

Wayne was hobbling at speed from the van.

"I told you to wait," said Jimmy.

"And I told you to go to A&E if things got worse," said Sacha.

"Got worse?" said Wayne.

"Him?" said Jimmy, thinking fast. "No, he's fine. I just think maybe the brace needs a bit of an adjustment. It's a bit, er, wobbly. It's those spring clasps."

Sacha sighed loudly. "Yes, they were always a problem." He looked from Wayne to Jimmy. "Come in. Yes, but only for five minutes."

As they followed the vet inside, Jimmy whispered to Wayne. "I told you to wait."

"I'm fine."

"But probably best if you don't mention your 'superpowers' to him, yeah? We don't want him to take them away, do we?"

"No!" said Wayne, horrified. "He wouldn't do that, would he?"

Sacha led them through to his surgery. "Come on, sit on the table where I can have a proper look."

Wayne hoisted himself up onto the steel table without assistance. The man thought he was weightless and clearly there was something in that mind over matter mantra.

Sacha bent to inspect the leg. "Oh my God. What on earth have you two been doing?"

Wayne was filthy dirty from adventures in ghost trains, seal sanctuaries and from sleeping rough. His skin glistened with an unhealthy sheen from what Jimmy suspected was an infection. His leg brace had become remodelled into a very different shape from when Sacha had fastened it on.

Sacha began to take his vitals: an electronic thermometer in Wayne's ear, listening to his chest with a stethoscope. "It doesn't look good at all."

"You spoke to Jacinda today," said Jimmy.

Sacha hesitated for just a moment. "Yes, but only to tell her that Miss Applewhite had come asking questions."

"Sam Applewhite knows nothing."

"She's got Wayne's missing trainer."

"My Yeezys?" said Wayne, excited. "Have you got it?"

"Er, no, Wayne." Sacha looked pointedly at Wayne's missing foot. "But even if she did..."

"You don't need to worry about Sam Applewhite," said Jimmy.

"Yes, but I do," said Sacha. "You are running a very high temperature, Wayne."

"I feel fine," said Wayne.

"You might be tempted to ... go to the police," continued Jimmy.

No hesitation from Sacha this time, but the formality of his movements as he listened to Wayne's chest and then assessed his leg betrayed his nervousness. "And if I went to the police?" he said lightly.

"That would be a really bad idea," said Jimmy.

Sacha nodded. He squeezed Wayne's leg through the hoof brace and dressings. "Does that hurt, Wayne?"

"No," said Wayne cheerily.

Sacha applied more pressure with his thumbs. "Now?"

"Nope."

Sacha dug his thumbs right in and pressed violently, like he was trying to break into an uncooperative orange peel. Fluid seeped through Wayne's dressing. A viscous pus, the colour and consistency of runny custard.

"I think I'm healed," said Wayne.

Sacha swore softly in the language of whatever long-lost country he had originally come from. "Yes, but if the police come knocking at my door?" he said to Jimmy without looking round. "With a brace designed for a horse attached to the leg of a man who should have gone to the hospital last week? It is a big clue, no? Damning evidence?"

"Is that what you're worried about?" asked Jimmy.

The vet tapped the leg brace with his fingernails. "This is a smoking gun."

"And that's the only worry you have?"

Sacha stood and faced Jimmy. "Yes, but I also have expenses that need paying."

Jimmy smirked. "You want paying off?"

"A one-off payment," Sacha assured him. "Thousands. Not tens of thousands. Unless your Wayne is covered by pet insurance."

Jimmy weighed it up and nodded. "That sounds very reasonable."

"Yes, it is," said Sacha. He turned back to Wayne. "Right, my man. I am going to need to take this brace off you."

"My bionic leg?" said Wayne.

"It is broken. Uncomfortable." He reached for the clasps binding it to Wayne's lower leg. "It will need to come off if I'm to make you all better."

Wayne batted Sacha's hands away. "I don't want to."

"All better soon," said the vet.

Wayne's meaty hands grabbed Sacha and hauled himself up. "You said he wouldn't take my superpowers, Jimmy!"

Sacha pulled back automatically. Wayne, refusing to relinquish, dragged him into a furious bear hug that lifted him up and onto the table. "You. Are. Not. Taking. My. Powers!" Wayne grunted as he squeezed. Sacha wriggled and kicked. A flailing foot caught a half-open drawer and medical utensils flew up and out in a shower.

"Gentlemen! Gentlemen!" Jimmy shouted, trying to restore order.

Seriously ill or not, Wayne was slowly squeezing the breath and life from Sacha. In response, the vet's hand had found a scalpel that had fallen on the table surface. He jabbed it down into Wayne's thigh. Wayne didn't even notice. Swearing violently, Sacha reversed it in his hand and stabbed at Wayne overhand. By chance, it found Wayne's eye. Apparently, Wayne still had some feeling in his eyeball. He let go of Sacha as he clutched at his injured face.

Sacha leapt back, half propelled by Wayne's jerking motion, somehow landing on his feet. There was a desperate, terrified and energized look to his face. He swung the scalpel – his hand dripping with blood and eyeball juices – swung the scalpel back and forth between Jimmy and Wayne.

"Madmen. Madmen," he panted.

"Easy, Sacha," said Jimmy. "Let's not get upset..."

"Jimmy," Wayne keened softly, hands cupped to his ruptured eyeball as though trying to catch falling tears.

"Upset?" Sacha jabbed at Jimmy to force him back. "Madmen. I *am* going to the police."

"You can't go to the police," said Jimmy. "You are in as much trouble as—"

"Yes, but I will confess my part!"

Jimmy lunged for Sacha, tried to grab the scalpel. Sacha swung. How he missed Jimmy's fingers, Jimmy couldn't tell. The two of them collided, bounced against one counter and then another. There was a high pitched squeak as Sacha's foot slid in eyeball fluid. Together they toppled.

"I think I need to go to a hospital," Wayne whimpered.

Jimmy and Sacha rolled, Jimmy ending up on top. The scalpel slid away from Sacha's hand. The vet battered at

Jimmy. They were of similar sizes, but a lifetime of poking pet hamsters and sticking hands up horses' bums did not compare with a life of physical labour. Besides, it was Cold Jimmy in charge now. Cold Jimmy swatted Sacha's blows away and reached for something with which to end the treacherous man.

His eyes fell on that weird gizmo of steel and plastic. Eighteen inches of pointed steel. The horse-inseminating gun. Cold Jimmy picked it up, assessing its potential as a murder weapon. It was heavier than it looked.

Sacha saw the intent in Jimmy's face. "Wait! I'll not tell—"

"Not up to me anymore," said Jimmy.

He hefted the strange tool. With a double-handed overarm strike he plunged the length of it into Sacha's open mouth. Sacha gurgled in shock and pain. Jimmy angled it upwards. The little TV screen on the device was on. Jimmy sought out the soft palate at the roof of his mouth and brought all of his weight down on the gun.

Sacha's gurgle briefly shot up in pitch as Jimmy pushed harder. He felt the steel rod crunch through layers of bone, cartilage or whatever he had penetrated until its entire length was buried up to the trigger hand. A rasp escaped Sacha's throat, then he was silent.

"Wow, look at that," said Wayne.

Above him, Wayne (ruined eye still cupped by a hand) stared down over the edge of Sacha's table at the little television screen. It showed a scene of gloopy mess, white and red and grey.

"It's his brain," said Jimmy.

"Can you see what he's thinking?" said Wayne.

Jimmy didn't know whether to laugh or vomit. He opted for both. "Great," he murmured once he'd regained control of himself.

"Can we fix my eye now?" said Wayne.

"Yeah, sure."

Jimmy looked round at the mess they'd made of the place. Blood, bodily fluids, equipment. It couldn't look more like a fistfight in a surgical theatre if he tried. At least all the mess would be taken care of when he torched the place, he decided.

He wiped his mouth with the back of his hand and looked round for some accelerant. He went outside to check out the other small buildings between the clinic and the stables. He was looking for cannisters of gas or cans of diesel. He was certain Sacha would have one or the other, being out here in the sticks. He paused outside a metallic shelter. At first glance the contents were unpromising, nothing but a large machine of some sort, but he went inside to check it out and flicked on the lights.

The machine was essentially a large container with a pulldown hood over it. It had an enamel badge on the front declaring it was a HELIOS 5000. A separate badge directly below said DEFRA APPROVED. There were some other controls, including a timer and a temperature setting.

"Temperature..." Jimmy looked at the large chimney that went up through the roof of the shelter and smiled. "Oh, this is perfect."

He hurried back into the clinic, where Wayne was still watching the live transmission from inside Sacha's skull case.

"We doing my eye now, Jimmy?"

"Yeah." He searched cupboards until he came up with a roll of bandages. "Here," he said and began to wrap the bandages around Wayne's head like an eye patch. "Just pop ... pop that bit of your eye back in and ... yeah, that's it."

Jimmy wrapped it round a half dozen times to hold it in place.

"Will I get a bionic eye too?" asked Wayne.

"Later, mate." Jimmy indicated Sacha's body. "Can you help me with this first?"

"Sure." Wayne climbed down from the table. He looked a little shaky, but Jimmy steadied him.

Jimmy pointed at the horse inseminator. "We need to pull this out first of all."

Wayne grasped the trigger and pulled. "Pe-yow! Oh, hey...!"

On the screen the video feed showed something cream-coloured mingling with the gore on screen. Jimmy wished he could unsee it.

"I just spunked in his brain," said Wayne, awestruck.

Jimmy helped Wayne pull the gun out from Sacha's mouth. It gave a long sucking slurp as it emerged, inevitably followed by gushes of blood pouring over the dead vet's chin and onto the floor. More cleaning up.

"Can you pick him up?" said Jimmy. "We need to take him somewhere."

Wayne bent over and plucked Sacha off the floor. "Here we go Sacha," he said conversationally to the corpse.

Jimmy led him out and across to the shelter. It took him a moment to work out how to open the hood. He spotted a hoist above it, understanding why it was designed like that.

"What is it?" asked Wayne, nodding at the machine.

"It's an animal incinerator," said Jimmy. "I reckon you can get a whole horse in here, so this should be a doddle."

Wayne dropped Sacha inside and Jimmy shut the hood. He studied the controls. There was a timer. Was an hour enough? The temptation to google for an answer was powerful, but it didn't do to leave traces of your presence all over the internet.

55

Marvin brought dinner to Sam in the living room.

"Is it your turn to cook?" she asked.

"Do we have a rota?" he said with a shrug. "You look busy."

She had, she realised, been sitting with a laptop in front of her ever since she'd returned home in the late afternoon. And now the sky was dark and the local evening news was on the TV.

"Sorry. Miles away." She looked up but couldn't see over the tray. "What is it?"

"In honour of your day at the beach," Marvin declared and put the tray on the settee next to her. Toasted cheese sandwiches, a circular formation of them around a mound of salad.

"*Sand*wiches," she said. "Side-splitting. You should have had a stage career with material like that."

"If only," he sighed. He positioned himself on the settee on the opposite side of the tray and took one of the toasted sandwiches.

"Did you know that E-type Jags can go for fifty thousand, even if they've not been serviced?" she said.

"Is that what you've been doing all evening?" he said. "Looking at how much money you'd get for my car?"

"How much money *you'd* get."

"I'm not selling it."

"You said you would."

"In my own sweet time."

She could feel the argument brewing and consciously stopped herself. "I was just looking. I've not been doing it all evening. No, I was frustrated by this other thing."

"What thing?" said Marvin.

"Edith Vamplew."

"Nice name."

"Except I don't think she exists." She looked at her dad. He was watching her, probably watching the cogs go round in her brain (or perhaps wondering why she had a swollen bump on her forehead). Sam closed her laptop and swivelled round to face him. "A customer of mine... She's gone missing."

"Did you personally lose her? Like an escaped prisoner?"

"Nothing like that," she said, "and we call prisoners 'service users', not customers. This is just a meals on wheels customer who vanished in the night. There was this list of names in boxes, in rows, on a notepad, and it went missing too. And I've remembered one of the names, only because I did a house check for a man with the same surname. Edith Vamplew."

"The man was called Edith?"

"The name in the box."

"Sounds quite an old name," said Marvin.

"Maybe." Sam took a bite of sandwich and was surprised. It was easy to forget how delicious hot melted cheese could taste. "Mmmm. If she's old that would explain why I can't Google her. No Edith Vamplew on Facebook."

"We older people aren't into your Facebook stuff."

"There's nothing but old people on Facebook," Sam countered. "Young people wouldn't touch it with a bargepole. Soon be more dead people than living on Facebook."

"Is that so?"

Sam took another bite. "She doesn't come up in searches for local news stories. Which is odd. All you have to do round here is attend a charity event or jumble sale, and they'll have your face and name in the Skegness Standard."

"Have you tried looking her up in the telephone directory?" he suggested.

"When did you last see a telephone directory, dad?"

He munched on his toasted sandwich and thought. "It's been a while since we've had a Yellow Pages delivered, too."

Sam gave him a look. "I think they stopped printing those years ago."

"Is that so?"

She sat back in the settee cushions. "Maybe I remembered her name wrong..."

"Of course, there is another avenue of enquiry," said Marvin.

"Yes?"

"Vamplew's an unusual name, isn't it?"

"Mmm-hmm."

"And you say you met a man called Vamplew."

"Ah."

"You could just – gosh, I dunno – go and speak to an actual human being."

"Ask him," she said.

"Might be his aunt or his cousin or..."

Sam looked at the time. Too late to be making house calls now. "That's actually a very sensible idea, dad."

"I have them from time to time."

Sam looked at her schedule for the following day. It looked pleasantly light and definitely had enough gaps to allow her to visit Mr Vamplew.

"It's a good plan," she said and ate the final toasted sandwich. She needed a fork for the salad and her dad had neglected to bring cutlery through. She pushed herself off the settee to go to the kitchen. "Cup of tea?"

"Sounds smashing," he said.

She made for the kitchen for cuppas and cutlery. "I'm just going to take a photo of the car too," she called back.

"I'm not selling it," Marvin replied.

"Just for valuation purposes."

The garage was attached to the side of the house. A stubby branching off from the long and winding bungalow. It was accessible through an unutilised utility room: a sort of twin-tub graveyard where household appliances went to die. It was a room Sam had yet to tackle in her zeal to sort out the house and she had to squeeze through a minor maze of clothes horses, defunct hoovers and old mops before reaching the garage door.

"I said..." Marvin called after her, loudly.

Neatly avoiding putting her foot in a Vileda Super Mop bucket, she reached the far door, unlocked it and felt around for the garage's light switch. The strip light inside flickered as Marvin pushed and shoved his own way through the utility space behind her.

The garage, built in an age when cars were narrower and apparently in need of a room to call their own, was a dusty space with large wooden folding doors she assumed hadn't been opened in a decade. Brick dust and cobwebs and ancient oil spills covered the floor. The garage was otherwise empty.

Marvin stood in the doorway next to her.

"The car," she said. "It's gone."

Marvin nodded. "Sold it two years ago," he said quietly.

"But..."

He patted her arm. "As you said, I needed the money. Bills to pay."

"Oh, dad." Sam stared at empty floor.

Marvin turned away. "Come on. Your salad's getting cold."

56

T hank you for buying the Helios 5000 top-loading high capacity incinerator with integral secondary chamber. The Helios 5000 is DEFRA 'Type Approved' and conforms to EU safety regulations (142/2011). The arched lid and low-level loading bed make this model ideal for equine or bovine cremation, or for multiple medium-sized pet carcasses.

Jimmy turned the instruction leaflet over. "No indication of cooking times for people," he noted irritably.

"Whack it on high," suggested Wayne.

Jimmy turned the oven up to maximum. His hand paused over the start button. "There's room for at least another person in there," he said.

"What?" said Wayne.

"We could put Mrs Skipworth in there too."

"Be nice," said Wayne. "Company."

It was hard to be sure with Wayne, but Jimmy thought his mental faculties were definitely deteriorating.

"We would clean up the evidence in the clinic," he mused out loud. "Then we could collect the old lady from the ghost train."

"Won't it be closed for the night?" said Wayne.

"That's sort of the point," said Jimmy.

Jimmy spent half an hour cleaning the clinic rooms. This was made all the easier by there being mops, buckets, bleach cleaners and handwipes aplenty. By nine, they were in the van and on the road back to Skeg.

Jimmy parked on Scarborough Esplanade and walked past the entrance to the funfair. The gates were closed. Everything was dark and silent. The nearest signs of life were from the burger drive-thru up by the main road. The locks on the fairground gates looked formidable, and there were at least two CCTV camera looking down on from on high.

Jimmy could see the ghost train from the fairground gate. It was secured with a padlock on a fairly lightweight hasp. Wayne would have that off in seconds with a crowbar. Jimmy sniffed the air. Could he smell the decomposing body from out here? He thought perhaps he could. It was definitely time to sort it out. Jimmy reckoned they could use the van to block the CCTV overlooking the site. If they moved quickly there was a good chance they could be away without anyone bothering to check.

"Spooky out here, isn't it?" said Wayne at his shoulder.

"Christ!" Jimmy hissed. How was it possible for a one-eyed, one-legged man to sneak up on him?

Jimmy moved along the bar and retail units surrounding the fairground until he came to a tattoo parlour. It was one of the row's few unshuttered premises. Maybe they thought they had nothing worth stealing.

"There," he said, pointing.

"We getting tattoos?" said Wayne.

Jimmy tutted. "The shop has two entrances. One this side, and one in the fairground. And—" he gave the place a cursory glance. "—no burglar alarm. We can sneak through and bypass the main gate. Get a crowbar. And the roll of bin bags."

Jimmy's housebreaking skills were crude but effective: punching out enough of the glass door to gain entrance, then repeating at the back.

"I could get an alligator tattoo on my leg," said Wayne as they moved through the darkness. "Or a tiger."

"Shush," said Jimmy.

"I don't remember the tiger all too clear anymore. Was there a tiger?"

Jimmy ignored his ramblings and led the way through the dark and silent fairground, up to the locked ghost train.

"We need to get that padlock off so we can go and get Mrs Skipworth," said Jimmy, handing the crowbar to Wayne. He held it gleefully, but staggered back and forth a few times, waggling it ineffectually. He looked as if he was having problems focusing on the doors, never mind the padlock. Eventually, he had it inserted it at the back of the hasp. He pulled down and snapped it away from the door, bringing chunks of part-rotten wood away with it. He grinned at this minor achievement.

Jimmy turned on his phone torch.

They soon found Mrs Skipworth. As the light hit her body, a cloud of flies rose up.

"Wayne, do you reckon you can fit her into these bags?" Jimmy asked, opening the first bin bag wide.

"Sure, Jimmy."

Jimmy held the light. It didn't matter if he looked or not. The sounds of squelching, dragging and crunching were unavoidable.

"Something went on my hand, Jimmy!" complained Wayne.

"Never mind," said Jimmy. "Get it in there."

Wayne folded and stuffed. Jimmy unspooled a second bag to get the feet end.

The corpse was tidied away into the bag, leaving only a broad, glistening stain, with some unidentifiable, gloopy fragments on it.

Wayne picked up the bag and lumbered out of the ghost train. Jimmy steered him towards and through the tattoo parlour, trying to stay upwind of both the corpse and Wayne. They loaded the bag into the van without incident.

As they drove away, Jimmy wound down the window. The smell was overpowering, and he knew it would linger in the van for days. He wondered if he could create a worse smell to mask it. If he got Wayne to soil himself, maybe? No, that wouldn't be bad enough. If he could get hold of a skunk with halitosis, feed it kippers and laxatives for a week before having its anal glands squeezed in the back of the van, it still wouldn't be enough.

Jimmy's conscious mind retreated and let Cold Jimmy

take over. Cold Jimmy didn't mind the smells. He was too far down in the dark to notice them.

Cold Jimmy drove them back to Hogsthorpe, an eye on the wing mirrors at all times just in case, for some inexplicable reason, the police were onto them. He slowed as he neared Sacha's clinic, checking to see there were no more vehicles parked up there before turning in and driving round to the shelter out back.

"Let's get her loaded in," said Jimmy.

"Right-o, Jimmy," said Wayne.

Jimmy opened all of the doors of the van wide to let the smell out, while Wayne carried the bag into the shelter.

Jimmy raised the hood of the Helios 5000. Sacha was still there, which was both comforting and horribly unnerving at the same time. Sacha's mouth and eyes were wide. Messy red blood coated his lips, like he'd been surprised in the act of eating a jar of strawberry jam.

"Pop her in where there's space," said Jimmy, with a vague wave of his hand.

Wayne placed the wrapped corpse on the oven bed. "Lots of room in here for both of you," he said, cheerily.

"You want to jump in with them?" said Jimmy, offhand, wondering if Wayne was so delirious he might even consider it.

Wayne wobbled, a grin on his sweating face. "Good one, Jimmy."

"Yeah." Jimmy fastened the door closed and set the controls. Full heat, four hours. That'd be enough.

57

F riday morning. After a team briefing with Doug in the DefCon4 office, Sam decided to pick his brains over the thorny issue of her dad's finances.

"It's not as if I really know why he's got these money problems," she said. "I can see his incomings and outgoings. His investments and pensions just aren't covering the bills and repayments. Maybe he was mis-sold payment protection insurance."

Doug Fredericks, being a cactus, considered this stoically and didn't hurry to give an opinion.

"Got caught in some BitCoin scam?" she said. "Made friends with the wrong Nigerian prince?" Sam shook her head. "I always assumed he was too clever to fall for that kind of thing."

Doug said nothing.

"But the thing is, am I actually damaging our relationship

by sticking my nose in? He's getting on a bit, but maybe he can make decisions for himself still? What do you reckon?"

Sam's mobile rang. It was Delia.

"Good talk," she said to Doug and answered the call. "DefCon4, clown control and mine-clearing our speciality."

"Oh, good, I hope you can help me," said Delia deadpan. *"I've got some out of control clowns down here."*

"Fancy French ones with conical hats, or nightmare grinning ones with red noses?"

"Does it matter?"

"Different rates for different clowns."

Delia broke first and laughed. *"I assume you're not having a very busy day."*

"A shocking accusation. I have written a detailed report on the effectiveness of the drone tests, and later on I am going to represent the company at a local awards ceremony."

"Ah, yes, I wanted to ask you about that."

Sam noted Delia's tone. "You don't want to go?" she asked. "We only signed you up a few days ago."

"I just— I just don't know if I fit in. Is it going to be glitzy affair?"

"Glitzy? This is Skegness. All we do is superficial shine." Sam sat back in her chair and stretched. "You think you don't fit in? It's not the Oscars. It's not even Crufts. It's a bunch of caravan salesmen and pub landlords making an excuse to get togged up in their finest, eat vol au vents, quaff cheap fizz, and pretend they're business moguls."

"Yeah. Yeah, you're right."

"Good," said Sam firmly. "Cos you'd better bloody go since I voted for you."

"*Did you?*" said Delia in squeaky delight. "*Oh, I'll get my best frock on then.*"

"I said I voted for you. Not sure anyone else even knows who you are."

"*Yeah, but yours is the vote that counts.*"

"Don't think that's how democracy works…"

There was a distant ding on the line. "*Customer's come in. Look, I'll see you later. Can I come round yours so we can go in together?*"

"Sure," said Sam.

"*Gotta go.*"

The line went dead. Sam pretended to put the phone down on an old-fashioned receiver and gazed at Doug for a long moment.

"Gonna go out and find this Edith Vamplew," she said. "Let's see if she knows what happened to Wendy Skipworth. Or the one-legged man."

She felt as if she was trying to convince herself, that she was following clues to a mystery no one wanted solving and which, theoretically, wasn't a mystery at all. Nonetheless, with only mindless paperwork (written in DefCon4's byzantine corporate-speak) to otherwise occupy her, she found it very easy to summon the energy to leave the office and seek out Mr Vamplew at Lavender Court (or possibly Lavender Court House).

She found the right house on the second attempt. The door was once again answered by the disinterested teen in headphones.

"Yeah?"

"Hi," she said. "You might recall. I was here before. I was with the woman who took the turkeys. I spoke to your dad."

"Yeah, they've gone," he said.

"The turkeys?"

"Them too. I meant my folks. Out."

"Oh," said Sam. "I was hoping to ask your dad about the Vamplews."

"That's us," said the teen.

"Yes, I gather. And there aren't many of you."

"No. It's a stupid ass name."

"I don't know. It's got 'Vamp' in it. That's a bit..." She made a spooky noise. "Isn't it?"

"Do I look like an emo or goth to you?" said the teen.

Sam did not consider herself to be an old adult. She was only thirty. On optimistic days, she'd even describe herself as a young adult. But she wasn't up to date with teen trends. To her eyes, the lad looked at least a bit goth-ish, a tiny bit emo-ey. She had hoped to speak to a Vamplew with more gumption, but if he was the only Vamplew on hand... "I'm trying to locate an Edith Vamplew."

The lad nodded, then shook his head. "Nope."

"No aunts or cousins?"

He shook his head slowly, his fringe swaying.

"Maybe a grandma?"

"I've only got two."

"Right. Right. It's not a very common name. Edith. Probably an old person's name."

"My sister's kid's friend is an Edith. In fact, I think she knows two."

"A child?"

"A toddler."

Sam was surprised but, she supposed, the old names did circle round, find new life. She thought about the names in the boxes. Could they be baby names? But why?

"I suspect this Edith is going to be an older person," she said.

"Sorry," said the teen Vamplew. "I reckon any old Ediths are long dead. Dead and buried."

"Right," she said. Then, struck by a thought as powerful as a physical blow, exclaimed, "Sam Applewhite, you are an idiot!"

"What?" said the teen.

Names in boxes. Neat rows. Dead and buried. Sam could have slapped herself at her stupidity but narrowly decided against it.

"Applewhite?" the teen was saying. "Like the magician guy?"

Sam was already nodding when she remembered to frown. "How do you know about Marvin Applewhite? He stopped being famous before you were born."

"Nah, the old guy from the YouTube videos. Does that close-up magic stuff. My mate says he lives round here."

"He's my dad."

"Cool," said the teen, though without much enthusiasm. "Know any tricks, then?"

"A couple," she said. "Right now, I'm going to ask the dead to help me solve a missing persons case."

"You're weird."

Sam took that as a compliment and left to fetch her van.

58

Jimmy learned a lot about cremation from his first personal experience of it.

Four hours on full heat was definitely enough to cremate an inconvenient old biddy and an untrustworthy vet. But that was just the cremation. They had to hang around for another couple of hours, in the near silence of the shelter, for the remains to cool enough for them to be handled. The remains, on what Jimmy thought of as the oven tray, weren't a small and convenient pile of ashes. They were a collection of mostly fragmented bones, laid out in the approximate shape of two sloppily intertwined human beings.

Wayne had advocated sticking the oven back on for a few more hours, but Jimmy suspected this was as good as it was going to get. The charred bones had the colour of cremation ash. Maybe, in the proper crematoriums, this was how ashes started out. Maybe the undertaker had to smash them up.

Maybe the undertaker had a special food blender or smoothie maker for turning bones into ash.

Jimmy found a shovel outside along with a horse-feed sack. Together, he and Wayne scooped the remains into the sack. Jimmy noted the largest fragment of skull, a curved smooth piece of bone. He had no way of knowing if it was Sacha's or Mrs Skipworth's, but he was struck by how thin the bone was, and touched by an almost satisfying thought that, with skulls so thin, it was no wonder people died easily, and they really had no one to blame but themselves.

The bag of remains was heavier than he'd expected, a good ten pounds or more of bones. But it was a damned sight less stinky, and far more transportable, than Mrs Skipworth's manky corpse had been.

With dawn more than an hour or two away, they made their way back to the van with their still-warm spoils. Jimmy checked the clinic rooms one last time to make sure his clean up job was good enough, trying to make the place look like Sacha had simply tidied up and left for the evening.

Sacha's car keys were in his coat by the door. Jimmy put the coat in the car and drove it round the back of the stables. It was hardly hidden, but it gave the superficial impression Sacha had left the premises. Only then did he climb in the van with Wayne and declare they were done.

"We gonna scatter the ashes then?" Wayne asked.

"Not when they're like that," Jimmy replied. "But I need some shut-eye first. Then we'll get them sorted."

Hours later, Jimmy woke in the Shore View container house, the one with actual proper windows and doors, rather than the fake ones adorning all the other containers. His clothes stank like a bonfire. Ash stained his trouser legs.

He looked across and saw Wayne laid out on a bed of fibreglass rolls. The big man was pale and perfectly still. Jimmy watched his chest for signs of movement, hopeful that he had stopped breathing; that he had succumbed to his injuries in the night. Jimmy watched him for a long time and couldn't be sure. It suddenly became very important to Jimmy. Rather than going over and prodding the fat lump to see if he would wake, Jimmy lay quite still, lining up the curve of Wayne's belly with a seam in the plasterwork and trying to assess if it was moving.

Jimmy didn't know how long he had lain like that, observing, measuring, when Wayne spoke.

"If you had a bionic eye, would you want it to be a real eye?"

"What?" said Jimmy.

"A bionic eye. Would you want it to look like your real eye? Or would you want it to be like a robot eye, like the Terminator?" Wayne turned his head to look at Jimmy. The dressing Jimmy had wrapped around Wayne's head and ruptured eye was now stained light brown with dried blood.

"You could have whatever you wanted," said Jimmy.

"Yeah, but I was just thinking."

"Sure." Jimmy sat up. "You want breakfast?"

Wayne shook his head, his sweaty head squeaking on the plastic coating of his makeshift bed. "I don't think I'm hungry any more."

"Any more?"

"There's less of me than there used to be. Maybe I don't need as much food."

A Wayne who didn't want food? Maybe Wayne's body was hitting a tipping point, hanging over the precipice of terminal decline, like a zebra going limp once it knows the lion has caught it.

"Okay, mate," Jimmy said with honest good cheer. "No breakfast. But we've still got a job to do."

"Yeah?"

"The bag of remains. We've got some paddle mixers over at Welton le Marsh?"

"Should have."

"Excellent. Let's saddle up."

It was nearly noon by the time the two of them set out. There were a couple of lads on site, painting the exteriors of the new containers. They actually looked passably pleasant from a distance, like post-war pre-fab houses or beach huts, but the grim reality of these houses would probably be all too obvious close up. Jimmy gave the lads a nod and a wave which they returned. Neither appeared to care that he and Wayne had spent the night there, or that Wayne was looking increasingly like a war-wounded soldier.

"I can drive if you like," said Wayne, once Jimmy had got him in the van.

"Drive? You can barely see."

"Bionic eye, remember?" said Wayne and tapped the bandage.

"Right."

"But I *want* to drive." Wayne grabbed for the steering

wheel as though he could haul himself over to it or it over to him.

Jimmy rapped the back of Wayne's hand sharply. "You need to be calm. And you need to sit where you're told."

Jimmy drove to the Welton le Marsh construction site. His life for the past week, for as long as he could remember, had been a ragged diamond, ten miles to a side, between Anderby Creek, Welton le Marsh, the Frost house at Friskney and Skegness itself. Hell, if it existed, didn't need to be any larger than that.

"I'm bored," said Wayne, clearly still sulking that he'd not been allowed to drive.

"Uh-huh."

"Can we play I-Spy?"

Jimmy looked at his one-eyed colleague. "I-Spy?"

"Yeah. What you do is you look at something and say, 'I spy, with my little eye—'"

"I know how it's played," said Jimmy. "Sure. You start."

Wayne made a big show of looking round at the rural landscape: the thick grassy verges, the golden brown fields. "I spy, with my little eye, something beginning with *r*."

"Road?"

"Wow, yeah! Your turn."

Reasonable Jimmy might have been howling with frustration fifteen minutes later, trying to entertain a giant idiot who thought *fence* began with *a*. Eventually, Jimmy realised Wayne thought that *fence* and *offence* were the same word. He didn't bother pointing out neither of those words began with *a*.

Incriminating human remains in the back of the van or not, Jimmy couldn't get to Welton le Marsh fast enough.

There were no teams working at the development today. Many had been diverted to Shore View. The first houses here were close enough to completion that house buyers could begin looking round next week. There might have been a bit of a rush job on some of the work, but the cracks in the plaster weren't going to show for a few months yet. This was acceptable. One problem at a time.

"Now mate," Jimmy said to Wayne, "I need to go and sort out Mrs Skipworth and Sacha. I need *you* to sit tight in the van. You can do that, right?"

"Oh yeah, I can do that."

"The thing is, Wayne, I know you sometimes forget, don't you?"

Wayne shifted uncomfortably. "I know Jimmy, I don't mean to."

"And I don't need you wandering around drawing attention to us."

"I understand." Wayne frowned. "Have we had breakfast?"

Jimmy nodded. "We had a delicious breakfast, yes. Now, I have an idea that will make sure you stay here." He dipped into the door compartment of the van and pulled out a bundle of cable ties. "See these? I'm gonna put one round your wrist then attach it to the steering wheel. That way, it's going to be a handy reminder that I need you to stay here. Got it?"

Wayne grinned as Jimmy tied his right hand to the

steering wheel. Jimmy tried not to recoil at the touch of Wayne's bloated off-colour flesh.

"Nice and tight," said Wayne.

"Good," said Jimmy and hopped out.

There were brickies' supplies in what would be the last completed house. Jimmy had a sack full of bone fragments to grind down. It would be tempting to put them in the cement mixer drum, but that wouldn't break them up sufficiently. Jimmy sought out a paddle mixer, a power tool with the handles and body of a pneumatic drill, and a head that was essentially a giant whisk.

Jimmy tipped the sack of cremated remains in a heavy duty tub and turned on the paddle mixer. When he dipped it in the tub, it immediately threw up clouds of ash. That was fine. The ash could go where it wanted. It was the bone fragments he need to work on.

Bone clattered and crunched beneath the spinning paddles.

The noise and vibration meant he almost failed to notice the phone ringing in his pocket. When he did, he quickly patted the worst of the dust from him and answered.

"Jacinda."

"Did I wake you?" she said, snidely condemning.

"It's been a long day already," he said. "I've settled the business with—"

"No names! No names!" she cut in.

"You think someone's listening in?" he sneered.

"I have an Alexa in the office. Of course someone's listening in."

Jimmy could have laughed. He attempted to pat further ash from his clothes but it was a pointless endeavour. "Fine!"

he said. "I've *settled your bill* with the vet and, on top of that, I've *closed our account* with the old woman. I'm just tidying away *the final paperwork* right now. That good enough for you?"

There was a thoughtful silence.

"*It's the least you could do, as you well know,*" she said. "*Anyway, is there not another* aspect *that still needs dealing with?*"

"Little Miss Marvellous."

"*Who?*"

"DefCon4."

"*Yes, that,*" said Jacinda.

"We don't need to bother. What clues are there for her to follow?"

"*What about W— I mean, what about our, er, bipedally-challenged friend?*"

"Visually-challenged too now," said Jimmy.

"*What?*"

"The man's likely to kill himself by accident if I leave him unsupervised. I could just leave him in a room with a whole bunch of horse tranquilisers— Hang on."

There was a box of stick-on Fentanyl patches still in the van. A half dozen had nearly killed Wayne before. The full twelve would send him to sleep and then to the grave in seconds...

"Leave it with me," he said.

"*The DefCon4 woman...*"

"She has nothing to go on. It's not like she's going to turn up here and start questioning our road alterations, is she?"

59

Sam parked the Piaggio at the bottom of Mrs Skipworth's drive.

An idea – an answer – buzzed in her head and, though she couldn't let it go, she didn't want to relinquish it too soon. She looked at the bay window of the empty house and then across to the churchyard.

"You saw ghosts," Sam murmured. "Playing silly buggers at night."

Sam crossed to the churchyard. It was surrounded by a simple fence of stout wooden stakes and barbed wire, enough to keep wandering sheep or pigs out. Just enough to declare itself as a border. Sam found the gate and stepped inside.

The church, a squat rectangular thing, was a common enough type round here. Not large or ostentatious, drawn in on itself as though it knew how wicked the winters round here could be and didn't want to offer any of itself up to the elements. She went to the church door. There was a notice on it.

ST MATTHEW'S CHURCH – PART OF THE BURGH PARISHES – SERVICES BY ARRANGEMENT

SHE WASN'T EXACTLY sure what that meant, but it didn't sound like it was a busy or regularly attended church. The churchyard itself was overgrown and scruffy. Those graves which were simply horizontal stones with no marker were almost entirely invisible. A couple of raised tombs and a copse of headstones marked out the other graves.

"Names in little boxes," said Sam.

The graves were all old, barely any later than the First World War. Lichen covered engravings that might have been from the seventeen hundreds, if only Sam could make out the numbers.

She worked her way through the graveyard, looking from grave to grave. Certain surnames cropped up time and again. Whole families buried across the decades and centuries.

Then she found it.

Edith Vamplew, died 1862. Next to Benjamin Greening, died 1897. Next to that, Thomas Osmond, died 1899. The names from Wendy Skipworth's notepad.

"I asked if they were coming to your next birthday," she

said and suddenly felt like crying. At one simple memory of the woman no one else seemed to care about. At the thought that, in all likelihood, Wendy Skipworth was now dead, like these people.

Mrs Skipworth had come to the churchyard and made a note of all the gravestones in this corner, right up against the fence and the narrow tarmacked road squashed up to the other side. Sam couldn't quite work out why she had done that.

Then she noticed the odd texture of the grass in front of Thomas Osmond's grave. The grass had not been cut for several months, maybe even a year, and where the grass grew against gravestones, the blades were longer, sheltered by the wall of stone. However, the grass directly in front of these graves was shorter, flatter, bent inward.

Sam crouched and touched the grass. Not only was it flatter, blades of it were bent over and trapped under the gravestone, as though caught when the century-old gravestone was slid into place.

"What the—?"

Sam looked along. The same was true for all of these graves. She looked beyond them. Under the boundary line of the fence she could see narrow strips of fresh turf. The gravestones had been moved – and the fence too, she realised – moved inward by less than a metre.

"Someone has been playing silly buggers," she said emphatically.

Not far away a car horn beeped repeatedly, but Sam was too mesmerised to pay any attention.

Someone had moved the gravestones – moved the whole graveyard – a foot or two away from the road. She looked at the narrow road leading onto the half-built housing development beyond. The tarmac was black and shining; the road was new.

60

With a splash of water to damp down the worst of the ash dust, Jimmy had ground the bone remnants into a sludge with the consistency of wet plaster. There was a tugging temptation to pour it out somewhere on site where another half inch of cement or screed was needed, but that was foolish. He would take the tub away, find a stream or a drain a suitable distance off and pour it away there.

Happy with the results of his labours, he turned the paddle mixer off. In the silence he heard the van horn.

Wayne was in the cab, halfway between the passenger and driver seats, bouncing up and down, alternating between pounding the horn and pointing excitedly across the way. Jimmy looked where he was pointing.

Jimmy didn't see it at first. His gaze travelled along the housing development's cul de sac, but saw nothing. Then he glimpsed movement beyond the little road. By the access road, beyond the narrow verge, the relocated fence and relocated gravestones, there was someone in the churchyard. His initial reaction – a dismissive 'so what?' – was immediately replaced by shock when he recognised the figure moving among the graves.

"Sam fucking Applewhite," he gasped hoarsely.

It was shocking that she was here. It was incomprehensible she had somehow stumbled onto the business with the relocated gravestones. It was utterly galling that Jacinda had been right.

Cold Jimmy flexed and stretched. One more piece of business to attend to then.

He jogged down onto the main road and doubled back through the churchyard gate. There was nobody around at all. Sleepy village in the early afternoon. His best bet was to try to grab her and get her in the van, but could he manage it without her screaming? There were people living nearby who might respond to a woman's screams.

Sam had crouched by a gravestone, brushed lichen from its eroded face. The hours Jimmy and Wayne had spent, levering up and repositioning those old stones. The woman had no idea what effort and time had gone into this scheme. Jimmy's temper rose and the Cold Jimmy wrapped its tentacles around it, like a volcanic sea vent – hot, sulphurous, energising.

As he approached, his boot scuffed lightly against a flagstone and she turned and saw him. Her reaction told him everything he needed to know.

Her mouth hadn't half-formed the word, "Jimmy" when she leapt up and bolted directly away from him.

He gave immediate chase. She dodged around the gravestones, but the grass was long, it wasn't ideal for getting up speed. Jimmy was certain he could catch her if they were running out on the tarmac road, but this stuff hid all sorts of obstacles – like fallen headstones and tiny iron railings edging the grave plots.

"I know what you did!" she shouted as she ran.

He no longer gave an actual fuck if she knew what he'd done. His focus was entirely on the chase.

He could see she was running in a loop around the churchyard, ignoring the thick barrier of trees and barbed wire at the rear, trying to get all the way round the building and back to one of the lanes leading to the main road. At the edge of the church yard was a waist high fence. She hurdled it at speed, catching a toe on the barbed-wire top, stumbling onto her hands and knees, then bouncing up again.

Jimmy lumbered after her, knowing he wasn't quite as agile. He stepped over the fence and continued the chase. Sam ran down the lane towards the centre of the village. There was a pub, The Wheel Inn, further up and a very real danger she might find help if she made it that far.

She jinked left to cut the corner, nipping around the back of a house. Jimmy followed. He could hear her breathing now, an exhausted rasp. She wasn't a long distance runner then. He sprinted through the side gate and grinned wolfishly when he reached the back garden and found that, beyond the flower beds and a lawn with the children's pop-up goal post, there was a high fence which prevented her escape.

Jimmy saw Sam in the process of hauling a wrought-iron

bench over to the fence. She saw him in return, realising that moving the bench had cost her too much time.

"I've already called the police!" she yelled. With a grating clatter she dragged the bench a few more inches into place. Jimmy ran forward. As she climbed onto the bench he grabbed her by the knees and pulled her back.

She bounced heavily on the patio. The air knocked from her she yelped rather than screamed.

She glanced to the patio doors of the house. Jimmy did the same. Nobody had appeared.

"Get off! Help!" she yelled.

Jimmy clamped a hand over her mouth. Next to him was the pop-up goal post, made from some sort of spring-loaded plastic, with a mesh netting stretched across it. He reached for it with his free hand, rolling Sam inside the thing, his hand coming off her mouth briefly.

"What the hell are you doing!" she yelled. "And a net? A *net*? Are we in a comic or what?"

She thrashed and resisted. While the net was not a foolproof restraint, it definitely provided enough tangled resistance that Sam couldn't put up any kind of meaningful fight. There might be fire in her voice, but there was also fear. Jimmy liked to hear the fear.

He hauled her wrapped body, feet first, down to the edge of the garden and the road, He heard a vehicle coming. He edged behind a trellis. Sam tried to make as much noise as she could, but it was no more than a muffled whine.

His own van appeared, Wayne somehow hanging onto the steering wheel in a very unnatural-looking way.

"Oh, you fucking beauty," breathed Jimmy. He stepped

out and held up a hand for Wayne to stop. The van braked hard, skidding past a dozen yards.

"Fuck's sake," he mumbled. He ran after it, dragging Sam roughly over the tarmac. He opened the back doors and heaved her inside. "Settle down."

"See what I did there, Jimmy?" called Wayne from the front. "I saw her. I saw her and then you got her and I drove round and bam! What a team!"

"Yeah, like clockwork," muttered Jimmy.

He used an elasticated bungee cord to fasten the mesh more securely. There was a rag on the floor of the van. He popped it into her mouth. "You'll be fine."

The lie came as easily as the violence.

Sam screamed through the gag, muffled. Jimmy liked that. Muffled, reduced, robbed of a voice. Maybe he'd do that to Jacinda when the time came.

That thought came as a surprise to Jimmy. It had come from Cold Jimmy in the darkness at the bottom of the sea. He could almost feel Cold Jimmy putting an avuncular tentacle across his shoulder and pointing out that, yes, obviously Jacinda would have to die at some point. Not for a while yet, not for months or even years, but he would have to kill her eventually. They were co-conspirators in murder and fraud. They were tied up together in this deal. But there was no written contract, and a verbal agreement wasn't worth a damn.

Sam said she'd called the police. He searched her pockets, left then right, and pulled out her phone. It was unlocked. He scrolled the call history. Nothing to the emergency services. The last call was from a contact called D*ELIA* – J*UNK* S*HOP* and that was nearly an hour ago.

"Lying bitch," he muttered, pocketing the phone.

Jimmy reached over to a tool caddy for more cable ties, but the van lurched forward.

"Shit." He hissed, kicking the panel at the back of the cab. "Wait up!"

He jumped out, slammed the back door closed and ran round to the front. He tried to climb into the cab, but he found Wayne sitting in the driver's seat. "How the hell did you—?"

"Someone's coming Jimmy. Don't worry, I can get us away," said Wayne.

Jimmy looked up. A man, an old duffer in a wax jacket, was walking towards them on the pavement. Wayne had a point, but this wasn't how he'd have chosen to tackle things. The van shot forward and Jimmy clambered across Wayne's arms and shoulders so he wasn't thrown from the door. He wriggled over to the other side and righted himself, sitting on the passenger seat. He saw Wayne's right arm was still fastened to the left side of the steering wheel. He'd slid across to sit in the driver's seat, but his arm was tightly clamped between his belly and the steering wheel, leaving his left arm to do everything else. It wasn't working out.

"It's a bit tricky," said Wayne, hurtling forward on a fixed trajectory towards a row of parked cars. "The steering wheel is hard to move like this."

Jimmy grabbed the wheel and yanked it to the left.

"Ow!" Wayne yelled, as his arm followed it round, his whole upper half twisting downwards.

"Back off the accelerator!" Jimmy shouted.

"I can't feel my leg!" Wayne said.

"You shouldn't drive."

"Nah, I'm fine."

Jimmy tried to lift the handbrake, but he couldn't get to it with Wayne draped sideways. He straightened the steering, which hauled Wayne part of the way up, but the van was accelerating towards a junction, still in first gear, the engine screaming. Jimmy yanked round to the right, taking the turn much faster than he should have. Somehow the van made it round. It was a quiet street, but there were ditches on either side.

They zig-zagged down the road for a distance. Every time Jimmy straightened their course Wayne would yank them back again, complaining loudly.

"Fuck's sake, Wayne, we cannot have an accident right now!"

"Best get a move on then."

"Stop the van."

"I'm not sure how."

Wayne grunted and shifted position. It resulted in increased acceleration. They were still in first gear and the engine protested with an ear-splitting whine. They shot across a crossroads where they didn't have right of way.

"Are you steering or am I?" asked Wayne.

His cable-tied hand had been twisted round and the plastic dug into his flesh. His hand, circulation cut off, was turning a rich purple.

"Do something with your legs!" snarled Jimmy. "Brake damn it!"

Jimmy held the steering wheel and rummaged again for any possible purchase on the handbrake beneath Wayne's bulk. The A158 main road to Skeg was ahead. No chance of avoiding traffic there.

"Turn!" yelled Jimmy. As Wayne leaned right, Jimmy found and yanked the handbrake. The van skidded in a turn just before the junction and ended up, engine stalled, facing back the way it had come, the side of the vehicle half-mounting the knobbly roots of a tree.

Wayne turned the key in the ignition to restart it.

"Don't!" yelled Jimmy. "Just leave it for a minute, Wayne."

He searched in the glovebox and found a cheap folding multitool that he'd got from a petrol station ages ago. He unfolded it into the shape of pliers and, with some persistence, released the cable tie from Wayne's arm. The dark discolouration of Wayne's blood-engorged hand began to ebb away.

"Thanks, mate," sighed Wayne. He made to turn the key again.

"No," said Jimmy, placing a hand possessively over the steering wheel. "I'm going to drive."

"Aw."

"I'm going to walk around to that side and you're going to come across here, understood?"

"Yes, Jimmy."

Jimmy jumped down and walked round the cab. A car had slowed down to see what had happened. "It's all right, just swerved to avoid a squirrel," said Jimmy, waving, and climbed into the cab.

With Wayne back in the passenger side, Jimmy started

the engine and edged the van away from the tree before pulling onto the road and accelerating away. There was a crimp in the wheel arch that was rubbing against the wheel, but as long as the tyre held they should be fine.

From one point in the landscape of Jimmy's nightmare week to another, it was not a long drive from Welton to the Frost house at Friskney. It felt long to Jimmy. From the scraping of the damaged wheel arch to Wayne's mumblings and moronic comments to Sam thrashing and squealing against her gag in the back, Jimmy felt as if he was chained to the noisy memories of his crimes. He stared at the road ahead, the straight road out to the fens. The vista before him was a single line separating land from sky. Cloud hung thickly and the sun was invisible in the uniformly grey afternoon sky. Hell, he thought, would be this road without end; an eternity with bleating and protesting in his ears and no meaningful destination ahead of him.

He tried to retreat to the cold cave of his mind again but, right now, it was hard to find. Cold Jimmy wasn't needed right now, but would be soon enough. When he put Wayne and Sam out of his misery.

Once they were parked up in the yard between Jacinda's house and the office shed, far from any public gaze, Jimmy told Wayne to take Sam into the office shed.

"Make sure she's tied up properly as well." He handed Wayne more of the cable ties.

"Sure," said Wayne. Struggling to co-ordinate without the correct number of limbs or eyes, he bumped into the van door before grabbing Sam and slinging her over his shoulder.

As Wayne carried her over to the shed, Jimmy used the opportunity to put his latest idea into action. There was indeed a box of the fentanyl painkiller patches still in the van. Sacha had told him that more than a couple of patches at once could be potentially fatal, although the vet had not been one hundred percent certain. He was used to giving them to horses, not people.

The drugs came in two by three tearable sheets, fabric backing on one side, covered adhesive on the other. Each square patch in the sheet (according to the box) contained two and a half milligrams of fentanyl. It was clearly powerful stuff. There were two sheets left in the flat pack. More than enough.

Jimmy stood in the open door of the van as he worked. He dug out a pair of builder's work gloves from a tool caddy and turned them inside out. He cut apart the fentanyl blocks and, with a nearly exhausted tube of superglue, stuck a patch on the first knuckle of each fingerhole, arranging them like the studs on a knuckleduster.

By the time he'd affixed the last one, the other nine were dry. He ripped off the adhesive covers and carefully turned the gloves inside out again, so the patches were on the inside. The tricky part was keeping the gloves loose enough that the patches didn't immediately stick one side of the fingerhole to the other. They seemed to be okay.

"Hey, Wayne," Jimmy muttered in mock rehearsal, "can you help me do the thingy? Put these on. Yeah. That's great. They feel sticky? I'm surprised you can feel anything."

He grinned.

Ten patches. The big imbecile would probably be dead before he walked a dozen yards.

There was the crunch of shoes on the chalk yard. "What the hell are you doing?" demanded Jacinda.

He turned, unfazed by her angry outburst. "Making plans for the future," he said. "Nice dress."

She was wearing a long sleek number with a slit up one leg. The dress was black with points of glitter that twinkled when she moved. The dress had more life in it than she did.

"Don't change the subject," she snapped. "I'm getting ready for the businessperson of the year awards and I discover you've brought Sam Applewhite – a prisoner! – to my home. To my fucking *home*, Jimmy MacIntyre!"

"We had to take her somewhere."

"I told you I didn't want to be part of this! I need full deniability!"

He grunted, a laugh. "You're one of us now, Jacinda. You want Shore View to go off without a hitch? Then you get your hands dirty like the rest of us. Besides—" he gestured to the world around them: the RAF bombing range and the sea in one direction, the endless fenland fields in the other "—no one's going to know what goes on out here."

"Sacha?" she said.

"Reduced to a bucket of paste," he said, realising he'd left the tub out at the Welton site. "The old woman too."

"And then Wayne?" She nodded towards the office shed.

"Long John bloody Silver in there is next on my list," he replied. He carefully folded the gloves and put them in his jacket pocket. "I'll make it humane. Now, come inside and meet Sam. Let's find out what she knows."

61

The one-legged man carrying Sam stank.

Everybody had their smell. From the top to the bottom of society, everyone had an odour, and Sam had long accepted that some people were smellier than others. But this guy stank. It went beyond the regular 'man who hasn't showered in a week' whiff. It was more than the 'dude with a poor attitude to personal hygiene and underwear rotation' guff. It was something deeper, something that had layers and texture, a complex aroma with so many notes – bass whiffs and high stinky quavers – that even a seasoned wine-expert or perfumier would require a month and a vulgar thesaurus to decode and describe it. The man smelled of death itself.

He dropped her roughly into a wheeled office chair. Her arms were secured to her sides with the bungee cord from the van. He wrapped some extras around the back of the chair and tied them behind. Cable ties held her wrists together. She was glad when he was done and she could get the full blast of his stench out of her nostrils. At least she'd managed to spit the disgusting rag out of her mouth when he hauled her over his shoulder.

The building was a single room, the size of a small warehouse. The walls, up to the start of the roof, were lined by walls of free-standing breeze block. Like someone had attempted drystone walling but wasn't going to mess with any of that natural stone nonsense. Throughout the room there were cobbled together pedestals, also of breeze block, and on some of them what looked like junk from a house clearance: pottery, knick knacks, souvenirs. The floor was littered with crumbs of breeze block and the shattered remains of more household ornaments. Despite the worrying situation, Sam found herself insanely wondering if Delia would recognise any valuable junk shop potentials amongst these ruins. Her thoughts were giddy, wild, and Sam recognised that although she was able to function mentally, her conscious mind was nothing but a raft on a sea of terror. These people were going to kill her. There seemed no doubt.

"She secure, Wayne?" asked Jimmy MacIntyre, entering the building with Jacinda Frost at his side.

"Yes, mate," said the stinking injured man. Wayne had a look on his face, halfway between teeth-gritted determination and dreamy delirium. Sam wondered if it was an effort for him just to remain upright.

Jacinda's resting bitch face occasionally broke out in

fleeting moments of panic and anger. She definitely wasn't happy with this situation.

Jimmy's face, by comparison, bore almost no emotion at all.

Sam couldn't quite work out the dynamic here, or the circumstances which had led them to kidnap her. But given that only one of them seemed to be regretting the situation, she guessed she was in a lot of danger.

"Jacinda. Jimmy," she nodded, putting on as brave a tone as she dared. "Nice to see you both. Off to the awards ceremony tonight?"

Jacinda tried to pretend she wasn't there and turned to Jimmy. She opened her mouth to speak, stopped, held up a finger for silence and went to the home hub smart speaker on her desk. She unplugged it. Only then did she speak to Jimmy.

"Find out what she knows and then…" She made a mostly incomprehensible but unsubtle series of gestures that Sam guessed added up to a cowardly instruction to have Sam killed.

"You want to know what I know?" said Sam. "Maybe I've got questions too."

"Shut up," said Jimmy.

"And I understand most of it."

"Shut up."

She fixed him with a look. "You brought me here alive. I'm not worth any ransom money. My dad's skint and my rich boyfriend left me. Well – I left him. It was sort of mutual, I think. Point is, you want me to talk."

Jacinda put a silencing hand against Jimmy's chest. "Talk, then."

Sam tried to line up the pieces of the puzzle in her mind. She didn't want to get any of them wrong. If they thought she knew everything, though it might mean she was in more danger, it would give her some dominance over them. If they thought she held all the cards...

"You moved the headstones in Welton le Marsh. That's what this is all about."

She looked from one to the other. No flickers of denial.

"You had to make your own plans, change things to save your building project?" She modulated the tone of her voice at the last moment, making it more of a statement than a question. "What was it?" She thought about what she had seen beyond the rejigged boundary of the graveyard. "Was your road not wide enough?"

"She's dead clever, in't she?" said Wayne.

"Shut up, Wayne," said Jimmy and Jacinda as one.

"Is that it?" said Sam. "Your road wasn't wide enough?" She almost laughed. "Is that it? What? Didn't it meet the customer's specifications, or the planning regulations or something?"

"You don't have to say it like that," said Jacinda.

"Like what?" retorted Sam, channelling some of her fear into anger. "Like, it's the stupidest bloody reason for killing a woman I've ever heard?" She looked from one to another to another. And, with that, the floodgates opened. Pure emotional, whistling fury, poured through her. "You did! You killed Wendy Skipworth! You murdered a defenceless woman because she happened to notice that you were playing silly buggers in the graveyard! You went to her house and ... and..."

She would have whirled on each of them, arms outstretched in rage, if she wasn't actually tied to an office chair.

"What did you do? *Which* of you did it?"

Before she could remember herself, remember she wasn't the one who had been kidnapped, Jacinda half-raised a hand to point to Wayne.

Sam glared at him. "Fucking monster."

Wayne blinked (or maybe winked – he only had the one eye) and looked like a kicked puppy: shocked, bewildered, distraught. "I didn't mean to. She surprised me and I only gave her a tap."

"A tap?"

"But Jimmy said—"

"Enough," said Jimmy.

"And we tried to do the right thing by her," Wayne continued. "We took her out of the ghost train and put her in that big oven."

"Enough!" barked Jimmy.

Sam was starting to get the measure of them now. Jacinda was the boss, the company owner, notionally in charge. Wayne was the muscle – all brawn, no brain, and with only fifty percent of the normal number of legs and eyes. But Jimmy... Jimmy was the will of the group, the driving force. If they were caught and tried one day, he would plead he was only doing what Jacinda told him and that all the grisly deeds had been carried out by Wayne. But without him, none of this would have happened.

"We're the ones asking questions here," he said.

"I think I've heard enough anyway," Sam sneered.

"She knows too much," said Jacinda. "What are we waiting for?" She put her hands on the shotgun lying broken open on the office desk. Beneath it were maps and plans. Even from this angle, Sam could see Shore View in cross-hatched yellow, further similar sites also drawn in up and down the coast.

"Obviously she knows too much," said Jimmy. "Point is, who else knows?"

"Like I'd tell you," she said.

Jimmy rushed forward and, with a speed she did not expect, slapped her hard across the face. She heard her own teeth clack together like the roll of dice. She was stunned, mentally and physically, and it took far too long for the pain to arrive. It came slowly, like a huge locomotive, signalling its arrival with distant whistle toots. But when the pain train arrived at Sam Station, it was enormous and overwhelming.

"Jesus," she whimpered and wished she had the saliva to spit. Her mouth had dried in an instant.

"Who fucking knows?" Jimmy yelled.

Sam blinked tears and looked past him at Jacinda, wondering what the woman would make of the man's sudden violence. Shit. There was excitement gleaming in Jacinda's eyes, evil vicarious excitement. The woman was a bloody psycho. For the first time, Sam happily wished death on all three of them.

"What about your weird friend from the beach?" said Jimmy. "You tell her?"

"Delia?" Sam shook her head. "Just a business contact."

"Your dad."

Sam forced a mirthless laugh. "He's senile. Doesn't know what day it is."

"That's not what you said before."

"I lied," she growled, finding some old fire, and spit to wet her whistle. "It's a nice lie, to pretend everything's okay."

"She's told no one," said Jacinda.

"What about work colleagues?" said Jimmy.

Jacinda grunted. "I don't know if anyone else works at that office."

Sam shook her head automatically.

"Right," said Jimmy, then hesitated. "Doug. There's a Doug."

"Doug Fredericks," said Sam.

"You tell him anything?"

Sam looked up at him and realised the vision in her left eye, just above where he'd struck her, was blurry. She shrugged. "Yeah. I tell Doug pretty much everything."

Jimmy spun away from her, swearing. "Shit. Shit shit shit!"

"What's the matter?" said the dumb oaf, Wayne.

Jimmy, hatred etched into every line of expression, pointed a finger at Sam. "You'd better not be fucking lying, sweetheart."

She sighed and tried to work her throbbing jaw. "I'm not. I showed him the shoe."

"Have you got my Yeezys?" said Wayne.

"I showed him the shoe. I shared my theory. I told him about Edith Vamplew and other names on the graves." This was all remarkably close to the truth. She saw no reason to mention Doug Fredericks was a cactus.

"Fuck!" said Jimmy. "Then we're screwed."

"No," said Jacinda with greater calm. "You picked up this bitch while she was looking at the graves. At the point when she realised you'd moved them."

"On your instructions," said Jimmy.

"When she realised *you'd* moved them. She hasn't told this Doug character the whole story. She didn't even know the whole story herself until you helpfully filled in the blanks."

Jimmy was silent for a moment or two. "He might not know anything at all, really."

"We could question him," said Jacinda.

Jimmy moved towards Sam. She flinched, expecting another assault. He didn't hit her. Instead, he went through her pockets and, from her jacket, took her office keys.

"What are you going to do?" said Jacinda.

"You stay here," he said to Wayne. "Don't let her move."

"Sure thing, Jimmy," said Wayne.

Jimmy turned to Jacinda. "I'll go speak to this Doug Fredericks, pretend I'm a prospective client or an old friend. I'm good with people."

Jacinda snorted at that.

"I'll be subtle," he insisted. "Keep her here and alive until I know what's what."

"I have an awards ceremony and an award to pick up soon," said Jacinda, as though that somehow mattered in the scheme of things.

"Oh, I'm sure Cinderella can go to the ball," said Jimmy

bitterly. "Let me check out the lay of the land and then – *only then* – will we deal with her."

Sam didn't bother to ask what 'deal with her' meant. It was all perfectly clear. She had as long as it took for Jimmy to work out that Doug Fredericks was a cactus and then she was dead.

62

Jimmy drove into Skegness and parked up on the broad sweep of pavement outside the DefCon4 office. It was just a doorway between a café and a tattoo parlour.

"Easy," Jimmy told himself. "Go in. Genial chat. Ask a few questions and—"

There was a rap on the window. It was that copper from the StoreWatch, the one with a seal bite on his hand. Hackett. Sergeant Cesar Hackett. Jimmy cracked the window. "Hi."

"This your van?" Cesar asked.

Jimmy held himself back from any sarcastic retort about him clearly sitting in its driving seat. "Yes."

"You've had a prang," said Cesar, pointing at the wheel arch that still scraped on the wheel.

"Ah, yes. I'm off to get that fixed in a short while."

Cesar looked down at the wheel, then peered in through

the window, taking in the van's interior. Jimmy had the sinking feeling he was about to be busted. He wasn't sure what the cop had picked up on, but something had caught his interest. Could he take out a police officer as well? It would be a lot harder to get away with.

"It's your lucky day," said Cesar.

"Sorry?"

"I see you've got nothing in your van that could pull the bodywork away from the wheel. It's making quite a noise when you drive along, did you know that?"

"Yes, I was aware."

"Well it just so happens that I have the very thing." He pulled a baton from his side. "I bought my own off the internet because it looked better than the ones we get issued with. It's made from aluminium, see?"

Jimmy could see he was expected to admire Cesar's baton. It wasn't the way he'd expected things to go, but he could roll with it. He reached through the window and rapped it with his knuckles. "Yeah. Quality."

"Allow me," said Cesar. He bent down to the wheel, inserted his baton under the arch and levered upwards, intending to bend the crumpled metal away from the wheel. The baton snapped in half.

Cesar looked crestfallen but tried to put on a brave face. "Ah. Hmmm."

Jimmy climbed out of the van. "Well, look at it this way, mate. Better you tested it before you tried to use it on some villain, yeah?"

Cesar straightened. "You're right. Yes. Thank you. I'll

leave you to it then." He picked up the two halves of the baton and sauntered off.

Jimmy went to the office door and tried it. It was shut, locked. Jimmy tried the bell. It rang, but there was no reply.

Nobody in. Time for a rethink. Jimmy looked at the café. Yes. He'd sit in there with a cup of tea and watch the entrance to DefCon4 until Doug came back or came out. He'd find a way to casually bump into him on the street. That would work.

63

Wayne sat in a folding chair opposite Sam. They faced each other directly. She watched him. She couldn't be sure what he was watching, whether he even remembered she was there. He was burbling quietly to himself. Possibly semi-delirious from his injuries. His missing foot had been replaced with something that looked like one of the little fences that were sometimes put round trees in a park. It had been squashed out of shape, and a mass of dirty bandages and black-brown lumps squeezed through the gaps. What had happened to his eye? Whatever it was looked bad, as there were rotten-looking fluids crusted on the bandages sagging from his face. He was a fat bloke anyway, but his whole body had a jaundiced and bloated quality, like something that had been dead in a river for weeks. He didn't look well. He looked barely alive.

Off to Sam's side, Jacinda was still in the room, sitting at her desk, working on a document. Presumably it was her acceptance speech for the award she was so certain she was about to win.

"Hey, Wayne," said Sam quietly.

His head snapped up, a surprised look on his face. "Hi!"

"I really liked that shoe of yours. Yeezys, right?"

Wayne grinned at her. "Yeah! You've got the other one."

"I have."

"I really want it back."

Sam nodded enthusiastically. "Why are they so special?"

Wayne shrugged as if it was really obvious. "They're like a collectors' item. Kanye designed them. Not easy to get hold of."

"Ah, nice. I had no idea. I would love nothing more than to re-unite you with your lost Yeezy."

He nodded, his head bouncing. The man looked so sickly she wouldn't have been surprised if it rolled off its rotten mounting and fell to the floor.

"Let's have a think about how we could make that happen," she said.

"I'm getting a bionic eye soon though."

"Uh-huh." Sam didn't know what to say to that. He clearly wasn't orbiting this particular planet right now. Sam weighed the likelihood of Wayne being a biddable ally versus the likelihood of him keeling over unconscious at any moment. He was obviously built like an ox to have got this far.

"I'm really good at I-Spy," he said.

"Oh. Right."

Sam considered her needs. She was tied to a chair, although if she was left unsupervised for any length of time, she reckoned she could loosen those bungees enough to hobble away and find something to cut the cable ties. She needed to know where they were. The way they'd been talking, it was somewhere remote, but it wasn't that far out of Skegness. What about phone or internet access? Maybe Jacinda's desk had something.

"How about you start?" Sam said. "It's pretty boring in here though. Do something you can see out of the window."

Wayne's brow knotted in thought. "Yeah but ... but how will you guess it?"

"Let's see how smart I really am," said Sam. "Go on, let's give it a try."

JIMMY WAS fifteen minutes into a phone call with DefCon4's unhelpful phone line.

"*For purchasing, press one,*" said the electronic voice. "*For contracts renewable, press two. For contracts foreclosing, press three. To hear about our Y2K coverage package, press four.*"

Jimmy stabbed at the asterisk and zero.

"*You have made an incorrect selection,*" said the voice. "*For purchasing, press one...*"

He gritted his teeth at the thing. "I don't want any of them. I just want to speak to Doug Fredericks."

"No joy?" said the woman at the counter. "Another pot of tea."

Jimmy looked at his empty cup. He was awash with the stuff, but he needed to keep his spot at the only table with a clear view of the doorway to DefCon4.

"You could do with a book to read, the amount of time you've been sitting there," said the woman.

"Not sure I've got the time to read," said Jimmy. He didn't want to engage in conversation. People expected you to look at them while you were chatting and he knew he couldn't afford to miss anyone leaving or arriving at the office.

"Oh, we should all make time for reading," said the woman. "Although I need to be careful what I read while I'm writing my play. I read a Dan Brown novel while I was working on one of the scenes and would you believe I found myself with a subplot about the Knights Templar?"

Jimmy didn't respond, hoping she would take the hint. He pressed two on his phone.

"You are through to the contracts renewable menu. If you have a two-year contract press one. If you have a one year contract press two..."

"A lot of people want to know what my play's about," the woman continued as she brought a pot of tea over.

Jimmy willed himself to be silent to ignore her but a stubbornly polite "Uh-huh" slipped out.

"All I'm prepared to say is that it's going to be the one play that *everyone* will love. It crosses genres, you see."

Jimmy didn't see. What's more, he didn't want to. He continued to stare at the doorway, the phone pressed to his ear.

"If you don't know who your account manager is, press seven."

"Of course, when they press me about what kind of play it is," said the woman, "I'm going to suggest that it belongs in every genre. It's got dragons for the fantasy fans, big guns for anyone who likes military stories, and I've started to realise that it's a multi-generational family saga as well, so it would make an excellent TV adaptation. Although I don't watch that kind of thing myself."

"Do you know Doug who works next door?" Jimmy asked. He wanted to shut her up as much as anything else.

"Oh Doug. Mmm, yeah. Been there for years."

"Any idea what sort of hours he keeps? Maybe it's too late in the day to catch him?"

"Doug? No, I don't think so. He's in the office pretty well all of the time. It's worth trying now, definitely."

"The door's locked. I rang."

The woman shrugged went back behind the counter.

Jimmy left a fiver on the table and went out. He had the keys to the office. If Doug wasn't going to come out....

Sam had quickly run up against the limits of Wayne's vocabulary and spelling. She had failed to guess the word that began with 'b' and Wayne had taken great delight in telling her that it was 'pagoda'.

Sam was genuinely lost for words for a few moments. "An actual pagoda?"

"Yeah, it's a big one as well."

Sam couldn't think where there was a pagoda in the Skegness area. There might have been a small one, little more than a model, in the ornamental gardens by the boating lake. Nothing that would have been visible from a distance.

"Like a helter-skelter?" she suggested. "Or a lighthouse?"

"No, silly."

"Not something you see every day. Describe it for me."

"Right. Well it's big." He illustrated with some hand gestures, indicating largeness.

"Uh-huh. What else? What's it made of? What colour is it?"

Wayne hobbled over to look, causing Jacinda to look up from her work.

"What are you doing, Wayne?" she called.

"Looking out the window," he replied.

"Well, don't."

He went back to his chair and flopped into it. The perspiration was more than a sheen now, it had started to drip off him and pool underneath him in his chair. "It's made of wood. It's wood-coloured."

"Right," said Sam. She wanted to believe there genuinely was an oversized exotic tower outside that she had not noticed when she was being bundled in here – that would give her a strong clue as to her current location – but she was starting to suspect Wayne just had the wrong word. "Has it got a plant growing up it, Wayne?"

"Yes, a blue one."

"A pergola," murmured Sam.

Jacinda stood up, smoothing her dress, and stepped clearly into Wayne's field of vision. "I am going to Carnage Hall now," she said in a slow, contemptuous tone.

Wayne nodded. "Yes, Miss Jacinda."

"I'm going to the awards ceremony. Jimmy will be back here before long."

"Where's he gone?"

"To talk to a man."

"About my bionic eye."

"*Until then*, Wayne, it's your job to stay here and make sure she doesn't move from that spot."

"That spot?"

"That spot."

"Or do anything at all. If she tries to leave..." Jacinda made a complex and not very clear mime of murdering someone and stabbed a finger in Sam's direction. "Is that clear, Wayne?"

Wayne frowned.

"Is it clear?" she demanded.

He nodded.

"You know, it might be better if you refrained from speaking to her as well," said Jacinda over her shoulder as she left the room.

Sam watched her go out the door. Less than a minute later she heard the soft purr of an engine, then even that was gone. There was only Wayne now. And no more than ten feet from her, a desk with a telephone and a scissors and all manner of potentially useful things on it.

"Does that mean no more I-Spy?" said Wayne.

"Yeah. I believe so," said Sam. She looked at the smart speaker on the desk. If Jacinda hadn't unplugged it, maybe she could have shouted to it to call for the police. Thoughts of phones and smart devices sparked an idea in her mind. "You know," she said, "if you're bored, I do have a drone."

"A drone?"

She nodded slowly, enticingly. "A drone. You just need to download the app on your phone."

Without a question, Wayne followed Sam's instructions

on downloading the MySky drone app. "A hundred percent!" he declared in delight. "And then I can bring it here?"

"Once you've logged into the app with my ID."

"Right, right. It's here."

"My login is Sam dot Applewhite at DefCon4 dot net."

"Sam dot....?"

"Applewhite. A. P..."

64

J immy stared round at the large open-plan office. There were four desks but no people. It was clearly not a paperless office, as a multitude of wire trays and upright folders held printed sheets and brochures. Jimmy picked up the top sheet from a nearby tray. It had the DefCon4 logo at the top and the address of the central office in London.

Memo: From 5th September, all timesheet codes will need to be prefixed with the location identifier of the primary contact for the appropriate cost centre. A full list of identification codes can be downloaded from MoSD.

The acronym was underlined, and the rest of the sheet was taken up with handwritten notes where someone had attempted to unpack what it meant.

Manager of ???

Ministry of ???

MOSSAD?

He put the sheet back. There was a line of folders labelled reference material. Many of them looked like user manuals for software from several decades ago.

Then there was the only desk with a nameplate. Doug Fredericks. Doug was not at his desk. The desk was oddly empty, apart from the nameplate and a tall spiny cactus. He'd heard no sounds from the rest of the office, but he walked through to see if perhaps Doug was in the toilet, or in a store cupboard or something. It turned out there was no store cupboard, only a tiny kitchenette. The toilet cubicle was empty.

Back in the main office, Jimmy looked around. If there were personnel files, then maybe he could find a home address for Doug. He pulled open a filing cabinet. He flicked through brochures for contract services of every kind. He wondered who else worked in the office. Clearly somebody was providing crowd control and prisoner transport. He couldn't picture Sam Applewhite doing those things, capable as she was.

"I'M IN!" exclaimed Wayne, jigging so excitedly in his seat it sent him off-balance and he crashed to the floor. Sam craned forward. It would not be a massive shock if he was in a coma or dead. What was more of a shock was how on earth he kept going in his ravaged state. He levered himself back up off the floor.

"Can't wait until Sacha gives me my bionic eye," he said

apropos of nothing. He frowned at his own words, as if remembering something that troubled him. "Can we make the drone come here?"

"I reckon so," said Sam. "There should be a set of commands available and one of them is 'return to base'. That will bring the drone to you."

"I can turn its lights on and off!" yelled Wayne.

"Er, yeah. Good. But the 'return to base' thing..."

Wayne hobbled rapidly over to the window and scanned the skies. "Where is it?"

DELIA RANG THE BELL AT *DUNCASTIN'*. After a minute, the door was answered by Marvin.

"Delia," he said and didn't get much further, apparently entranced by her dress. "That's..."

"Pauses generally aren't a good thing," she said. "Is it too much?"

"No, not at all," he said. "It's intriguing. That's what it is. Come in, come in."

Delia followed Marvin through into the kitchen.

"I made it to represent my business," she said, giving him a bit of a twirl and a swish. "It's very practical and down-to-earth at its core, which is why the base of the dress is made from agricultural feed bags."

"Is it really?"

"Yes. Then I wanted to show it also involves a lot of creative flair and recycling, which is the reason for the Capitalist Whore utility belt."

"Yes, that was the part which caught my eye," said Marvin, eyeing the row of naked plastic dolls. "What is in your utility belt?"

Delia reached down and patted the woven tape forming the pockets. She'd found that if she made a loop of the correct size, she could slide in a Capitalist Whore, and the unfeasibly large breasts would stop it sliding through any further, neatly wedging it into place. She pulled one out.

"We have here the bottle-opening Capitalist Whore," she said, holding it upside down to demonstrate that its lower half had been supplemented with a metal bottle opener. "There's another one that is a corkscrew."

"It's ideal for a party then? Or an awards ceremony," Marvin said.

"Yes, but it's so much more than that. I have a hammer, a screwdriver and a set of pliers in here as well."

"In case some minor DIY needs doing while you're there."

"I'm hoping that I might whip up a frenzy of demand tonight, so that people come by the shop, wanting to buy one for themselves."

"What will you charge?" Marvin asked. "You must remember to factor in all of the time it took you to make them."

"Well, in that case, we're looking at around four hundred pounds, all in," said Delia with a laugh.

"Sam will love that," said Marvin.

"Is she here?" Delia said, realising with a jolt she clearly wasn't.

"No. She's not been here for a while. Work, I guess."

"But we've got an awards ceremony to go to."

"Maybe she's been held up?" suggested Marvin. "If you're planning to wait for her, perhaps I can show you something?"

"Ooh, is it a magic trick?" said Delia, pulling her phone out.

"Well, if there's time, maybe I'll show you the everlasting jug. You'll like that one. No, it's something else. One moment."

Marvin disappeared and Delia checked her phone. It was odd that Sam hadn't sent a message if she was delayed. Maybe they wouldn't make it to the awards ceremony after all. Delia really wasn't sure how she felt about that. It was clear she was out of her depth with other business people, but she'd gone to all the trouble of making a Capitalist Whore Utility belt now, and it was unlikely she'd ever get another opportunity to wear it.

"Here we are," said Marvin, dumping a large box onto the counter. "I've sorted out some of Linda's old outfits. I wonder if you might take a look and see if you think they might be worth selling?"

Delia pulled a garment from the top of the box. Sequins and cutaway panels with flesh-coloured inserts featured heavily. The one in her hand was an elaborate body suit decorated with a peacock design. Up close it was impossibly gaudy, but Delia knew it must have looked wonderful to a theatre audience.

"I've seen some interest in things like this," she told

Marvin. "I'm sure someone found one of Mary Wilson's outfits in a French flea market and she paid a lot of money to get it back for her collection."

"Mary Wilson from The Supremes?" Marvin asked. "I think I might have danced with her at a London Palladium after-party. Lovely girl."

"It's the story that goes with it," said Delia. "It's part vintage outfit, and part social history. "Where is Linda now? I bet she has tales to tell."

"Oh, I'm not at all sure about that," said Marvin. "She moved to the States years ago. We probably shouldn't be bothering Linda with things like this."

"Whatever you say." She was momentarily distracted by an arrhythmic tapping and a faint buzzing sound. In an older house like this, it was probably just the heating system. "Well, let me take these with me and I'll do a little bit of research," she said. "Then I can let you know what I think about selling them."

"It's a win-win situation," said Marvin. "Sam will be delighted to see me getting another box of theatrical gubbins out of the house. The Swedish have a word for it."

"For what?" said Delia, picking up the box.

"*Döstädning*. Death cleaning."

"Eh?"

"Getting rid of all your clutter before you die to make things easier for your family."

"I'm sure that's not what this is about."

Marvin raised a silver eyebrow at her.

"I'll just go and put them in my car," said Delia uncomfortably.

Delia carried the box outside, pausing briefly when she heard the tapping sound from another room again. She dumped the box in the boot of car and, noting the lateness of the hour, gave Sam a call.

65

Jimmy was taken off guard when Sam's phone buzzed in his pocket. He'd checked every folder in the filing cabinet, but there was nothing relating to personnel. He was currently standing on a chair, so he could drag a box off a high shelf. All it contained was workwear in varying sizes, embroidered with the DefCon4 logo. He pulled out the phone and answered the call.

"Hello?" he said.

"*Oh,*" said a woman's voice.

"Hello?"

"*Hi. I was looking for Sam.*"

It was that Delia woman, Sam's friend.

"She's not here," he said.

"*She's at work. Is that Doug?*"

Jimmy needed to think of some way he could use this call to extract more information about Doug, without giving away anything was wrong.

"Uh-huh," he said.

He stepped down off the chair, scanning Doug's desk for any personal items that might provide a useful discussion point. He stepped forward and his foot snagged on something. It was caught under a loose carpet tile. Automatically, he attempted to lift his foot up to rip it free but it was unexpectedly gripped by the tacky underside. He found he was observing himself in slow motion, making moves that were almost balletic. Stymied, his raised foot could only come down. This unbalanced his back leg and his knee buckled. He automatically pushed himself forward to try to stay upright and he pivoted over his trapped foot. His mouth opened to scream and the small, detached part of his brain watching this weird, slowed-down movie realised he was about to slam into the desk surface, face first. Except there was a cactus there.

His mouth was suddenly filled with cactus. Not just his lips – his tongue, the roof of his mouth, his tonsils, his uvula – until he felt the rounded tip touch the fleshy back of his throat, and his lips kissed the soil of the plant pot. He instinctively rolled aside as he impacted, bringing the plant with him, the pot poking out of his mouth like the handle from the world's most bizarre sword-swallowing act.

He tried to scream at the fucking horribleness of it all. Nothing would come but a strangled squeak.

His mouth was jammed around the enormous bulk of the cactus, as if he'd taken on the mother of all gobstoppers, but this was so much worse. How the hell was he going to get it out? He sobbed at the thought of the extra pain that would bring, but then sobbed at the thought of choking on a cactus.

Could he breathe? Was he breathing now? He didn't even know.

"Hello?" said a distant voice on the phone. *"Hello?"*

He pushed himself to his knees, drooling spittle and blood on the floor, and found the phone. He pressed the button to end the call. He did not want anyone witnessing this appalling agony. He looked for the phone's camera feature. He held it up to his face and turned on the front camera. It was so much worse than he'd imagined. He stabbed at the phone to turn it off. He heard the sound of it taking a picture instead. He threw the phone up the wall. He'd seen an image of his face horribly distorted, like that painting *The Scream*. It wasn't just that his mouth was filled with a fucking plant though. The bottom of the pot was congested with emerging roots from the plant, and it looked as if alien tentacles were emerging from the cavernous maw that had replaced his face. It was fucking horrific. He had to try and pull it out. He gave it a tentative tug. It hurt so much that he sobbed again, but he had to do it.

He pulled much harder, and – yes, thank god! – it came away in his hand. He looked down in bewilderment. He was holding an empty plant pot. He had only managed to pull the pot off the plant. He still had a face full of cactus. He put his head in his hands, ready to die, but cold distant Jimmy told him to pull himself the fuck together. He raised his head. He could do this. He grasped the soil ball. It crumbled in his hands until there was nothing to hold onto. He had no choice. He grasped the cactus itself, spines driving into his palms. He pulled, howling with pain, ripping the insides of his mouth and shredding his lips until he ripped it out.

Dragging it free of his mouth with a half-scream, half-vomit. The cactus was flung away, many of its remaining needles tipped with blood.

Whether it was the sight of blood, or the initial surprise passing, but the pain came anew. The pain of a mouth pinpricked from front to back with agonisingly fine needles.

"*Haaaaaoooooaaaaggggghh!*" he hollered in pain, coughing and ejecting dozens of bloody needles in the process.

He retched, he spat, he rolled around screaming, but nothing would shake it. Every movement of his mouth brushed needles against each other, wormed them deeper. His throat burned and his mouth drowned.

DELIA WASN'T sure what to make of that call. It didn't sound particularly good. Sam was obviously preoccupied in some way, but whoever had answered the phone was making no sense at all. Hanging up had just been plain rude.

"Marvin," she called as she went back into the house. "Have you ever spoken to that Doug person?"

"Pardon?" said Marvin from the kitchen.

She went through to repeat herself but stopped at a door just off from the front. The tapping sound she had noticed earlier was louder and more definite now. She recalled this door was an old-fashioned cloakroom with nothing more than coats and shoes.

"You got an animal in here?" she said and opened the door.

A black shape flew out at her. For a moment, she thought she was being attacked by a trapped bird of prey. Before she actually shrieked in alarm, she realised it was Sam's drone. Delia stepped back hurriedly as the drone glided out of the cloakroom, into the hallway, and headed directly for the front door.

"Er, Marvin?" Delia watched the drone. She could accept one weird thing, maybe even write it off. Someone else had answered Sam's phone. While there were multiple reasons for that not to mean anything odd, or anything at all, now there was this. "Marvin!"

Sam's dad hurried through.

"Marvin, the drone wants to go out."

"Sorry?"

"The drone—"

"Like it needs the toilet?"

"It's bashing at the front door like it's on a mission."

Marvin glanced at Delia's face. Oh crap, was she looking agitated or alarmed? She channelled all of her efforts into looking serene, but it was too late.

"You think something's up," Marvin said.

Delia shrugged and said, "Yes," anyway.

"Where's Sam?"

Delia shook her head. "I was thinking about letting it out and following it to see where it's headed."

"I'll get my coat," said Marvin.

STUMBLING, whimpering, bleeding, dribbling, Jimmy pulled out his own phone and tried to call Wayne. He hadn't dared take another look at his face, he was way too scared of what he might see. There were spines from the accidentallyfellated cactus embedded in every part of his mouth. He had become hyper conscious that if he swallowed, he was likely to get them caught in his throat as well. As a consequence, he somehow triggered a swallowing reflex every time he tried to think about not swallowing. He kept his lips parted, so he didn't mash the spines in further, but that was becoming more difficult too. He had a strong suspicion parts of his mouth were swelling up at an alarming rate.

"*Hi, Jimmy,*" said Wayne cheerily.

Jimmy put the phone to his ear and tried to form words. It hurt more than he's anticipated. "He-awwwwww!" It trailed off into a low moan as he realised his tongue was almost immovable.

"*Jimmy?*" said Wayne.

"Aa-aaaaa. Eeeuurghhh."

"*Jimmy? I can't tell what you're saying. Are you a ghost now, Jimmy?*"

Weeping, Jimmy ended the call.

66

S am watched Wayne with interest. His brow was creased with confusion.

"Something the matter with Jimmy?" she asked.

"Dunno, he sounded funny."

"Maybe he butt-dialled you," said Sam, lightly hoping that he'd fallen down a well and Wayne had heard his gasps of life as he sank below the surface. This situation was in danger of turning her into some sort of monster, but she didn't care.

"Oh, look," Wayne said, waving his phone.

"Is it Jimmy?"

"It's the drone!" He showed her the screen, though he was too agitated for her to see anything in detail. "The drone's coming!" he yelled.

"Cool," said Sam.

Wayne dragged himself to the window and craned forward, looking for the drone in the fading light.

Sam set about wriggling free of the bungee cords. With a struggle they came apart and fell to the floor with a small thump. She glanced over anxiously, but Wayne was too distracted.

"I can see it," he said. "Oh no, that's a seagull. Now I can see it! Oh no, that's another seagull."

Wayne was so completely fixated that Sam was able to get up from the chair and very daintily side-step across the office. She could see the scissors on the desk quite clearly now she was standing, and she made the journey as quickly as she could.

"'Nother seagull," noted Wayne.

The hardest part of the escape attempt was getting the scissors inside the cable tie, then finding a way to get enough leverage to cut through it. Sam used the surface of the desk. She leaned down and the scissors closed, cutting her wrists loose.

"There's a lot of seagulls here, aren't there?" said Wayne, turning back to her. "Oh no! You can't do that."

The scissors had skidded free as they snipped her wrist ties, and her feet were still bound.

"I'm just going to release my legs now," she told Wayne, as though it was the perfectly normal thing to do.

"Jimmy's going to be mad about this," said Wayne.

"To hell with Jimmy," said Sam under her breath, tottering around the desk as quickly as she could. A computer cable tripped her bound feet and she crashed to the floor, but she could see the scissors. She used her elbows to propel her faster, wriggling at speed. Wayne's crash-thumping gait was closing on her.

She grabbed the scissors, snipped through the tie around her ankles and turned, scissors in hand.

Wayne was almost on her, roaring like the Hulk. Sam rolled upward and to the side, jabbing blindly at Wayne as hard as she could. The scissors were ripped from her hand. She scrambled away.

The desk was now between them, but she needed to be on the other side to get to the door. There was the shotgun, open on the desk. If she had any faith her own reflexes and ability to shoot, she might have tried to grab it. She had neither. Wayne didn't seem to have noticed it, but nonetheless his bulk was blocking her escape. If he managed to grab her then his wild, delirious strength would be enough to end her.

Wayne frowned and lifted one arm. The scissors were buried in his armpit up to the loop of the handles. As he raised his arm, a narrow stream of arterial blood sprayed out.

"Ow," he said softly.

If he'd done the obvious but stupid thing, and tried to rip them out, he'd have probably bled out in moments. Instead he did something unobvious and possibly sensible: squeezing his arm against his side, trapping the scissors and the wound.

"That hurt," he said.

Sam feinted one way, then ran the other. She sprinted for the door. She wrestled briefly with the latch, hoping to God it wasn't bolted. After a couple of moments it opened and she ran outside.

"Come back!" Wayne shouted, following.

Sam ran past the pergola (not pagoda), registering she

was in a large garden. There was an expansive and uncared for lawn that offered no cover at all. Jimmy had driven off in the van, Jacinda her car. A ride-on mower was the only vehicle in sight. The garden was surrounded by a ranch-style fence, so she ran towards the furthest end, with a vague plan of getting some distance between her and Wayne before looping back towards the road and flagging down a car. She clambered through the middle of the fence, glancing back. Wayne was following, but his movements were hampered by his many injuries. She watched in horror as he clambered onto the ride-on mower and started the engine. Was he seriously planning to chase her on that?

"Cool!" he shouted as it surged forwards.

Sam ran across the uneven loamy ground. A short distance further on was another fence, easily crossed. On it was an official looking sign – *RAF Wainfleet: Military Air Weapons Range*. More arrestingly, a yellow triangle sign next to it warned of unexploded ordnance in the area.

"Great," she sighed.

This had to be one of the coastal bombing ranges. Somewhere was the sea. She considered turning back, or taking a different angle, when she heard Wayne rev the mower's engine. There was a huge splintering sound as he burst through the fence. She didn't bother looking back, hoping it had stalled the mower, or impaled Wayne with a broken fence post. Knowing Wayne's dumb luck had kept him alive so far with injuries that really should have killed him, a minor collision was unlikely to signal his demise.

Sam ran on, desperate to put uneven ground between her and Wayne. She tried to keep track of where the fence had been, where the boundaries were, to give her some bearings between sea and road. But the light was fading, the fence already lost in gloom. Marshy mud sucked at her feet. Behind her, Wayne shouted and cheered.

The ground beneath her feet changed and she almost fell. There were concrete foundations. It looked as if a building had been here at some point, maybe an RAF observation station, or maybe even a bombing target.

The ground fell away quite sharply on the far side of the concrete slab. She decided to use that to her advantage. She flung herself to the ground on the far side, knowing Wayne would be unable to see her until he caught up. While she was out of sight she crawled along the edge of the foundation. With a bit of luck he would go speeding past (as speedily as a lawnmower could go), and fail to see where she was. She made it to the corner and peered around it.

Her heart sank. The mower was hurtling straight towards her, exploding out of the muddy field and across the concrete surface. It made a horrific noise as the blades connected with loose stones and concrete edges. Sam realised the danger of being hit by a ricochet was probably greater than the danger posed by Wayne. She ducked back down. Moments later the mower, with Wayne on board, shot off the edge of the foundation, soaring briefly, before ploughing into the ground, nose first. Sam hoped for a small explosion, as promised by so many Hollywood films, but there was merely the tumble and jangle of crunching metal.

Wayne might have had the decency to break his neck in the fall, but after a moment he pulled himself clear of the wreckage. The dressing over his ruined eye was pulled around, blinding him. He yanked the dressing upwards, revealing the gaping horror underneath. The gloopy mess of an eyeball hung from the upturned dressing. His head swivelled in an exaggerated arc as he used his good eye to scan the surroundings.

Sam ran. He lumbered after her. The expanse of grey mud before her became spongier, her feet sinking with every step. People drowned in this stuff. But Wayne was still coming. In the boggy fenlands between land and sea there were hidden pools and slicks of mud not solid enough to support human weight. Coupled with a tide that came in at a sprint over the flat shore, the prospect of getting trapped and drowned by rising waters was very real.

Sam stumbled once, twice, then came down in the mud of a small, unseen watercourse and sank straight up to her thighs.

"Not good, not good."

She pulled on her feet, then remembered that struggling was the worst thing she could do. This was confirmed as she slipped down another couple of inches. She heard Wayne's heavy breaths not far away. She could not afford to get stuck here, completely at his mercy. She took a deep breath and folded forward into the mud, flinging her arms as far forward as she could. She felt extremely vulnerable, face-down in mud determined to suck her under. Then her hand found something to grab. She wasn't sure what it was, but she hauled herself gently forward, and was rewarded with a sense of her legs being buoyed up by a small degree. She tried to keep her cool and repeat the action by tiny increments.

She was still stuck though, and Wayne must have caught up by now. She couldn't afford to be distracted by what he was doing, so she pushed it from her mind. After a few long moments she could feel the earth was more solid beneath her arms. She levered herself up and out of the mud. She risked a glance back and almost laughed. Wayne was nearly upon the mud, but he'd paused, his head turned to the sky.

She followed his gaze. Her MySky drone was flying over.

"Come on Wayne!" she shouted. "This way!"

He tore his eyes away from the drone and lumbered towards her, heading straight for the mud. Sam stood waiting for him to get stuck, so that she could make her way back to civilisation while he was rendered immobile. Wayne walked towards the silty mess, trotting directly over it and started up the slope towards her.

"What the...?"

The treacherous mud must be treacherous only in patches! Sam was stung by the unfairness, but she had no time to think about it. She turned and ran. The chill of the wind was making her extremely cold now. She was coated in grey mud and soaking wet. She looked back and saw Wayne. She faltered in the face of his unstoppable drive. How the hell was he still going? He was almost on her.

As he closed in she realised sand flies were clustering around his head. Were they drawn by the smell of blood and sweat? He wasn't even batting them away as they crawled in and out of his eye socket.

"Why can't you just leave me alone?" She turned to run. Betrayed by the landscape one more time she slipped on the mud and fell. Wayne caught up with her. She kicked out at him and in the confusion, a series of stumbling accidents, he grabbed her by the ankle.

"Wayne, you need to let me go!" she shouted.

"No! Jimmy said I gotta—"

Wayne put down his prosthetic foot and there was a deep, metallic clunk. Whatever Jimmy had said was temporarily forgotten.

"Uh, I'm stuck," said Wayne.

Sam twisted in his grip so she could see what was going on. Wayne was grunting in an effort to get his leg loose.

"It's stuck on something."

Sam craned to get a better look. Wayne was holding onto her with the arm which had scissors stuck in the armpit. With every one of her jerks an additional spurt of blood further soaked his top. But Wayne's attention was solely on the spur of metal that was jammed inside his elephant's foot leg brace. The metal spur was attached to a cylinder just about visible above the surface of the mud. Something about its dull matt finish said *military*.

A bad feeling didn't so much creep over Sam as drop on her out of the sky. Unexploded bomb. Wayne continued to tug violently.

"Stop moving! It's dangerous!" she yelled.

"None of this would have happened if you'd just stayed and played I-Spy," he moaned. "Hey!"

The MySky drone was descending. Sam, in among all her more pressing thoughts and concerns, wondered if the homing drone was going to clonk him on the head the way it had her. Wayne half-smiled and reached for it with his free hand. The engine stuttered. Cocktail sausage lumps of fingertip cascaded down around him.

"Oi!" he said, more irritated than anything.

The grip on her ankle loosened a moment. Sam kicked at the fingers holding her. She wriggled free, already vital inches out of Wayne's reach.

"None of this would have happened if you hadn't murdered Wendy Skipworth!" she spat and ran, ducking to avoid the drone, which with one rotor out of action was trying to remain airborne, and failing.

67

J immy answered his ringing phone, although he knew he was incapable of meaningful speech.

"*Jimmy, I think I might have a bit of a problem,*" said Wayne.

"Oo ot o-unnnn?" Which was all Jimmy could manage. He blew spit and blood way from his lips.

"*She got loose and ran away. She went across the army land.*"

"Uhhh?"

There was the sound of wind on the line. Shit. Sam was free and Wayne had gone after her. Jimmy had been trying to pull needles from his hands so he could drive. Such niceties would have to wait. Phone to ear he hurried to the stairs.

"*Well, I had to go there to try and catch her and now I'm stuck. My leg's caught on this metal thing.*"

"Eh-al?"

"*Looks a bit like the tank for a welder. It's stuck and I can't...*"
Wayne started to grunt, rhythmically. Heaving. Yanking.

"Ih a onnnn!" Jimmy shouted. "Op ooing!"

"It's a bad line, Jimmy. Don't worry. Once I've got free I'm get her and..."

Jimmy forced his lips together to allow him to make a plosive 'b' sound. "Bonn! A onnnn!"

He stumbled to the door and the street. Only Wayne could have achieved this level of fucked-upness.

"I had hold of her as well Jimmy, but she's got free and she's running away."

If Sam Applewhite had any sense, she'd be legging it as fast as she could.

"I've got some scissors, Jimmy. I – unh! Ow – I'm going to try to prise it off."

"Oh! Oh, oo uck!"

Jimmy went to the van. Through vision narrowed by tears and pain and anguish, he could just about see to drive.

On the phone, Wayne said, *"I think I can wiggle it in here. Right tool for the—"*

SAM HEARD the blast and immediately fell to her knees. It was more a feeling than a noise, a thrumming through her very core. She looked back. There was smoke and flying dust. Something – an arm? a leg? – was pinwheeling high into the sky, still on an upward trajectory. A hundred metres behind her was a steaming, hemispherical crater in the soft ground.

She got slowly to her feet and checked herself for injury, surprised to note she had survived utterly unscathed. A high-pitched whine struck up and she looked round for the source before realising it was her own ears. She stretched her jaw and yawned.

"Can I hear? Can I hear?" she said to herself, checking she hadn't been struck deaf by the blast, deciding the hearing impairment was minimal and hopefully temporary.

In the sky, among the dozens of birds startled into the air by the explosion, something tumbled down, looping like a stricken kite. It was a length of bandage.

Sam turned about, took a best guess at where the sea was, and headed inland.

68

On his mad dash back to the Frost home in Friskney, Jimmy had hit several things, but he kept the accelerator to the floor. With his limited field of vision, he wasn't even sure what it was he'd hit, but he had to get to Jacinda's place and pick up the threads Wayne had dropped. He needed to keep his chin high so he could see where the road was, but that was making him gag on the spines at the back of his mouth. He had to keep dropping it and driving blind.

Had he just shot over a junction? It didn't matter. He couldn't stop now.

He reached for Cold Jimmy, detached Jimmy, but the pain, intimate and unshakeable, anchored him in the here and now.

Above his own wheezing breath he heard a siren. Blue lights flickered in the blur of his wing mirrors. He couldn't lead the police directly to Wayne and Sam. He slowed down and pulled to the side of the lane.

Jimmy blinked at the car in his mirror and reluctantly stepped down to meet the officer walking towards him.

It was the idiot cop with the crap truncheon.

"Sir, are you aware that you— Oh, my goodness!" Cesar Hackett stumbled in his tracks, gawping at Jimmy.

"Uaad?" said Jimmy.

"Your ... your face, sir. It's..." Cesar stared at Jimmy, at his much dented van, then back the way they'd come, perhaps at the destruction Jimmy had left in his wake, and finally back at Jimmy. "Was it a wasp?"

Jimmy mumbled, uncomprehending and incomprehensible.

"A wasp," said Cesar. He became quite animated. "They do say a lot of unexplained accidents are caused by insects flying into the car and distracting the driver." He narrowed his eyes as he stared at Jimmy's face. "Did you swallow it? Them?"

"Uaad?"

"There's a lot. Were you transporting wasps? Wasp hives? Do wasps have hives?"

Jimmy didn't have time for this. He probably only had moments before Wayne killed himself and Sam ran away to blab to the first person she found. He groaned in annoyance.

"Sir. Sir! I think you might be going into anaphylactic shock," said Cesar. He put a hand on Jimmy's chest to reassure him. "I'm going to sit you down and call for an ambulance."

Jimmy shook his head violently, regretting it instantly. He felt the needles in his throat worm their way in more deeply.

"It's okay," said Cesar, a big idiotic smile on his face. "It's all part of the service."

Jimmy might have tried to politely indicate he was unable to speak due to cactus needle mouthwash. He might have usefully suggested he could write down some key facts to bring Cesar up to speed. But lacking the time or the will, what he did instead, because he'd taken enough shit for one day, was headbutt Cesar violently. Cesar staggered back, dazed. Jimmy grabbed him again, pulled him into a fresh headbutt that hurt Jimmy like buggering hell but knocked the cop unconscious. He dragged Cesar's unconscious body into the back of the van and slammed the door. He walked back to the police car, turned off the ignition, closed the door and tossed the keys into a field.

When he climbed into the van, he was pleased to recognise Cold Jimmy was back at the wheel.

SAM WALKED CAREFULLY, placing her feet with delicate slowness. Eventually, she came to an established vehicle track and jogged, to keep warm as much as anything else. Her wet, caked clothes were heavy, and though it was many weeks until winter she imagined it was possible to die of exposure out here when night fell.

A wave of relief washed through her when the track passed through a barbed wire fence marked with the RAF warning signs. She was out of that particular danger and heading in the right direction. Not long afterwards, the track met a long, low hedgerow and the main road.

She hung back, behind the hedge. It would be a terrible thing if the next car to come along was Jimmy or Jacinda. They were sufficiently out in the sticks here, and it was entirely possible. She heard a car's approach and she peeked carefully. For some unfathomable reason, it looked like Delia's car. Sam stepped out. It *was* Delia.

The car wobbled on the road and braked beside her.

Sam actually squealed with delight as Delia pulled open the door. Even more bizarrely, her father was in the passenger seat.

"What the hell?" said Delia.

"I am so glad to see you two," said Sam. "How...?"

"Following a drone."

"I summoned it. I was—"

Sam didn't know where that sentence was going and didn't get to end it because her dad got out of the car and flung his arms around her, pulling her into a giant hug.

"I'm pretty muddy, dad," she said. She'd covered him with the vile grey sludge that coated her front.

"Not to worry, sweetheart. It's only mud."

"That man we spoke to on the phone seemed a bit suspicious," said Delia as Marvin took off his coat to put round Sam.

Sam thought. "That'd be Jimmy MacIntyre."

"Who?"

"The hunky builder."

"Who's hunky?" said Marvin.

"He kidnapped me and brought me out here."

Sam got into the back of Delia's car. She'd been concerned about marking the upholstery, but she realised the back seat was covered in several layers of newspapers and bags for life, so there was no chance she'd get it dirty.

"I think someone needs to explain what's going on," said Marvin.

"It all started with the meals on wheels," said Sam. "And we need to get back to Skegness, pronto."

Marvin was both deeply perplexed and concerned. "Is this what you do for a living, Sam?"

JIMMY RAN into the office shed at the back of the Frost house. The chair where Sam had been tied was still there. Bungee cords and a cut cable tie lay on the floor. The spread of the debris suggested action and hurry. No sign of Sam or Wayne. Oddly, neither of them had thought to take the shotgun from the desk.

Jimmy grabbed it, ignoring the pain in his stiffening hands. He pocketed a handful of shells, loaded two into the breach, snapped it shut and went outside.

In the near dark, he could make out the new marks on the lawn and the damage to the far fence. The lawnmower? One of them had taken it. Hardly a fast getaway vehicle, but a very Wayne thing to do.

So, they'd gone out towards the sea. Sam, if she'd had any sense, would have looped swiftly back to the main road. That's where Wayne was, either dead, dying, or still stuck in a piece of military hardware. Well, fuck him. Jimmy wasn't going to waste any time going to find him, dead or alive.

No, what Jimmy needed to do was find Sam before she got back to civilisation. Failing that he needed two things: a load of ready money and the means to get miles away from here before looking for medical attention. He would confront Jacinda and get her to give him a payoff. Whatever, all roads led to Skegness.

69

S am could feel her skin tightening underneath the drying mud, but she'd assembled all of the pieces and been able to explain them to her father and Delia.

"So, this all started because the access road to their housing estate wasn't wide enough?" Delia said. "That's cold."

"Despicable," said Marvin.

"It's certainly no reason to kill an innocent old woman."

"I don't think they meant to kill her," said Sam. "But as they got deeper in, they had to kill the vet, and they were definitely going to kill me."

"We need the police to take it from here," said Marvin. "We're taking you home."

"Er, awards ceremony," said Sam.

"I know I'm dressed up and everything," said Delia, "but I don't think I was going to win anyway."

"I meant Jacinda Frost is there."

Marvin had his phone out. "I'm calling the police now. Let them deal with it. Besides, you're in no state to go to a glitzy ceremony like that. You know I love you like a daughter, but you do smell a bit funny."

"There's some spare clothes in the back that you can use," said Delia.

Sam looked over the gap where the parcel shelf should be and saw a familiar-looking box with sequinned costumes spilling out of the top. Her initial enthusiasm was wiped away in an instant. "Oh. Linda's stuff. I see."

"There might be something in there that you could use," said Marvin. The tone of his voice suggested it would be a minor miracle if she found anything suitable. "Ah, police please," he said into the phone.

Sam unbuckled her seatbelt so she could lean over and retrieve the box. Once it was on the back seat she could more easily sort the contents. She made one pile for bodysuits and one for other accessories. It was all rather ... skimpy.

"It would be nice to warm up a bit," said Sam.

"Think layers," said Delia.

"Layers," said Sam. "Like feather boas in six different colours, you mean?" She held them up like streamers.

"Yeah! It works for birds, doesn't it?"

Sam had to hand it to Delia. She'd taken on the role of cheerful optimist and was determined to see it through. Whether polyester feather substitute had any insulating properties was hardly worth debating in the face of Delia's insane cheeriness.

Marvin, busy chatting to someone, waved away a

wafted boa.

"I've got some wet wipes you can use to clean the worst of the mud," said Delia, handing the packet across the seatback.

Sam opened the packet to find it had suffered the fate of all wet wipes kept in cars. More or less dehydrated, all that remained was a packet of stiffened tissues, but Sam used them to scrape off as much mud as she could. She littered the footwell of Delia's car with discarded wipes as Delia drove on towards town.

Marvin ended the call. "Right, the police are informed. Not sure they fully understood everything I told them."

"But they're going to arrest Jacinda?"

"There are police at Carnage Hall already. Well – a couple of those pretend police bods."

"PCSOs. They don't like it if you call them pretend police officers."

"Anyway, them."

"And I know Cesar is going to be in attendance."

"*And,*" said Marvin with a showman's emphasis, "I told them about Jimmy MacIntyre, and I definitely heard one of them say he'd been pulled over by the police less than an hour ago. So, problem solved."

"Arrested? Wow. And what's to happen to us?"

"They're going to get the boys in CID to speak to you. They've got this number, so all's good."

All's good. Sam laughed at that.

"You okay, hun?" said Delia.

"Never better," said Sam, not knowing whether to laugh or cry. So she laughed again.

After Sam had done as much as she could to remove mud

with the rubbish wipes, she turned back to the clothes. She wriggled out of her current top and into a sequined body. There was no way she could fasten the gusset at the bottom, both because of the confines of the car and the fact Linda had been a much slimmer woman. Sorting through the box had yielded little that might serve as a decent bottom half of an outfit.

"There are no bottoms here," she said, partly as a way of complaining to the world at large, but also hoping that the world at large might have some suggestions.

"There's that one with the feathers," said Delia, without looking.

"Er, no. Not that." Sam said. "There are some things that make nakedness look like an appealing option."

"It will be fine," said Delia. "Once it's on you won't even notice them. They will be behind you. So to speak."

Sam stared at Delia's eyes in the rear view mirror, looking for tell-tale signs of mockery, but Delia's face was deadpan.

With a heavy sigh, Sam pulled the feathered bum-dressing from the box. She'd often looked at this garment and wondered what alignment between popular culture and crazed designer had spawned the monstrosity. As its foundation it had a pair of sequinned shorts with a tiny skater skirt. The back of the garment was the problem. The styling borrowed something from the bustles of Victorian fashion, originally designed to extend the bottom of a lady, so her skirt would hang elegantly backwards. This particular structure, while a similar shape, served only to support a colossal fleur-de-lys that extended above and beyond the shoulders when worn. It emulated the worst excesses of a bunny-girl outfit, without the discreet cheekiness of a bunny tail. Like peacock feathers springing from a giant, artificially-enhanced butt, and Sam was not impressed. She sat back in the seat, the feathers pressing against her back. She draped herself with the feather boas, but she was still cold. There were no capes in the box, but there was a large velvet cloth which, in Marvin's act, had been used to drape over various boxes, tables and (presumably) Linda as the occasion demanded. Sam wrapped it around her shoulders, aware she probably looked like a giant bat with its wings folded, as the feathers stretched out beneath it.

"I look ridiculous," she announced.

Delia glanced back and gave a nod of approval. "You look … quirky."

"Oh, crap. That's not good."

"It's wonderful." They were approaching Carnage Hall along the promenade lit by seaside illuminations and gaudy shop fronts. "It looks busy round here. I'm going to drop the two of you outside and then find somewhere to park the car further down."

"You must allow me to accompany you," said Marvin.

"I think Sam is the one who's most in need of moral support," said Delia.

Sam nodded in silent acknowledgement. She climbed out of Delia's car and took the arm Marvin offered. She could feel the heavy feathers swaying behind her. She ignored the odd feeling and tried to walk tall. They stepped into Carnage Hall and a bustling lobby. A stand declared that the Skegness and District Local Business Guild Awards were being held in the main auditorium.

"Through here," said Sam. "We need to find Cesar, or the PCSOs."

"The police have everything in hand," Marvin reassured her.

The auditorium had been set out conference style, the banks of theatre seating pulled back into the walls. A bar was set up along one side, and side doors had been folded back to reveal a wide balcony, backing onto the pleasure gardens and fairground beyond. The floor was already thronging with what passed for the great and good of Skegness. Tuxes and cummerbunds and dresses more suited to a night at the opera abounded among the tinsel drapes and café tables.

"Even here I feel oddly over-dressed," Sam muttered.

"And I under-dressed," said Marvin, gesturing to his mud-smeared jumper. The man was still wearing his indoor slippers.

"You didn't need to come and find me," she said, squeezing his hand.

"You were running for your life across a minefield. I think we did."

"You know what I mean," she said. "Jacinda Frost is here somewhere. She's not going to get away with this."

"She isn't," he said and squeezed her hand back.

Sam felt a boiling lump of emotion in her core, restless and violent. If she took a while to interrogate it there might be nuances of fear and trauma and horror, but right now she felt it primarily as a barely controlled rage. Whatever else she had said, whether the police had arrested Jimmy or not, she was here to see justice done.

"Let's split up and do a circuit," she said.

"I might try to drop in on my mate, Tim."

"What?"

"Nothing. A quick turn about the hall each, eh? You take this in case the detectives call." He passed her his phone. "And we'll meet back here in a few minutes. Delia should be here by then as well."

Sam headed off, searching the crowd for a sign of Jacinda. But first she was drawn to a mirrored column by the bar, so she could see just what she looked like. She suspected she might regret it.

The velvet drape she wore did indeed look like bat wings, but not in any kind of sexy superhero way. More like an aging pantomime bat whose wings had turned saggy and dusty.

She whipped it off and draped it over her arm. It wasn't so cold inside the building. She realised the makeup she had put on that morning had migrated down her face, after the mud-soaking and subsequent clean-up efforts. She dabbed a finger on her tongue and tried to make it look more like a style choice than an accident.

"Hey, Sam!"

She turned. It was Rich. Of course, it was Rich. Sneaking up on her while she looked like an Alice Cooper cosplay fail.

"Hi," she said weakly.

"Fascinating outfit you're wearing."

"Please don't."

"It really suits you."

Sam had no idea how to take that. It was either massively demeaning – this was as good as she'd ever looked – or a compliment that she was able to carry off such a bold choice. She decided not to enquire.

70

J immy pulled up in the car park between the fairground and Carnage Hall. He'd decided to leave the van a short walk away from the Hall in case the copper woke up and made a noise. He climbed out and pulled out the shotgun, draped in a piece of tarp. Just a builder going about his business with some supplies, he told himself. On a Friday night. With a mouth full of blood and a face like a permanent sneeze. It would have to do.

As he shut the door, he saw someone getting out of a car nearby. He didn't so much recognise the woman as the bandolier of ugly dolls around her waist. Capitalist Whores. It was Sam's friend. Delia.

If Sam had fled, this woman might know where to find her. He acted instinctively. Cold Jimmy was nothing if not opportunistic and decisive. He strode over, shotgun levelled, seeing the alarm in her face as she clocked him.

"Oh, God. It's you!" Her alarm shifted into a different kind of shock when she saw him clearly. "What did you do?"

Jimmy raised the shotgun and let four inches of it poke out from the tarp. "Uaaurhh," he gargled.

"Sorry?" she said.

"Uaaurhh!" he repeated, frustrated by his limited range of sounds. He jabbed her with the gun for emphasis. The jab unnerved her. Her eyes widened. Good, he thought. Keep her in her place.

"I don't know what you're saying," she said.

"Uueer unh aah."

"You clearly want something."

Jimmy nodded and scowled at the same time, causing a fresh bolt of pain to shoot from his inflamed face right through his body. He grunted with the pain.

"Okay," she said and smiled.

"I annh Sthhhanh."

She half-uttered the name 'Sam' before she thought not to, but it was too late to play dumb. "I don't know where—"

He cut her off by shoving the gun under her chin. She was dicking with him and he wasn't taking any more of this.

"Okay, Jimmy," she said.

She was doing that thing of using his name and smiling. It was the old salesman trick, and Jimmy wasn't falling for it. "Nnnaa!" he insisted.

"All right, all right," she said, trembling. "You're very certain I know where Sam is, clearly. Would you like me to get in touch with her, perhaps?" She gestured carefully at her phone. "I can call her."

He lowered the shotgun slightly and stepped back to give

him a decent firing arc if she decided to run. There were dozens of other vehicles in the car park but no one around. No one to see this scene play out.

She dialled a number. "Hey, Marvin?" Delia said. "Is Sam with you?" She paused for a moment. "Oh, you're with Cesar? What, he's got an armed response unit with him?"

Jimmy made an abrupt barking noise. He was unable to vocalise the word *bullshit,* but he hoped he conveyed the sense of it with a sharp, cautious shake of his head. He held out his hand and took the phone. There was no call active on the screen.

He thrust it back at her and tried to increase the level of menace in his face. It hurt enough to make him cry, but it seemed to do the trick.

"CAN I GET YOU A DRINK?" asked Rich. "My mixologist, Cleopatra, has developed a recipe called *Call of the Wild* with feathers as a stirrer. It would go really well with your outfit."

Sam smiled but was too tired to put much of an effort into it. "Maybe later."

"I'll hold you to it."

"Please don't. Listen, it's good to see you," said Sam.

"I wish it was true," said Rich. "Your voice says one thing, but your eyes—"

"Look, I just need to find Sergeant Hackett. Or any policeman."

Rich frowned. A frown never looked good on his face. It didn't make him look stupid as such, but on a face permanently set to 'fun mode' it didn't look right. "Is there a problem?" he said. "You're not in trouble?"

"Me? No. Someone else. In fact, I need to mention something about the awards. You're still presenting tonight, aren't you?"

"I am indeed!" he declared, taking a small bow.

"There's something you should know—"

"What do you reckon?" said Marvin, sliding up next to Sam. She did an actual double take. He was now wearing a tuxedo jacket and suit trousers, with the just a hint of celebrity sparkle on his shiny lapels.

"Do you carry a spare suit with you?" said Sam.

"I asked Tim." He gestured to the rotund and white-haired man a step behind him. "Tim's worked in props and storage here since the days of King Arthur."

"Longer," agreed the man, Tim, in a broad local accent.

"And I thought he might have had some of my old clobber here."

"Jeez," said Sam. "Not just cluttering up the house, but the local theatre."

"See? I told you what she was like," Marvin said to Tim as though a previously discussed point had been proved. "It's not just me," he said to Sam. "Tim and I were just taking a look at the props that Tony Winters—"

"Antoine de Winter," Tim corrected.

"Whatever – is using in the supposedly psychic show they've got on at the moment. He's doing the old Pepper's Ghost trick with a piece of kit I'm sure I sold to him."

"Did they not have any shoes for you back there?" Rich asked, nodding at Marvin's feet.

Marvin flexed his toes in his tartan slippers. "I remember chatting to Peter Cushing and Mark Hamill. Seventy-six I think it was. Had lunch together. Apparently, Peter did all of his scenes in Star Wars whilst wearing carpet slippers. Refused to wear the shoes they gave him. And if it's good enough for Peter..."

"We're meant to be looking for Jacinda Frost or the police," Sam reminded him. "Not looking through the prop bag, or reminiscing about old times."

"Some of us with the gift are capable of doing more than one thing at once," said Marvin sniffily. "I found a couple of your PCSO pretend coppers back there. They should be— Ah!"

A pair of Police Community Support Officers, hi-vis tabards over blue shirts, unhurriedly weaved through the crowd towards them. As they did, Marvin's phone buzzed in her hand. It was Delia's number. Maybe she was unable to find them in the throng of business folk, hangers on, and people who went to regional business functions for kicks.

"Is this the woman who needed to speak to us?" one asked Marvin.

"Excuse me." Sam put the phone to her ear. "Got lost?"

"Not exactly," said Delia. *"I'm outside and your man Jimmy has a shotgun on me."*

"Cock," breathed Sam, her chest clenching in alarm.

There was a moaning, like someone was doing an impression of a horror movie mummy.

"He's not making all that much sense," said Delia. *"His face is... Jesus, I don't know."*

"Are you okay?" said Sam.

"Did I mention the gun?"

Sam heard an incoherent gargling sound in the background, presumably Jimmy expressing something. Sam was viciously pleased to hear him incapacitated.

Delia translated. *"It's not totally crystal clear, but I think the general idea is we're not to do anything, er, hasty."*

"No causing a scene, huh?"

Rich tapped her arm and pointed over his shoulder, mouthing, "Got to go. Speech."

"Yep," she said as he backed away and then, to Delia, "Hang in there, okay?"

"Oh, I'm hanging."

Sam muted the call. "Parking problems," she said to Marvin. She looked at the PCSOs and then pulled a weary face. "Sorry, officers, is my dad up to his tricks again?"

"The gentleman here said you had a crime to report. Something about you being kidnapped."

"Dad," she said with heavy admonishment. "You can't keep doing this." She looked to the two PCSOs. "He thinks it's funny. Likes wasting your time. Calls you glorified traffic wardens."

One tutted. "We've heard it all before."

Sam thought her dad might argue, but he was sharper than that.

"Just one of my little jokes," he grinned.

"You were never funny," said the other one. "Even when you were famous."

When they were gone, Marvin scowled at Sam. "There had better be a bloody good reason for that."

"There is," she said, and with a wave to Tim put her arm

through his and steered Marvin away. "Jimmy has Delia at gunpoint."

"Bloody hell."

"Way I see it, they must be close by, outside somewhere. We can go out and try to help, but, as I say..."

"Gun, yes."

"Which is a problem if he sees us." She put the muted phone to her ear. "Line's still open."

"Here," said Marvin and passed her an earbud. "If Delia's bugged then let's keep listening in."

Sam slipped the earphone in. Currently, there was little more than grunting and heavy breathing on the line.

Past the bar, down near the front of the stage at one of the better appointed tables, Jacinda Frost stood among a small cluster of men and women. Out-of-towners: their faces unfamiliar to Sam, their suits and dresses more modest, less gaudy. Sam could see Jacinda schmoozing her moneyed guests, smiling and topping up their wine.

"Those'll be the investors for Shore View."

Marvin nodded. "Paying her to ship the benefits claimants from their cities here. Making their problems our problems."

"The poor aren't a problem to be fixed, dad. They're people."

"Fine sentiments," said Marvin, though without gusto. "And what are we doing exactly?"

"Making our problem her problem," said Sam and tapped Jacinda on the shoulder.

The woman turned, glass in hand, smile lingering in her

eyes until she saw Sam. Her large, heavily made-up eyes widened further.

"Surprise," said Sam.

Jacinda stared, composed herself and then, bad actress that she was, said too loudly and too woodenly, "Who are you? We've never met before."

"Oh, you have to do better than that," said Sam.

With a smile of apology for her cronies, Jacinda stepped away from the table, propelling Sam with her.

"What the hell do you think you're doing here?" she hissed once they were out of earshot. "How did you...? Where's Wayne?"

"Oh, here and there," said Sam casually.

"That's funny," said Marvin, "because you see, he stepped on—"

"Shut it, granddad," Jacinda snapped and returned her full attention to Sam. "You don't belong here. Dressed like an attention-seeking slutty peacock and hanging out with someone who's old enough to be your dad—"

"Actually —" Marvin started.

"This is Carnage Hall not the Folies Bergère, Miss Applewhite. Where's Jimmy?"

Sam almost laughed. Jacinda expected Sam to have tabs on her henchmen. "It's Jimmy I wanted to mention. He's outside, making a scene with a shotgun. Your shotgun, I guess."

Jacinda looked like she wanted to be sick. She kept control and glared at Sam. "It is terrible that my employee has decided to steal something from my house and is now a danger to the public." She was scanning Sam up and down.

Looking for a wire, Sam wondered. "Have the police been called?"

"He has my friend hostage. You can tell him I've not called the police."

"Me? Talk to Jimmy?" Jacinda forced a laugh and gestured at the room about her. "Tonight? Of all nights? This has nothing to do with me!"

"The police will spot him soon enough. I'm sure he'll tell them everything."

A man in a tuxedo came along and touched Jacinda on the elbow. "Your guests are waiting for you."

Jacinda gave Sam a final, withering look before stalking off, taking out her phone as she went.

71

Jimmy's phone rang. It was Jacinda. He groaned, knowing there was no way he could explain the situation. He handed the phone to Delia.

In the darkness between two parked vans in bays close to Carnage Hall, Delia stared at the lit screen. "Want me to get that for you?" Delia asked, as if she was a helpful assistant, and not a hostage who feared for her life. It was troubling Jimmy how perky she was.

"Ungh." Jimmy nodded at the phone. Delia put it on loudspeaker.

"Hello? Can I help you? Jimmy is indisposed."

"Who the hell is this?" said Jacinda sounding more pissed off than ever.

"I'm just an innocent passer-by," said Delia.

"What's the matter with Jimmy?"

Delia blew her cheeks out. "Where to start? To be honest, if he'd been taking part in a world record attempt for who can hold their head inside a wasps' nest the longest, then I'd place him up there as a finalist. His face looks a bit like a Halloween pumpkin without the charisma and warmth—"

"*Enough!*" said Jacinda curtly. "*Where is he, right now?*"

"Er, about eighteen inches in front of me. Up close and personal. Did I mention the halitosis?"

Jimmy growled a warning at Delia.

"*And he has my shotgun?*"

"That he does."

"*Tell him not to do anything stupid.*"

"Uh annn eere, ou ngow," Jimmy managed to say. He didn't want Jacinda to think he was deaf as well as dumb.

"I'm all in favour of people not doing anything stupid," said Delia.

"*I have an award to go and collect, and I don't want anybody spoiling my achievement – or putting off anyone investing in our tiny starter homes. I hope that's clear.*"

"You are more concerned about houses than my life?"

"*I'm talking to Jimmy, lady. Jimmy, I am here in Carnage Hall. Sam Applewhite is here. I don't know what criminal activities you've been up to—*"

Jimmy groaned. The stupid bitch was talking like her every conversation was being recorded.

"*—but I want you to come to Carnage Hall and* sort everything out. *You hear me? I want you to* do the right thing."

Her unspoken code was clear. Though Jimmy had no idea what he could do about Jacinda's situation. Do the right thing? Get in there, silence Sam and then this Delia. He had two shots with the shotgun and, even though he had a pocket of shells, his injured hands didn't feel up to the task. He could probably do it if he put in the requisite effort.

He wondered, how many murders did you have to commit before it made no difference to the punishment you were due? The thought almost made him cheerful, in a perverse way.

Jimmy looked to the theatre. The stage door was ajar, possibly left open by a staff member on their fag break. He shrugged.

"I think we're coming in by the stage door," said Delia. "Is that the plan, Jimmy?"

SAM HELD the earbud close to her ear. "Stage door," she said.

"You sure?" said Marvin.

She nodded tersely. She had heard everything on the still open call with Delia's phone. Muffled from within Delia's dress pocket, but she'd heard it. "We know where he is."

"We going to call the police now?" said Marvin.

"We've got two PCSOs here, unarmed. No idea where Cesar is. The nearest Tactical Armed Police unit is in Nottinghamshire."

"How do you know this stuff?"

"I may have a stupid job, dad, but it does make me privy to some occasionally useful information. Lincolnshire Police will have a firearms car on patrol somewhere, but the chances of reaching us in time..."

Marvin tapped the side of his nose. "I think I've got an idea."

"Will it get someone killed?"

"It will buy us some time, and if this Jimmy is toting a double-barrelled shotgun... Yes, it will work."

"What will?" asked Sam, but he was already leading her across the floor.

Up on the stage, Alistair Green, chairman of the Skegness and District Business Guild had taken to the podium.

"Ladies and Gentlemen. I would like to welcome our keynote speaker for this evening. He's certainly our area's biggest success story in the world of business. As if we didn't need reminding that he's genuinely multi-talented, he's going to talk to us this evening about the business lessons his current position has taught him. As many of you will know, he's spending some time as a volunteer lifeguard on our beautiful, award-winning beach. How is it possible that there are crossover skills? Well, I will leave that for him to explain. Please put your hands together for our distinguished guest, Mr Richard Raynor."

"Lifeguard?" Marvin mouthed at Sam.

"I think he bought the Skegness lifeguard crew as a sort of hobby," said Sam. "Where are we going?"

"Looking for Tim again."

"Hi everyone!" said Rich. He waited for the ripple of applause to die down before launching into a speech on planning and creative thinking.

Marvin led Sam to the round figure of Tim the props guy who had parked himself at the shadowy end of the bar.

"Tim!" called Marvin.

"Have either of you met Cleopatra here?" said Tim. "She's a sorceress with cocktails." He raised a glass of something milky-white and swirling. "And this is.... What is this called?"

"Pepper's Ghost," said Marvin.

"It's an *Unquiet Spirit*," said Cleopatra the mixologist. "But I like your name for it."

The crowd laughed at a joke Sam didn't hear.

"What's another thing I've been reminded of?" said Rich. "Let me talk to you about being humble. A lifeguard's there to help the public, right? Is that lifeguard too important to help any of those people? No. Absolutely not."

"What's he blethering on about?" said Tim.

"Doesn't matter," said Sam. "The longer he talks, the better. They announce the Businessperson of the year award when he's done. Jacinda won't leave until it's announced. Win or lose, things might turn ugly after."

She looked back across the hall. Jacinda was still on the phone in a discussion with Jimmy that Sam could half hear through her earbud.

In the car park, Jimmy seemed reticent to go to the stage door and was trying to explain a complex concept through simple mimes.

"I don't think Jimmy is your obedient slave anymore," said Delia. Jimmy nodded vigorously. "You're worried that your investors will get wind of the murders and fraud—"

"I've no idea what you're talking about," said Jacinda swiftly. *"I'm a respected woman and I need to keep it that way. Tell Jimmy if he goes down, I'll make sure he's amply rewarded. As, er, loyalty for his years of service. Seriously, he might need to put himself in the line of fire for me, and he knows how much I value that."*

Jimmy cut in with some expansive and stretching motions. Delia understood.

"How much?"

"What?"

"How much do you value that?"

"Is Jimmy asking?"

"Uh-huh!" said Jimmy in a loud, drooling affirmative.

"Ten thousand," said Jacinda. *"Bring everything to a* satisfactory conclusion *and—"*

Jimmy spat derisively.

"That's not going to cut it," said Delia.

"A hundred then," said Jacinda without pause.

Jimmy spiralled upward with the barrel of the shotgun.

"I'd go for a round million if I were you," said Delia and gave Jimmy a wink, like she was his agent or something.

Jacinda scoffed on the line. *"A million?"*

Jimmy nodded.

"A million," said Delia. "A million, or he comes in there and blows your tits off himself."

Jimmy jerked back, looking like he wanted to slap the phone out of Delia's hands.

"A million," said Jacinda. *"A satisfactory conclusion for a million pounds."*

Tears ran out over Jimmy's puffy cheeks. Delia wasn't sure if they were from pain or joy.

"I have to go. He's going to read out the winner in a minute," said Jacinda and hung up.

Delia stabbed the phone. "Wow, she's pretty bossy isn't she?"

Jimmy nodded carefully.

72

Backstage, Marvin and Tim huffed and groaned as they shifted panels around. Sam peered round the wing curtains at Rich.

"But now it gives me great pleasure to announce the winner of this year's Skegness and District Business Guild Businessperson of the Year," he said.

Marvin and Tim weren't ready with their props.

"Too soon, too soon," Sam muttered. In an act of unconscious desperation she threw the wad of dried face wipes she was still carrying. It fell a good ten feet short of Rich's podium, but he saw it. Sam waggled her feathery butt to draw Rich's attention. When she had it she made spinning, hand over hand motions for him to keep talking.

Rich paused for a moment, then, a little too loudly, said, "But before we get onto that, perhaps we need to reflect on the ups and downs of the business year in Skegness. Let's, er, start with the, um, clothes bin controversy..."

There were murmurs from the hall. From her position in the wings, Sam could just about see Jacinda at her table, fists balled in tense frustration.

"Yes, it was an eagle-eyed volunteer from one of our town's charity shops who spotted some higher value garments being sold for profit by the private contractor who was tasked with emptying the bins and distributing the clothes," Rich was saying.

Marvin's phone buzzed in Sam's hand. She was still on the open line to Delia but there was a call waiting. A withheld number. Probably the detectives.

"It seems he'd made several hundred pounds before being intercepted," Rich continued. "So let's give a big hand to Maureen in the Cat Shelter Collective, shall we?"

The applause was lacklustre, the mood restless, and Rich had apparently exhausted the local gossip and raised the award envelope.

"So, I know you're all waiting eagerly to hear what awaits in this special gold envelope. And I'm sure you'll join me in congratulating the winner." He opened the envelope slowly, either to heighten tension or to give Sam more time. "It's Jacinda Frost, of Frost and Sons!"

There was applause, even a restrained cheer or two, but the loudest noise came from Jacinda herself, an orgasmic growl of victory as she rose to her feet.

"It's time," said Marvin, tugging at Sam's arm.

JIMMY ORDERED Delia up the steps and to open the stage door. In truth, he dribbled some word-shaped sounds, but she got the idea. A shotgun pressed against the spine was a great focuser of the mind. Inside, a long bare brick corridor led to the backstage area. Jimmy could hear, deadened and distorted by distance, the sound of Jacinda Frost giving a smug acceptance speech. As they made their way forward through the dimly lit corridor, echoes conspired and synchronised to give moments of clarity.

"...considerate building practices..."

"...affordable housing up and down the coast..."

"...a construction legacy to be proud of..."

Jimmy would have laughed, but his throat wasn't working properly. A construction legacy? Bob Frost would have hung his head in shame at what his daughter had become. It was only then that Jimmy realised he was holding the very shotgun Bob Frost had killed himself with. And he knew Jacinda was going to be on the receiving end of it. Like father, like daughter.

"Jimmy!" called a voice from the far end of the corridor.

His vision was a tiny sliver of what it once was, but he could see well enough to recognise the woman in the outlandish feathery outfit. It was Sam Applewhite! She had some brass neck coming out here and facing him. Didn't she realise he held all the cards?

"I need you to let Delia go," Sam called. "She's no part of this."

"Uurh I ow."

"What?"

"Urg ivv ow!" Jimmy rasped.

"What?"

"'She is now!'" Delia translated. "I mean, I. I am now, is what he meant."

Jimmy would have rolled his eyes if his face was capable of such movements.

Sam adopted a firmer stance. "Let her go, Jimmy. I'm the one you're really bothered by."

"Unh oo!"

"And Jacinda's not pleased. She's angry with you, not me."

He could see the woman was trying to rile him. Jimmy knew he couldn't afford to lose his cool. Cold Jimmy was in charge, and Cold Jimmy knew that hostages were his ticket out of here. But he couldn't possibly take everyone hostage. Perhaps, right now, he could kill Sam Applewhite and get Delia into the van. It was actually quite doable – especially if Jacinda got her skinny arse outside so the two of them could sort something out. The corridor was all shadows, but a bright light around Sam made her a perfectly clear target. Jimmy couldn't miss with the shotgun, even if the swelling around his eyes closed them completely. He aimed over Delia's shoulder.

Sam raised a hand in surprise, as though she wasn't expecting this – stupid bitch – and he pulled the trigger.

His clumsy injured finger unleashed both barrels at once. Sam Applewhite flew apart in a hundred shards.

73

Sam felt the patter of glass fragments against her arms as she raised them to protect her eyes. The tall mirror, set at forty-five degrees in the corridor, was reduced to a jagged-edged frame.

Above the distant but growing sound of shouts from the auditorium, Tim muttered, "Well, Antoine de Winter ain't getting that back any time soon."

"He shot both barrels," Marvin said to Sam. She'd heard it too.

She poked her head round into the corridor putting herself properly into Jimmy's view. "He's out of ammo!" she yelled at a stunned Delia. "Run!"

Delia slipped out from under the barrel of the shotgun. Jimmy made a grab for her. Delia pulled something from her belt – a Capitalist Whore corkscrew – and stabbed it through the back of his hand.

Jimmy bellowed like a stuck cow.

"Run!" shouted Sam.

EVEN WITH HIS COMPROMISED SIGHT, Jimmy could see what had happened wasn't right. He'd not shot Sam. There was no corpse, and now he had a perky knock-off Barbie impaling his hand. He roared, not just with the pain, and ran down a side corridor to his right, towards the sound of screaming. He stumbled into the wings of the auditorium stage almost immediately, running onto a stage where Jacinda, wild-eyed, clung to a podium in a room of startled people.

"It's nothing!" she was shouting into the microphone. "It's nothing! I was telling you about investments for the future! It's just ... just shut up and listen! It was probably only a car backfiring! The future—"

She saw Jimmy and fell silent.

Oh, he liked it when she was silent. Cold Jimmy loved all manner of silences. The silence of the deep. The silence of fear. The silence of the dead, their lips sealed.

He stalked across the stage, gun raised to blast her, before remembering he'd spent both shots.

"Sfffit," he muttered, broke the shotgun open, expelling two smoking cartridge shells, and tried to get the spares from his pocket.

The doll jammed in the back of his hand made it impossible. He huffed, raising the hand to shove the doll's head between his swollen lips. With a bite and a twist he ripped the thing out of his flesh. The pain was a point of hot bright consciousness that only heightened his anger. He fumbled for the shells in his pocket. Fingers that would not respond properly simply spilled them across the stage.

This was a cue for the audience to hide or scatter. Seeing his struggles, Jacinda found her voice again.

"You stupid man!" she shrieked. "What are you doing? You're ruining everything!" She turned to the retreating investors. "Wait! Mr Branston! Donald! Kerry! Come back! It's okay! He's with me!"

At the door, the bottleneck of business folk trying to get out met a trio of police officers forcing their way in.

"Drop the weapon!" one hollered. Her colleagues were close on her heels, one with a baton ready, the other with taser drawn.

Ah, the fucking British bobbies, thought Jimmy. Ready to go up against an armed man with sticks and zappers.

He looked at the shells scattered on the floor, at his injured hands, calculating whether he'd be able to reload before they reached him. With a snarl, he hurled the shotgun at Jacinda's face and ran for the balcony behind the bar.

SAM HELD onto Delia until Delia insisted that Sam let her go.

"I'm so sorry," said Sam. "So, so sorry."

"It's okay," said Delia. "I'm fine."

"Really?"

"No. I'm going to need a shitload of counselling, probably."

"But as a guild member, you do get a discount off local

business services, and I hear Dr Almeida's a brilliant therapist—"

Delia clutched at Sam's feathers. "The award!"

"What?"

"Well, you voted for me."

"I think it's been announced..."

Arm in arm, they returned to the auditorium via the stage wings. Rich was righting the podium while two PCSOs carefully collected the dropped shotgun and loose cartridges.

"Now, the police have told us all to stay here while they deal with the gunman," Rich said to the audience. He looked at the gun in the PCSOs hands. "Well, not a gunman anymore. The ... man. We're all going to stay here."

The audience didn't look like they were in the mood for glitzy regional business events right now.

Rich thought on his feet. "I've put a tab behind the bar. Drinks are on me until the police get back."

The audience changed its mind very rapidly and there was a sudden rush for the bar.

Rich saw Sam, Delia and the two older men coming through the stage area. "You all right?" he said. "No injuries? I know CPR."

Sam saw Delia give the millionaire a quick up and down before she sighed. "I'm a married woman."

"She's here!" yelled a voice in the hall.

As Sam looked, fingers were pointed at Jacinda Frost, trying to sneak her way to the exit, while holding what appeared to be a bleeding and broken nose. A grey-haired lump of a woman leapt out and powered Jacinda to the ground.

Rich shaded his hand against the stage lighting to see clearly. "Well done that woman," he said. "Everyone – give it up for Maureen from the Cat Shelter Collective! Again."

74

J immy ran between Carnage Hall and the fairground. There were blue flashing lights up on the promenade, and a cluster of figures around one end of the car park near where his van was parked. There was a heavy thumping sound, and the shouts of someone telling that idiot copper they'd have him out soon.

Jimmy kept down to the right, in the shadows of the closed shop units alongside the fairground. He followed the building round and into the darkness of Scarborough Esplanade. He was having trouble seeing exactly where he was. On the one hand, he wanted to stay out of the light, but on the other, he could barely see anything anymore. Cold Jimmy knew this was bad, but that he'd survived worse. Probably.

He stumbled into a concrete wall. He heard the sea slurping on the sand. He was down near the front. Jimmy worked his way along, found a metal railing and then a set of stairs. Wooden stairs. He climbed, realising where he was. He'd made his way round to the pier and onto the open boardwalk that jutted over the beach, now closed for the night. As he edged along he looked back at the illuminated town. The lights around Carnage Hall, the extravagant illuminations on the parade, the bars and arcades that were still open: the warmth and innocence of it all sickened him.

He saw swinging torch lights on Scarborough Esplanade. He made his way further out. Out to sea there was only the blue-black of night and the occasional pinprick light of a passing ship. He would be trapped if they decided to search up here. The tide was lapping around the supports below the pier. If he climbed down, he could paddle or swim up the coast. He'd only need to go so far as Ingoldmells, or the north end of Skegness, to bypass all the search efforts.

It was a bold plan. Cold Jimmy approved. He grasped the rail and clambered over, immediately realising the cold slippery metal presented a greater risk than he'd anticipated. He clung to the railing and fumbled in his pockets. Gloves! He forced his aching hands into them feeling much more secure. He found a grip further down and lowered his feet onto one of the diagonal supports. It was so dark he would have to do most of this by feel, so he wasn't necessarily impaired by his injuries. Also, the more he used his hands the more the pain receded.

He was delighted by this. He could feel how straightforward it would be to simply trust to instinct, like a jungle creature. Maybe he would scamper through the forest of cross beams head first, just to embrace his new abilities. As he reached for a new support, he felt a tug at the hairs on the back of his hands, remembering too late the drugs patches he'd glued in the gloves earlier.

"Fuhk," he murmured, although he didn't feel as panicked as he knew he ought to. Cold Jimmy and a massive dose of horse tranquiliser wrapped him in their protective embrace. He let go. He felt so light, he thought he might just soar towards the water, then swoop upwards again, shrieking like a seagull.

He hit the water hard and plummeted beneath the surface. His feet kicked at the sand mere feet beneath the surface. Giddy and near unconsciousness, he thought he'd best breathe through the gills he knew were there somewhere, if he could only remember where. He swallowed sea water, gagged and spat as it burned along his ruined throat.

He splashed towards the shore, but his arms were weighed down, clothing soaked, limbs losing all sensation.

There were two figures on the shore. They stood in near darkness, no torches. Not the police. Night time beach drinkers? Teenagers looking for a bit of privacy? He splashed and shouted to them, but only a desperate hooting noise emerged from his throat.

"What's that?" said the thin one.

"What?" said the thickset one.

The seawater around Jimmy was simultaneously freezing cold and a comfortingly warm blanket. Cold Jimmy's tentacles coiled around his legs and torso and tried to pull him down into the dark, safe depths. Jimmy fought against it and cried out to the two figures.

"It's just a seal," said one.

"Careful," said the other. "A seal can bite a man's hand clean off."

"Bollocks."

"I heard that the other day. Happened to a bloke at Seal Land."

Jimmy dipped below the surface. Stinging seawater flooded his nostrils and mouth. With failing effort, he bobbed up again. He'd have coughed, but he'd forgotten how. The two figures were still there. The thin one looked stooped and frail, like an old woman. The heavy one had a fat, shaved head and the slouch of a happy-go-lucky moron. They looked like they were waiting for him.

A low wave broke over Jimmy and the tide pulled him back. Better Cold Jimmy and the dark than those two. He let the water take him.

75

Time heals all wounds, and alcohol does a pretty good job too. Cleopatra presented Sam and Delia with a pair of shimmering cocktails.

"*End of the Night*," she said.

"Far from it," said Delia. "We've only just got tonight back on track. There better be karaoke before the evening is through."

"Guild events aren't renowned for putting on karaoke," said Sam.

"We'll soon see about that, won't we, Tim?" said Marvin. "We'll go find the sound engineer."

"Some ABBA!" Delia shouted after them.

The women leaned against the bar and drank.

"Definitely the two best-dressed gals in here," said Delia eventually.

Sam compared her feathered monstrousness with Delia's

seed bag and cannibalised toy construction. "Positively smoking," she agreed.

Up on stage, Rich was deep in debate with the guild chairman. On a table nearby, a couple of people were sifting through voting forms.

Rich waved Alistair Green away and took to the microphone. "I would very much like to get this ceremony back on track for you, ladies and gentlemen," he said. "The police assure me that the building is now secure, and we can safely continue."

"Is there still a free bar?" someone shouted out.

"I'm a man of my word," he replied. There was much applause.

"There remains the difficulty of the award, which has been removed from the previous recipient, so we're just conducting a recount." Rich looked over at the table to see if they were done, and got a headshake in response. "However," he continued, "I do feel as though our humble awards ceremony has been eclipsed by the heroics of a very brave woman this evening."

Sam felt her cheeks redden.

"Let's show our appreciation one last time for Maureen from the Cat Shelter Collective!"

"Unbelievable," said Sam. She applauded nonetheless.

A piece of paper was handed to Rich.

"I can now reveal that we've run the numbers and we have a clear winner, after removing the entries for the recently arrested Jacinda Frost." He looked at the paper. "With a staggering one vote, it's Delia from *Back to Life*."

The audience generally had no idea who Delia was, but it

was a night for cathartically enthusiastic applause and they gave it some welly. Delia looked genuinely astounded and was frozen to the spot.

"Come on," said Sam. "This is for you."

She dragged Delia to the front, while Delia mimed shocked and delighted *me?* gestures all the while. Sam propelled her to the podium. Rich gave her a small but perfectly formed trophy plaque and a kiss on the cheek. Delia stood before the microphone and waited for the applause to die down.

"Now, I won't be making a speech, because, quite frankly I have no idea how. But I think it's fair to say that this evening has not turned out how I expected. I love our town for that. It's always got a curveball to throw at you. Mind, I'm beginning to think Sam Applewhite is a one-woman curveball all on her own."

Delia paused and Sam did a little curtsey of thanks.

Delia raised the trophy high. "That's it. Let the karaoke begin!"

There were blank expressions. The guild chairman was clearly about to explain they didn't do karaoke when the intro to *Dancing Queen* struck up over the PA system.

Delia passed Sam the podium mike and whipped a Capitalist Whore out of her belt as a pretend microphone for herself.

"Told you yours was the vote that counted."

AFTERWORD

Many thanks for reading book one in the Sam Applewhite series. You can find the link to book two in the coming pages.

We're grateful to all of the readers who continue to support our work and help us to keep writing.

If you can find the time to share your thoughts in a review, it not only helps us, but it helps other readers too.

We're very busy writing new books, so if you want to keep up to date with our work, you could subscribe to our newsletter. Sign up at www.pigeonparkpress.com

Heide and Iain

ABOUT THE AUTHORS

Heide lives in North Warwickshire with her husband and a fluctuating mix of offspring and animals. Iain lives in South Birmingham with his wife and a fluctuating mix of offspring and animals. They aren't sure how many novels they've written together since 2011 but it's a surprisingly large number.

ALSO BY HEIDE GOODY AND IAIN GRANT

Doggerland

There's something very wrong at the Otterside care home.

When Sam Applewhite tries to help a friend who's lost a beloved pet she finds that it's just the first in a series of seemingly unconnected deaths. Is it her imagination, or do all of them somehow point back to the same residential home for seniors?

Sam's skills are in demand elsewhere however, as she must orchestrate a safety drill with animal actors, cook dinner on an abandoned oil rig and keep an eye on those vikings who are building a longship.

When the police don't see the pattern, it's all down to Sam, and the closer she gets to uncovering what's going on at Otterside, the more danger she's in.

Doggerland

Clovenhoof

Getting fired can ruin a day...

...especially when you were the Prince of Hell.

Will Satan survive in English suburbia?

Corporate life can be a soul draining experience, especially when the industry is Hell, and you're Lucifer. It isn't all torture and brimstone, though, for the Prince of Darkness, he's got an unhappy Board of Directors.

The numbers look bad.

They want him out.

Then came the corporate coup.

Banished to mortal earth as Jeremy Clovenhoof, Lucifer is going through a mid-immortality crisis of biblical proportion. Maybe if he just tries to blend in, it won't be so bad.

He's wrong.

If it isn't the murder, cannibalism, and armed robbery of everyday life in Birmingham, it's the fact that his heavy metal band isn't getting the respect it deserves, that's dampening his mood.

And the archangel Michael constantly snooping on him, doesn't help.

If you enjoy clever writing, then you'll adore this satirical tour de force, because a good laugh can make you have sympathy for the devil.

Get it now.

Clovenhoof

Oddjobs

It's the end of the world as we know it, but someone still needs to do the paperwork.

Incomprehensible horrors from beyond are going to devour our world but that's no excuse to get all emotional about it. Morag Murray works for the secret government organisation responsible for making sure the apocalypse goes as smoothly and as quietly as possible.

In her first week on the job, Morag has to hunt down a man-eating starfish, solve a supernatural murder and, if she's got time, prevent her own inevitable death.

The first book in a new comedy series by the creators of 'Clovenhoof', Oddjobs is a sideswipe at the world of work and a fantastical adventure featuring amphibian wannabe gangstas, mad old cat ladies, ancient gods, apocalyptic scrabble, fish porn, telepathic curry and, possibly, the end of the world before the weekend.

Oddjobs